Some Other Time

A Novel

Diana Richmond

iUniverse, Inc.
New York Bloomington

This is a work of fiction. All of the characters, names, incidents, organizations, and dialogue in this novel are either the products of the author's imagination or are used fictitiously.

iUniverse books may be ordered through booksellers or by contacting:

iUniverse
1663 Liberty Drive
Bloomington, IN 47403
www.iuniverse.com
1-800-Authors (1-800-288-4677)

ISBN: 978-1-4401-5785-1 (sc)
ISBN: 978-1-4401-5787-5 (hc)
ISBN: 978-1-4401-5786-8 (ebook)

Library of Congress Control Number: 2009932243

Printed in the United States of America

iUniverse rev. date: 08/19/2009

To my mainstays, Al and Kavana

1996
Sunday

In high spirits, Sunday Morgan drove vaguely northward out of Boise. The conference had gone well and had ended. He had no more obligations before flying home tomorrow afternoon. It was a late Saturday afternoon in April. The winding, two-lane road paralleled a river bordered by aspens, just leafed-out, their new green back-lit by the slanting sun. With him was Marsha, a colleague he had known and liked for years, who for once had come to the conference without her husband. They had decided to drive out into the country a bit and then return for dinner. After dinner, who knew? The afternoon billowed with possibility like a spinnaker. Suffused with a sense of well being, he hung his arm out the driver's window, registering how good his eggplant-colored shirt looked against his dark, sun-burnished skin.

Marsha fed a Bruce Springsteen CD into the player. "Nostalgia," she smiled. She was just that much younger than he. Nostalgia for him roused Marvin Gaye and Tammi Tarrell, maybe The Four Tops. Marsha crossed her bare pale legs and leaned back, her fingers beating a small rhythm on the handrest between them. He glanced over at her breeze-blown sandy-colored hair, no gray yet. And few wrinkles, except at the outer corners of her eyes when she laughed, or furrowed her brow to think over a point in conversation.

"Do we know where we're going?" She asked.

"Yes. We're following this river to see where it leads."

"Perfect."

And so they wound their way into the dusk, watching the glinting aspens and river on their left and occasional farms on their right. There were almost no other cars on the road, which made the two city-dwellers feel privileged and quite apart from their normal lives.

After some distance on the curving road, Sunday spotted a vehicle in the distance behind him, a pickup truck. It gained on them steadily, apparently some local intent on getting home for dinner. Then it was on their rear bumper, aggressively close. Sunday searched for a wide shoulder on the right so that he could pull over and let the impatient truck driver pass. But for some distance the road snaked on narrow turns and afforded no place to pull over. Finally, as the road straightened a bit, Sunday could see a small dirt road leading off to his right, ahead of them. He lit his turn signal and headed for it, to let the truck pass.

As the truck slid by them, Sunday glanced to his left. A pale, raw-boned man with eyes squinted in anger glared back at him. 'Dirty nigger.' Sunday could read this on the truck driver's lips without even trying.

Instead of speeding ahead, the truck pulled in on the right shoulder ahead of Sunday and Marsha.

It started to back up fast. Dust swirled around the rear of the pickup.

Instinctively, Sunday closed the windows and locked the car.

"I think our drive is over." As quickly as he could, he put the car into reverse to turn around and drive back. But the truck pulled in aslant in front of the car and stopped, blocking them. The driver got out. He loped toward them in a country walk. 'Scrawny' was the word that came to Sunday as they watched him approach. He wore a faded red plaid shirt, unevenly buttoned, with one side hanging out over his loose, hip-sliding jeans. On his left side was a leather sheath for a long knife, with a bone handle sticking out the top. The driver fingered it twitchily.

"Open the fuckin' window, nigger." He leaned over the driver's side of their car.

Reflexively, Sunday opened it, just as Marsha started to tell him not to. "Sunday, don't do it. Let me try to talk to him," she was saying. Sunday's mind was quickly receding into Mississippi, slowing him, mesmerizing him.

"Whatcha think you're doin' in my country with your white 'hore. It makes me sick."

"We are old colleagues and good friends. I'm here because I want to be, and I'm not anyone's whore," Marsha told him with quiet authority before Sunday could string any words together. "We didn't do anything to bother you and would appreciate you're leaving us alone."

"Bother me," he screwed up his face as if from a bad smell. "It bothers the shit out of me that you two come up here and think you can do your dirty business in my country."

Suddenly the driver had their door open and was pulling Sunday out, his right hand clutching Sunday's neck. The foot-long knife was in the driver's left hand. He gripped it as if it were part of his own body, pointing it first at Sunday's neck and next at his groin. The blade was filthy and crusted. Idiotically, its filth terrified Sunday, as if it mattered whether he would be dismembered by a clean or filthy knife.

All self-possession, Marsha was out of the car on the passenger side, holding her cell phone aloft.

"I just dialed 911. If you put that knife down, get back into your truck and drive away right now, we'll forget this incident happened and nothing bad will happen to you."

"Heh." The driver spat. "You think you're goin' to git any reception on that thing here? Just try." In an instant, he was in front of her. He seized the cell phone and threw it into the ditch behind her. He backslapped her face with his right hand.

"You stay outta this, whore."

Though taller than the driver, Sunday felt impaled in place, without strategy. He caught Marsha's eye and signaled her with a tilt of his head to run, just as the driver circled their car and pointed the knife again at Sunday's throat. All he could think of was his inevitable brutal death in the next few minutes or hours. He smelled sweat and stale alcohol on the driver's breath.

"Keep her out of this." Sunday recovered his voice.

The driver swiftly kneed him in the groin. As Sunday doubled over, he took a hard blow to his chin, knocking him to the ground. Another idiotic thought flitted through Sunday's brain: he had never been in a fight before in his whole life. So this is how it was. He crumpled into a lump on the ground, knees under him and arms around his head. He thought he could hear Marsha running away, back toward Boise.

With a flick of his knife, the driver split open Sunday's shirt, along his spine. He waited for the man to start carving up his back. What should I be doing, he kept asking himself and finding no answer.

"Heh. You're a fuckin' coward, too." With that, he kicked Sunday in his right ear. Sunday's legs reflexively stretched out, accidentally tripping the driver. He toppled like an old fence post. There was an elongated moment of stupid surprise on both of their faces. Then Sunday was on his feet. In falling, the driver had dropped his knife. Now Sunday grasped it in his right hand, testing his grip and the effect it had on the driver.

"I'm going to give you a second chance to stay out of trouble. Get back into your truck and drive away."

The driver sat with his legs bent in front of him, his arms on the ground beside him. Sunday did not know whether he was going to spring up and charge him, walk to his car, or just sit there and taunt him some more. The driver squinted, his lips curled down, hate emanating from him like a stink. Sunday realized slowly that he was shaking and that the man was not moving. He stood and the other man just stared at him for what seemed an eternity. Would he have to use this knife to save himself?

A sound intruded from outside the lock of their attention. An approaching car. The driver cocked his head, disbelieving. He got up slowly, wiping his hands on the dusty legs of his jeans.

A county sheriff's car loomed fast upon them, screaming to a stop between them and the road. The officer leapt out with gun drawn. For an instant, Sunday wondered if now he would be shot, since he was holding the knife. He lifted his arms slowly. Then he noticed Marsha in the car.

"Hold it right there." The officer was talking to the driver, not to Sunday.

The driver started to run for his truck.

"I said 'hold it right there!'" He raised his pistol. The driver did not stop.

The pistol cracked out two shots. The driver, one leg on the driver's seat, dropped the other, his left jeans leg darkening toward his ankle.

Marsha was out of the car, her arms around Sunday. "I felt so bad for running away; can you ever forgive me?" He looked at her in disbelief and started to heave. His shoulders shook uncontrollably. He wept. He wept until he had to seize breath and hiccups began.

"Forgive you? You have it all wrong. I was a coward. You were a lion compared to me."

Soon there was a siren, a second county sheriff's car, and the driver was taken away in handcuffs in it. Police tape was strung up, officers walked the area, searching the ditch. Sunday was helped into the sheriff's car while Marsha walked to their car. "This way, Sir," the officer had said to him. Sir: he was not expecting that. On the way to the Boise police station, he passed into a temporary but deep sleep. On waking, it was as if he had not slept. He read the words on a billboard they passed on the way into the city: "Find Your Best Life Here."

Sunday apologized again to Marsha at the police station. She was quiet but still apparently calm. He asked to call his wife. He was told they would need to give statements first. Randomly, he wondered if he could ever feel carefree again.

At the police station, he and Marsha were separated and each questioned in separate rooms. Sunday remembered the courtesy of the officers, the fact that they brought him coffee and a hamburger, but not much of the statement he gave. He and Marsha were released separately late that evening and driven separately back to their hotel.

He telephoned Paula from his hotel room. At the sound of her voice, his voice broke. He could barely tell her what had happened. "Come home," she told him, again and again, her strong voice a balm. Without seeing Marsha again, Sunday caught his scheduled plane home the next afternoon.

Prologue

1
August 1945
Norma

If anyone had told Norma she would be a mother within a year, she would have thrown back her head and laughed dismissively.

She was thinking of now, not a year from now.

The boundaries of her world had just broken open. Until now, she had existed in roughly the perimeters she could walk – the park at Lake Michigan on the east, the stores on Wisconsin Avenue to the South, Rick's house across Teutonia Avenue on the West (he'd walk her home through Union Cemetery at night), and Center Street on the North. Everyone she knew lived inside this tiny sector of North-Central Milwaukee. Norma was eighteen and lived with her parents in a bungalow just four blocks away from her fiancé Will and his family. She and her family walked each Sunday to Holy Ghost Church, *Heilige Geist Kirche, estab. 1896* engraved on the cornerstone, hearing the old bells calling them to service and home again for Sunday dinner of roast chicken and red cabbage.

Until now. Train wheels clacking in the groove

of metal track underneath carried her in an uncertain, sometimes lurching, relentless rumble westward. Outside the perimeter for the first time, and traveling essentially on a dare, she breathed rapidly, clutching her arms as if to contain her exhilaration. Depending on whether Karla had kept her word to call him, Will might or might not know she was on her way to meet him. When she arrived tomorrow at Nellis Army Air Corps Base outside Las Vegas, she would tell him that they would elope rather than marry in church with their families next month.

Aspens fluttered golden next to the track. A hawk drifted over an open meadow below forests of deep green spruce massed in shadow. The sharp white light of early morning highlighted the barren mountain peaks. For hours and hours there had been nothing but cornfields and then wheat fields, with only an occasional silo relieving the monotony. Crossing those fields, she began to doubt whether this country held anything but the flat landscape of the Midwest, to doubt whether her impulse could take her anywhere that would be different. These mountains left familiar territory far behind. Cliffs like ruins of ancient dwellings loomed beside the track. Some of the cliffs tilted at a steep angle, only the trees on them upright. Norma felt certain she was coming into her own life for the first time.

From early childhood, she had known she did not belong in her family. The lives of her parents and her younger siblings Britta and Bruno existed in some other realm that belonged to all of them but not to her. Her parents treated her kindly, as they would an adopted stray, but at a distance too, as if they had taken in a kitten and found themselves with an ocelot. Yet Norma knew she was not adopted. After punishing her for running away from home at age ten (she'd been found a day later after spending the night in the hayloft of a nearby barn), her father told her in some detail how her mother had almost died in labor with her. That episode eight years ago earned her thirty-one hours alone in her room - the same number of hours she had been away. With a pained expression, her mother had brought plates of cold food to her room after the rest of the family had eaten.

"Why don't you just put the plate on the floor?" she had taunted her mother.

Now Norma was hungry. The train had stopped before dawn in Denver. Jolted awake and stiff from sleeping upright in her seat, she had emerged into the cold, vaulted station and immediately smelled frying bacon. Having denied herself dinner because she had only $7.50 left in her purse, she wondered - but only for a moment - whether she could afford breakfast. She indulged in a Denver omelette (she liked the sound of the name), orange juice and coffee. That brought her down to $6.37. Breakfast was three hours ago, and her stomach growled.

Facing her across the aisle sat a Negro soldier with sergeant's stripes on his Air Corps uniform. With a jowled face and full chest and belly, he looked stuffed into his uniform. He'd boarded somewhere back in the Midwest, she forgot where, but she did notice he carried several large paper bags. Last night he emptied one of the bags and very neatly removed wax paper wrappings from three pieces of fried chicken, two pieces of corn bread and an apple, which he'd eaten with slow and deliberate relish. Now, with military posture and full concentration, he was downing the contents of his second bag - two full chicken sandwiches, a small bowl of potato salad and a thermos of coffee. She found herself staring at him as he ate. His ears were small and round and his skin was mahogany, shining in the warmth of the car. He caught her glance and she looked away instinctively.

She wished she had at least brought a book or magazine; even the mountains failed to distract her from hunger.

"Pardon me, ma'am," he was standing beside her seat now. "Would you like one of these?" In the pink of his hand was a large ripe peach.

She hesitated, embarrassed, but only for a second. "Yes, thank you."

"My sister grows them, just outside Springfield, Illinois. I have more." He gestured toward his paper bags. "Take this, too." He gave her one of his sandwiches.

"You're very generous."

"No, ma'am. I got extra, and you look hungry."

The sandwich was delicious, with tightly packed pieces of chicken and mayonnaise on home-baked bread.

"Where are you stationed?" she asked, to make polite conversation.

"Nellis Army Air Corps Base, Las Vegas. Just returning from hardship leave. My pa just died. I got a squadron just two weeks from finishing flight training. I was set to go with them, but now it seems the war is almost over."

"Yes, isn't that great! About the war, I mean. I'm sorry to hear about your father." She stumbled over her words.

"Thank you, ma'am." He nodded soberly, not volunteering any more.

"I'm going to Nellis myself."

She caught him glancing at her belly, which was smooth and flat. He gave a noncommittal response which could be mistaken for clearing his throat.

"My fiancé is there."

"Looks like he'll be freed up soon."

"That's why I'm here. His name is Will Reinhardt. Do you know him, by any chance?"

"Billy - the artist! Yeah, he's in my unit." He laughed. "He even drew my portrait; I have it stuck up in my locker. Quiet fella, good man." And so they began a conversation, never moving from their positions across the aisle.

Some hours later, their conversation having drifted away, Norma napped. In her sleep, she was riding this train, bound for Las Vegas, but at a stop in western Colorado, Rick boarded the train. Her heart skipped at the sight of him, his black silky hair and the languid tilt of his head. He looked around the car, as if for her, then headed toward her and sat down. Without even saying hello, he leaned over and kissed her, inserting his tongue between her lips. Remembering where she was going, she started awake, shook her head and recovered a sense of where she was and how she got here.

Two days ago, on August 6, the first atomic bomb had disintegrated Hiroshima. At home, her family clustered around the large wooden radio on the bookcase in the front room. Her mother quietly wept, then prayed. Her father put his arm on her shoulder: "Etta, stop. This will end the war." Her twelve-year-old sister Britta cooed, "Now Billy will come home and we'll have a wedding," looking at her older sister for approval. "It's Will, not Billy," Norma snapped.

None of them had any clear idea of why this bomb was more powerful or special than all the others that had been dropped on other cities in this war. The Milwaukee Journal carried photographs of a large mushroom-shaped cloud rising high over Japan and descriptions of this scientific marvel developed in secret. There were no photographs of the city on which the bomb had fallen, no statistics on how many people had died. On page two, fashion ads sat next to photographs of the scientists who had brought this wonder to light.

That same evening, Will's younger sister Karla had called and suggested they go downtown the next day to celebrate on Wisconsin Avenue. Yesterday morning Norma had put on her favorite summer dress, which she liked despite the fact that her mother had sewn it for her. Patterned with big, blowsy peonies, it had a full gored skirt and a fitted bodice. She could twirl in it and show off her good legs. She stood for a moment staring into her savings jar, debating how much to take. It contained exactly $63 in savings from her job as a hospital aide. She took a $20 bill, the most crumpled of the three in the jar, and put it carefully into her purse. Perhaps she would splurge on a new dress. She met Karla and together they took the trolley downtown to Wisconsin Avenue, expecting hordes of celebrants. Instead, the streets were disappointingly subdued. Passersby looked distracted, puzzled. People bought out all the newspapers and stood on the sidewalks reading them intently.

Karla and she stopped for root beer floats at Hoffman's and chatted about her wedding.

"You know," Karla said, "my mother is still trying to persuade Billy not to marry you."

She put her soda down and looked pointedly at Karla. "What does she say?"

Karla's eyes widened as she caught Norma's interest. "She says you think you're too good for us, that you don't love him enough. She wrote to Billy that she wouldn't be surprised if you ran off and left him some day."

"What did she do, read the letter to you?" Norma felt a surge of heat from deep inside radiating to her skin. She also wondered if somehow Karla and her mother had found out about Rick. She knew her own mother would never disclose something so shameful, so private, but Karla was nosy and may have had an inkling of her own.

"Actually, she did. She asked me what I thought." Karla paused.

"What did you say?"

"I told her I thought she was wrong, that you love Billy as much as he loves you, and that you were meant for each other." Norma knew enough not to believe her.

"When did she send this letter?"

"About a week ago, but never mind, Billy knows she can't help intruding. He won't let it get to him." Karla's face suddenly brightened.

"Wouldn't it be funny if you simply ran away and married Billy, without anyone knowing? That would shut her up."

She slowly finished her soda and deliberately slurped the last sips from the bottom of the glass. Karla's mother, Brunhilde Reinhardt, deserved such a surprise. Hilda, as she was called, belittled everyone, including Karla and her own husband Friedrich. Everyone, that is, except her gentle son Billy, whom she adored. The first time Norma had been invited to dinner to meet Will's parents - she alone called him Will because she thought it made him sound strong and independent - Hilda had pronounced before dinner, "You look a little scrawny; you could use a good dinner now and then." In reaction, Norma had pointedly not eaten all the food on her plate, silently returning the insult. She spurned the dessert altogether, a tall, buttery torte Hilda had spent the day making, telling Hilda politely that she had eaten too much already. Will tried to appease his mother by suggesting that Norma take some of the torte home to her family.

At that same dinner, Hilda berated her husband as soon as he sat down.

"Friedrich, look at your hands! You can't sit at my table with those filthy nails." Friedrich, a cabinetmaker, simply laughed a strange laugh, a loony hoot, at once embarrassed and ridiculing. He did not move from his seat.

"Ma, quit it," Will said gently.

Norma had been most surprised by Karla that evening. Ordinarily a sarcastic loudmouth, Karla was meek and obedient at table. The conversation consisted mainly of Hilda's lecturing Norma on how talented a painter Billy was, and how he had last year won the Milwaukee Journal high school art calendar prize; his painting of a white-tailed deer was on this year's cover of the calendar. As if she did not know. The calendar hung on the door of her closet at home.

"Karla, what do you think the train fare is between here and Las Vegas?"

The two girls walked the few blocks to the train depot and inquired about the fare. "The California Zephyr is what you want. Round trip or one way?" inquired the young Negro behind the counter. "One way," she'd said without pausing. She purchased her ticket for $12.50 without even looking back at Karla. The train was to leave for Chicago in half an hour, then from Chicago for Las Vegas and Los Angeles at 1:30 that afternoon.

They spent that half hour together, nervously waiting, not saying much.

"Call Will and tell him I'm coming," she directed, looking straight into Karla's gray eyes, "and don't tell your mother."

She was not at all sure she could trust Karla, but there was no one else who could help. Karla looked downcast, confused and slightly fearful. When the train pulled in, she pulled a five-dollar bill out of her own wallet and put it into Norma's hand.

"Thanks." Norma stepped bravely onto the train.

"You can pay me back when you get home." And Karla vanished down the walkway, running as if from the scene of a crime.

"We're almost there now," the chunky sergeant advised her, as he got up to fetch his duffel from the overhead rack. He caught the heavy long bag gracefully with his shoulder and told her the best way to get to the base was to hitchhike. Since they stepped out of the train together, they found themselves walking awkwardly side by side but as though not together. Yet he led her to the road in front of the station and helpfully showed her a likely place to catch a ride. Backing away from her, he murmured that she had best catch a car by herself. He waited a distance, watching until she caught a ride with a couple in a shiny Plymouth. Then he stepped up to the road and held out his thumb.

2
Bill

Bill was stunned to see Norma in the base waiting room. He rubbed his eyes. Never one to adjust quickly to change, he was still puzzling over the Hiroshima bomb when he learned about the second bomb today on Nagasaki. Dumbstruck by the magnitude of becoming a bombardier in less than two weeks, he wondered if he would have to drop one of these new bombs on another Japanese city. The enormity of consequences he could not foresee made his thoughts diffuse. Despite all the talk on the base that the war must now be virtually over, he wondered.

And now Norma sat not thirty feet away, on the base, in the middle of all this confusion. He paused beyond her line of view, taking in the improbable fact of her presence. She sat with her arms and legs crossed, one leg swinging energetically up and down. There was the proud head that he had touched and drawn and held lovingly. Her determined straight nose in profile defined her. That perfect oval head, with its thick, wavy dark hair, green eyes, inquisitive brows and full pouting lips both excited and disturbed him. That this beautiful woman had agreed to marry him felt at times too good to be true. Not that he didn't know she could be difficult -- so too were his mother and sister, and, for all he knew, every woman. It was more a sense that he hadn't earned this good fortune. There was more to this woman than he could fathom. This intimation made him cautious, sometimes almost inert.

He swung open the door.

"Will!" Norma leapt toward him. As they kissed, he smelled smoke in her hair and sweat from her days on the train. She tasted eager. He wrapped himself around her, trying to embrace her certainty.

"How did you get here?"

"Raw nerve." She laughed. "Didn't Karla tell you I was coming?"

His confused look was her answer.

"Never mind. I'm starving. Let me tell you the whole story over a good plate of food."

So he took her to the canteen, where she devoured a large bowl of strawberry ice cream and told him all the details of her long train ride. As to what had made her board the train, she skipped Karla's comments about his mother and told him how the bomb would free them both. Her eyes glittered with the relish of her impulsive journey. She searched his face.

"Why aren't you more excited?"

"I'm trying to figure out where you can stay tonight. There's no place on base, and I can't leave."

A glance at her face told him these details had not occurred to her.

It was while they were sitting in the canteen

that the news erupted. The PA crackled with the announcement that Hirohito had ordered a surrender.

"You see," Norma beamed, "I came at just the right time." She leapt up and held him tight.

Yells and whoops of joy reverberated from everywhere on the base. Men collided, embraced each other, danced around in circles. Lines formed at the telephones. Someone broke the locks on the beer kegs, and the canteen soon filled with raucous drinkers. One soldier grabbed and embraced Norma. "Me, too!" another yelled. "Form a line!"

Bill rushed her out of the canteen before the place became a riot. She followed him to the barracks, where he packed a duffel bag with his civvies and overnight gear. Getting leave was no longer an issue. They joined the hordes of soldiers who decided to hitchhike into Las Vegas to celebrate.

The streets of Las Vegas were so chaotic that even Norma was frightened. Wild-eyed men in cowboy hats brandished pistols and shot them skyward. Everyone staggered about drunk. Bill and Norma escaped the crowds as soon as they could and spent the night in a cheap motel with wooden sidewalks flanking the tiny airless shacks. Lizards darted unpredictably over the walls.

What struck Bill then for the first time was Norma's desperate energy. Although they had made love before, the occasions had been stolen, furtive and brief. He'd had to persuade her each time, and his adolescent urgency hadn't roused her beyond reluctance and regrets afterward. On this the first time he had ever spent a whole night with her, everything was different. She unzipped and removed her dress before he could do it. She wrapped her legs around him. All without words, her tongue in his mouth, not letting him speak. Afterward, as he stroked her breasts, she molded her body next to his, as still and warm as a purring cat. Late in the night, the high white moon woke them. In the slightly cooler air, she climbed on top of him and drained him of all the longing of these past months. When he woke the following morning, his face was nestled in her thick hair.

So it was with no reluctance that he found a justice of the peace to marry them the following day. His only doubts surfaced when he suggested they should call each of their parents first, but Norma insisted on surprising them afterward.

Bill walked down the block to a phone booth to make the call to Hilda while Norma showered. His dad answered.

"Pa, I want you to know that Norma and I got married. She came here on the train after she got news of the bomb, and we got married yesterday."

"Your ma better hear this," was all he said before he dropped the receiver and yelled that Bill was on the phone. He repeated the news to Hilda.

"I figured that's what she did." Hilda sighed, before launching in. "Do you realize she told her parents she was going downtown with Karla? Then she roped Karla into helping her buy a train ticket to visit you and made Karla promise not to tell anyone."

"She was supposed to call me, but she didn't."

"Don't interrupt!" Hilda explained that Norma's father had called the first night, worried sick about where Norma was, and asked if Karla knew. "Karla felt she had to keep her promise to Norma, so she told us all that she had left Norma at the bus stop at five that afternoon. Only later when Norma's father was on the verge of calling the police did Karla tell us Norma had jumped on a train."

"She's sort of headstrong..."

"For Chrissake, Bill, that's like calling a tornado headstrong. When you see one coming, you go for cover."

Part of him wanted to say that he hadn't any warning, but he didn't want to make excuses for himself or Norma.

"Ma, I was going to marry her anyway. Can't you just wish us happiness?"

"Billy, do you have any idea what you're getting into?" She hung up.

He kicked a piece of gravel at his feet. It pinged off a car fender at the curb. It wasn't fair for Norma to have left her parents in the dark about where she was. He imagined how frantic they must have felt. Norma should have called them before getting on the train. She should have called them before now. He kicked some more of the gravel at his feet. Even now, if he asked her to call them when he went back to the room, he knew she would find some reason to postpone it.

He picked up the receiver and called them himself. Better for him to tell them than for Hilda to do it.

Helmuth answered, his voice heavy. Bill apologized. He said he was sorry for getting married this way. He apologized for not letting them know where Norma was. He apologized for not letting them have a wedding. It wasn't supposed to happen this way. He took all the blame.

"It's not your fault," Helmuth told him.

Etta got on the line.

"We love you, Bill." She could hardly speak. She started several different sentences and stopped after two or three words. Finally, she said, "Come home soon."

Norma was dressed and brushing her hair when he got back to the room. She looked at him provocatively.

"Not now," he grumbled, and went to change his shirt, which was already damp from his sweat.

The War officially ended within a few weeks of Norma's arrival in Las Vegas, and it was only a few weeks later that Bill was mustered out of the service. They spent all that time together and, after much searching, found a tiny cabin with a tin roof to rent. The only real room was the bathroom, a small extension from one side of the otherwise square building. The entire floor of the bathroom sloped toward a drain in the middle, and it was impossible to take a shower without dousing the sink and toilet at the same time. Quick little lizards gravitated toward this room, and invariably as either Bill or Norma reached for the light to enter, they would hear the tiny scuttle of a startled reptile. They slept in a Murphy bed, and one wall made a sort of alcove for the sleeping area. Opposite this wall was what passed for the dining table. Just big enough for the two of them and a few plates, it flipped down on a hinge from the wall. They heated food on a kerosene stove. Mostly Norma would ask Bill to light it for her; when she had to do it herself, she closed her eyes in fear of an explosion. The bottom of the kitchen sink was stained with rust, but the water flowed freely and tasted good. Though cockroaches infested the kitchen, fortunately they saw no snakes. The lizards became their friends, and Norma grew to enjoy watching their darting movements.

Norma was generally cheerful about keeping this little house. She sewed red and white checked curtains for the kitchen windows and made a matching table cloth. She regularly picked fireweed and other desert flowers and put them into a bottle on their table. Sometimes they hitchhiked into Las Vegas itself, just so Norma could absorb what she called its "raw Western energy." Too daunted to gamble in the new casinos, Bill and Norma wandered the boardwalks, just watching the glitter and gusto about them. One evening they took in a movie and watched a newsreel of the formal Japanese surrender. That all those years of explosions and killing should end with men in top hats and morning coats signing papers in leather books was bewildering.

One day they packed a picnic lunch and hitchhiked into the mountains, where he painted and Norma wandered among the cacti and colored rocks. When clouds massed in the sky, they headed home and were lucky enough to catch a ride before a hailstorm began. They treated themselves to a glass of whisky and listened to the hailstones batter the tin roof while a rare cool breeze caressed them

They talked about where to live after his discharge. To him, it was obvious that they would return to Milwaukee. He would find a job and they would look for an apartment.

"Let's stay here," Norma urged, "away from our families. We already have our own place to live. You can use the GI bill to go to college here."

"If I go to college, we'll have to live with our parents to save on rent. We need to go back."

Norma relented grudgingly. "Only fifty-eight days," she said as they left.

Vacant apartments were scarce that fall. No new homes had been built during the War and thousands of returning soldiers searched for places to live. He and Norma tracked down apartment ads, but people stood in lines at available living spaces. Meanwhile, they stayed with Norma's family in what had been Norma and Britta's room. Sixteen-year-old Bruno slept in the adjacent room, from which they could hear even small sounds, like a pencil dropping on his desk. They tried to imagine privacy. Mercifully, Norma's parents slept down the hall. Britta was displaced to what had been a sewing room. Everyone used the same bathroom. Everyone was uncomfortable.

3
Helmuth

Helmuth Beckman eased his small frame onto the davenport next to his pipe stand. He picked up a packet of tobacco. As he slowly packed his pipe, he sighed inwardly at how seldom lately he'd been able to enjoy this simple, solitary pleasure of a pipe before bed. Although occasionally he would listen to a mystery on the radio while he smoked and contemplated his day, usually he would sit in total contented silence. Now with Norma and Bill in the home, no one was ever alone in a room. It was almost as hectic now as during the Depression when his brother Walter and his wife and children had stayed with them for seven months.

It had been only one month - but a long one - since Norma returned home following her makeshift wedding. If you could call that a wedding. She was supposed to have been married, as she had been baptized, by Pastor Heutchenreuther in Holy Ghost Lutheran Church, when Bill returned from the service. Helmuth exhaled an audible sigh, as he had on so many occasions since Norma's birth. Her having disappeared without telling the family - and not even calling for three days - was only the most recent of the troubles Norma had caused him and Etta. Since birth, she had been a difficult child. Etta's labor had been so prolonged and painful that she had been afraid to have another child. Fortunately, Bruno and Britta had been easier. Even as a baby, Norma was hard to please, squirmy and cranky and seldom smiling. Etta, as warm and nurturing a mother as he had ever seen, could rarely get Norma to cuddle with her. As an older child she sulked while the rest of her family played canasta in the evenings. In school, Norma sometimes defied her teachers, and he and Etta would have to meet with one of them and promise to get her to be more obedient.

In her first three years of high school, oddly, they had had a reprieve. Norma's beauty emerged. She became popular and found a group of friends. She started dating Bill in her junior year. Helmuth smiled to remember the first night Bill had come to the house. Etta and he could hardly believe what a good and gentle young man she had found. When Norma and Bill became engaged following his graduation, at the end of Norma's junior year, he and Etta were relieved at the turn of events. They'd had no idea what disaster Norma would create in her senior year.

Bill joined the Air Corps during the summer following his graduation. Norma's senior year was marked by her restlessness, which they naively attributed to her missing Bill, and by her spending most evenings out with her friends. Not until the spring did they learn that Norma had taken up with Rick Larkin, a smarmy young man with shiny black hair and handsome looks. He seduced her. Worse, it was Bruno who accidentally came upon them, kissing on a bench in Lincoln Park. Bruno, who idolized Bill, came home grumpy and snapped at Helmuth at dinner. When he took Bruno into his room after dinner to upbraid him for talking back to his father, Bruno confessed what he had seen that afternoon. "She should be ashamed," he spat.

Helmuth put his arm around Bruno's shoulder, assured him that Norma should indeed be ashamed, and told him quietly to go to his room.

Then he bellowed as never before or since for Norma to come down that instant.

"You slut! You filthy whore!" he sputtered, slapping her across her lipsticked face. Helmuth's face reddened even now as he recalled the depth of his fury that night.

"You betrayed your future husband, your family and your honor. Gott in Himmel, how could you!" Incredibly, she glared at him, and he slapped her again. Then she slumped into a chair and curled up in tears.

"Don't you even know what a sin this is!" He snorted out each word separately. "After all these years in the church -- in this family, how could you!"

After ordering Norma to her room, Helmuth slumped to his knees and prayed. He prayed for Norma's redemption, and for forgiveness for his own outburst. Then, as now, he had smoked a long pipe and pondered what to do. The next day, he and Etta decided to remove Norma from school, where the temptation had arisen, and to keep her at home until Bill married her. They told the school Norma had become very ill. They told Bill nothing.

To this day, they did not know if Bill knew about Rick.

Perhaps it was better after all that Norma had not had her church wedding.

Helmuth noticed that his pipe had gone out. After dumping the ashes and cleaning the stem by habit, he debated for a moment whether to light another. He did, savoring his solitude.

Fifteen months after the debacle over Rick, Helmuth looked a bit more charitably on the situation. He wanted Norma to be happy with Bill and to have a decent life. She seemed to love him. Soon, inevitably, they would start having children. As much as Etta would enjoy helping with her first grandchild, he realized this house could not accommodate them all for long.

4
1946
Norma

Her first inkling was that peculiar twinge in her breasts. Standing in the middle of the grocery store, surrounded by stacks of bananas and little pyramids of oranges that were back in the market now, she held a pair of rutabagas in her hands and wondered what surge had overtaken her body. A thousand little currents suddenly drawn toward her nipples, as if by some lunar magnetism, momentarily riveted her in place, staring vacantly at the pale vegetables in her hands.

She didn't know what to make of it, but when she later thought to look at her calendar, where she routinely recorded her menstrual periods, it suddenly made sense. She flung the calendar at the wall, as if doing so would banish whatever djinn had taken up residence within her body.

Hilda learned of it almost more quickly than her own mother.

"I *told* you that would happen as soon as you got married!" Hilda stood with her hands on her hips, shaking her head. “And you don’t even have a place of your own to live in.”

“We will soon.” If only she and Will had stayed in Nevada! A dry, warm air would greet them as they opened the door to their little cabin, and silence would surround them. Why had Will insisted on coming back here?

“This will make it impossible for Billy to go to college, and even harder for him to make time to paint. His talent will go to waste.” Hilda fussed over some cookies she was shaping on a baking sheet.

What about me? Norma wanted to scream, but said nothing. She had talents too; why shouldn’t she be able to go to college? She began to save her arguments with Hilda. Pregnancy sapped her energy, left her feeling defeated by circumstances. She felt tired, pervasively tired.

“Have a cookie,” Hilda urged, as she took her own meticulously shaped works of art off the baking sheet.

“I’m too nauseated,” Norma lied. She had not had a single day of nausea, nor had she lost her appetite.

Curiously, Will was the one who seemed to welcome the pregnancy most. At his parents’ home, he defended Norma from Hilda’s verbal barrage. At home he thought to do extra things for her. He didn’t seem to mind when Norma asked him to go downstairs to get the book she had forgotten to bring up to bed with her, even though he’d been working all day. He’d gotten himself a job assembling metal tools at Harnischfeger Corporation. She knew he found it boring, but he didn’t complain. In the evenings, she watched him build a rocking cradle and then lovingly paint it pale green, with pine branches and colorful birds decorating the sides.

Hilda found a way to use the pregnancy to advantage. She phoned one day when Will was at work.

"I've found a job for Bill," she announced. She described a notice in the Journal of an opening for an artist apprentice at the Milwaukee Museum, and veterans would be given preference. "I'm putting together a portfolio of his work, and you and I are going together tomorrow morning to an interview with the director."

"Why me?" Norma murmured, "why not Will? Shouldn't he be the one to go?"

"Do you think for one moment that Billy could tell someone else to hire him?" It was not put as a question. "Don't tell him about this. I'll pick you up at nine tomorrow morning. And Norma," she paused significantly, "look pregnant."

So she and Hilda had dressed up, interviewed with the museum director, an ornithologist by background, and impressed him with Will's bird paintings. By the time he interviewed with the director himself, the job was already his. At least he found work he really loved.

By the time she was seven months pregnant, Will had already made friends with his supervising wildlife artist at work, Jim Thanatopoulos, whose wife Helen was pregnant with their third child, due only a month before hers. They invited Will and her to share a weekend in early June at their lake cottage.

"Wonderful!" She told Will. "It'll be like Nevada without the lizards - and away from my parents." They'd almost not gone, due to tornado warnings on that Friday. But Saturday dawned clear and fresh, and they drove to the cottage in high spirits.

Jim came to the door of the cottage with his six-year-old daughter Demi on his back, half choking him but laughing. He growled at her lovingly to get down, but he neither released her legs nor she his neck. Helen came out with both arms outstretched, four-year-old Themis huddling close to her hip. Her face, like her body, was broad, solid, balanced. She had eyes like black olives, spaced far apart, with long straight lashes. A mane of straight black hair, glisteningly clean, hung nearly to her waist. Behind her smile were big front teeth, with a slight gap between them.

"I've been waiting to meet you." She took one of Bill's and Norma's hands in each of hers. "Welcome."

"What took you so long?" Jim complained with a feigned grumpiness. "The fish are waiting." He led them to their bedroom, facing a screened-in porch and the lake. Pine trees just outside their window rustled gently.

Demi burst in and bounced on the bed while he and Norma began to unpack. "When are you having your baby?" she demanded. "You're not as big as my mom. She's due next month. I'm hoping for a sister, but mom thinks she's so big it must be a boy. Can I touch your belly?"

Norma recoiled visibly from the girl, turning away to put her clothes into a drawer.

"Demetra!" her mother commanded in a smooth voice. "Let our guests relax and put away their things. Come help me in here."

"I'll be back," Demi promised mischievously.

To Norma's relief, the men took Demi fishing

with them. Helen, Themis and Norma went down to the water's sandy edge with a pitcher of lemonade and an umbrella. Themis sprawled under it to nap on the sand. The two women watched the rowboat recede while Demi chattered away in the bow. Helen settled into a hollow into the sand she dug for herself, close to her son. Every so often, she reached over and stroked him gently, on his hair or arm or foot. Norma found her own hollow in the sand, somewhat apart. Its warmth soothed her back, which ached often these days from the weight of her belly.

Helen was easy company. She exuded calm, talked without demanding a reply, and listened thoughtfully.

"I wonder what personality this little one will have," Helen mused. "You see how different Demi and Themis are." She paused, her hand tracing an aimless furrow in the sand. "It was obvious from the moment they were born. Demi squirmed so much I couldn't even keep her in swaddling, and Themis was calm and affectionate from the first day."

"Didn't you ever worry what sort of child you would have?"

Helen looked at her with her wide, reassuring face. "It's normal to worry about everything, especially with your first."

"It's hard for me to imagine being a mother." She drew spirals in the sand with one finger, erasing them with her palm and repeating herself.

"Yes, it's a whole new life after you have a child."

"Is it ever difficult to love your own child?"

"No. It's the most automatic, compelling

feeling.... No, not at all." Helen smiled into the distance, her hand on her own huge belly.

She wondered if she could ever feel that way. She was anxious to give birth, if only to get rid of this unwanted weight, this burden on her freedom. She couldn't really visualize herself as a mother and found herself trying to think of anything else. In her mind she was as light and lithe and free as the young woman who boarded the train on a dare last August. Her body was a disgusting appendage she refused to recognize.

The men and Demi returned later with fish. Demi carried them on a string, excitedly racing up the pier to show her mother. As she held them in front of her, water dripped onto Norma's leg, and she moved it pointedly, hastily wiping the drops off her calf with the towel. Helen sent Demi to ask her father to teach her how to clean them, and she ran off as eagerly as she had come.

Later in the afternoon, the men waded in the water with the children while Helen disappeared into the kitchen to prepare dinner. She helped Helen bring the dishes to the table: a big platter of fish baked in olive oil and lemon, with potatoes alongside, a bowl of spinach with lemon, and a basket of bread. Demi helped Themis take the bones out of his fish. Norma absorbed the harmony of this family even as she could not imagine it for herself.

After dinner, she and Will took a walk along the lake shore. As they walked, the silhouette of pines against the pale yellow horizon gradually disappeared into an inky darkness. Stars emerged above, multiplied, and fireflies dazzled fleetingly in front of them. An owl hooted. Will told her how much he would like to have a place like this someday; wouldn't she? She admitted she would. When they returned to the cottage, she sat on the stoop while Will wiped the sand off her feet. She giggled unexpectedly, tickled by his gentle touch. The screen door slapped behind them as they went in to bed. She listened again for the owl as they lay together, with Will curled around her back, resting his hand on the beach ball that was now her belly. She fell asleep quickly. They awoke the next morning inhaling the piney air, and after breakfast everyone went into the water, she and Helen just wading in their shorts. By the time they left to drive home, she felt happier than she had in months.

Six weeks later, Will answered a phone call after dinner from Jim. She watched his face crack into shards. "Can we visit her?"

"What happened?"

"Helen's child was stillborn." He sighed and looked away before continuing. "Helen is still in the hospital. Nothing's wrong with her physically, but she's ... *tormented*, was the word Jim used. He asked us to visit her. He told me Helen would like to see you."

She looked up at him mournfully and said spontaneously, "She was lucky."

Immediately she regretted it. What she meant was that *she* would feel lucky if she could lose this ungovernable weight growing like a tumor inside her own body. But she couldn't say that to Will; he wanted this child so much. There wasn't anything she could say. Of course it was a tragedy for Helen. She was a natural mother.

"You can't mean that."

She looked up at him plaintively. *He* had never

carried a rock around in his belly or had his life defined by taking care of a child.

Will slammed the door as he left the house. She never learned what explanation he gave Helen for her not coming to the hospital.

Her own baby arrived a few weeks later, on a steamy August Saturday. She stood up from a chair in the back yard to reach for a glass of lemonade. Warm water spilled in a torrent down the inside of her legs, soaking her shoes. She shrieked. Her mother came out, took her arm gently and told her it was time to go to the hospital.

5
Bill

Ten hours after they arrived at the hospital, the doctor emerged to tell him he was the father of a healthy seven-pound baby girl. But before the doctor would allow him in to see Norma, he asked Etta to come in. Etta came out again after a little while. She looked drained, but she smiled encouragingly at him. They hugged each other. "Your daughter is lovely," she said, "and I know ... you'll be a wonderful father." He saw fatigue in the slump of her shoulders. "Norma's fine," she managed, "but...." Her face crimped.

The doctor allowed him into the nursery to see his daughter, but he too had a sort of vague, quizzical look, causing Bill to ask again about his wife.

"She is ... well," the doctor said, picking his words. "She's sleeping now; you should wait until morning to see her. But your daughter is superb. Here she is. You can hold her if you like."

The doctor picked up the tiny bundled child, a gauze cap over what seemed to be tiny brown curls on her head. Her round sleepy face bore a peaceful, beatific expression. When she briefly opened her eyes, she gazed into his own eyes, which instantly became wet with joy. The doctor's queer look showed some relief.

Although it was one in the morning when he arrived home, he did not go immediately to bed. He took out the painted cradle and began to fill it lovingly with cushions and blankets. After rearranging them several times, he placed the cradle next to Norma's side of their bed and collapsed into a deep, happy sleep.

He awoke surprisingly early, refreshed and excited to see Norma and their daughter. When he arrived in Norma's room, she was trying to eat breakfast, but the left side of her face seemed oddly stuck in a downcast expression. Her hair unkempt, she stabbed at her eggs with the fork. Their baby was not in the room.

"Look what happened to me," she snapped, "half of my face frozen from having that child. The doctor won't tell me when - or if – I'll be normal again." She threw down her fork and began to cry bitterly. "I never wanted to get pregnant. I wanted to get away and make my own life with you. Now what's going to happen to me?"

"I love you," he stammered. "We'll have our own life, even our own home someday. And you'll feel better soon," he tried to persuade himself.

"You did this to me!" She glared at him.

He backed out of the room, tears of another kind welling in his eyes. He went to the men's room and stood for a long time leaning his head against the cool tile wall. When he felt more composed, he went to find the doctor.

"The palsy is temporary," he explained. "She doesn't believe me, but her muscle control will be back within a few days or a couple weeks at most. What is more troubling is her depression. Some women suffer a bleak post-partum depression that can last as much as several months. You can't believe all she says. Many women come out of this kind of thing embracing parenthood. But in the meantime, you'll have to pull a little harder on the oars as a parent. She'll come out of it," he concluded unconvincingly.

"Your daughter is doing fine," he brightened. "Do you want to see her again?"

"Of course." Again he cradled his daughter's little warm head in his hand; again her eyes opened and locked with his.

The doctor proved correct about the palsy. Within two weeks, Norma's face and muscle coordination returned to normal. But she had no interest in holding or caring for their child. He caught her several times looking at the tiny baby with disgust. He moved the cradle to his side of the bed and Etta taught him how to sterilize bottles and mix formula. He and Etta took turns taking care of the baby's simple needs, each of them eager to touch and smell and hold the fragile child.

At some time while Norma lay in her paralysis of regret, he named the child Gretchen. He couldn't have explained why; it just came to him as a lovely German name. He painted her name onto the cradle he had made. He found himself exhausted but quite happily taken up with the small burdens of feeding her and lulling her to sleep.

He watched as Etta tried gradually to get Norma to hold the child and feed her, but Norma was plainly disinterested. "No, you do it," she would say. "She doesn't want to take the bottle from me."

There was some truth in what Norma said; the child would not readily take the bottle from her. She'd purse her lips or turn her head and squirm. When Etta or he took Gretchen, the baby's body relaxed and she opened her mouth eagerly.

No one even tried to get Norma to change Gretchen's diapers or wake her in the middle of the night. Occasionally, he caught a curious look on Norma's face as she bent over to watch him feed Gretchen. "She looks strange," Norma said, "not at all like me, or you either. Even Britta was pretty as a baby." He held the baby a bit more closely and said nothing. To him, she was perfect.

Jim had asked if he and Helen could see the new baby. Bill had told him not to come to the hospital, since Norma was embarrassed by her palsy, but that excuse soon evaporated. After some weeks, he began to tell Jim at work one day why he had not invited them to see the baby. They were painting side by side on a large diorama. "The doctor says it's post-partum depression," he began, and described how Norma seemed totally disinterested in the baby. He did not tell Jim what Norma had said when Helen's child was stillborn. He would never tell Jim about that; but also, he had vowed never again to bring Norma anywhere near Helen.

Jim said nothing for some minutes, while he continued painting. Bill knew he was not ignoring him.

"We never think how dangerous it is to have a child. We just do it, like these animals." He gestured toward the elk standing in the diorama.

"Why don't you bring Gretchen over some evening. It'll do Helen good to hold a healthy baby again, and we'd all like to meet her."

It was easy for him to take Gretchen for the evening to visit Jim and his family without Norma. She seemed to welcome the time by herself. Jim picked up Bill and Gretchen after work, so he could hold the baby while Jim drove them to his home.

Demi was the first to insist on holding the baby, and Helen bent over her to make sure she cradled the baby's head, explaining that the baby didn't yet have the muscles to hold up her own head. Demi bent to show Themis, and Gretchen smiled at him. "She likes me," he beamed. Helen asked to hold Gretchen, and he could feel her exquisite tenderness as she took the baby from Demi. Helen glanced up at him, and their eyes locked in an instant of silent, mutual understanding. He looked away, his eyes wet.

Everyone enjoyed that evening. Bill basked in the company of a family who all treasured the new baby, and Jim's family appreciated an interlude with the new life they had craved. Even Norma seemed more cheerful when he returned home. She had had a chance to read a novel by herself.

They made it a regular ritual: once a week he took Gretchen for an evening with Jim's family. Gradually, their ritual grew into a weekend at the lake cottage every three or four weeks during the summer months. When Gretchen was baptized, Helen and Jim became her sponsors, even though they were not Lutheran. Norma balked at attending the baptism, and he dissuaded Helmuth from requiring her to come. Gretchen's four grandparents and Helen and Jim circled the baptismal font while he held his daughter and the pastor dripped water on her moonlike sleeping face.

6
Norma

They say a woman is attuned to the slightest sound from her own child. It was true even for Norma. Early in the morning, when the baby began to wake – it would murmur or make some other quiet, small sound, not even a cry – she would awaken and just lie still, her own eyes closed, and wait. Will also awoke at the baby's first sounds, she knew, and at first he'd waited too, to see if she would respond. After the first few weeks, though, he'd stop waiting for her. He knew. He'd roll out of the bed gently, trying not to disturb her as he tended to his daughter.

By this time Gretchen was eight weeks old. What an odd name Will had given the baby. To her, the name recalled some innocent in an obscure German fairy tale, the sort of child to whom unspeakably bad things happen. Will had moved the cradle to his side of the bed. Tending to the baby came to him naturally, she thought, as it never would to her. He molded her small body to himself protectively and stroked her back with his long fingers. Norma watched him admiringly when he was not looking. Sometimes in the evenings he'd lay the infant lengthwise on his lap, its head at his knees, and gaze at her with wide eyes, making a sound like a cat's purr or audible, contented sigh.

It was better this way. The helpless little thing really was his daughter, and it deserved someone to love it. The baby relaxed in her father's or grandmother's arms and not in her own for a good reason. You can't fake it, she thought; even a newborn recognizes who loves it just by how it is held.

As she lay still in the bed, wanting Will to think she was still asleep, Norma wondered if Etta had felt this way about her as an infant, intruding on her need to recover from the labor that, as Norma had been told so many times, had almost killed her. Yes, better for the infant to be held by someone who loves her.

She drifted back to sleep after Will took the baby out of the room. For the first time in her life, she was sleeping late, and she liked it. Morning dreams drifted lazily in and out of her consciousness. Sometimes she would be walking across the Nevada desert in early morning, watching the sky turn from peach to pale lemon to a white blaze of sunrise. Usually what woke her was the klop-klop and bells of the gray horse that pulled the wagon of the raggedy old man who collected leftover goods. "Rags, bags, bottles and iron," came the mournful cry from the white-bearded man who had seemed ancient even when she was a child. In the evenings, her mother put out on the curb used bottles and bound newspapers and the occasional broken tool. When Etta forgot, it used to be Norma's chore to run out in the morning with the castoffs and hand them to the man. His fingers were always gritty and dark, and she dreaded facing him. Now the task was Britta's and Norma enjoyed the luxury of lying in bed listening to the horse and the bells.

Part One

7
1951
Gretchen

Four-year-old Gretchen ventured into her mother's bedroom one day and clambered up onto the chair in front of the vanity, attracted by the array of lipsticks. She opened one after another of the golden metal tubes, replacing the caps and trying to line them up as she had found them, until she uncovered a bold pink one that looked irresistible. With whatever accuracy she could muster, she smeared it over her mouth, then rubbed her lips together as she had watched her mother do so many times before she went out in the afternoon. Just as she paused to admire herself with this new color on her face, her mother entered the room.

"What are you doing!" she snarled, baring her teeth. Her arms flew up and her fingers curled like claws.

Gretchen dropped the lipstick tube. When it hit the floor, the colored part broke off from the tube and left a pink smear on the carpet. Instinctively, Gretchen shrank toward the corner, away from her mother.

"Now look what you've done!" she shrieked. "Nothing is safe from you, you clumsy little brat!" Norma wrenched Gretchen by the arm and flung her small body against the wall.

"Now get out of here while I clean up your mess."

Gretchen ran down the stairs as fast as she could, to get as far away from her mother as possible. She opened the door to the basement. Her chest heaved with tears. She sat down on the top stair, crying in the darkened stairwell. As she gradually calmed down, she could hear the washer downstairs. That meant Grandma was probably working down there. She carefully made her way down the stairs, holding onto the railing.

Lights were on at the far wall, where Grandma Etta stood next to the two big cold sinks feeding clothes slowly through the wringer washer. Gretchen loved this contraption, a big round bin on legs that wobbled as it washed the clothes. There Grandma stood patiently feeding each piece of clothing through the double wringers after she pulled it from the bin.

"I see I have company," she said gently. "Come on over, dear."

As Gretchen approached, Grandma Etta must have noticed the lipstick, now smeared over more than the area of Gretchen's lips.

"Oh-oh, I bet I know where you've been. Is it your mother's or mine?" she inquired amiably. "I remember when your mother used to get into my make-up; in fact, I can even remember doing it myself when I was a little girl." She chatted on while watching the clothes. As Gretchen came close and put her arms around her Grandma's legs, Grandma Etta looked into her teary eyes.

"Did you yell at Mama when she did it?"

"Probably," she allowed, "but it's not serious. Your mama knows all girls do this at some time or other."

"But I broke it," Gretchen started to cry again. "Mama probably wasn't so clumsy when she used your lipstick."

Etta pressed her foot on a pedal at the base of the machine, and the wringers separated. She knelt down and put her plump soft arms around the trembling small girl.

"You're not clumsy, dear. You're just a little girl, and a very fine one at that." She lifted Gretchen, who was almost too heavy to be held like a baby, and held her tightly.

Putting Gretchen down, Grandma Etta invited her to help pull the clothes out of the wringers. Gretchen eagerly lifted her arms to the task.

"Grandma," she asked after a little while, "why does Mama always get so mad and yell at me?"

"It's not you, dear," she said, pausing as if to say more, but she didn't.

"Make sure you keep your hands away from the wringer, dear," she instructed, as she and Gretchen continued at their task together.

Norma

Norma wished she hadn't yelled at Gretchen, but the girl had broken a new, expensive lipstick she had just bought for her interview this afternoon with a modeling agency. The lipstick had cost as much as a day's groceries. She had justified the expense by telling herself it would get her a modeling job, which would allow her to save some money so that she and Will could get out of her parents' home and find a place of their own. No one knew about the interview, not even Will, but her mother had looked at her suspiciously as she walked out of the house all made up and dressed as if for a party. Etta had not asked for an explanation and Norma had not offered one. Never mind. The stylish woman who ran the agency had liked her and arranged for a photographer to take a series of photos of her for their portfolio. Soon she would have modeling assignments and some spending money to spare. Maybe her picture would be in the newspaper in some classy ad. She promised to tell Will only after she brought home her first paycheck. And, she promised herself, she would hide her cosmetics better so that Gretchen wouldn't find them and she wouldn't have to feel bad about yelling at her.

Gretchen

Five-year-old Gretchen stood in the doorway of the attic. Inside, tucked under the steep slant of the pitched roof, her father was painting. This was his "studio," the only room the family could find where he could be alone with his big tilted desk and do what he loved best. He sat so still, with his back hunched over, that he could be sleeping upright, except for the small movements of his hand she could see in the mirror on the sloping ceiling just above him. It was late afternoon, and a warm light slanted across the wooden floor, giving him a long shadow. Because the only window in the room was below the height of his desk, he had installed the mirror over him so that he would have some reflected natural light.

There was almost total silence in the room, except for the occasional clink of his brush on the small rinsing can. She could smell the turpentine. On the desk in front of him, reflected in the overhead mirror and next to his painting, lay a small, brilliant orange and yellow lump. She wanted to see the thing with the intense color, but hesitated. Gretchen knew her father liked to be alone when he painted.

She edged into the room. Her shoes creaked on the floor. She nestled up to her father, who slipped his arm around her shoulder gently, without turning around.

"Hello, liebchen." He continued to paint. The orange thing was a dead bird, its wings folded into its side, its tiny feet curled and withdrawn, lying on its back. All but its color was lifeless. On the canvas was the same bird, but lively, its wings spread, beak open and obviously calling, feet poised as though to land. Next to it was what looked like a long, brown, fuzzy balloon, hanging from the branch of a tree.

"What's that?" she said, pointing at the long balloon-like thing.

"It's a weaver bird and his nest. He's just built it out of tiny branches and vine pieces so that he can get a wife. Inside, he puts soft feathers for the eggs and mother bird."

"What's he doing?"

"He's flapping his wings and showing off his nest in order to attract a wife." She looked at the painting with her head cocked to one side, her indigo eyes pensive.

"May I touch it?"

"Very carefully." He pulled her up onto his

lap and placed the brightly feathered bird into her cupped hand. She petted it with one finger, touched its beak. Bill smoothed a bit of her hair behind her ear. She leaned up against him.

"Daddy, if he couldn't build a nest," she pondered, replacing the bird on the desk, "would he be able to get a wife?"

"Probably not."

8
Sunday Morgan

Jorge was coughing in the bed next to his, but there was nothing new about that; Jorge was always coughing. The nuns gave him cough medicine before he went to sleep each night, but it never lasted all night long, and the coughing began again before it got light in the mornings. Five-year-old Sunday hoped he would not catch Jorge's cough. When Russell had had a bad cough, they took him away to the hospital and he never came back. Sunday looked up at the clock with its glowing numbers on the gray wall. The small hand was on the five, a long time before the nuns would come in to wake them with clapping hands and their orderly voices, even a longer time before it would get light outside.

Sunday often awoke this early, his first thoughts always what day it was. If it was Tuesday or Thursday or Saturday, it meant he would see Sequoia. On Mondays, Wednesdays and Fridays, she had classes all day long and she had to go to work in the evenings. Today was Saturday.

That meant the nuns would come in at seven rather than six, and early mass would be at eight rather than seven. After mass, there would be oatmeal for breakfast and then, for those children who had families who visited them, visiting time with their families. The other children were herded off to the big room before the families came, so they wouldn't see the visitors. There they played games or did chores or went outside to play if the weather was okay. Sunday looked at the window high up on the wall, but it was too dark to see what kind of weather they would have today. It would be cold; he knew from the wind he could hear rattling the windows even at this hour.

He missed Sequoia. She hadn't been here since last Saturday, when she told him she had exams this week. She needed to study hard so she could become a teacher and get a home for the two of them. She told him he should study hard this week too and practice every day on the piano with Sister Mary Margaret, which he had done. He wished he could practice this morning too before Sequoia came, but the piano was in the big room where the children without families would be all day. He liked Sister Mary Margaret and he could tell she liked him. When she gave him piano lessons, it was as if she were letting him in on secrets of the piano. If he touched the keys just this way, the piano would 'sing to him.' That's what she said. He wanted to play for Sequoia today and show her what he had learned this week, but that would have to wait.

He hoped she would bring cookies today – peanut butter, not oatmeal raisin like last week. He told her they had oatmeal every morning in the winter and he didn't need any more of that. Sequoia would take him downtown today and they would go hear music; she promised.

He woke to a gentle hand on his cheek and

smiled before he even opened his eyes. It was Ruth, the new nun, who came in without clapping her hands and woke each boy gently. To be touched like that....it was such a fresh and amazing feeling. None of the boys let on to each other or anyone else that Ruth did anything out of the ordinary.

Sunday dressed quickly, ate and then raced to the waiting room. He was the first one there. Gradually, the other boys with families wandered in, still wiping the sleep out of their eyes or bumping each other good-naturedly. Jeremy's aunt and uncle arrived first, looking stiff as always, but they had Jeremy's cousin with him and the two boys tore off at once, like puppies biting the same sock. Sunday watched each of the boys leave with their families and looked for the hundredth time at the clock. Sequoia was late. She was never late. But today she was not here. The attendant got up from her desk and came around to the chair where Sunday slumped, looking at the floor. She asked if he would come with her to the big room. Before he answered, he felt a blast of cold air and looked at the door. Sequoia burst through it as if she were rescuing a trapped miner.

"I'm here; I'm here, Sunday." She grabbed him up against her. "I'm so sorry I'm late." He felt the cold air on the outside of her wool coat and tried to open it so he could hold the warm middle of her. But she was so agitated she wouldn't stop moving, wouldn't stop apologizing to him and to the attendant. He just clung to her leg until she stopped. Gradually, she slowed down, bending down to kiss him on the cheek. "I won't let that happen again. I promise," she said. She snapped his cap around his ears, zipped his jacket, tied his scarf around his neck and put on his mittens. He noticed that she held a big paper bag and he bent over to smell it. Peanut butter cookies. The bag was warm and spotted with butter from the cookies.

Out on the street Sequoia told him they would take a bus downtown to the dime store, where he could pick out a toy. Then they would have lunch and go to the jazz concert. "Are your exams over?" he asked. Yes, she assured him, and she thought they went well. She would graduate in another year, and next week they would be back to their regular Tuesday, Thursday and Saturday schedule. A year sounded like a long time.

She couldn't stop apologizing for being late. She had overslept.

"I've never done that in a month of Sundays." She shook her head, then smiled at him. "How could there be a month of Sundays? There's only one of you."

"Koya," he couldn't quite say her full name. "How did I get my name?" The nuns had asked him this. He watched her closely, not sure he could hear her on the street with other people around. She blinked a little, as if some dust had blown into her eye.

Sequoia shuddered imperceptibly, an unwelcome memory leaking into the front of her mind. Their mother lay stinking on a hospital mattress. A nurse stood close by, holding her newborn baby brother, hesitating to place the baby next to his hung-over, irritable mother.

"What is his name?" the nurse asked.

Their mother looked up absently. "What day is it?" she asked.

"Sunday," the nurse told her.

"Well, that's it, then," their mother said, and closed her eyes.

"Sunday is the most blessed day of the week," Sequoia told him, taking his hand on the sidewalk.

"That's just what the nuns told me."

9
Gretchen

It was the first week of December, and already both grandmothers were busy baking. Grandma Hilda and her two sisters had made the first three batches of Christmas cookies and were busy on the next three. It was the one time of year Gretchen could eat as many sweets as she wanted, and these tiny, buttery cookies were the best. Even the tins were special, printed with St. Nick or Christmas trees. Inside, tucked on top of a lace doily, were little jam-filled sandwich cookies, shaped cookies with sprinkles, balls covered with nuts, gingerbread men, chocolate-covered circles, and fingers covered in powdered sugar. Grandma Hilda bragged that she and her sisters made fifty different kinds of cookies one year. There were stollens, too. Grandma Hilda's was rich and heavy, a flat cake dense with raisins and other fruits. Grandma Etta made a stollen that looked more like a frosted bread, and they ate it at breakfast with butter on it.

Gretchen could smell the yeast even from upstairs, and went down to ask her Grandma Etta if she could help. There were two big bowls on the kitchen counter, with dish towels covering them.

"Ssshhh," Grandma Etta said gently, "the dough is rising and we mustn't disturb it." The centers of the towels were above the level of the bowls.

"How does it rise?"

"It's the yeast." She looked down at Gretchen, who clearly did not comprehend.

"The yeast is what you smell now. When you put it into hot water with sugar and then add that to dough, it blows air into the dough and makes all those little holes or spaces you see in bread."

"Can I blow air into the dough?"

Grandma Etta laughed, but in a kindly way. "No, only the yeast can do it." But once the dough had risen, she let Gretchen help fold in the sticky preserved fruit and the slivered almonds.

"Now punch it." Gretchen looked up as if to ask why.

"Like this." Grandma Etta brought her fists down so hard on the dough that Gretchen jumped. "You do it." Gretchen took her turn at pounding her small hands on the dough. Grandma Etta laughed with delight, and Gretchen started to laugh too.

"This will give it a good second rising."

The family Christmas tree was downstairs in her grandparents' part of the house, because there was not enough room for one upstairs. They decorated it on the afternoon of Christmas Eve. Grandma Etta always let Gretchen put on the first ornament, because, as she said, Gretchen was the first grandchild.

"Will you have more grandchildren?" Gretchen asked. Grandma Etta handed her another ornament.

"Probably when Bruno and Britta grow up and get married," she answered, her back to Gretchen.

"What a good job you did!" Grandma Etta told her when they had finished. Gretchen felt proud of her tree decorating until a few hours later when she saw her mother re-arrange the ornaments she had hung.

After the tree was decorated and the tinsel hung, the whole family (including Aunt Meta, Uncle Bruno and Gretchen's great aunt Esther) ate a simple, early supper – a big bowl of pea soup – and then went to church together. Gretchen sat between Grandma Etta and her father, who held their hymnals as they sang carols. Gretchen hardly needed to look at the book; she knew the words and loved to sing with Grandma Etta, whose singing voice was clear and high. Her father kept his voice low, because, he told her, he didn't have a good singing voice. Her mother refused to sing.

It was the best time of the year, not even counting the presents waiting at home. This year, her parents gave her a Viewmaster, a black plastic contraption that she could look into and see pictures. Her grandparents gave her several rings of slides to use in the Viewmaster. Gretchen put the contraption to her face and, as she pressed a button, saw for the first time a cable car on a steep city street, a tall orange bridge over water, and trees so wide that a car could drive through the trunk. "Where's California?" she asked. Her father told her it was a state at the far west of the country, very far away. No one in their combined families had ever been there. To them all, California existed only on a map or in these slides.

10

1953

Gretchen

Just after Gretchen's seventh birthday, her father bought their first car, a slightly-used 1951 aqua Ford Fairlane. "The color of the sky on a perfect June day," he announced proudly. To Gretchen, it was the sky car, better than a carnival ride. Every evening after supper for the remainder of the summer, they drove it to Koszinski Park, slowly wound along the wooded roads, and counted rabbits in the twilight. Gretchen was the best rabbit spotter. "That's nine!" she would yell as a cottontail bounded into the bushes.

Her mother loved the car too, perhaps more than anyone else in the family. Bill taught her to drive while Gretchen stayed home with her grandparents. Norma learned quickly; it wasn't long before Gretchen began to ride to the supermarket in the front seat with her mother. Even Gretchen could see the look of quiet excitement radiating from her mother when she took the car out to drive. Norma never picked on her in the car; she was too intent on the pleasure of driving.

On Labor Day weekend, the three of them drove all the way to Door County, taking a picnic lunch with them. Gretchen played with the wing window next to her seat; she could make it whistle if she angled it properly. She pretended to be soaring through the sky. Her mother drove part of the way and even sang to the music on the radio.

"Remember the picnic in the Nevada hills near our cabin?" Norma leaned toward Bill and put her hand lightly on the back of his neck. Her voice crooned. Gretchen watched her mother intently; she had never heard her mother use this tone of voice before. Her dad leaned over and kissed Norma. They talked about the painting he had started that day, about the rain, about the tiny cabin.

"How come you didn't bring me?" Gretchen asked to the front seat.

No one answered. They began to sing a song together about a dusty trail. Her parents laughed.

Gretchen leaned forward.

"Why didn't you bring me?" She asked more loudly.

Her parents looked at each other and laughed.

"You weren't born yet, dear," her father leaned around and patted her cheek. Her mother stopped singing. But she continued to talk to her father with that odd, lilting voice that didn't belong to her at all.

Gretchen was silent for the rest of the drive, punching out and dressing paper dolls in the back seat but furtively watching her parents up front. It dawned on her that her parents had had some other life to themselves, not involving her at all. She knew, of course, from as far back as she could remember, that her mother wished she had never been born, but this was the first time it occurred to her that her father too might have preferred that earlier time. Gretchen's stomach cramped, as if she were going to be sick, but she said nothing.

They picnicked at an old one-room school house. While her mother laid out the food on a blanket, she ran to the swings. Pumping furiously, she soon swung high enough to be weightless for a moment at the top, staring up into the sky instead of down at her parents. She imagined taking off into that moment, floating up into the puffed-up clouds, where she would disappear - floating, bodiless - just eyes and thought. She would watch her parents scurry around below, wondering where she was, her dad worrying for a while, and then, when satisfied that she was really and truly gone, the two of them would dance around together in joy.

Gretchen felt arms on the chain of her swing, slowing her down.

"Whoa, girl, that's a bit too high to be safe," her dad said gently.

"DON'T TOUCH ME!" She flung herself off the swing at its highest arc, stumbled to her knees, and ran to the back of the schoolhouse. From its steps she could see the sky car. What if she got into it and just drove away? Would her mother be more glad to lose her or sad to lose her precious car? She could hear steps coming around one side of the schoolhouse, so she jumped off the stairs and ran around the other side, bypassing the car.

Her mother was fussing with the food, her skirt spread out in a circle around her on the picnic blanket.

"I made you a sandwich," her mother said into

the air, as though Gretchen had no body or face to look into. Her mother's voice had no feeling in it; that awful crooning was gone, but at least she was not angry.

Her father came around from the other side of the schoolhouse and sat down close to her. He cut an apple and handed her pieces, looking at her searchingly. She kept her eyes down but took the apple.

11
Norma

Norma smiled whenever she heard Gretchen call it the sky car; it was such a good name. "Makes me feel high as the sky," she admitted to Will and Gretchen. Driving the car invariably lifted her mood and allowed her some of the freedom she craved. Will took the bus to work and left the car for her to use whenever she wanted. She was getting modeling assignments now with some frequency, and she drove to them, without telling anyone except Will. He seemed dubious about the work but grateful for the paychecks she handed him.

"You know you don't have to do this," he told her more than once, as if her working cast some discredit on him.

"I like it. I get paid to stroll down a runway wearing beautiful dresses and even mink coats." No need to mention the department managers who felt entitled to lay their hands on the dresses while she wore them. "And I get discounts at the stores."

"Our parents would consider this a bad idea," he told her, as if that would dissuade her.

"Don't tell them; it's that simple." Yet she knew it might not be simple for much longer. She had just done her first photo assignment, an ad for Nibel's Furs that was to appear in the Journal. Maybe her parents wouldn't notice the ad; certainly no one in her family wore furs.

"Savings for our own apartment," was her confident refrain that always ended the discussion.

Often, when she was not working, she would just take off impulsively for aimless drives into the countryside while Gretchen was in school. She'd decide only after she sat behind the wheel whether to drive north or west and then maneuver onto winding country roads. Where the land rolled gently or lay flat, farms claimed the landscape, tall silos and imposing red barns marking their dominion over the surrounding orderly rows of corn or meadows of Guernsey cows. Where the land was hillier, thick forests still proclaimed the wilder history of the region. Norma found herself at peace on these drives. No one could watch or correct her. She could sing to the radio if she felt like it, and no one could remind her that she had an awful singing voice. As a child she'd had to sing in the church choir, although the director used to tell her she had no sense of key. She'd wondered why her parents had insisted on her doing something for which she had no talent. She wouldn't impose that on Gretchen. She knew she wouldn't ever be the world's most devoted mother, but Gretchen sometimes inexplicably made her happy.

Fall was the best season in Wisconsin. The humidity and mosquitoes had gone, the air smelled crisp, and the trees blazed into color. Maybe next week, when Gretchen was home from school for teacher conferences, she would drive her to an apple farm and they could pick apples together.

12
Gretchen

Home from school for teacher conference day, Gretchen was rearranging the furniture in the big dollhouse Grandpa Helmuth had made for her. The dollhouse family was seated at the dinner table in the dining room, but the daughter was in the attic, playing alone. Gretchen decided to put the twin beds from the grandparents' bedroom into the parents' bedroom, and move the big bed from the parents' room to the grandparents' room, so they could hug each other and keep warm at night.

"Get your jacket; we're going out for a drive." Her mother thrust herself into the room. Her voice had that edge to it that told Gretchen she had no choice in the matter. She'd overheard her mother yelling at Grandma Etta over something about modeling, but she'd tried to ignore it and stay out of the way.

Gretchen went to her closet to fetch her jacket. Her legs tingled from having fallen asleep under her. She could not feel one foot at all, but she struggled to move normally. Her mother was in no mood for delay.

As they left the house, Norma went back toward

the kitchen to say something to Grandma Etta. Gretchen could smell oatmeal cookies. She wanted to run into the kitchen herself to get one, but her mother's voice stopped her.

"Don't you *ever* tell me again what I can't do!" Her mother yelled as she swung the kitchen door shut. She stomped out the door. Gretchen followed as unobtrusively as she could. Why was her mother yelling at Grandma Etta?

Her mother backed the car out of the driveway without looking, stopping just in time to avoid backing into a truck. The truck driver honked. Gretchen glanced at her mother, who cursed under her breath. She was afraid to ask where they were going and wished she had sat in the back seat.

Before long they were out of the city. Fortunately, they lived at its edge, and the busy streets soon became a country highway, with farms and silos and cows and only a few cars. Gretchen sat very still, glancing sidewise at her mother from time to time. She thought there were tears coming down her mother's cheeks, but there was no sound and no movement in her face. Her mother was driving very fast. Gretchen held the armrest as tightly as she could.

After a while, the road became winding and hilly. Gretchen thought she recognized it as the road to the orchard where they sometimes picked apples on their way to a tall hill with a monastery on it. Scary-looking men in hooded brown robes and sandals lived there. You could climb one of the church towers and look around the whole countryside. Her parents had taken her there last fall to see the colored trees on the hills all around. She hated it. The wind howled in from the outside, and Gretchen felt as if it would blow her out one of the steeple windows. Instead of the red trees, she saw an image of her bloody body splatted on the cobblestones below.

Gretchen had to hold onto the seat to avoid sliding toward her mother when they rounded the curves. Her mother was driving much too fast. But now she looked happier; she had that soft look that appeared only when she was driving the sky car.

"Remember when we took you to Holy Hill last October?"

Gretchen shuddered. "Is that where we're going?"

"We're going to pick apples," her mother said dreamily. Gretchen dared to turn her head to look at her. Her mother's mind was somewhere else; she was smiling slightly, a peaceful look on her face. Gretchen let the tightness in her body ease. She allowed herself to look out the window. A gray cat stretched itself against a window of a blue farmhouse as they drove past; an old lady leaned forward in her chair to glimpse the car. Ahead of them the road wound gradually up a steep hill. Huge maples and elms lined the road. The wheels crunched on fallen leaves as they whizzed along. They had left the farmhouses behind, and now they were in a colorful woods with yellow elms and red maples and green pines.

All too slowly, Gretchen realized they were heading toward a huge tree on the right side of the road; her mother was not turning with the road. Her mother's eyes were closed, a smile still on her serene face. Should she grab the wheel?

"Mama!"

Her mother opened her eyes, without surprise,

and shifted the wheel slightly to the left. The dreamy smile never left her face.

Gretchen clamped her eyes shut. What she heard was crunching, metal and wood. What she felt was a spray of glass, like stones pelting her. Then the windshield hit her hard on the front of her head. What had she done to the sky car to make it hit her? Or was it her mother who had hit her? What had she done to get hit so hard? When she woke, she lay shivering in wet red leaves. Someone was lifting her onto a stretcher. She could hear a siren, and then all went black and silent again.

Gretchen woke up again, screaming. She thought at first it was the siren, but it was her own screaming. She stopped when she saw her father's face, though it scared her too. He looked sad, as if she had died, though he changed his expression right away when he saw her look at him. He bent over her hospital bed, his long fingers stroking her cheeks. His lips were cool on her forehead. His touch was gentle.

"Honey, you're okay, you're safe. Grandma and Grandpa and I are here. You're in the hospital, but you'll come home soon. Everything's going to be fine." His face contradicted his words, and she closed her eyes again.

"Where's Mama?" She felt his hand twitch, then tighten on hers.

"She's here, too, honey. She got hurt a bit, and she'll have to stay a little longer, but we'll all be home again soon."

Gretchen started to cry. It got worse and worse; soon her whole body was wrenched with her sobs and she couldn't talk. Her father held her tightly.

"It's my fault!" she sobbed. He put his hand on her mouth to still her. She jerked her head away.

"Daddy, I should have turned the steering wheel. I saw the tree coming and Mama didn't. Mama had her eyes closed and didn't even see it until it was too late. Daddy, why couldn't I stop it?"

He held her so tightly she almost couldn't breathe and she couldn't look up at him.

"You didn't cause that accident, and you couldn't have stopped it. It was absolutely not your fault." He spoke through clenched teeth in a very controlled voice. She could feel the anger in his body as he held her, but it didn't scare her like her mother's anger did.

"Believe me, liebchen, that will *never* happen to you again. I will *not let* anyone hurt you again, so help me." Now his body jerked as if he had hiccups. She felt a tear drop onto her cheek. It was his. She let herself go limp against him. Grandma Etta and Grandpa Helmuth also came to her bedside. Grandma knelt and said their usual nighttime prayer, "Ich bin klein; mein herz ist rein...." She was small, but her heart didn't feel pure at all. Grandma Etta stroked Gretchen's hand and arm and kissed her forehead gently. Her father read her back to sleep.

Gretchen left the hospital after five days, recovered from a light concussion, though a curved inch-long scar on her forehead would remain throughout her life, like an expression of surprise over her left eyebrow. Her mother stayed for fourteen days. She had broken three ribs and her shoulder and had suffered a more serious concussion. The sky car was never seen or spoken of again. Eventually, they bought another car, but her mother was not allowed to drive it. For months afterward, Gretchen never went anywhere with her mother without also having her one of her grandparents or her father come along.

Not being allowed to drive became just one more thing that added to her mother's edginess. When Gretchen came into the house after going to the park or somewhere else with Grandma Etta, she could feel her mother's mood as she entered the room. She'd overheard arguments between her parents about her mother not being allowed to work, but she didn't feel she could ask either of them what was going on. Often, her mother's seething hit her like static electricity, without even touching her. It made Gretchen very quiet, very eager to avoid being in the same room alone with her.

The Sunday after the accident, Grandma Etta took Gretchen to church with her. Church was much better than Sunday school because no one called on her to say anything, and the singing was pretty. Also, her Grandma had so many of her "girls," as she called them, friends she had known from her own school days. Hertha, Meta, Hilda and Ida, all of them with big, soft, welcoming bodies like giant buffers against the world. Each of them hugged her as they went into services, and Grandma Etta stood next to her as they stood to sing, one arm over her left shoulder, holding one side of the hymnal as Gretchen held the other. Gretchen could smell her Grandma's lavender soap. They sang one of her favorite hymns: "when other helpers fail and comforts flee, help of the helpless, oh, abide in me." It was the first time the hymn was more than just words she sang by rote. Grandma's voice was soft, with a high sweet pitch.

Church was a place where Gretchen could just sit with her own thoughts. The rhythms of the service flowed past her calmly - hymns, creed, sermon, hymns and then the doxology signaling the service was coming to an end.

On this day, some distinct words emerged from the sermon. "You can't love someone you fear." The pastor had said something real and true. It was the first time meaning had come through the words of the sermon. It was like permission. She could not love her mother because she feared her. It was impossible to love where there was fear. She rolled it around in her head. Loving was gentle, sheltering like her Grandma's body or her father's touch. Just looking at her mother was often scary. Gretchen tried to reach back to the pastor's words to hear more of what he had said, but she had heard only the one sentence.

As she thought about it over the days and weeks that followed, she wondered why the pastor would say that. Jesus was loving, gentle, not scary at all. But the pastor taught that God should be loved, and the father of Jesus was often frightening. Each of her Bible stories had something scary about God, like his telling Abraham to kill his son on the altar. How could you love God? Had he actually said 'you can't love someone you fear'?

13
Sunday

When Sequoia came to take him home from the orphanage three weeks ago, she brought him clothes, as the nuns had instructed. His school uniforms were left behind, as were his flannel pajamas; even his shoes were set next to his bed for a new boy to shape to his own foot. He carried almost nothing out, just an oversized envelope with his toothbrush, a school notebook and a score for the piano that Sister Mary Margaret had stuffed in at the last minute.

Now he had Things of His Own, three different plaid shirts and two pairs of jeans in the drawers of a wood dresser in his own room, and even a pair of high-topped sneakers on the floor next to his bed. Sequoia let him pick out his own bedspread, and he chose one with bright colors - dark reds and orange and brown – just because he had never seen so much color in a room before. There was a window in his room. It faced an alley, but it took in the morning sun. Sequoia sewed him curtains; they were orange too, but they let in the light and his whole room looked warm.

From the very first night at home, Sunday knelt

beside his bed to pray before he climbed in to go to sleep, and he prayed every morning as soon as he got up. He could tell Sequoia was surprised at first, though she didn't say anything. Now, when she came in to read to him in bed, she waited while he got out, knelt to pray, and then climbed back before she kissed him goodnight.

Sometimes he got up before she did, and he went into her room to wake her. She welcomed him into the bed with her and hugged him. But when she got up, she went straight to the bathroom without ever saying a prayer.

At breakfast he asked her if she had the Habit of Prayer.

"Habit of prayer," she repeated, as if she had never heard the words before but knew she should understand them. She rubbed one arm up and down the other, something she did when she was thinking. "I don't, honey; but don't let that stop you from praying."

"Do you miss going to church?" She asked, after getting him his cereal.

Sunday didn't know how to answer. It was a sin not to go to church, he knew, but he didn't miss anything about the orphanage. He squirmed, as if he had found tacks on his chair.

"Do you want me to take you to church?"

He shrugged.

A few days later she told Sunday they were going to go to church the following weekend, and she bought him a pair of 'good pants' to wear to the service. It turned out to be Palm Sunday, and the church was crowded. As she and Sunday walked up the stairs to the entrance, he was struck by how all the other women were dressed. There were no nuns here. Flaming red dresses with hats to match, trailing feathers in the breeze, blazing yellow capes and blowsy flowers. Sequoia wore her work clothes, a dark-colored skirt and a clean white blouse. He'd never seen women in big hats – never in such colors. The men too were decked out, with bright ties and some of them in sky-blue or deep purple suits. Sequoia hesitated as she reached the entrance with Sunday in hand. A deacon greeted them and held out a palm frond for her to bring inside. It was as tall as Sunday. Sequoia offered it to him, but he shook his head. He remembered them from Palm Sundays in the orphanage.

"Is this your son?" the deacon asked in a booming voice.

Sequoia and Sunday looked at each other. "Yes," she said, tentatively. Sunday felt a smile come over his face. "Yes," she repeated, more emphatically.

"Welcome, sister." The deacon hugged her, his large warm body scented heavily for the occasion. Sunday never let go of her hand.

14
1957
Gretchen

She and her parents were on a family vacation at the Thanatopoulos' lake cottage. Jim and Helen had lent the cottage to Bill while they went to visit Helen's parents in Chicago. Gretchen, now eleven, sat at the round oak dining table, painting. Her pale hair hung like a curtain around her bent head. Her father had lent her one of his fine-tipped brushes, so she could paint details with more precision. She was painting a Baltimore oriole, angled downward on an elm branch but looking up. Her mother was in the adjacent kitchen, making potato salad for lunch. Celery crunched fiercely on the chopping board. Her father came in with a colander of bluegills he had caught and cleaned that morning. Intent on getting just the right orange and happy with the jaunty angle on the bird's bright head, Gretchen barely noticed her mother come up behind her.

"Baltimore orioles don't have orange heads, Gretchen."

She cringed, instinctively pulling her arm around the edge of the paper to protect it from view.

"Better clean up soon and set the table for lunch."

Bill glimpsed Gretchen hunched over the table.

"Do we have time to pick blackberries for dessert?" he asked Norma.

"Go ahead, but I have to stay here and fry the fish."

"Gretchen, will you be my helper?"

"Sure!" She closed her watercolor box, washed her father's brush, blotted it dry and gave it back to him. She crumpled up her half-completed painting and threw it into the trash bin.

He handed her a yellow child's sand pail and took a splotchy blue tin bowl for himself. Once in the woods, they walked without words. He had taught her as a young child to 'walk like an Indian,' breaking no twigs, moving as silently as possible for one entering another's world. The blackberry patch was on a small rise at the sunny edge of a bog.

She reached as high as she could to pick the berries, stripping the sunniest of the canes. The berries she tasted were compact and sour. Occasionally, she reached deep into the mass of canes to pick a bunch that had ripened in the shade. These were plumper, softer and sweeter, also harder to find. They stained her fingertips, and the canes plucked at her sleeves with their thorns. Her father bent to pick his berries, usually deeper into the bushes where his longer arms could reach. Smiling, he held out his hand to her, three especially plump berries in his palm. They burst on her tongue with warm juice. His arm had tiny beads of blood in a row from the reach of a cane. They picked in contented silence.

She felt his hand on hers, just a touch to get her attention. She looked at his face; he tilted his head slightly to the right. Not twenty feet to the right of where they stood, a red fox sat watching them, its ears perked, black whiskers working like a rabbit's, eyes intent. As soon as it caught Gretchen's eyes, it rose and darted back into the woods, its tail vanishing like a scarf into a magician's sleeve.

Thanks, she smiled at her dad, still not breaking the silence that had given them the fox.

After a while, she paused and watched her father. He peered into the bushes from one side and then another, reaching in each time to pull out more berries. His bowl had twice as many berries as her pail, though he had seemed to move very little from where they had started.

"Dad, how come you have twice as many berries as I have? I've been working just as hard."

He chuckled. "After you finish picking a stretch, come back at the same bush from the opposite direction. And then when you finish that, start looking at it from the bottom up, then from another direction. They hide in there. You see more each time you look from a different angle."

She looked back to her left at one of the bushes she had already picked. A cluster beckoned from under one of the branches she thought she had already plucked.

"It's the same thing I do when I paint," he added softly.

They walked back to the cottage, his free hand resting lightly on her shoulder.

* * *

A month later, the Braves made the World Series. Grandpa Friedrich, as usual, was glued to his television set, and everyone had to talk around him. Grandma Hilda had Gretchen up on a table, wearing a dress Grandma was sewing for her. Running her appraising hands along the seam that went from just under Gretchen's nipple to the top of her hip line, Grandma Hilda complained loudly that she was 'flat as an ironing board.' "I'm only eleven," she wanted to say, but Grandma Hilda was not someone who could tolerate correction. Fortunately, her dad was in front of the television and her mother was somewhere else, out of earshot, probably reading in another room.

"No; they can't do that!" Grandpa Friedrich yelled angrily. Gretchen could hear him bang television set with his flat hand. Probably the picture had flickered.

"Pa, wait; leave it alone. It's not the television."

Gretchen could hear different voices on the television, more level than those of the baseball announcer.

"My God, everyone come here!" It was her dad's voice. Gretchen got down from the table, taking care not to sit on any of the pins in her unfinished dress. She walked into the living room. Walter Cronkite's face was on the screen, announcing that the Russians had put a satellite into space. Sputnik, it was called, a small rocket into the future. Why, Gretchen wondered, would they interrupt the World Series for this? Her grandpa apparently wondered also, for he began to yell again that he didn't want the Russians to spoil this game. Gretchen and her grandma went back into the kitchen. Gretchen climbed back onto the table and Grandma finished pinning her hem.

Within a few months, Gretchen would learn in school why Sputnik was important. The Russians had got ahead of the United States, and we needed to catch up. New, national tests were administered in her class, and Gretchen was placed into accelerated math and science classes.

15
Sunday

Sequoia was making dinner for them, pouring tomato sauce into the hamburger and onions for sloppy Joes. Their little television sat on a counter between the living room and the kitchen. She had put it on a lazy Susan, so that when they sat in the living room they could watch it from there and she could turn it around to watch it from the kitchen while she worked in there. Sunday was doing homework in the living room, half-listening to the news at the same time. His arithmetic homework was so simple that he wanted to occupy his mind with something more interesting. When Walter Cronkite began to speak, Sunday noticed immediately that his voice carried an undercurrent of excitement, which was strange.

"Sunday, get yourself in here!" Sequoia didn't bother to hide her excitement. He marked his place with his pencil and stood behind her in the kitchen.

They both gaped open-mouthed at the spectacle of a rocket soaring straight up into the sky like a huge firecracker.

"Is that the bomb?" He asked. The announcer

seemed so concerned that this rocket was put up by the Russians, that he wondered if this was the bomb for which they did air raid drills at school, hunkering under their desks. He knew from school that the Russians 'wanted us dead' and had nuclear bombs that could take out whole cities. He'd already read about Hiroshima in the encyclopedia that Sequoia was buying in installments, and he knew the desk routine was so ineffective as to be silly. Only underground shelters with a clean air supply would save them. Some people had bomb shelters but he and Sequoia didn't. "Do we need to go to a shelter?"

"No, child. It's not a bomb." She put her arms around him and held him tightly. He'd begun to shudder. "No need to be afraid. It's not going to hit us. It's gone into outer space. The reason the announcer is so excited is that Russian scientists figured out how to do it before we did."

"They won the space race?"

Sequoia grinned to hear him use the phrase. "No, Sunday, I think this is just the beginning. Both our country and Russia want to put a man into space someday. We're just gonna work harder and faster now to do it first; you'll see."

He set the table while they listened to the rest of the report. He wondered whether he would ever want to ride a rocket into outer space and look down at the earth. They waited to eat until the news was over. No television at dinner, was Sequoia's rule. Dinner was for discussion, and tonight she wanted to talk about schools.

"I don't care so much about whether we put a man into space as I do about improving our schools. Maybe we'll finally get more money for schools like yours. I want to see you challenged more." She was starting to rant. He watched her stab at bits of the meat that had fallen out of the bun.

He started to laugh. "You look like you're trying to kill mosquitoes with your fork."

She smiled but wouldn't laugh. "I just want to be sure you get the education you need to go to college."

As the months passed, he read in the newspapers and watched on television about the changes being made in schools around the country to ramp up their science and mathematics programs. Nothing changed, however, at 34th Street School, where Sunday was in fifth grade. According to Sequoia, nothing changed at Washington High School either, where she taught music. "Same lame science," she complained.

16
1959
Gretchen

Gretchen's thirteenth birthday fell on Friday the thirteenth of August. It looked like a bad beginning for her teenage years and, sure enough, on her birthday her mother made her scrub all the floors in the house. It had been her job to do, and she had dodged it all week, but she held a good grudge over having to do it on her birthday. Nothing else bad had happened for two weeks, though as a thirteen-year-old she was on the lookout for it.

As she hurried to get into the house, Gretchen scraped her calf on the bike chain. She was late, and she had known for the whole ride home she was going to be late. The Menominee Pool had been such a relief from the humidity, and she had learned to dive backwards off the diving board. She'd waited in line to repeat the dive several times to make sure she could, and, once satisfied, she went to the changing room where she noticed the clock. To lean backward into space just far enough to cut a smooth arc - to trust herself and that space without seeing the water below – and then to hit the cool blue water without pain or a big splash, was the best thing she had done all summer. But all good feeling evaporated on the ride home. Her tongue stuck to the top of her mouth as she raced home on her bike. To make matters worse, both sets of grandparents were coming to dinner tonight to celebrate both her birthday and her father's, which was three days later. Her mother was cooking for all of them. Her mother had been cranky since before she left for the pool in the morning.

"I'm sorry I'm late," were Gretchen's first words as she opened the screen door. Both grandparents and her father were seated at the table. Her mother was carrying a platter of T-bone steaks into the dining room.

"Sit down," her mother said with a clenched jaw.

"I just want to change my shirt; I'm all sticky." Her tee shirt stuck to her like peanut butter, revealing the outline of her training bra, which had slipped up on one side. As Gretchen moved toward her bedroom, her mother swung around and grabbed her arm, slamming the steak platter onto the counter with the other hand. The platter broke with a crack, and red juice from the steaks began to run into the opened drawer below. At this point her mother turned into a tornado.

"Look what you did!" she screamed, her nails digging into Gretchen's arm. As Gretchen tried to pull away, her cheek burned from a fast slap. Then she was down on the floor, trying to pull herself into a ball. Her mother pulled her pony tail, and it felt as if her scalp were coming off. As Gretchen used her arm to free her hair, her mother wrenched her arm sideways. Gretchen felt a shooting pain in her elbow and kicks to her side.

Part of her felt removed, as if she were watching some awful drama in a movie. There was screaming, not only from her mother, but also from Grandma Etta. Both grandfathers yelled at her mother to stop. Grandma Etta was crying and calling her mother's name. Still it did not stop. Where was her father, who had promised to protect her? Finally, Grandma Hilda grabbed Norma by both arms from behind and pulled her off.

"Haven't you done enough damage to this family already?" Hilda shouted. Her mother whipped around and tried to hit her mother-in-law, but Grandma Hilda was stronger. She held her mother and pulled her away, leading her forcibly down the hall to her parents' bedroom.

Gretchen ran to the bathroom and locked the door. She shook too much to do anything but sit on the floor and cry. Her right arm felt useless. Sharp pains shot upward if she moved it all. She couldn't even hold toilet paper to blow her nose. Grandma Etta knocked gently on the door and asked to come in. "Honey, let me help you." This made Gretchen cry all the more. How could she have such a good Grandma and such a frightening mother? Gretchen unlocked the door with her left hand and collapsed into her Grandma's arms. For a long time, she just sobbed on her Grandma's lap. Grandma Etta stroked her hair and soothed her. When Gretchen could sit by herself, her Grandma took a wet washcloth, wiped Gretchen's face and cleaned up the bicycle grease and blood from her leg. Then she gingerly pulled the rubber band out of Gretchen's hair and combed it slowly, lovingly.

"Thank you for being here. Can I come live with you and Grandpa?"

"Hush, my dear; we'll talk about that later," her Grandma whispered. Even as she heard Grandma Etta's words, Gretchen knew it would not happen.

Instead, her mother went to stay with her own parents for a few days, to "cool off" as everyone said. Her father drove Gretchen to the hospital that evening, where her arm was x-rayed and put into a cast. On the way to the hospital, her father hunched over the wheel, looking abject and saying almost nothing. Gretchen stared at him as hard as she could, demanding with her glare to know why he hadn't protected her. But he avoided her look, and she refrained from asking the question aloud. The doctor asked her how it happened, and she just looked hard at her father.

"She fell off her bike," he explained.

"Too bad," said the doctor abstractedly, putting away the casting materials. "There won't be any more bike riding this summer."

Gretchen stared at the floor, knowing that if she looked up the doctor would see her fury. After not protecting her from her mother, now her father even lied to protect his wife. Why didn't they just send her to her grandparents? Maybe her grandparents didn't want her either.

The next day, her father moped about the house, apparently avoiding her. She assumed that he missed her mother, and that he too believed Gretchen was an obstacle to his having the life he wanted with her mother. She wanted to know why he had failed so completely to protect her, but she was more afraid of his answer and didn't ask the question. That evening, he made them scrambled eggs for supper and they ate in near-total silence. Gretchen remembered her birthday present for him, stuck away in a corner of her closet, and asked to be excused from the table for a moment. “Of course,” he said gently, his head bowed. Gretchen fetched the present, a large sketch of a deer in flight. As she pulled it out, she felt a twinge of the pride and pleasure she had had in making it for him, and relief that her mother was not here to criticize it.

As he took off the ribbon and unrolled the sketch, she watched closely as he studied the drawing appraisingly. She knew from his eyes and the faint nod of his head that he approved. “I like it very much. I knew you could draw well, but an animal in motion is a real challenge and you did this very, very well. I’m so proud of my young artist daughter.” He put his arms around her and held her reassuringly. She fought off her tears. Afterward, he took her out for ice cream, and while they both slurped on cones of butter brickle, she told him about her backward dives.

“I want you to show me,” he said proudly, and then glanced down at her cast and lost his smile.

“Why didn’t you stop her?” Gretchen blurted. His face crumpled. She watched the lines around his eyes and mouth curl and reform in different arcs as different expressions flitted over his face.

“Part of me couldn’t believe what was happening.” He paused again. “I can’t believe this is the woman I married. It *isn’t* the woman I married.... I’m so sorry. I just sat there refusing to believe my eyes. I should have helped you.” He put his head into his hands. “I wish I were a better father for you.”

“Why don’t you just leave her!” Gretchen yelled.

He looked shocked, as if the thought had never occurred to him.

"I can't," was all he said.

When her mother returned home a few days later, her father brought her flowers, as if it were an occasion to celebrate. Gretchen learned to stay mainly in her room, and rarely spoke at the dinner table. When they next visited her Grandparents Reinhardt, Gretchen felt more warmth for her stern Grandma Hilda than ever before; but before Gretchen could find a moment to thank her, Grandma Hilda reverted to her most critical self, at one moment telling Gretchen that she was so flat-chested it was hard to believe she was a girl.

Gretchen's arm gradually healed. But while the bone set, quiet and still inside the cast, her mind roiled. She wished she herself could sit still inside some hard protective cast for the next five years, until she was grown and could get away. She was now convinced that there really was no one to protect her. Her father would yield every time to her mother, afraid that her anger would turn on him. Her grandparents Beckmann were kind but too gentle to face her mother. And her grandparents Reinhardt might help in a crisis, but only to thwart her mother, not to protect her; they seemed to have no real interest in her.

On bad days, when she could hear her mother banging angrily around the house, Gretchen took refuge in her closet. She'd arranged a soft corner where she sat on her keds and leaned against and partly inside of her winter coat. It was the most still place in their house, and Gretchen would close her eyes and imagine where she would live when she grew up. It would be in another city or state, as far as she could get from here. Sometimes it would be an apartment in a big city, and she would be a successful working woman, coming home to her own home, with sunshine yellow walls. Other times it would be a cabin in the North woods, where she could be alone and read in perfect peace.

At the dinner table, Gretchen continued to speak only when spoken to and avoided controversy. She tended to look down at her plate, never at her mother. One evening, while her father was away deer hunting with his father, Gretchen sat slumped as usual over the dinner table. Her mother began to criticize her posture, telling her no one would want to meet such a slumped-over girl. Gretchen said nothing but sat up straighter. She flinched as her mother got up from her own chair and swung suddenly around the back of Gretchen's chair. Her mother rammed a yardstick from the kitchen cupboard between Gretchen's elbows and her back, forcing her upright. Of course, she could not eat. When she tried to raise her fork to her mouth, she dropped food on her lap. Her mother laughed, cold as a slippery rock.

"Look at you," she jeered, "slumped over and sloppy. No one would guess that you were my daughter."

There were interior responses to this kind of comment, but they never came to Gretchen's lips. In fact, she trained herself so that no expression crossed her face. *I don't want to be your daughter. Someday I won't have to be your daughter.*

That evening, Gretchen was allowed to finish her dinner only after she had cleared the table and washed the dishes and her mother had gone into the living room to read. While her mother sat on the sofa reading Vogue magazine, Gretchen finished her cold spaghetti in the kitchen. After that, she managed to get invited to friends' homes on the weekends her father went hunting.

This was the year that Gretchen began to stutter. It mortified her to hear herself stumble over words she knew well. It came up at school, when she was called upon unexpectedly. It happened during a spelling bee, when she was asked to spell "exacerbate" in the final round. The rules required her both to pronounce and spell the word. She spelled it correctly but could not say the full word, though her teacher gave her half a dozen attempts. It also happened when a boy asked her to the October sock hop. He looked as if he wanted to change his mind when she said "y-ye-ye-es." Oddly, the stutter was barely noticeable at home; when she and her father spoke, she did not stutter. When her mother yelled at her, she rarely spoke back.

Her teacher, Miss Appelbaum, took her aside after class one day and offered to arrange for an after-school tutor to help cure the stutter. Gretchen looked at her gratefully and asked how she could sign up for this help. "I'll call your mother and set it up if she agrees." That evening, Gretchen heard her mother answer the telephone and speak to Miss Appelbaum. "I haven't noticed any stutter," she replied irritably, "and besides we can't afford to hire a tutor." That was the end of the conversation. Miss Appelbaum spoke to Gretchen again after class the following day.

"I'm sorry, Gretchen. Regrettably, tutoring is not a service the school can offer without charge."

As if picking her words, she added, "Your mother told me your family cannot afford it."

"Can you ask my dad?" Gretchen pleaded. "Call him at work," she added.

Two days later Miss Appelbaum told Gretchen that her father had also said there was no money for a tutor.

"I'm so sorry; I'll see if I can find some class that's offered without charge." Gretchen could tell her teacher did not believe her parents' excuse, and that she wondered what lay behind it.

"Thank you for trying" was all she could tell her.

Soon, a neighbor asked if Gretchen was available for babysitting, and she began to babysit for a four-year-old boy most weekends. He was an unusually quiet child who loved word games, and Gretchen enjoyed playing with him. After he went to bed, she could do her homework in a safe and quiet place. And she began to earn money, nearly all of which she saved. She began to work as well for other neighbors, too, babysitting or doing other chores around their homes.

After several months, Gretchen approached Miss Appelbaum after class and asked if it was still possible to arrange for a tutor to cure her stutter. She wondered how much it would cost and explained that she had babysitting money to use. Miss Appelbaum put her arm around Gretchen's shoulder and assured her that it could be arranged, and Gretchen began after-school tutoring. It went unspoken between her and Miss Appelbaum that nothing would be said to her mother. Miss Appelbaum handled the finances, just telling Gretchen how much money to bring each week. The amount was so modest that Gretchen suspected Miss Appelbaum must be paying part of it, but she never asked and Miss Appelbaum never mentioned it. The tutor taught her to slow down before responding under stress, taught her to pronounce slowly and distinctly, and tried to teach her how to relax. Some letters were easier to cope with than others; she compensated quickly for "s." But "m" words were more challenging. When the tutor asked her to repeat "My mother makes mince pies," she stuttered over the word "mother" every single time.

17
Sequoia

Sunday was practicing on his drum set in his bedroom. He had just started lessons a month ago, and the rattling from his room was loud and ragged. Sequoia was trying to compose a song on the piano in the living room and finding it impossible. The thin walls rattled with an irregular, staccato beat. Bars of a melody had come to her in music class today while she was teaching, and they had remained in her head all the way home. Now she wanted to make something of them, and couldn't concentrate.

So she went to her desk to pay bills and balance her checkbook instead. Sunday will be in bed soon, she thought. He went to bed earlier now that he had a paper route at four-thirty each morning. The route paid for his lessons. She sighed. At least the upstairs neighbors didn't complain. For nine years now, she had been teaching him piano, and he played well. He could become a musician, she thought. But six months ago, after seeing a movie about Gene Krupa, Sunday asked if he could switch to drums. How could she not say yes? She found a set of drums at a pawn shop and gave them to him for his birthday. Their deal was that he would have to earn the money for his lessons. So far, he had been diligent to a fault about his paper route. And he practiced whenever he could, which was after his homework was done and on weekends and when he was not reading. She'd never seen a child read so much, and so independently.

Sequoia worried about Sunday. He didn't get enough sleep. He sped through his homework – his school didn't challenge him – and he either read or played music all the time. So far as she knew, he had no friends. For a thirteen-year-old, he was remarkably cheerful. He helped her in the kitchen and he told her in detail about his days at school. He ate well but remained as thin as a cattail. She and his books seemed to be the sole population of his universe. He had begun to read Frederick Douglass and Richard Wright and James Baldwin, and she had been reading them too, just to keep up with him, but she couldn't keep up with him, really, and she wanted to do more. She couldn't make friends for him, though, not that she herself was a model for having lots of friends. Where was the time? And she knew that, when he would attend Washington High School, where she taught, there would be one or two teachers who could challenge him, no more. If she could save more money, maybe they could move to a better school district, but most of the good schools were all white, and she couldn't expect him to make more friends there. She also worried about how to send this child to college.

Sunday's voice hadn't yet changed, and she could hear, behind the drumbeat, a thin high melody he was humming to himself.

Part Two

18
1964
Gretchen

Sunday Morgan entered Gretchen's high school in Milwaukee at the start of their senior year. Not counting the Nigerian exchange student a year earlier, he was the first Negro at Northern Bay High. He arrived like a piece of charcoal dropped on someone's white linen skirt.

Gretchen saw him the first day. His locker was four doors down from hers. She couldn't help staring. This was as close as she'd ever stood to a black person, except for bus drivers or cafeteria workers. Negroes lived in another part of the city, closer to downtown, where her parents used to live when they were in high school. The new student's skin was almost as black as the Nigerian's, but he was much taller, maybe six-four, and so thin he looked spindly. The Nigerian was much shorter and rounder and friendlier than this somber stranger.

Sunday waited helplessly at his locker. Doug, the varsity halfback, jammed his locker door wide open, blocking the front of the door to his right, which belonged to Sunday. Doug took his time, as if choosing a book from the library, though the idea of his even thinking about a book was ludicrous. Finally the new student quietly said, "Excuse me."

"Can't you see I'm getting my books?" Doug took one more book as if in slow motion and then slammed his locker.

Sunday gathered his books as fast as he could and walked down the hall.

It started to happen every time Doug and Sunday were at the locker at the same time. Invariably, Sunday just waited until Doug slammed his door, just before class began. Sunday had to run to avoid being late. Gretchen seethed at Doug and wondered if there was anything she could say to him that would make him stop, but he ran in a different crowd and wouldn't have paid any attention to her.

Gretchen's friend Jenny used the locker just to the left of Doug's. Jenny was the first in their school to wear black tights and straight black skirts and her hair straight and long over her shoulders, like a New York folksinger. Gretchen told Jenny about Doug's stunt.

"That's simple," Jenny said. "Wait 'til the next time Doug's here at the same time as me."

Just before third period, Doug strolled to his locker while Gretchen and Jenny stood talking. Jenny's locker door stood open against the front of Doug's. She leaned against it, facing Gretchen.

"Hey, I need to get into my locker."

"Can't you see I'm not done?" Jenny said, still not facing him. Jenny took a sweater from her locker hook and put it on slowly, one sleeve at a time, pulling each blouse sleeve down, and then cuffing the sweater so that each sleeve had the exactly the same inch of blouse showing at the bottom.

All this time Gretchen just stared at Doug, who looked like he was about to tackle Jenny. When she finished with her sweater, Jenny bent over to pick out a book, putting one back and then taking another out of the bottom of her locker. Finally she shut her locker door, reset the combination and looked at Doug for the first time.

"Your turn."

Gretchen wished the new student had been there to see it. By now he'd adjusted by coming to his locker as seldom as he could, carrying most of his books around with him all day long. She never saw anyone walk with him or even speak to him, except teachers in class. When he walked down the hall, the wave of other students parted in front of him, as if he were a boat creating its own wake. Walking in that wake behind him one day, Gretchen felt engulfed in an isolation altogether other than anything she'd experienced before. Her own solitude was an absence, a longing for more friends like Jenny to understand and buoy her and for parents who would protect her. This was different - a malignant presence, a disgust, an active avoidance, a shunning. She gulped and tried to blink away her sadness.

Gretchen smelled something awful near her locker, like someone couldn't get to the toilet in time. She'd just been in the girls' bathroom across the hall and knew the stink wasn't coming from there. She glanced around at the floor but couldn't see anything there. She took her books and began closing her locker door when she noticed one of the lockers to the right of hers was smeared with wet brown feces. Sunday arrived at the moment she noticed it was on his locker door. He muttered something under his breath and laid his books on the floor very slowly, like someone taking an extra moment before spinning around to punch someone.

Gretchen dropped her own books and ran across the hall to the bathroom to get some paper towels. She came back with towels stuffed into each hand. She shoved the ones in one hand at him and began to use the ones in her other hand to wipe off the door. Sunday took over with the others. As she carried the stinking towels back to the bathroom, she noticed Doug coming toward her with two other football players, joking loudly and looking in the other direction. Gretchen paused just as Doug passed her, brushing the soiled towels onto the white sleeve of his letter sweater. As she opened the girls' room door, she glanced back. He hadn't noticed. Perfect. She knew he would later.

Gretchen went back to get her books.

"Thanks," said the new student as she stood up. He wouldn't even look at her directly, and his thanks were mumbled.

"I'm going to tell the principal," she told him.

"No; don't!" Now he looked at her directly, and she couldn't tell if it was anger or fear she saw in his eyes.

All through the next period, Gretchen wondered whether to tell the principal. Dr. Bach was intimidating and distant, and she had no way of knowing what he would do. The new student had told her not to; maybe he knew *he'd* get in trouble for it. And if he'd get in trouble, chances are she could too. Doug had read her stare the other day and could easily figure out who had put the shit on his sleeve. But it was such a disgusting stunt; it shouldn't be ignored. She thought of telling Mr. Vitelli, her honors English teacher, who would know what to do. But a day went by, and then two, and finally she said nothing about it, except to Jenny, who discouraged her from telling anyone else.

"Shit on the sleeve is the best revenge," she said.

But revenge was no salve.

In early January, their high school gave its first jazz concert. Gretchen knew nothing about jazz but Jenny persuaded her to go. The school band played a range of music from Dixieland to contemporary ballads from Miles Davis and Dave Brubeck. For Gretchen, what stood out about the concert, apart from the startlingly unfamiliar music, was Sunday Morgan's drumming. Complexly rhythmic, often fierce, textured and passionate, it came from a different place than the quiet and controlled person who inhabited her classes. Afterward, she went out and bought a Miles Davis record. But she didn't say anything to Sunday.

Only Mr. Vitelli, their honors English teacher, treated Sunday with respect. Mr. Vitelli was also the only teacher who got away with teaching *Othello*, with its black king and white wife, while the other English teachers taught *MacBeth* or *Romeo and Juliet*.

Mr. Vitelli called on Gretchen and Sunday to read together from *Othello* in front of the class. This was a routine of his; he told the students they would learn new dimensions from hearing literature read aloud. Sunday was asked to play Othello, she was to be his wife Desdemona and another student was to read Desdemona's father Brabantio, who lamented his daughter's having fallen in love with "what she fear'd to look on." Gretchen stood up thinking *anyone but me* and worrying for a second that her stutter would return.

Sunday stood up straight as he began to read. His unfamiliar voice sounded deep and resonant, with the quiet authority of someone much older. Gretchen was so caught up in his voice that she heard only the last two lines he read:

She lov'd me for the dangers I had pass'd,
And I lov'd her that she did pity them.

Riveted, Gretchen read without stuttering to Brabantio:

And so much duty as my mother show'd
To you, preferring you before her father,
So much I challenge that I may profess
Due to the Moor, my lord.

She blushed as she read "the Moor," not knowing if it was an insulting way to describe the black king. She glanced involuntarily up at Sunday. He stared at her, his deep-socketed eyes intense and focused. She reddened even more.

"Well read; the perfect innocent," Mr. Vitelli pronounced as he released her and called upon someone else as Iago to read further with Othello. Sunday continued in that mesmerizing voice. She closed her eyes and let it flow through her.

"Ah, that is a voice that commands!" Mr. Vitelli praised as Sunday finished. "You should audition for drama. Only put more feeling into your body as you speak." Gretchen heard snickers from the back of the room. Mr. Vitelli stared hawklike toward the back of the room, silencing them.

At the end of class, Gretchen and Sunday reached the doorway together.

"You read well," she found her voice to say. She had no idea of how to start a conversation with him.

"Thank you."

He drifted away down the hall, but since they were both going to study hall in the library, it was awkward to avoid walking together. There were only two open seats, and they were next to each other. She sat down. He looked around the room as if seeking rescue before sitting down next to her. Gretchen glanced up at the student across the table, who wouldn't meet her eye. She felt the collective eyes of all the other students, waiting for something bad to happen.

Gretchen took out her chemistry book and tried to make sense of the assignment for tomorrow. It was a difficult course for her, and she always struggled with it. She needed at least a B to hope for the scholarship she'd need to get away to college. Getting away to college had been her driving force throughout high school, and she had nearly a four point average. Distracted by that worry, she couldn't concentrate or make sense of the assignment. Sunday worked steadily next to her, his chemistry book open. Glancing over at him, she was amazed to see that he was already working on the last page of the assignment.

She took out a piece of paper from her notebook. Curling her left arm in front of the paper, she wrote: *will you help me with chemistry?* She folded the paper into quarters and pushed it toward Sunday. The student across from her blinked, as if trying to ignore what she was doing.

Sunday opened her note. He hesitated and then wrote a single word on it. Pausing again, his wrist above the paper, he wrote some more and folded it up before passing it back to her.

The bell rang for the next period, and everyone packed up their books.

Gretchen opened it once she got to her history class. *Yes. Meet me at the Korner Kafe right after school.* She thought she could hear her heart beating. She folded the note and waited for the end of the last period, trying to slow her breathing as if she were poised at the top of a high diving board, trying to look outward and not down.

The Korner Kafe was just far enough away from school that no one went there. When students hung out after school, they went to Jimmy's, which was closer.

Sunday was already at a booth when Gretchen walked in. His chemistry book and notebook were spread out in front of him. She sat down across from him, and he smiled tentatively at her. She couldn't read whether he was being friendly or superior or something else.

"'Why don't you set up while I get us cokes. Want anything else?"

She shook her head.

He came back with two cokes and a plate of fries.

"You can see better if you sit next to me."

So she moved. Gretchen ate almost all the French fries while Sunday explained the principles of the assignment in a way that made more sense to her than anything their chemistry teacher had said.

"Your turn." He'd used the same words as Jenny did with Doug in front of his locker and for a split second she wondered whether Sunday had been there or magically knew about it. She licked the grease off her fingers until she noticed him watching her intently and then used her napkin to finish. As she began to do her equations, he propped his head on his elbow close enough to watch what she was doing. She listened to his slow breath close to her ear. When she was able to slow her breathing to match his, she began to concentrate and solve the equations.

"There," he pointed, and his arm brushed hers as he pointed out a correction. She suddenly wanted him to put his hand on top of hers and guide it wherever he wanted.

"Tomorrow?" he asked as they were packing up.

She nodded.

"You sure?"

She nodded more emphatically.

Next door to the Korner Kafe was a music store. Sunday told Gretchen he was going in and asked if she wanted to come. She followed him.

19
Sequoia

The instant she saw Sunday and this pale girl standing next to him in front of the jazz rack, poring over albums, Sequoia sensed the attraction between them. She wondered whether she'd made a mistake in transferring Sunday to this new school. At Washington, there were white students too, but they were outnumbered and there were more than enough black girls for Sunday to take out. She'd thought somehow that Sunday would keep his friends from Washington. Curtis and Jake were solid guys – nowhere near as sharp as Sunday but they didn't make an issue of it - and she'd assumed they'd remain close. But they'd drifted away from each other this semester. Maybe it was just too far away. When she asked Sunday if he'd seen them lately, he said maybe he'd give them a call, but she never saw them together. So far as she knew, Sunday had no friends at Northern Bay. And this one might not be a good start.

"Hey, Sunday, what's doin'?" Sequoia draped her long reddish brown arms around his shoulders and gave him a big hug. The girl blinked and stepped back.

"Hey, Koya, get outta my tree!" Sunday grinned broadly as he pushed away her big arms. She could tell he was squirming inside.

"Gretchen, my sister, Sequoia. Sequoia, this is Gretchen."

Wide-eyed, Gretchen blurted: "Is that your real name?" And then blushed.

Sequoia laughed comfortably, her head tilted back. "It sure is, honey. You think a boy with a name like Sunday is going to have a big sister with a name like Susan or Kathy? And besides," she teased, "'Gretchen' didn't exactly come out of Dick and Jane either."

Now Gretchen laughed too, and Sequoia found herself warming to her despite her reservations.

"Baby bro', be home by six, ok? I have to run. Gretchen, you come over sometime and we'll trade name stories." She strode toward the door, without stopping for the record she'd wanted to buy, wondering why she'd been so friendly.

"So who is this girl?" she asked Sunday at dinner.

"She wanted help with her chemistry."

"Is that a safe place to meet her?"

He shrugged. "Got a better suggestion?"

She pulled a cheese string from the piece of pizza Sunday lifted from the plate and helped herself to a second piece.

"You could come here." They lived just at the edge of the Northern Bay school district, and there were some white folk on their block and in their general neighborhood. "It might be safer here."

Sunday shrugged, and they didn't pursue it. Maybe this wouldn't go anywhere, she hoped.

20
Gretchen

Gretchen hoped she hadn't stared at Sequoia - the tallest woman she'd ever seen - loping across the aisle of the music store with the odd grace of a giraffe. In her first look at the two of them, she blinked once, her large round eyes calm and long-lashed. When Sunday talked to Sequoia, he dropped all that stilted talk he spoke in class. His shoulders sloped at a looser angle and he looked relaxed. When he smiled at Sequoia, he beamed.

Sunday must have seen the questions all over Gretchen's face.

"Yes, she's really my sister but she's been like a momma to me. I came to live with her when my momma died. She got me into your school."

"It's your school, too," she reminded him.

"You've seen enough to know better." He left it at that.

That first day, he bought her Miles Davis' "Sketches of Spain." She played it that first night and then every night. Its muted trumpet ached with longing.

Sunday invited her to study after school at his

apartment a few days later. "It's all right," he said, "Sequoia will be there." He lived a short bus ride south of their school, on the second floor of a plain Milwaukee cream-colored brick fourplex with small trimmed evergreens lining the walk. It looked like her parents' first apartment after they moved out of her grandparents' house.

Sequoia emerged from the kitchen, which smelled like popcorn.

"Come on in, girl. Just leave your boots outside." Gretchen took off her slushy boots and walked inside, where everything looked different from anywhere she had lived. Instead of white walls, the living room was painted dark red. An upright piano dominated one wall, with photos of jazz musicians above it. Sunday's drum set occupied the far corner, and a Southwestern-style blanket draped over the back of the sofa. Stacks of large pillows sat on the floor. A small television on a cart with wheels sat in another corner.

Sequoia hugged Sunday and looked for a second as if she would hug Gretchen too. But she turned around and led them into the kitchen. A big table covered with a flowered oilcloth took up most of the room. Sequoia put a big bowl of popcorn in the center, shook a big salt shaker over it and plopped it next to the bowl before she left the room. Sunday took off his track jacket with a shrug of his shoulders and draped it over the back of the chair as Gretchen set up her books on the table.

"Chemistry again?" He grinned at her, teasingly.

"It's the only one I can't get," she came back defensively.

"I wasn't tryin' to put you down. I struggle with calculus myself."

"I heard you were a prodigy; that's how you came to Northern Bay."

"Yeah, I'm a real prodigy at making friends." He laughed suddenly, at having said something stupid, and it was such a childlike laugh that it made her laugh too.

He asked her where she was applying to college. When she told him Radcliffe and the University of Chicago, he asked why. She told him Radcliffe because it was the best and Chicago because it was generous with scholarships. She didn't tell him she couldn't even afford the application fees for more colleges and her parents wouldn't help her. They'd told her she should go to UW-Milwaukee. She didn't tell him how desperate she was to vault herself into a different life than her own. He told her he'd applied to Harvard because Sequoia had told him he should try for the best and Howard and Morehouse because they were the best black colleges.

"I bet you get into Harvard," she told him.

"Why?"

He asked why to almost everything she told him. She liked that. It made her think again about her reasons and it made her feel that he cared to know.

He asked her again to study at his house, and again she went, this time taking the bus herself and meeting him after his track practice. Sequoia invited Gretchen in and invited her to sit at the kitchen table and talk while she waited for Sunday. Sequoia asked if she had any brothers or sisters.

"No, I think my mother thought one was bad enough."

Sequoia looked up from cutting celery, as if to contradict Gretchen or ask if she really meant what she'd said, paused, looked down again and resumed slicing, as though she'd thought better of it.

"Do you and Sunday have any other brothers or sisters?"

"None that I know of." Now it was Gretchen's turn to look quizzically at Sequoia.

Sequoia didn't volunteer an explanation.

Going to Sunday's house to study after school became a regular event. When Sunday had track practice, Gretchen arrived before he did, and Sequoia always made time to sit and talk with her, asking her about her school day or what interested her or her plans for college. Gretchen found herself trying to arrive before Sunday did, to have these times to talk, to bask in Sequoia's attention. When Sequoia asked Gretchen about her parents, Gretchen began with her dad.

"He's an artist at the Natural History Museum and a loving, gentle man – too gentle for my mother."

"What's she like?"

"A Harpy. She wishes I'd never been born." The only other person who'd ever heard this from her was Jenny, and Gretchen felt excited, eager to have Sequoia hear her story. "Once she almost killed me."

"Mmm. What'd she do?"

Gretchen launched into the story of her mother's driving the Sky car into the tree. She relished every word, feeling spiteful and released.

"On my thirteenth birthday, she broke my arm.

My grandmother had to pull her off of me." Gretchen embellished on the details, her cheeks flushed with eagerness. Sequoia handed her a glass of ice water, and Gretchen took a few sips. "The worst part was when my Dad took me to the hospital and told the doctor I'd fallen off my bike." She began to cry and then to sob, covering her face in her hands. Sequoia stood behind Gretchen's chair and placed her warm hands on Gretchen's shoulders, rubbing them gently.

"Honey girl, you've had a hard childhood."

Gretchen leaned back into the shelter of Sequoia's hands.

One day in March, Gretchen had an appointment after school for her Radcliffe interview. Sequoia and Sunday had both given her encouragement the day before, and she was feeling almost optimistic. The interview was across town. She'd asked her parents to borrow the car so that she could drive there after school. Her mother said no; she needed the car herself but she would pick up Gretchen after school and drive her to the interview. Her mother was driving again, despite her father's promise a few years earlier. It seemed he had nothing to say about anything anymore. About halfway through the school day, it occurred to Gretchen that her mother might not show up. There would not be enough time for her to catch a bus to the interview after school. By the time she left school, she'd become convinced her mother would not be there.

Snow fell in wet, heavy clots, trying to be rain. As Gretchen waited under the sheltering eave of the school entrance, other cars came, picked up students and left, but her mother did not appear.

Close to panic, Gretchen telephoned Sequoia and told her what was happening.

"Honey, I'll be there in ten minutes. You call that college lady and tell her that your momma got sick and a friend is bringing you. You'll be just a little late." Gretchen did what she was told, and the woman sounded understanding. Sequoia arrived faster than Gretchen thought possible. In the car, Gretchen started sobbing.

"I hate her; I hate her; how could she do this to me?"

In a very firm, quiet voice, Sequoia said, "Gretchen, you've got a job to do this afternoon, and that job is to let this woman know why you should be in the next class at Radcliffe. Leave your momma out of this, and do your job. I know you can." Sequoia drove slowly and deliberately, avoiding the risk of swerving in the slushy streets, and she got Gretchen there only fifteen minutes late. Just before Gretchen got out of the car, Sequoia put an arm around her shoulder.

"Sunday and I are pulling for you. Just know that."

The interviewer was a really pleasant woman. They sat and drank tea in the woman's library, which had floor-to-ceiling bookshelves on three walls of the room, and a Chagall poster on the fourth wall. In the poster a young woman floated across the sky. Gretchen felt comfortable in that room and hoped when she grew up she could live in such a place. When the interviewer asked her about her parents, she explained that her father was an artist at the museum.

"And your mother?"

"She teaches music at Washington High School,"

Gretchen lied, imagining how life would be different if Sequoia were her mother.

Sequoia was waiting in the car outside when the interview was over, as Gretchen knew she would be. She felt good about the interview.

"I knew you'd do well," Sequoia told her.

"I don't want to go home," Gretchen pronounced after a few minutes.

"What are you going to say to your momma?"

"There's nothing I can say that would make any difference. And my dad won't help; he just fades away when she's there. I need to get out of there."

"I can see why you say that, but you can't do that today. When you start college, you'll leave her behind and start your own life."

"How can I wait that long?"

"Because you got to."

When Gretchen let herself into her house, her father came quickly to the door.

"Where's your mother?" He sounded worried.

"Where's my mother! What about 'How did your interview go?' Is she all you care about? She never even showed up! Why couldn't you drive me there! I hate you both!" She slammed the door to her room. And fumed. And waited for her father to come in and give her some excuse, some comfort. But he didn't come in, and she didn't come out. She got hungry but wouldn't leave her room. After a long time, she realized it was getting late and her mother wasn't there and her father probably didn't know whether Norma had tried to wrap herself around a tree again. Gretchen went to bed hungry and disgruntled, and woke up around midnight, when she heard the outside door. Then her father's worried, pleading voice and her mother's, strident and unapologetic. Now he knows what it feels like, she thought.

After that, Gretchen went to Sunday's house after school almost every school day and ate dinner with Sequoia and Sunday whenever she could. Sunday drove her home after dinner. Her parents rarely even asked her if she'd be home for dinner. Gretchen noticed that her mother acted more disgruntled with her father these days and didn't bother Gretchen as much. Her father seemed preoccupied with her mother.

Sometimes Sequoia, Sunday and Gretchen watched the news on television before dinner. Gretchen squirmed as they watched police dogs bite the legs of civil rights marchers in the South or black people felled by fire hoses as they gathered in the streets to demonstrate against segregation, while she sat here in Milwaukee with a woman she wished were her mother and a young man who was something between a brother and a boyfriend. None of them said anything. Gretchen picked the pills off her sweater, feeling ashamed and wishing she could say this was another country.

"Believe it or not," Sequoia broke the silence one evening, "this is progress."

Gretchen found her college notices one night when she came home after dinner at Sunday's. A thin envelope from Radcliffe and a big one from Chicago told most of the story before Gretchen opened the envelopes. Dejected by her failure to get into Radcliffe, she tried to blame it on her mother's failure to get her to the interview on time, but she knew better. Thinking about her mother's no-show was just a way for her to salt her wound. That she was granted a full scholarship at the University of Chicago - which meant she would finally make her escape and have the chance to make her own life – made no dent in the wall of her bad mood. Her mother cemented a few more bricks in that wall by telling her she'd know all along Gretchen wasn't good enough to get into Radcliffe and that she'd have a hard time keeping up at Chicago. Gretchen recognized what a perverse incentive her mother created. Determination had been bred into her.

When she phoned Sunday she assumed from the buoyancy in his voice that he had been admitted to Harvard. She tried to mask her own foul mood and forced the word 'congratulations,' but there was no enthusiasm in her voice.

"So, you're off to Harvard?" she said, and heard an undertone of jealousy in her words.

"Not that good, but I have a full scholarship at Howard! Sequoia and I be dancin' 'round the pad." He'd never spoken in street slang to her before. She felt distanced by a language that belonged to him and Sequoia but not to her. Preoccupied with herself, Gretchen dashed some more salt into the wound by reminding herself that she and Sunday would be half a continent away from each other in college. It did not even occur to her that his acceptance also meant he would escape being drafted.

"Did you have good news?" he asked tentatively. He must have heard her tone of voice. When she told him, he blurted, "That's wonderful! Chicago is a great school!"

In the background, Gretchen could hear Sequoia talking happily, singing. She felt only that the world had dealt her a personal blow. "If you think so," she said finally. Sunday tried to humor her. He told her he was only unhappy that they would have to travel so many miles to see each other. At that, she began to cry. Then to laugh at the same time.

"I just thought of something," she said.

"Tell me."

"A few summers ago, my dad and I were picking blackberries at the cottage. I found a bunch that were deep in the brambles, beyond my reach, and I told him. He told me that some things were worth reaching for, and he leaned way over to get them. He lost his balance and fell into the brambles. At first he swore. After he got up and untangled himself, you could see little red dots all over his arms and chest, where he'd been prickled. For a few days, he looked like he had a rash. But right after he got up, he said to me, 'It's still true; some things really are worth reaching for.' And he gave me the squashed berries in his hand."

Sunday chuckled. She found herself beginning to laugh with him.

"You broke my bad mood."

A few days later, while Gretchen was helping Sequoia make dinner, Gretchen started to confide her newest grievance about her mother.

"You sure have some hard feelings for your momma."

As Gretchen was about to continue, Sequoia interrupted. "Did Sunday ever tell you about his momma?"

"Only that she was very sick and died when he was little."

"Hmmph. That's only part true. She could still be alive, but there's almost no way of knowing."

Gretchen stopped cutting green beans and stared. "I don't suppose he told you what made her sick."

"No."

"Alcohol and heroin. She sold herself to pay for the drug." Gretchen slumped, knowing that whatever Sequoia was going to tell her would dwarf her own problems.

"It started gradually. She migrated up from Georgia in 1928 with my dad, who was a foundry worker in Gary, Indiana. He was part Cherokee, which I suppose is how I got my color. Our momma was coal black like Sunday. My daddy died when I was ten, of lung cancer he probably got from working in the foundry. What I remember of him mostly is he was always tired. On weekends he'd sleep until noon and Momma had to keep me very quiet, which of course I resented. I wasn't a quiet kind of child."

Sequoia had been staring out the kitchen window as she told the story. Now she turned quickly toward Gretchen, as if to check whether she was still listening. Gretchen watched her raptly, ignoring her task with the beans.

"What happened after he died?"

"Momma had to go to work. Lucky for us, it was during the War and there were plenty of jobs for women, even black women. She worked on an assembly line in a munitions factory. But after the War ended and the men came back, she lost her job. I was thirteen then."

Sequoia spoke very quietly, as if talking to herself. Riveted, Gretchen leaned closer to Sequoia to hear her better. She had the feeling Sequoia was telling this story for the first time.

"I remember her coming home one day, moving

a bit too slowly as she fried up some eggs for our dinner. In a croaking voice, she told me she didn't know how she could take care of me anymore; she had lost her job. She tried hard for a while to get another job, but there's wasn't anything available. She cleaned houses, she took in laundry, the usual things a colored woman did. But we had no people in Gary and she never was very good at reaching out to others for help. I started to work myself. My teacher had a cousin with a shoe store, and I started to work there after school and on weekends, in the back room, matching up the shoes and putting them back into their boxes after people had tried them on.

"Momma got more and more listless. Sometimes she'd barely look up when I got home. I cooked our dinners and went to the store for our food. When I started high school, she was often out when I got home. She began to show up at odd times, completely unpredictable, and she got mean. When I got home each night, I began to hope she'd stay out 'til after I was in bed, so I wouldn't have to see her or listen to her. And that became the pattern. Even on weekends I hardly saw her, because I was either at the library studying or at work, and she was out nights."

Gretchen winced as she remembered how often she'd complained to Sunday or Sequoia about her mother.

"How did you get to college and become a teacher?"

"I was very lucky. My English teacher, Miss Rose Ann Walker, took me aside and encouraged me to apply to college. When I told her I had no money, she helped me apply for a scholarship. I went to the University of Indiana on a full scholarship. I left home at eighteen and never moved back. Sometimes you need to protect yourself by getting away."

"What about Sunday? Where was he?"

"That's a story for another day. You need to cut the rest of those beans, and we have chicken to fry."

Sunday came in from track practice, his skin glistening like a wet black beach stone.

"I beat my time in the 100 yards!" He grinned.

"Hey, that's great!" Sequoia hugged him with her big cinnamon arms.

Sunday invited Gretchen to a movie that coming Saturday afternoon. They arranged to meet downtown and go into the theater separately, but they sat together to watch "Dr. Strangelove," sharing popcorn from the same container but not once touching each other. Afterwards, they jokingly imitated the famous salute and compared memories of the Cuban missile crisis. At her school, news reports had been broadcast almost continuously over the PA system, classes suspended, while everyone sat tensely awaiting the outcome of the showdown. At his school, classes continued, interrupted by caustic jokes about the bomb and living under the Russians.

Afterward, they took a long walk through Lake Park. Gretchen tried to find a way to get Sunday to talk about his mother.

"What was your first memory?" she asked, with a deceptively cheery smile.

Without much pause, he answered, "Sequoia feeding me. There are different memories and they come together and then separate again, but she is always there feeding me – like she still does today." He grinned. "In one, she is trying to show me how to lick an ice cream cone. She puts out her tongue and licks the glob of ice cream and then holds it in front of me. I try to put my mouth around it and of course it's too big, so I have strawberry ice cream on my nose and cheeks. She laughs and I laugh and then she licks it off me like a mother cat."

"Was that after your mother got sick?"

"Yeah," was all he said. He started to kick a stone, first nonchalantly and then, each time they came up to where it had landed, with increasing force and anger.

"Did Sequoia tell you about her?" His look was almost threatening. "Damn," he said quietly.

"Yes. And I owe you a big apology. All this time I've been complaining about my mother, you listened so sympathetically. You had it much worse. I'm sorry. My problems are nothing by comparison."

He stepped in front of her, blocking her step. "What she does to you is *not* trivial. Don't ever say that." He looked at her full on, his eyes intent on hers. She began to smile, and he started to step away.

"Wait," she said, and impulsively brushed her finger along his cheek. "Look," she admired, "it's a perfect little spiral." On her fingertip was a tiny ringlet of his hair. He looked at her again, just as intently, and kissed her. His lips surrounded her surprised mouth. Then she opened it and kissed him back. Then they both looked around, to make sure no one had seen them.

They began to walk again, toward the beach. A ribbon of foam lined the shore. A cold wind blew off

Lake Michigan, its gray-green water full of white-caps. Gretchen's cheeks colored.

"Even when I was in the Catholic Home, I always had Sequoia. She came to visit me every day she could. She..."

"Home? Sequoia didn't tell me that."

"It's stupid, but I think she still feels guilty for putting me into the orphanage. When our mother got so bad that Sequoia couldn't leave me alone with her, she had no other choice. She couldn't go to school and work and watch me at the same time. So I went to the Catholic Home while she was in college. She visited me every day she was allowed, and she took me out every weekend. She never abandoned me. She promised to come get me when she was finished with school and had a job. As soon as she became a teacher, she got an apartment and took me in with her.

"In a way, I was luckier, because I always had Sequoia. You've only had her these past two months."

They held each other for a long time, standing like two saplings grown too close together, their upper branches caught, tangled and intertwined for life.

21
Gretchen

Gretchen looked around at the neighborhood where her parents had grown up. Rows of sturdy, brick, pitched-roof houses built in the twenties, with front porches and small front lawns, lined the streets where her parents must have sat on such porches and walked to Washington High School together. Now only black families lived here. A muddied late snow clung to the ground. Gretchen shivered, and Sunday put his arm over her shoulder.

"Nervous?"

He was taking her to a party at the home of Curtis, one of his friends from Washington, another track runner. Unfamiliar music blared from the party house.

Gretchen nodded her head.

"Me too. Let's hope they treat you better than *your* friends at Northern Bay."

She punched his arm with her mittened hand. "Well, that really gives me confidence." They both laughed, and he kissed her.

"Hey, Sunday, my man!" Curtis hugged Sunday and then gripped his right hand in some fast sequence of different handshakes. "Lookee here,"

Curtis said to Sunday when he saw Gretchen. He eyed her up and down.

"Gretchen, this is Curtis. Curtis, Gretchen." Curtis made an exaggerated swoop and kissed her hand. Gretchen pulled back her hand as soon as he released it. Mumbling 'hi Curtis,' she felt an immediate urge to go wash her hand.

Sunday's other friends welcomed him as he led the way in. They did a double take when she followed, said "hey" to her too in a subdued, tentative way. She was the only white person there. Gretchen flinched, sensing a pall over the room. The music had stopped.

Someone put on a new record and almost everyone else began to dance. She stood alone for a dazed moment while Sunday went to get her a beer. The dancing was sinuous, captivating, entirely unfamiliar to her. Sunday returned with a beer for each of them and draped one arm gently over her shoulder as he let her take it in. He waited a while before asking her to dance, continuing to stand at her side with his arm over her shoulder. She felt eager and yet frightened to dance with him.

"Wanna start with a slow dance or a fast one?" His smile teased. His fingers tapped gently on her right shoulder.

"Dunno. Slow, I think."

And so he waited. "If this world were mine," she heard a female vocalist begin as he led her onto the crowded floor. He led with his hips, not his hands. Since he was so much taller, his pelvis fit just under her ribcage. With a shock, she felt the swell of his groin against her belly. In the same instant, she wanted to run away and to press herself closer to him. She glanced around with panicked eyes.

Everyone else was dancing the same way, swaying gently and not moving around much. His chin rested close to the top of her head. "Relax," he said gently, close to her ear.

It was easy to follow him, his warm hand resting just below her waist. She folded into him, moving with the music, moving as she had never even imagined, as he added steps. At the end of their first dance, he simply put both his arms loosely around her and held her to him. Her face molded into the curve of his shoulder. He took deep slow breaths. After that, they danced fast, to the Four Tops, Marvin Gaye and Tammi Terrell, The Marvellettes, Jerry Butler. She caught on, they laughed, and one of his bolder friends even danced with her. At the end of "Ain't No Mountain High Enough," Sunday held her again, in the same way, with the same pointedly slow deep breaths. Then he kissed her, his lips circling hers.

He got her home in time to meet her parents' midnight deadline. Lights blazed on her front porch and inside, and she knew her parents would be inside, listening. Sunday thanked her, kissed her on the brow and told her to "be cool."

"How was your evening?" her mother asked with mock insouciance. Her eyes were penetrating, and Gretchen involuntarily dropped hers.

"Okay. I mean, good. A little strange. I was the only white person at the party. But they were okay. G'night." She disappeared into her bedroom. In the dark, she danced a while to music that was only in her head, her hand pressed between her legs.

On Thursday of the next week, Sequoia had an early-evening meeting at her school. She left pizza for Sunday and Gretchen. Gretchen had been counting days. She'd been with him and Sequoia each day since Monday, studying as usual and helping Sequoia prepare dinner, trying to act as if nothing had changed. On Thursday, she'd stayed to watch him at track practice, trying not to stare at his chest. His ribs showed, along with tight muscles down the center of his body. Tiny dots of hair dappled the area around his nipples. His arms were sinewy, with almost no hair. They took the bus to his home after practice.

As soon as he opened the door, Sunday laid his books on the kitchen table as usual but crossed the room to put "Sketches of Spain" on the record player. Without a word, he took her hand and led her to his bed. The afternoon sun shone through rust-colored drapes, giving an orange tint to the whole room. She lay awkwardly on her side, not knowing what to expect. He closed her eyes with his lips and then kissed the tips of her ears, her forehead, the center of her neck, her fingertips – all before he let her taste his wet lips. Then he leaned his leg between hers, where she was already burning, and she squeezed her legs around his. He placed her hand on his jeans, where he had grown big, and held it there. There was nothing she wanted more than for him to surround her. Sunday opened her blouse and kissed her nipples; she unzipped his jeans. When they were both naked, he sighed with pleasure and smiled as if the world were theirs. She began to kiss his chest, still salty from track practice, and then licked it for the salt. She nervously glanced down the length of his body. She'd never seen a penis before and it seemed too big to fit inside her. Momentarily afraid, she shivered. He began to rub it gently between her legs until both of them were slippery with their eagerness. After a number of pushes – one of them suddenly, intensely painful - he was inside her. Before long, she was lying in the surf at the edge of a very warm sea. From outside herself, she could see the two of them as wet, salty, overlapping beach stones, one pale, one dark. She'd never felt so powerful, so good. Afterward, they held each other tightly, his feet laced around hers. When he released her, he sighed deeply.

"I'm gonna love you for always," he said in that deep voice.

When Sequoia got home, she and Sunday were at the kitchen table, bent over their books, but Gretchen felt exposed. She did not know how to disguise how her body glowed. Her limbs felt as if they had no bones in them. Sequoia seemed tired and pre-occupied, going to her room and saying little other than, "See you tomorrow."

Gretchen and Sunday continued to thrive in school, each pulling mostly As. Usually they didn't sit together in study hall, since they had that time each evening at his home. Miraculously, Gretchen's parents didn't object to her being with Sunday. Even her mother seemed to like him. When he came to her house to pick her up, he'd talk books with her, and Gretchen could tell her mother was impressed with his intelligence.

22
Sunday

Sunday's knees were propped up like a grasshopper's against the dashboard of the VW bug. Sequoia in the driver's seat looked equally cramped.

"Do ya think you could have bought a bigger car?" He teased.

"Baby bro, when you're earning the money for this family, you can take us out for a nice long drive in your shiny hog. Until then, all you can do is push your seat back."

He turned around to look at Gretchen sitting crosswise in the back seat, her shorter legs fitting within the width of the car. She smiled at him contentedly. "Plenty of room back here." He'd just picked her up at home to take her to the All-City Track meet, to be held at Northern Bay High because it had the best track in the city. Her dad had answered the door, shaken his hand and wished him good luck. It was more than Sunday had hoped for. Every time he went to that door he hoped it wouldn't be Gretchen's mother, who made him feel edgy.

Everything was cooperating today except the weather, hovering in the mid-thirties even though a pale sun shone. He felt a springing energy coursing through his body and he wasn't cold, just eager, focused and confident. Sequoia had always told him he could do anything he put his mind to, and today he believed it.

He arrived before any of his teammates. Only four of Northern Bay's track team qualified for this event. He would do the hundred yards, and there was one man each for the mile, the four-forty and the two-twenty. Only he and Harold, the miler, had any reasonable chance of winning.

Harold sat down next to him, so close that their legs touched. Usually, only the coach would sit next to Sunday, the other players finding spots as close to the opposite end of the bench as possible.

"Trying to get warm?" As soon as he said it, Sunday regretted the edge in his voice.

"Yah, it's bad today. I'm glad the mile's first so my feet don't freeze."

Sunday glanced over at Harold's face. His goofy crooked smile made him look simple, but Harold was anything but. He and Harold were the only two Northern Bay men who had applied to Harvard, and Harold had been accepted. Harold clasped his hands under his armpits to keep warm.

"There's a team with depth." Harold pointed at the group of ten black men in purple-and-gold satin jackets sauntering toward them. "Where are they from?"

"Washington, my old school." As Sunday caught sight of Curtis and Jake, he leapt up and jogged toward them, expecting to give them a hug. But Curtis threw him a cool look and exaggerated the swagger in his step.

"Running for the white boys now?" Curtis

glanced around at the track appraisingly, his head cocked so that his eyes looked down, from the corners of their sockets. "Look at you; you even turning white." Curtis bowed his head and shook it with mock sadness as he gestured toward Sunday's white sweat pants.

Sunday stopped. One smile vanished and another took over his face. "Curtis, you're just jealous cuz my legs are longer and faster than yours. See you on the track." He turned around and walked back to his own bench.

Sunday could feel a change in his breathing as he sat down. Labored, halting, caught in Curtis' insult and lodged somewhere in his chest instead of flowing like wind through a tunnel, his breath refused to join him. Sunday coughed.

"I heard him," Harold said. "You're not running for us or Northern Bay or anyone but yourself. You've got a real chance of winning this, Sunday. Run your race and try to forget about what he said."

Sunday turned to face him. These were more words than Harold had said to him all year. His straw-stiff hair stuck out in every direction from his head and he held up his right hand awkwardly, waiting for Sunday to give him a high five. Sunday slapped his hand into Harold's. It was probably the first time anyone at school besides Gretchen or his coach had as much as touched him.

"Thanks, man."

When Harold got up to run his mile, Sunday gave him a high five and told him to run like the wind.

Sequoia and Gretchen sat in the bleachers above and behind Sunday as he waited. He could feel them like an August sun on his back. When he turned around to look behind him, he saw Gretchen huddled with Sequoia under Sequoia's red blanket, both of them sitting in a sea of black faces of other teachers and students from Washington. Northern Bay fans sat further down, on the other side of the first row of steps. Gretchen and Sequoia were laughing together. Gretchen looked completely comfortable.

At the sight of them, Sunday felt unaccountably happy. He envied them the blanket though, as he jumped from toe to toe, trying to get warm, stay loose. Harold ran back with a red ribbon around his neck, second place. Sunday slapped Harold on the back.

Sunday's race was called. Kneeling at the starting block, he wedged his left foot on the block and concentrated his energy on that foot, not on the knee on the icy ground. He curled his back like a coiled spring. Fingertips on the ground, all he felt was energy coursing through him. His lungs created clouds of steam around his head, and he inhaled the moist air like a surfacing dolphin.

Only vaguely aware that Curtis had knelt in the next lane, Sunday looked straight ahead. His legs twitched, like those of a cat eager to pounce. At the shot, he lunged.

The ribbon; he kept his eye on the ribbon as his arms pumped, his legs coursed. The cold air burned his lungs. He could feel more than see a runner pull too close on his left, an arm brushing his. He surged forward, veering slightly to the right of his lane, arching his chest forward and throwing his arms and head up as his chest tore the ribbon from its mount. His legs poured onward, slowing only yards past the finish line. He could feel a band across his heaving chest, an echo sensation of tearing the ribbon.

He knew he'd won, but he didn't understand the cheers from the crowd or hear the announcement. He looked at the crowd around him, standing and cheering. For him?

His coach ran up to him, shoving his stopwatch into Sunday's face, but he couldn't register the time. Coach threw his arms around him, lifting him easily off the ground. Sunday was already floating. A word came to him, just one. Joy. That was why he ran, not for Northern Bay or to beat Curtis or to prove what color he was. Joy. Only Joy.

Gretchen ran down from the stands and flung her arms around him. He twirled her; she was so light, so full of his joy. Then Sequoia wrapped her big arms around him. Her warm lips next to his ear, she reminded him, "Anything. You can do anything when you pour yourself into it." She grabbed his shoulders and held him slightly away from her. "I'm so proud of you!"

He'd set a school record. When he bowed to accept the blue ribbon and medal around his neck, he heard the announcement. Everyone in the bleachers stood, Washington, Northern Bay, the other schools, black and white celebrating together.

When he got home, even before he showered, he tore off his jacket and sweat pants and sat down in front of his drums. He sat still for a moment, slowly placing his left foot on the pedals. And then flew into motion, some incredibly fast staccato that left Sequoia just shaking her head in admiration.

For nearly an hour, the apartment thrummed, vibrated, reverberated.

The senior prom approached. Sunday and Gretchen went shopping together for her dress. They picked out a Mediterranean blue satin sheath, which she bought with her babysitting money. Sunday rented a midnight blue tuxedo. They danced together in his living room and felt themselves lucky. Dancing close, Sunday whispered into her ear, "Do you suppose if we were older, we'd get married?" She held him tightly.

"We'll have children who are all named after strong trees, like Sequoia," she replied.

23
Gretchen

On the Tuesday before the prom, Mr. Bauman, her history teacher, called her in to talk to him after school. To Gretchen's chagrin, her mother was also in the room.

"We are all concerned," he began, "about your relationship with Sunday Morgan. You appear to be too close for your own good." He went on about how young Negro men could not control themselves, and if she became pregnant it would ruin her life and become a school scandal. Gretchen sat stonily quiet.

"We're concerned that he may already have, uh, seduced you."

"He has not seduced me!" She blurted. Then she worried that she had admitted something by saying even that.

"Perhaps not," he continued, unfazed, "but we at the school believe it would be better for you and for the school if you and Sunday were not seen together as much. You know how high school students gossip," he said with a thin smile. And that was it, no questions, no punishments, just his insidious warning.

Her mother drove her home, and they were both silent. When they arrived home, Gretchen faced a new inquisition. This time she was not spared. Her father joined them, sitting apart like a silent judge.

"You're having sex with Sunday. It's dangerous."

"I am not; and I wouldn't tell you if I were. It's my own business." Gretchen surprised herself. It was the first time she had ever confronted her mother.

"Do you think it's your own business if you get pregnant or diseased?"

"I'm not and I won't be."

Her father spoke up, more gently than Norma, although almost anything would be more gentle than Norma.

"Honey, we know you want to go to college, and we don't want this relationship to interfere."

"Why would it? We're both good students. We study together; we help each other. Being with Sunday has nothing to do with my going to college."

Norma resumed. "That just shows how little you know about the world. We've decided, for your own good, that you can't see Sunday outside of school."

"No! No, no, no; you can't do this to me!" Gretchen flailed, one of her arms hitting the wall next to her. "This Saturday is the prom. I can't just back out of that." The prom was the least of it but the words raced out of her mouth on their own speed.

Surprisingly, her mother relented about the prom; she could go but had to be home by midnight, and that was the last date she and Sunday were permitted. No further pleading would do any good. Her mother had made up her mind. Her father sat silently, a sanctimonious cast to his eyes. Gretchen restrained an impulse to run over and hit him. Instead, she went to her room and cried furiously. Just when she had found the truest friend she could imagine, a man she thought she would love all her life, her mother stepped in to ruin her life. Her mother had found a new way to try to kill her; no one could blame her for this one.

Gretchen could hear her mother calling her to set the table for dinner. She stayed where she was, splayed on her bed, but listening now to her mother's agitated footsteps on the stone tile outside her room.

"Stop feeling sorry for yourself and set the table."

Gretchen flung open her door and her mother stepped back.

"You think just because you're missing your freedom you can take mine away too." She never thought she could say such a thing to her mother, and it energized her. "You can't!"

"You slut!" A bit of saliva shot from her mother's mouth on the 'sl,' and Gretchen backed away to dodge it, just as her mother lunged, her arms outstretched as if for Gretchen's neck.

Gretchen sidestepped into her room as her mother fell like a board onto the hard floor and lay still. Her father materialized from somewhere, kneeling next to her. She had made no sound after falling. Now she gurgled and spit out something. Gretchen saw pinkish spit on the beige tile and a little white bit of something in the spit. A tooth. Her father propped her up somewhat, facing Gretchen. Her mother's eyes bore a dazed, surprised look, not focusing on anything. Her jaw looked strange and a thin line of blood seeped from her slack mouth.

"Get a wet towel," her father told her.

Gretchen stepped around them gingerly and did what she was told. She saw her fingers tremble as she held the towel under the running faucet and wrung it. She handed it to him.

As he dabbed it under Norma's lips, she flinched. He tried again, very gently, but she pushed him away with one hand, starting to cry. She turned her head very slowly, up toward Gretchen and then down at the floor. She reached for the little bit of tooth and tried to pick it up, but her fingers wouldn't cooperate. She turned her head all the way around, slowly and stiffly, to face him.

"Look what she did to me," she gurgled.

"Help me get her to the car." Her father took hold of her mother under her shoulders, her head propped up against his body, and Gretchen picked up her feet, clutching her by the ankles. While her mother moaned, they managed, with some awkwardness, to put her crosswise into the back seat.

"Get in."

"Not this time." Gretchen backed away, shaking her head, first slowly and then more emphatically. "I don't want to hear you tell the doctor she fell off her bike." Gretchen turned around and stomped into the house, slamming the door behind herself.

Between the front door and her room, she could see on the tile floor the little blood-tinted wet spot where her mother's face had hit the floor. Grabbing toilet paper from the bathroom, she knelt to wipe away her mother's sputum. The tooth was still there. Gretchen picked it up and palmed it while she carried the wet toilet paper back to the bathroom and flushed it away. She opened her left hand and examined the tooth under the bright bathroom light. She could now see that it wasn't a whole tooth, but a big corner of her mother's front tooth, broken diagonally. She glanced up at the mirror and imagined her mother – or herself - without the center corner of her right front tooth. Grotesque. She turned away from the mirror, from the very thought of being so disfigured. Suddenly, she couldn't bear to hold it any longer. Tempted to flush it down the toilet, she dropped it instead into a drinking glass, walked to her parents' bathroom and left it there on the counter. She washed her hands, then walked back to her own bathroom to avoid wiping them on her mother's towel. She washed her hands again, automatically, forgetting she had already done so in the other room.

She walked into her own bedroom and sat down on the bed. Her knees trembled. Bracing them together as if to make them stop, she noticed her hands trembled also. Jumping up, she flung open her closet door and sat down in the corner where she used to take refuge from her mother's rants when she was younger. But the trembling only worsened. Standing up, she pulled her winter blanket off the top shelf, gathered it around herself and sat down again in what used to be her refuge. Only now it provided no refuge.

For a few seconds, somewhere in the sequence of this evening, she had felt emboldened – satisfied even – for having stood up to her mother and declaring her own independence. No longer the meek, terrified child, she'd defied her mother. For those few seconds, she'd glimpsed a world in which she did not have to flinch before Norma. In that tiny stretch of time she'd thought that if her mother's jaw was broken, it would be wired shut for weeks and she wouldn't be able to yell at her. Now all she could think of was that her mother's face would be forever disfigured. Her mother, who would not leave the house without spraying her hair perfectly into place, would now be unable to speak or even smile without revealing a jagged front tooth. And whose fault would that be in all the days and years to come?

Here she was, cowering in her own closet, cold even under the blanket in the stuffy air. Trying to talk herself out of her trembling, she said aloud, "In three months, I'll be out of here, on my way to college, beyond her reach." Speaking out loud helped stop her teeth from chattering. "It's true." She said it a second time, louder and more firmly than the first, and she felt slightly better. "Norma can't touch me once I get to Chicago."

But how to get through the next three months? Even her father wouldn't want her around after this incident. Grandma Etta now lived in another part of the city in a small apartment and could no longer see well enough to drive. She couldn't live there. Her grandparents Reinhardt lived just as far away. She saw them at Thanksgiving and Christmas and Easter and as few other times as possible. Jenny was a good confidante at school but Gretchen had rarely been to her home and barely knew her parents. She could not imagine asking them to take her in. She leaned her head back against the wall. She couldn't even imagine how to tell Jenny what had happened. Or Sunday. Or even Sequoia.

Gretchen heard the muffled ring of the telephone. Stumbling as she got up – her feet had fallen asleep underneath her and her right leg was numb as a stump – she rushed to answer the phone. Her father, she assumed.

"Hello."

"What's happening? You sound breathless." It was Sunday.

"Nothing. I ... I just ran in from outside. I didn't hear the phone at first."

"Something bad happened today." He paused, and she wondered how he could know. Was it the tone of her voice? Before she could think of what to say, he continued. "Mr. Bauman gave me a lecture today about why it wasn't a good idea for me to hang out with you anymore."

Gretchen gasped. "What'd he say?"

"That people were talking about us and I might be a bad influence on you. That this might jeopardize my scholarship to Howard." His voice was flat and so soft Gretchen had to strain to hear him.

"How could he say that! It's outrageous! And it's not true."

Gretchen heard him sigh. In a quieter tone, she told him, "He talked to me too."

"Oh no. What'd he say to you?"

Gretchen swallowed, totally unprepared for this conversation. "Pretty much what he said to you. My mother was there too. Was Sequoia there when he talked to you?"

"It was just me."

"What'd Sequoia say when you told her?"

"She got real mad but she didn't say much at

first. Just went around banging pots and slamming doors. She told me she wasn't mad at me but she didn't know what to say about Mr. Bauman."

"I can just see her doing that." Gretchen tried to laugh but it sounded feeble. "You're not going to stop seeing me, are you?" Her voice rose at the end, pathetically, she thought.

"What'd your momma say?"

Gretchen sighed. "You don't want to know."

"I think I need to know."

"Okay, but I won't let it stop me. You're too important to me."

"What did she say?"

There was no escaping it. "She told me I couldn't see you at all outside school after the prom."

"Yeah. I'm not surprised." His voice was flat.

"You're not going to let that stop you, are you?" Gretchen's voice wavered between a demand and a plea.

"We can handle the prom, baby, but I don't know about the rest of this."

"Let's talk about this at your house tomorrow after school."

Gretchen heard a faint sigh. "I don't think you should come."

Gretchen hung up the phone. Her voice had choked up so much she couldn't say more. Flinging herself onto her bed, she sobbed into her pillow until the muscles in her neck and shoulder hurt and tears no longer came. She sat up and looked around her. The room was totally dark. When she flipped on the light, her watch read eight forty. Thirsty, she opened the door to her room and lit the hallway light, also the outdoor light for her father, who hadn't returned from the hospital. In the kitchen, she poured herself some lemonade and stared at the pot of beef stew on the unlit stove. Realizing she was hungry, she touched the side of the pot, still lukewarm, and ladled some of the thick fragrant stew into a bowl for herself. That any food would taste so rich and savory at this moment came as a small surprise to her. She ate it greedily, without trying to make sense of the welter of her thoughts. As soon as she had finished, she felt overwhelmingly tired, spent. Leaving the bowl on the table (unthinkable under her mother's rules), she went to bed and fell asleep.

At some point in the night, she heard a door open and saw the shape of her father enter her room. "Now you see what happens when you cross her," he said, shaking his head, receding from the room like a ghost.

Gretchen woke at first light, the sky milky and unpredictable. She sat up with a start, remembering what her father had said in the night. Or had she dreamed it? After dressing quickly, she opened the door to her room and went to see if her parents were home. The door to her parents' bedroom was closed, and the car sat in the driveway. Normally, she was the first up and she left for school before either of her parents got up. Taking cereal from the cupboard at usual, she banged the door slightly and made more noise than usual, testing to see if her father would get up and tell her what had happened to her mother. But her parents' bedroom was silent.

By the time she gathered her books together to walk to the bus, she paused in front of her parents' bedroom, still silent. If she knew that her mother wasn't inside, she'd knock. But she had no way of knowing. She left the house. Walking to the bus stop, she wondered again about what her father had said in the middle of the night. Was it worse than she had imagined for her mother? Could she have died? Had she dreamed it? Her mind swirled almost as much as it had the night before.

She willed herself to think of school. First period was English with Mr. Vitelli. What was the assignment? She couldn't remember. Sunday would be there. She was catching a bus earlier than usual and might be able to speak with him before class.

Sunday didn't appear at his locker, even though she waited for him. When she walked into Mr. Vitelli's class, he was already seated, looking down at his book, and he didn't look up.

24
Sunday

He couldn't stop staring at her hair and her hands. He had the advantage of sitting slightly behind her in the next row of desks, which were slightly staggered to discourage cheating. But he was cheating now, stealing this time that was with her but not with her, imagining himself running his hands through her fine, yielding hair, and folding her hand around him. She had such warm slender fingers, and she touched him with such surprising curiosity, tracing the line of hair from his navel to his penis. She shifted in her chair, running one hand under her bottom to smooth her skirt. He had run his hands over that same place, but lingering over that fleshy entrance to that most exciting cave. She wouldn't turn around to look at him.

Somehow he had known all along it would come to this. He knew it the same way he knew in the orphanage that the boy in the next bed with the persistent cough would eventually disappear without explanation. For years he was afraid whenever he caught a cold and began to cough. In the first year he lived outside, with Sequoia, he'd caught strep throat. She'd thought he had a much higher fever because he couldn't stop trembling, but it wasn't the fever at all, it was the fear that he'd be taken away somewhere and just disappear out of life itself. Sequoia had stayed home with him, got him antibiotics, and sat in bed with him just holding him for hours at a time. It was the only way he could fall asleep. Now Gretchen was going to disappear from his life, and he felt the same leaden inevitability about it, an inertia so overpowering he could barely move his limbs. It wasn't even the specific fear that someone would intervene and take away his scholarship to Howard, although that would be its own catastrophe since Sequoia certainly couldn't afford to pay his tuition.

Gretchen's entry into his life was as golden as it was unexpected. She looked at him without guile or hesitation, but with an openness that accepted him for who he was. From the start, she sloughed the gossip and scorn of the other students with an indifference that mystified him. Her confiding in him so nakedly aroused a protectiveness he had never felt before. No one had ever confided in him like she did. If Sequoia ever felt vulnerable, she sheltered him from it. And yet Gretchen, even when feeling wounded, still had a spine of steel. She wanted to defy her mother and Mr. Bauman and whoever else wanted to keep them apart. Sunday doubted he could match her in that. Defiance was not part of his being.

"Sunday?" It was Mr. Vitelli's voice. He knew this would happen.

"I'm sorry; I don't know the answer." He'd never drifted away in class like this before. Mr. Vitelli simply called on someone else, but several heads turned around, including Gretchen's. Her eyes pled with him, and he looked down again.

Was it even possible for them to take away his ticket to Howard? Logically, he thought not, but he did not assume logic or even good luck would ensure his entry and scholarship to college. If anything, he was inclined to assume the worst. His thoughts went back to Gretchen, and he remembered how she licked the inside of his upper lip when they kissed. He shifted in his chair to disguise his hard on. Transfixed between his fear and his desire, he knew there was no solution for any of this.

25
Gretchen

Sunday had avoided her all day. She thought of watching him at track practice, but that would only protract her misery about him and perpetuate her dread about what had happened to her mother. So she took the early bus home.

When she opened the door, she was surprised to hear her parents' voices and meat sizzling in the kitchen. She smelled sauerkraut and pork chops. Hesitating, she listened for a moment to their voices. Although she couldn't hear what they were saying, the sounds were friendly, even cheerful, and companionable. As she walked into the kitchen, they looked at her as if not expecting to see her at home for dinner. Her mother's chin swelled like a ripe plum, but she otherwise looked normal. Her parents' conversation ended, and neither of them said anything to her.

"Are you okay?" Gretchen blurted, looking at her mother.

"It's what you see," she said, raising her chin. "And this." She opened her lips to reveal the disfiguring broken tooth, just as Gretchen had imagined it. "We'll get it capped," Her mother said without emotion.

"I'm - - I'm glad it's not worse." Gretchen stumbled over what to say.

Her mother turned around to tend to the sizzling pan. Gretchen saw two pork chops in it. Two, not three. She cast a look at her father, and she thought she saw a trace of conscience flicker across his brow. *They weren't even expecting her to come home.* Gretchen spun around to flee the kitchen, this house, this family that didn't want her as part of it. Her father reached out and clasped her arm.

"It's not what you think," he said firmly. "Norma's jaw is sore and she can't chew meat. The pork chops are for you and me, and your mother will have soup tonight." He pulled her toward him, trying to be gentle but also trying not to let her get away, and she limply allowed him to hug her.

"Go wash up and then help us by setting the table," he told her gently.

At dinner, her mother ate in almost total silence, occasionally wincing as she brought her napkin to her swollen purpled chin to dab up dribbles of soup. Her father tried to engage Gretchen in conversation about school, but she gave him monosyllabic responses. He even asked, lamely, if she was looking forward to the prom.

"How can I?" she answered, tears welling in her eyes.

The next two days passed almost identically both at school and at home. Sunday didn't look at her in class and was nowhere to be found outside class. Her parents tolerated her at dinner like a stray dog. Sunday didn't call her until Thursday evening.

"Where have you *been* all week?" she demanded.

26
Sunday

After track practice on Thursday, as he opened the door to his apartment, Sunday was acutely aware that only Sequoia would be home, that he wouldn't hear the gurgle of conversation between her and Gretchen that he'd grown to anticipate. He heard only the male voice of a newscaster on television. Sequoia greeted him with a hug and a sigh.

"I miss Gretchen," she confessed. "How is she?"

"Dunno." He turned away and went to dump his books in his room.

She was standing just outside his room. "Don't know?" *How could you not know?* said her look.

"I can't talk about it." He shut the door to his room. For two days he had not spoken to Gretchen at school, which entailed skillful dodging, although he had stared at her obsessively in class. He had not called her. What could he say? He wanted to be able to promise her that this would blow over, that once they graduated they could do whatever they wanted, that the two of them could brave the physical distance and her parents' disapproval and the sneers of passersby on the street and whatever else it would take. He couldn't say any of that. He didn't believe it. Yet he ached for her every minute.

The prom was the day after tomorrow. It seemed to him a kind of acute torture to allow them to be together on that evening, with an early curfew, and over-attentive chaperones for each dance together. They could be close but not really close, could catch the scent and touch of each other but only at a body distance. He was half tempted not even to go, as if that were a more bearable ache.

Now even Sequoia was on his case – the one other person on earth who wanted to let the two of them breathe and grow and love each other. When she called him to dinner, he sighed, knowing she would press him.

"Haven't you even called her?"

"Koya, *I don't know what to say to her."*

"Yeah. I hear you. But don't you think she wants to know you still care?"

"What good will that do? Aren't we just torturing each other?"

"Seems to me that if you do care, you'd tell her that waiting 'til after graduation isn't the end of the world."

"Then what?" He sank his chin into his fists, his elbow sending his fork klinking onto the floor.

"I can't answer that for you."

After dinner, he slumped on his bed and stared at the telephone. He wanted to hear her voice, *right here on this bed*, he wanted to touch her, he wanted to inhale the faint peppery smell of her armpits, he wanted to reassure her. He couldn't find any words to do it. He dialed her number and she answered on the second ring.

"Gretchen, I...."

"Where have you *been* all week?"

"Aching. I can't be with you and I can't stand not being with you."

"Me too, but at least you could have told me." She sounded slightly mollified. "I've been thinking. Why don't we dress for the prom and you pick me up and we just go to your house and hang out there? I bet Sequoia wouldn't mind."

"She probably wouldn't, and I know she'd like to see you...."

"That wasn't *exactly* what I meant."

"But what if your mom finds out?"

"I don't even think she even expected me to come home for dinner. Last night they looked surprised to see me, and had cooked food for only two people."

"Gretchen, ..."

"Check with her and call me back."

"Okay."

Sunday slouched in the doorway of Sequoia's bedroom. "What if we hung out here Saturday night instead of going to the prom?"

"You mean tell her parents you're going to the prom and then come here instead?" She shook her head emphatically. "Not on my watch. No. Not gonna happen."

He turned around without an argument and called Gretchen back.

"She said no." He waited for a long moment.

"Then let's make it one beautiful evening at the prom for you and me."

27
Gretchen

On the morning of the prom, Gretchen decided to do what she could to make herself beautiful for this last night, even if it took all day. She looked in the mirror at her narrow face, gray-blue eyes and long pale eyelashes. Her hair, the color of a dry cornfield in November, hung limply at her shoulders. Today, she would make it bouffant like the other girls'. She'd watched the other girls back-combing their hair in the school bathroom – 'ratting' was what they called it – so that the underhair balled up a bit and the strands on top lay smoothly over the mass underneath to give the effect of a beehive. Gretchen took over the bathroom, newly purchased hair spray in hand. Fortunately, her mother was away, shopping and getting her hair done. Her father was painting in his studio, as usual oblivious to the goings-on in the rest of the house. At first, she took too-large clumps of her hair and back-combed it so hard that she didn't have enough hair left on top to cover the mess below. When she tried to undo it, her hair snarled and it took a long time to get it smooth again. Then she started over. It was lunch time before she was done.

She brought sandwiches to her father in his studio, where they sometimes ate together on weekends. He took one look at her and started to laugh. "You look like a face inside a squirrel's nest. What did you do to your hair?" She started to cry.

"Oh, liebchen, I'm sorry. " He put his arms around her, as he used to do when she was little. "I know you want to look beautiful for tonight. But you don't need to do this." He touched her hair. "You have hair like shiny corn silk and eyes the color of the lake on a summer evening. You can't improve on nature."

She felt much better. She had never thought of her eyes as anything but plain and boring before. After lunch, Gretchen went back to the bathroom and took a second shower, washed her hair again and started over. Her hair did in fact shine. She wished she had mascara for her eyelashes and thought of using her mother's. She was in her mother's bathroom reaching for the mascara when she remembered having borrowed her mother's lipstick as a little child. Closing the drawer, she resolved to go as she was.

She heard her mother come home. Fortunately, she went first to the kitchen to put away groceries, and Gretchen slipped from the bathroom into her own room and closed the door.

"Gretchen, come up here and help put away the groceries."

There was no escaping her. Her mother stood in the kitchen, unpacking grocery bags. She took hold of cans with unnatural delicacy because her fingernail polish – Hawaiian coral – was still fresh. Her hair coiled in an artful bouffant. Gretchen silently put away the groceries, trying hard to avoid anything that could give her mother offense.

"I thought you were going to the prom tonight," her mother said breezily. "Aren't you going to pretty up?"

"I will as soon as I'm finished here." Her mother released her without further conversation, and Gretchen finished getting ready in her room, where she stayed until she heard the doorbell. She hurried to be the first to open the door.

Sunday stood in the doorway holding a white orchid corsage. He beamed at her as if nothing had ever daunted their loving each other. Her parents did not even come to the door, a small grace. No one snapped the typical prom photos. In the car, Sunday drove silently for a couple of blocks and then swerved to the curb and braked the car to a stop.

He leaned toward her, gently took each side of her face and kissed her. It was a long, searching kiss, as if memorizing every part of her lips.

"I just want you to know I love you; I will always love you no matter what. I had no idea someone like you would ever come into my life, and..."

"That's all you need to say. Let's make the most of this evening and pretend Mr. Bauman and all the others like him aren't even there."

"Maybe you can do that, Gretchen, but I can't." Sunday turned on the ignition and drove to school.

Pale blue and white helium balloons festooned the ceiling of the gym. Their strings hung like tiny life lines, brushing Sunday's head as they walked in. The dance floor was so crowded that Gretchen knew they could obscure themselves in the center and dance as closely as they wanted. But when Sunday took her hand to lead her onto the dance floor, he kept a discreet distance. Their arms and shoulders touched, but not their hips. His hand lay lightly on her shoulder, not on her lower back. He felt stiff. She stood on her toes and nuzzled his ear, whispering, "you don't have to keep this distance." He turned his head and spoke in a low voice into her ear, "I do, but none of this changes how I feel about you." She fought the urge to cry. When he took her home at midnight, he kissed her one long, last time.

"I will always love you. Our being apart won't change that."

"Sunday, I want to find a way to be with you. I don't want them to keep us apart."

He held her very tightly. "In some way, I will always be holding you. You ... touched me ... in a way I never imagined. Some part of you will always be with me." Then he let her go, brushed her wet cheek with his thumb and said goodnight.

From that moment until graduation a month later, he was nothing but proper at school. He was still her chemistry partner, but he spoke only of what they were doing in class. When they passed in the hall, he said hello. He stopped calling her in the evening.

Gretchen would not speak to her parents. She ate silently at dinner and kept to her room as much as possible. She could not look at her mother without venom, so she looked down at her plate.

Gretchen missed Sequoia almost as much as she missed Sunday. She telephoned Sequoia after school one day when she knew Sunday had track practice.

"I miss you. I can't stand this. I want to keep seeing Sunday. What can we do about this? Can I still come study at your house after school?"

"I miss you too, girl. I don't think I can help you in breaking your own parents' rules. You and Sunday need to decide what you're willing to risk to be together. I can't make that decision for either one of you."

Gretchen called back and spoke with Sunday. Edgily, he asked if her mother was there. "No, and I want to find a way to see you."

"Hold on," he told her, "until graduation, when the school could no longer hold over us the threat of interfering with college."

Gretchen tortured herself with questions. Was it really the fear about losing his scholarship? Did he think this relationship wasn't worth the risk? Had he lost interest and just 'seduced' her, as the school would have it? Why wouldn't he see her or even talk to her? She questioned his courage, questioned whether he actually cared or whether his words were empty.

By coincidence, she sat directly behind him at graduation, closer to him for a longer time than since the prom. For an hour, that straight dark stiff neck was within her touch. When they stood up after the ceremony ended, she caught the scent of his hair. He turned around and hugged her. "Congratulations," was all he said. He signed her yearbook with a message about how deeply she had touched him and how he would always remember her. Sequoia came over and embraced Gretchen tightly.

"Be strong," she said; "use your talents and go

shine on this world." And then she loped off to join Sunday.

A week later, Sunday phoned. "Could you come for dinner with Sequoia and me this Saturday?"

"I will, of course," she said. "I won't ask them."

"Ask them."

"No. What time?"

Gretchen showed up on Saturday, graduation gift in hand. She had bought him Miles Davis' latest album. She also brought a bunch of daisies for Sequoia, who seemed happy to see her, but solemn.

"Go off, you two; I know you have a lot to talk about and I'll be busy here in the kitchen."

He took Gretchen's hand and led her to his bedroom. This time there was no light behind the dull orange drapes; the sun had already set.

"I have some important news." His body radiated a resolve, a kind of palpable excitement she hadn't sensed in him for some time.

"My college is sending a contingent of students to Mississippi to help register voters, and they've opened it up to the incoming freshmen. I'm leaving next week." He went on to explain, almost breathlessly, how he'd live with a local family and hoped to make a difference at a critical time in history. She'd stopped listening to his words after "leaving next week."

"I'll go too. I want to help."

"You can't. I mean, not with me. This is just for Howard students." As an afterthought, he added, "Maybe Chicago is sending students too."

So it was him and the other Negro students. Not a place for her. This was about him, and history, and not about her. She strung together some words about how she admired him for doing this and how important it was. After mustering whatever words she used, she turned away so he could not see her eyes. "I'll go see if Sequoia can use some help."

Sequoia was banging pots with more than usual energy as she put dinner together. She cut her finger while cutting an onion. "Damn!" She pounded the counter. Gretchen ran to get a bandage.

Before Gretchen said anything about Mississippi, Sequoia gave her an intense look and said, "I bet you want to go too." Gretchen's look told her yes.

"I don't think either of you has a clue about how dangerous this is, but that probably won't stop either one of you. If you go," she pinned Gretchen with her dark eyes, "don't go because of him. And don't go just to get away from your family; you'll get away soon enough. Go because you want to do this, and don't even hang out together."

When Sunday sat down at the table, Sequoia practically slammed a pot of greens in front of him.

"I made you greens in pot liquor, so you can get used to Southern cooking." Her voice was not friendly.

"Don't you want him to go?"

"Gretchen, he's all the family I got. He has a beautiful future ahead of him. I want him to live to see it. I'm being selfish. No, I don't want him to go. But it's his choice. And I'll support him every way I can." She stabbed a fried chicken leg and plunked it on his plate.

"Sequoia," Sunday was dead earnest, "I think we can make a difference there. I want to go and be part of it."

"And you will. So let's talk about other things." She asked Gretchen about her summer job, which was dishing ice cream at Baskin-Robbins, and what she knew about her start of college in September. They made arrangements to postpone Sunday's drum lessons for the summer and talked about what to pack.

Gretchen liked the sweet, smoky greens even though she wasn't hungry. Sequoia explained how to cook a ham hock in water to make 'pot liquor' before throwing in the mustard greens.

As though something had just occurred to her, Sequoia put down her fork and knife and turned to Gretchen.

"You need a place to stay this summer?"

"Here?" Gretchen felt as if the sun had just come up. "You mean it?"

"Well, Sunday won't be here, so you won't be breaking any rules," she said with a sly smile, "and I'd sure love to have you." Gretchen put the heels of hands over her eyes and started to sob. She cried so hard she hiccupped.

"Yes, thank you, yes."

Sunday beamed as if some difficult equation had been solved, and Sequoia stood up and put her big arms around Gretchen's heaving shoulders. "You know you're family here," she whispered.

Sunday caught a train to Washington, D.C. two days later to meet his cohort, and Gretchen planned her own get-away. She thought about going to Mississippi. She knew this was an important effort, an effort to make a change in this whole country, not just between her and Sunday or other people like her, but all those people whose struggles were far more difficult than theirs – who couldn't even vote or go to a decent school or take public transportation without being humiliated. But she felt helpless too, overwhelmed by the enormity of the problem and completely at sea about how to join such an effort and what it would demand of her. She'd never even traveled outside Wisconsin – except to Chicago – and the South was as foreign and forbidding as Afghanistan or Cambodia. She made a couple of phone calls. From the University of Chicago, she learned that their cohort had already departed and did not include incoming freshmen anyway. From the local NAACP, she learned that she had to be eighteen to join, and she would not be eighteen until August. She didn't know who else she could call. But she also felt an inchoate relief as she contemplated the prospect of living with Sequoia.

Gretchen rehearsed several different departures before saying anything at all to her parents. One version was simply to disappear, leaving an empty room. But she realized that would probably motivate her parents to come look for her, and she would be only too easy to find. The version she liked best held a perfect mixture of drama and revenge and defiance.

At dinner one night, Gretchen announced to her parents that when she left for Chicago in the fall, she would never come back. She would make her own way. Her voice assumed more confidence with each sentence.

"Since I seem to be nothing but trouble for you, I've found a place to stay for the summer." Sarcasm and defiance and self-righteousness flowed from her lungs. "You can enjoy each other's company without me at last. You won't have to be embarrassed about my Negro boyfriend anymore. He's gone to Mississippi to help register voters. I'm going to live with Sequoia, who cares abut me. You won't be able to ruin my life any more."

Her mother, surprisingly, had almost nothing to say. She looked genuinely hurt, which pleased Gretchen. Gretchen noticed she'd been keeping her mouth shut more since losing part of her tooth. Her father, however, rose to the occasion.

"Are you finished?"

"Yes."

"No, you aren't. You owe your mother an apology. She made the hard decision to stand up to you in order to save you from destroying your future. She doesn't deserve this reaction."

Gretchen got up and jammed her chair into the table.

"I don't owe either of you an apology. You owe me a big one. She's been trying to trample me all my life and you haven't protected me. I'm leaving."

Gretchen took her clothes and left that night, feeling righteous, proud and brave. Sequoia fussed over her like a new chick. That night and for the rest of the summer she slept in Sunday's bed, smelling him on the pillow, remembering him there with her and waiting for when they would be back together. She played his music on the record player. "Ain't no Mountain High Enough" became a song she sang to herself to keep up her hope.

Sunday wrote letters and cards about twice a week. They were at first addressed to both Sequoia and Gretchen and full of news of his training in nonviolent resistance and of the family with whom he stayed. There were eight of them in three rooms, and they insisted on giving him one of the rooms all to himself because he was an important guest. The local people were kind and warm and at once eager, dubious and fearful about getting to vote. His host family had no TV. On the day President Johnson signed the Voting Rights bill, someone came running to the door of their home and knocked so hard that everyone got jittery and hid Sunday in a back room before opening the door. When they heard the news, his local family praised the Lord and hugged each other.

Gretchen dished ice cream during the days, including weekends, and at night brought home pints of jamoca almond fudge for her and Sequoia. They whooped together while eating ice cream as they watched the TV news coverage of the Voting Rights Act. Not that many days later, Sequoia and Gretchen watched the news of the disappearance of three young civil rights workers in Mississippi, not more than a few miles from where Sunday was living. Two were white, said the reporters, one a Negro. Andrew Goodman, Michael Schwerner and James Chaney. Not Sunday Morgan. Sequoia was hushed only until the report ended. She hit the television hard as she turned it off and stormed around the room, banging her open hand on the walls, then on her own face.

"I told him not to go! I knew something like this would happen. Those crackers!"

Gretchen went to Sunday's room. She wasn't angry like Sequoia. Shocked, frightened, relieved it was not Sunday. Underneath that, she felt admiration for what Sunday was doing, for his courage, the importance of what he was doing. She thought she understood what had moved him to go.

Sunday telephoned the next day, to let them know he was okay. He spoke only with Sequoia. Gretchen was at work. He reported that people were registering to vote; this was not going to stop them.

* * *

"Tomorrow's your birthday."

Gretchen's head jerked up in surprise. She and Sequoia were having breakfast on a Saturday morning in August.

"You think I didn't know?" Sequoia beamed. "Gimme a little credit. So what do you want to do? I wanna celebrate with you, girl."

Gretchen couldn't believe her own ears. She thought of that horrendous birthday five years ago. "No chores."

"That's a given, honey. What would you really like to do?"

"Go swimming," Gretchen blurted, and then reddened as she realized they couldn't go to the beach together. The Negro and white sections of the Milwaukee beaches were clearly separated.

"Hmm. Let me think. I may know a place. Do you know how to fish?"

"Are you serious? I grew up fishing at my dad's friends' cottage on Silver Lake."

"Well, girl, you are in for a challenge, because I am one fine fisherwoman, and we are going swimmin' and fishin' tomorrow."

Sunday called early the next morning. "Happy Birthday, Gretchen."

Gretchen sucked in a deep breath. She almost couldn't speak.

"Your voice. Say something else. I just want to hear your voice again."

"I'm doin' fine. I think about you all the time. I wish I knew a way for us to be together. I hope you and Sequoia have a good birthday planned; she's good at birthdays."

"I'm so glad you're okay. We didn't know what to think when they found the bodies. We each said a selfish prayer of thanks that it wasn't you. Let me get Sequoia; she needs to hear your voice too."

"Wait, just a minute." She could hear a little change in his inflection, as if the South were slowing down his speech.

"I mean it when I say I think about you all the time. I love you, Gretchen. I just don't know how to find a way for us to be together. It's a damn good thing you didn't come here with me, or it might have been us they found dumped in a river. We each need to go to our own schools and finish college, and I just can't figure out how we can do it together."

"I want to find a way, Sunday. Just keep your mind open to us finding a way."

"My heart is wide open, Gretchen, but my mind is finding it hard."

"I'll get Sequoia."

Sequoia came rushing in her chenille bathrobe, and Gretchen closed the door to her room so they could talk by themselves. She collapsed on the bed and big gulping sobs overtook her. He was safe. He cared. He loved her. But he was also saying they couldn't be together. Why wasn't he willing to try to find a way? She couldn't believe the obstacles could be that big. What happened to Chaney and Goodman and Schwerner was in Mississippi. This was Wisconsin. People could be unpleasant, but it wasn't that bad. She lay back on the bed where they had made love just three months earlier and put her nose into the pillow. It smelled only of her own hair, not his.

Sequoia packed a picnic lunch and drove them to a little hidden lake at the end of a dirt road. The lake had no beach, just cattails all around, and it was so small you could hardly call it a lake. But there was a pier that went beyond the cattails to the open water, and there was a wooden raft in the middle of the water. And the day was sunny, with drifting white clouds that held no threat of rain. There was only one cottage, which leaned like a faded old man against an enormous white pine. Hints of light blue showed under the eaves. Two wooden rocking chairs sat on its wide screened porch.

"Race you to the raft." Sequoia launched off the pier like a log into a river. Gretchen dove too but couldn't keep up with Sequoia. They lay on the raft until the sun dried their skin; when they grew too hot, they swam again. And laid again and swam again, until they were as relaxed as seals on a warm rock.

They ate egg salad sandwiches and watermelon on the porch of the old cottage.

"Know who owns this place?" Gretchen asked.

"No, it's been abandoned for years, I think. I imagine some old man whose family all died before him, living out his last days here, and nobody left to take over his home."

After lunch, they fished from the pier. On

the way, Sequoia had stopped at a bait shop for minnows, and she baited their hooks.

"You've got to do this so that the minnow can still swim."

"You sound like my dad."

Sequoia fished silently for a while, casting and reeling in slowly and evenly. Gretchen remembered that her father also had a birthday this week. As she fished, she both missed him and, at the same time, savored a bitter thought that he would not hear from her on his birthday.

"Do you think you'll ever forgive him?"

"I don't know." The word 'forgive' had not even occurred to her.

"Why should I? He promised to protect me but always chose to please her instead. I don't understand how he could do that."

"Wasn't he always kind to you? Didn't he make you feel special even though your mother didn't? Didn't he teach you a lot?"

Gretchen felt a tug on her line and jerked it too hard, losing both her fish and the minnow, which flopped in an arc over the water. Sequoia re-baited her line, and Gretchen cast badly, whipping the line into the water too close to the pier. "Easy," Sequoia reminded her quietly. Sequoia's own line tightened suddenly, and the rod bent with promise.

"Okay!" Gretchen watched as Sequoia kept the rod bent and reeled in a bass. It glinted in the sun as Sequoia took it off the hook, then threaded a line through its large jaw and gill. It swam futilely beside the pier as it tested its tether.

"I think we need another one like that for dinner. It's your turn." Sequoia put her rod aside and lay down on the pier.

Gretchen cast with more focus, remembering who had taught her and how gently he had coaxed her. The line went in where she wanted it. Again and again she cast, imagining herself as ten years old again and her father here with her, encouraging her. She felt calm and almost happy. Soon enough, her rod bent and she pulled in another bass, smaller than Sequoia's but big enough to keep.

She called her father on the next day for his birthday, but her mother picked up the telephone. Gretchen hung up without saying anything. On the following day, she called him at work and wished him a happy birthday. He thanked her, with a catch in his voice, but he also told her he didn't like her having hung up on her mother the day before.

Sunday returned home just two days before she was to leave for school. She and Sequoia picked him up at the Greyhound bus station. He wore a big white grin and a tee-shirt that fell too loosely around him. He hugged Sequoia first, and she lifted him up in her exuberance, turning around slowly.

"My baby brother's back," she kept saying. Then he hugged Gretchen, and she could feel how thin he was. He smelled different. She couldn't say how.

"I thought about you every single day," he whispered into her ear. He pulled the tip of her ear with his lips. "Every day."

They slept together in his bed the next two nights, and it was as if no time had separated them from that first afternoon behind the sunlit drapes. Their bodies twined like sweet licorice. But he wouldn't go out of the house with her. She'd suggested a movie for one of the nights, but he said no, he wanted to stay in, without giving any reason. He helped her pack. He touched her whenever he could, even if it was just brushing her hand as they packed or putting his fingers through her hair. He was not talkative, and he was not happy. His eyes had lost luster. When she tried to talk about visiting each other at school or coming home for Thanksgiving, he promised nothing.

"I don't know how we can carry on," he said.

28
Gretchen

Sequoia drove Gretchen to Chicago the day before Labor Day. Gretchen and Sunday had curled against one another all the night before, even though it was too humid to touch anything, or to sleep.

"I feel like one life is ending," she'd whispered, and he'd finished her sentence.

"Another one is beginning."

"I want you to be in the new one too," she'd told him.

"I will always be with you," was all he said. He said it again when he kissed her goodbye in the driveway.

Gretchen was mostly quiet on the drive. This was the weekend she and her dad always went to the cottage for the end of summer and helped Jim, Demi and Themis take in the pier. It was a ritual dismantling of the summer, comforting and bittersweet. It signaled the end of the annual two-week vacation of the two men and their respective children, like cousins by now, and the return to school. After taking in the pier, they packed their clothes, roasted hot dogs on sticks in front of the fieldstone fireplace Jim and Bill had built fifteen summers ago, and drove home. At the last small town on the country road before they turned onto the highway, they stopped at the fountain for ice cream. One life ending. Gretchen leaned against the window to hide her tears. They were just passing the state line.

This part of Illinois looked just like Wisconsin, rolling green fields, dairy cows, intermittent barns and old farmhouses, elm forests. The air smelled like alfalfa and cow manure. Chicago she thought she knew: Milwaukee but bigger. One life ending but not even going to a new place.

"I don't suppose I'd make any points with you by saying how lucky you are to be going to one of the best universities in the country, on a full scholarship."

Gretchen just looked at her with big eyes, wet and blue as a lake.

Their arrival on campus was blurred by all of the activity of students moving in. She was in New Dorms, a big, white U-shaped building around a grassy courtyard. The walls on the ground floor, the student union, were all curved, encircling sitting areas filled with excited students. As Gretchen and Sequoia got into a boisterous, crowded elevator, it fell silent, and the other students looked away, as if they thought it was tacky to bring her cleaning lady to help move in. Gretchen's room was on the third floor. She knew only that her roommate was named Carol Hagerty from Ann Arbor.

When she found her room on the third floor, it was obvious Carol had already moved into her half. Political bumper stickers lined the sideboards of the upper bunk: C.N.C.C., "I Have a Dream," "Make

Peace, Not War." Over Carol's desk was a poster of Stokely Carmichael.

Carol burst into the room like a gust of warm wind. "Welcome, Gretchen," she said, and gave her a big spontaneous hug. Turning to Sequoia, Carol shook her hand. "Hi, I'm Carol." She had direct, unblinking eyes, a loud confident voice, and a body that tumbled all over itself in constant motion. She rushed around the room showing Gretchen where things were. Sequoia and Carol both helped Gretchen hang up her clothes. And then Carol surged out of the room.

"You're gonna have a lot of company here," Sequoia whispered with a suppressed smile. Gretchen laughed despite herself. Sequoia hugged Gretchen and kissed her on the forehead.

"You can make yourself a good new life here. Nobody's going to hold you down. Let your light shine." She was out the door before Gretchen could thank her.

That first night's dinner in the dorm impressed her with the obvious: there were no parents here, only students, with choices of mass-cooked food. There would be many freedoms, limited only by her own choices. After dinner, the Dean of Students addressed all the freshmen. After stirring them up about all the opportunities they would have here to grow and explore, he warned them about traveling beyond the perimeters of the campus: go no further than 60th Street on the South, 50th Street on the North, Cottage Grove on the West. Ghettos surrounded them, and it was unsafe to go there at any time of day and always at night. He vaunted Hyde Park, though, as a model of racial integration, an island of sanity. But still, don't go out alone at night.

Orientation week was filled with entrance exams in all the core courses. If she passed any of them, she could move on to more advanced courses. Humanities I had three components: literature, art and music. Gretchen knew she knew the first two, but for music she had only what Sunday had taught her. She listened to Beethoven's Violin Concerto in D every day for the week before the exam, listening for the sample questions. Major or minor mode? Sunday had told her you had to listen for it; he couldn't explain it. Minor mode: listen for the slow, the sad, he'd said. She wished he was here to tutor her again. In between entrance exams, Gretchen wandered the campus and the neighborhood. There was a Frank Lloyd Wright home directly across the street from her dorm; it seemed to advertise how special this place was. Never had she seen more imposing, dignified buildings or uglier students. The Gothic quadrangle conjured up British students in black gowns, not these scruffy blue-jeaned students who slouched on the lawns and scratched their rumpled hair or armpits as they crouched over books. A haven for the peculiar, she thought. She discovered the lake, a long walk east but a pretty one, and the shore was a good place to just look out into space, when it wasn't too windy. On warm days, groups of young black men played conga drums, and the rhythms radiated for several blocks around.

At night Gretchen heard the strangest sound, like wolves howling against the dark. She heard it two nights in a row before she screwed up her nerve to ask Carol if she had also heard them.

"Oh, yeah," she said, "there's a brilliant animal behaviorist here who has a small pack of wolves in his research compound on campus." Gretchen gave her a skeptical look. "For real," she added.

Carol lived up to her first impression, a tornado of activity, most of it political, sometimes heedless. After her mathematics entrance exam, which Carol "knew she had bombed," she consoled herself by playing Bob Dylan on the record player. "Isn't he amazing? Everybody should hear this." She pulled up the window in their room, which faced the big courtyard, dragged the speakers up onto the sill, facing outward, and blasted the music out into the courtyard. Gretchen was so embarrassed she slunk out of the room. But when she got downstairs and went outside, the music really did sound amazing in the courtyard. "I heard the roar of a wave that could drown the whole world....And it's a hard, and it's a hard, and it's a hard, and it's a hard rain that's gonna fall" echoed grainily against the three walls. Students on the lawn cheered at Carol, and she waved back at them, as comfortable as a candidate for office.

Gretchen wrote to Sunday about the episode and her impressions in general. He wrote back with his own impressions of Howard and of Washington, D.C. "There are professors here from all over the world, and when I walk through the city I can hear people speak in more languages than I knew existed. I feel like a big door has swung open for me. I'd like to think there's room in this world for you and me together. Whatever happens, know that there will never be another girl who will touch my life as deeply you have." She read and re-read his letters for signs of hope for them, but they were all equivocal. Sunday tethered her by his letters, but Gretchen could not understand how someone who had been touched so deeply would not try harder to keep that connection.

Gretchen found Carol too overwhelming for a close friend, though she did allow herself to be carried into some of Carol's activities. Carol held seemingly spontaneous meetings in their room or in the student lounge, where she debated political issues like the U.S. sending troops to Vietnam, a country Gretchen knew almost nothing about. She allowed herself to be swept along to many of these meetings, where she would sit quietly and absorb different students' perspectives.

One morning during orientation week, Gretchen saw a serious young black woman sitting by herself at breakfast. Gretchen recognized her as someone who had a room just down the hall from hers, and she had sat next to her in the science placement exam the day before.

"May I sit here?"

The young woman looked up guardedly. "Sure," she said as if she meant no but couldn't say it. She had large, protruding, serious eyes. It seemed odd to Gretchen that someone so shy should have such outspoken eyes. Gretchen introduced herself and asked what she thought of the science exam.

"I've never had any exposure to physics, and I watched you fly through that part of the exam yesterday. I just ate my heart out." Gretchen was pleased to see she drew a smile from the other girl.

"Physics is my subject," she allowed. "That and math. What's yours?"

"I wish I knew," Gretchen smiled.

"I'm Latisha Moseley, from Carthage, Mississippi." She cocked her head, as if waiting for a reaction. "And I can assure you, Dido and Aeneas never saw this Carthage." They both laughed.

Gretchen and Latisha began to study together. Latisha had passed out of eight of the twelve placement exams, including physics and math. That meant she could graduate in two or three years, if she chose to. She became a patient tutor for Gretchen in her physics class. They had the same world history class and read Thucydides together. Gretchen was surprised, in a way that Latisha wasn't, that history was relative, shaped by the perspective of the recorder. They usually studied in Latisha's room; her roommate was almost always in the library and it was quiet there. But one night when Carol was out they went to Gretchen's room. Latisha walked straight to Sunday's photo on Gretchen's desk and asked who that was.

"He's my boyfriend, or at least he was in high school."

Latisha looked at her strangely. "How could he be?"

Gretchen didn't know what to say. She blushed and stumbled and began to explain that they had started by studying together, then went to parties and school dances. Latisha's eyes popped.

"You mean you could do that in your school?" she asked incredulously.

"Well, it didn't go over very well." Gretchen told her the whole story, lingering with some fury on her mother's injunction against seeing Sunday.

"My momma would've done the same thing," Latisha said, "and I would know she was doing it to save my life."

Gretchen spat out: "One thing for sure, she wasn't doing it to save *my* life."

Latisha let the subject drop.

Gretchen noticed that every Sunday Latisha got up early and dressed up for church. Nobody else here got dressed up for anything, and it was quite stunning to see this young black woman in a hat, red party dress and heels go off to church each week.

"Could I go with you sometime?" Gretchen asked.

Latisha paused and then looked at her, hard on.

"Only if you've got the right clothes," she said, with a broad smile. When Latisha smiled, her face lit like a door from a dark room opening into sunshine. Gretchen felt good that Latisha could tease her.

"I'm not sure I do. It's been years since I went to church, and where I come from, no one would dare wear a red dress to church."

"You white folks are just repressed, that's all." They laughed and laughed, their sides splitting with relief.

"Seriously, can I go without a hat?"

"Yeah, but you gonna look awful plain." And they laughed some more.

Gretchen cobbled together an outfit with a yellow skirt and sweater from high school, which was at least cheerful, and they took off by bus for Latisha's Baptist Church on 79th Street. She drew stares as she got off the bus with Latisha, but at the church she was greeted with genuine warmth. The service began with an organ blast of upbeat, jazzy rhythm. The choir, in golden robes, filed in two by two, belting out a celebratory hymn like Gretchen had never heard before. During the sermon, full of assurances that 'God loves you,' random members of the congregation would stand up and call out "Testify!" or "Amen!" Just before the end of the service, the choir and congregation together sang "Good to Know You, Jesus" at a pitch somewhere between shouting and singing. The sound vibrated through the large room, connecting each person's voice to the others, a river of joyous sound. The Jesus of Gretchen's childhood had been tepid and saintly, a pale victim. Had she felt she could "know" Him like this congregation did, she might have grown up believing in Him. It was the liveliest church service she had ever imagined, and it made her feel good all week. She went back with Latisha several times, and each time she came out feeling hopeful about life in general.

Gretchen told Carol about the services, and she seemed interested. "If you like that," Carol told her, "you might really enjoy the services held on Saturdays not far from here." She described how they were held in a converted theater and blended religious service, community action and political dialogue. She encouraged both Latisha and Gretchen to come one Saturday. "In jeans," she instructed. Latisha, who didn't own any jeans, wore a pair of smart black slacks and a light green sweater. The three of them took a bus west of Cottage Grove, then transferred to a northbound bus, both busses traveling in all-black neighborhoods. Of the three of them, Carol seemed the most confident; Gretchen felt tension from others on the bus, and Latisha sat so stiffly she must have felt uneasy also.

Their destination was indeed a theater, with an

unoccupied ticket booth, and a refreshment counter where people stood in line for popcorn and soda. Latisha nervously deadpanned that neither her church nor Gretchen's would allow popcorn. The sometime theater was crowded - they had arrived early enough to get seats but some people stood at the rear and others in the aisles. This church had no organ, but it had a fifty-person choir on the stage, all in bright purple gowns. When they burst into song, it was as if the whole theater vibrated. Everyone sang. When it was done, the choir director signaled the choir and congregation to silence, and the room hushed immediately. A young pastor with a round, handsome face, an Afro hairstyle, wearing a bright yellow dashiki with a swirling red, black and green design around the neck, bounded to the podium. The choir director announced: "I give you the Reverend Jesse Jackson!" as though he were announcing a television celebrity. The young pastor spoke of the tragedy of young men dropping out of school, sinking into drugs and alcohol. He preached self-respect. Every one of you, he said, can rise out of misery. Say after me: "I am somebody. I am Somebody! I am SOMEBODY!" Each time he pronounced the word with a different emphasis, and the audience became a rousing chorus of self-affirmation. By the end of the service, everyone seemed euphoric. People made way for each other and everybody smiled.

But when the three girls reached the theater doors, they could see about six police officers fanned along the curb outside, stroking their batons as if warming them for action. Latisha immediately hung back, pulling on Gretchen's sleeve so that she would also wait. But Carol had charged ahead, and she didn't hear Gretchen call out for her to wait. As if on cue, the officers converged on one young man with a silk rag on his head and a swaggering walk as he swung open the left door. Carol was at that moment walking out the door furthest to the right.

"Stop right there!" They grabbed the young man, swung him around brutally, yanking his left arm up so high that his hand was even with his neck. The young man yelled something, and another officer jammed him in the stomach with his baton. A middle-age black man in a suit demanded to know what the officers were doing, and two of them turned on him, jabbing him in the ribs with their batons and hauling him off to their patrol car. An old woman from the congregation – too far out of their reach for them to hit – yelled, "Can't you see we're leaving church!" The crowd began to seethe.

Gretchen caught sight of Carol approaching one officer.

"What did he do? Why are you doing this?" He charged at her, pushing her out of the crowd but at least not hitting her with the baton.

"You don't belong here," he snarled at her.

Gretchen remembered a side door out of the theater and led Latisha to it. They left, came around the corner of the theater and luckily found Carol outside the throng of the crowd. She was fuming, trying to catch and write down the badge numbers of the police officers. Gretchen managed to pull her away from the crowd, and the three of them got away safely. On the bus ride back, Latisha was shaking but said almost nothing.

Gretchen did *not* write to Sunday about that experience. It was getting close to Thanksgiving break, and she asked him in a letter if he planned to come home for the holiday. She hoped Sequoia would invite her back and they could celebrate the holiday together. Gretchen called Sequoia from time to time to catch up with her.

"How you doin'?" Sequoia would invariably greet her, full of questions about how Gretchen was doing in school, and what was on her mind. Gretchen would parade whatever academic accomplishments she could muster, talk to her about her courses, books she was reading or movies she had seen.

"What about you? What's new with you?"

Sequoia would tell her small stories from Washington High School or what music she was playing, but their conversations never went beyond this. Questions about Sunday hung in the air between them, the silences between their words. Sequoia never volunteered information about him and she did not invite Gretchen to come home for the holiday.

Finally, Gretchen asked, "Is Sunday coming home for Thanksgiving?"

In the beat before her answer, Gretchen thought she heard a sigh.

"No, honey, he's not. He decided it was too long and expensive a trip for just a few days. But he's coming home at Christmas," she added more cheerfully. No invitation followed.

Sunday responded to Gretchen's letter a few weeks later, during Thanksgiving week itself, to wish her a good holiday and good luck on her upcoming exams. He worried about his own exams and said he wouldn't be able to write as often until they were over. He wrote nothing about his Christmas plans.

Everyone had to vacate the dorms over

Thanksgiving and Christmas holidays. Latisha planned to spend Thanksgiving weekend with another student's family in South Chicago. Carol invited Gretchen home to Ann Arbor, where she was welcomed but felt overwhelmed by Carol's whole boisterous family. Her father, a political science professor, and mother, a member of the local school board, jousted all day long over political issues - local, national, and international. Even her younger brother, a high school junior, knew more about politics than Gretchen.

After returning from Thanksgiving weekend, Gretchen received a letter from her father. Just seeing his handwriting made her sad, and she held the letter for some moments, then put it on her desk and sat on her bed and stared at it before opening it.

Most of it was predictable. He described a new exhibit at the museum he had prepared and wished she would come see it. He missed her and hoped she might come home for Christmas. Then he described Thanksgiving dinner at his parents' home. The Reinhardts usually had Thanksgiving since Grandma Etta had Christmas. But then came the surprise. He wrote that her mother had been so rude at Thanksgiving that his mother had told her not to come back again until she learned how to treat her family with respect. Grandma Hilda had told Norma that she would lose her husband and the rest of her family, just as she had lost her daughter, if she didn't turn herself around. Norma had been so shaken by this pronouncement that he'd been able to persuade her to seek professional help. Her mother had met for the first time with a psychiatrist. "Please come home for Christmas," he wrote, "and help show your mother that she can turn her life around. We both love you. She's always had a hard time showing it, but she loves you very much."

Gretchen crushed the letter and threw it at the wall. Throwing on her coat and scarf, she slammed out of the room and went out to walk off her fury. Why should *she* be the one to try to help her mother, when she had tried to kill her as a child and then ripped her apart from Sunday? And wasn't it interesting that it was being rude to Grandma Hilda rather than trying to kill her own daughter that prompted this new professional treatment? Gretchen stomped in the new snow outside, realizing she should have worn boots but refusing to go back for them. Why had he not kept his promise to protect his own daughter? There was *no way* she would go back home for Christmas, no way. When she saw the puff of vapor around her face, she realized she had said "no way" out loud. No matter; she was alone on the dark street, headed for the lake.

What *could* he be thinking? Maybe he was at last trying to protect himself. Maybe her mother had behaved badly one too many times, and she might really be in danger of losing the one person she seemed to love, her own husband. Maybe he had even told her that he couldn't stand losing his daughter. Gretchen tried to imagine his saying that to her mother, but she couldn't conjure it. He was too meek to stand up to her. It was just who he was. Tears started to drip down her cheeks. It was so cold, her cheeks hurt. But she couldn't stop crying. Her feet were wet and bitterly cold inside her tennis shoes.

Gretchen turned around to walk back to the dorms. She was no longer alone on the street. There were two young black men who had been half a block behind her, and now she faced them. They walked with the swagger of the ghetto. They weren't talking. Gretchen clutched: had they been following her and should she cross the street? Wouldn't that just advertise her fear? She kept walking toward them, brushing the last of her tears off her cold cheek. As she got close to them, she could hear her heart pounding. Look them in the eyes, she told herself. The three of them exchanged wary glances as they passed each other in silence on the snowy sidewalk.

Once she got back to her dorm room, Gretchen peeled off her icy cotton socks and climbed into her bed to warm up and begin to study. But she couldn't concentrate. She went to the telephone and dialed Sequoia.

Sequoia sounded cheerful and glad to hear from her. Just hearing her voice was comforting. They chatted. Sequoia asked her about her courses and what she was doing outside class. Gretchen told her about the Saturday church service in the theater. She mentioned the Reverend Jackson and the popcorn but did not tell her about the scene afterward. She asked Sequoia about what she was doing. Sequoia told her with Sunday away she had more time now to see movies with friends and to play music. It registered on Gretchen for the first time that she had never seen Sequoia with any friends and knew nothing about her life apart from Sunday.

"I miss you," Gretchen confessed.

"I miss you too, girl. You kept me good company last summer."

After a pause, Gretchen asked if she could stay with Sequoia over Christmas. After a longer pause, Sequoia answered.

"I don't think I can do that, child. Sunday will be home, and ... and... I don't have three bedrooms." Gretchen could hear the discomfort in her voice. Sequoia continued, gently.

"Don't you think it's time to make up with your parents? I'm sure they miss you."

"Have you made up with your mother? Do you even know if she's alive?" Gretchen blurted. It was as if a snake had darted out of her mouth and sprayed venom. Gretchen hung up the telephone.

She cried herself to sleep. She was getting awfully good at burning her bridges.

By the next day, Gretchen knew she needed to apologize to Sequoia, but she did not want to risk hearing any more advice that she should go back to her parents. So she wrote Sequoia a letter. It took several drafts before she could avoid making excuses. Finally, she wrote: "I am so sorry for what I said. I know it must have been hurtful, and I had no right to say it. You've been so good to me, and you didn't deserve to hear this from me. It won't ever happen again." Sequoia did not respond. Gretchen told no one, not even Latisha, about this exchange with Sequoia.

29
Gretchen

Latisha came to Gretchen's rescue by inviting her home to Mississippi with her. "That is, if you don't mind an awful-long bus ride," she said. Gretchen was so grateful she hugged her. Latisha seemed surprised. It was the first time they had touched. Latisha seemed to look forward to taking Gretchen as much as Gretchen looked forward to going. Latisha teased her about how little she knew of Mississippi.

"Don't forget it'll be cold there," she said. "You leave your little bikini at home and take your scarf and gloves." Latisha hovered about Gretchen's preparations like a nervous mother. She even inspected Gretchen's suitcase to make sure she brought the right things.

"I see you brought your church clothes," she teased, and they both laughed. "You'll need them."

As a surprise, Gretchen bought sandwiches, apples, oranges and candy bars to tide them over the seventeen-hour bus ride. She showed them to Latisha after they had taken their seats on the Greyhound bus, and she seemed pleased. Gretchen wanted to know who would be there and how Latisha's family celebrated Christmas. Latisha told her they would have a simple dinner with just their immediate family on Christmas Eve – her parents, her brother Jeb, and her Grandma Paxton, now almost ninety – and then spend the whole evening in church. On Christmas morning, they would open gifts and then have a huge feast midday. "Half the town will be there." Latisha's father, Nathaniel Moseley, was the town's postmaster - the town's first Negro postmaster- and a deacon in his church, and his friends "from church and state" would be there.

Gretchen was impressed with how glowingly Latisha described her parents and her brother. Her father was "funny-looking and strangers underestimated him all the time, but he's sharp and plain-spoken and usually right." Her mother was a serious reader, very intuitive, very warm and loyal. And her brother Jeb, only fourteen months older than she, was a sophomore at Howard, brilliant, funny, her idol. Gretchen wondered if he knew Sunday.

They broke out the sandwiches and ate them, sharing an orange between them. When they stopped in St. Louis, Latisha got them cokes. They read for a few hours and Latisha napped. Gretchen realized she felt happy about this trip, excited to spend time with Latisha and her family. She tried not to think about her own.

Latisha's father met them in the Jackson, Mississippi bus station. He was shaped like a giant yam, with a large, misshapen rear end that jiggled as he walked and a small, almost pointed head. Gretchen wondered why he wore sandals in

December, but when she got close she saw he had big knobbly bunions that splayed his toes sideways. When he put his arms around his daughter, it was obvious that he couldn't bend much. It was equally obvious how glad he was to see her.

"Rebecca, Rebecca, I'm so glad you're home."

Rebecca? Gretchen didn't have a chance to ask. Nathanial Moseley turned to her and studied her with his intense protruding eyes. "Welcome," was all he said, but she believed he meant it. He put their suitcases into the truck of his very shiny, very old, Cadillac.

"Have you ever been to the South?" he asked, still sizing her up.

"This is my first time."

"Well, we'll just lead you down the Natchez Trace Parkway to our little town on the Pearl River. Carthage, Miss, population 1,423." He made conversation as though he were leading a tour.

Latisha asked if Jeb was home yet.

"Sure is, and Zeke's there too, waiting for you."

"Oh, Daddy, why did you do that?" Latisha moaned.

"He was good enough for you last year, and I hope you don't think you're too good for him now that you've gone up to Chicago." He pronounced Chicago strangely, the middle syllable like "cog," as if mocking it. Gretchen registered that Latisha had never told her about Zeke and assumed he no longer meant anything to her, if he ever had. On the other hand, she had also not told Gretchen her name was Rebecca, not Latisha.

They pulled into a gravel driveway alongside Latisha's home. Gretchen liked it at once. A big sloping roof sheltered a porch that surrounded the old wooden house. In one corner hung a bench swing. A huge, blooming poinsettia tree thrust up to the roof on one side of the front steps. The wooden porch boards squeaked as Latisha's mother came out to greet them. She was thin, like Latisha, and the same brown color, though her hair was nearly white and combed back into a tight bun. Her face had no lines except the lines of her broad smile at seeing her daughter. "Momma," Latisha called; "my baby," her mother responded. They petted each other like blind people connecting after a long absence. As Sarah Moseley introduced herself and welcomed Gretchen, she took Gretchen's hands in her own and looked her straight in the eye. "I'm glad you're going to spend the holidays with us." She had sparkling eyes the color of root beer.

They walked through the small house to the back, where Latisha and Gretchen would be sharing the sun room as their bedroom. In the front room sat an old maroon davenport with crocheted doilies on the armrests and a big rocking chair with chintz cushions. Behind the davenport were bookshelves, almost a whole wall full of books. To the left of the front room was a big old-fashioned kitchen with a built-in ice box (no longer used, Latisha's mother explained) and big sitting area looking out to the street. Behind the two front rooms were two bedrooms, one for Latisha's parents and one for her brother. The room Latisha and Gretchen would share was one side of the rear porch, with wood paneling below the porch rail and glass above. Behind it was a small yard, including a vegetable garden with frostbitten tomato vines, framed by large trees all around. It was private and sheltered. It reminded Gretchen of the sun porch at Jim and

Helen's cottage. Gretchen asked if she could take the outside bed, under the windows, and Latisha readily agreed. "It's too cold for me."

As soon as they were alone, Gretchen asked, "So who's Rebecca?" Latisha laughed a little into her hand, as if embarrassed.

"I got tired of having a biblical name like everyone else out here and called myself Latisha when I started college. It was kind of a new identity for my new city life in the North. My father doesn't like it," she added unnecessarily.

"And who is Zeke?"

Latisha shrugged. "Zeke was my boyfriend for the last two years. He was a local star basketball player and a decent guy with no future beyond Carthage. My dad fishes with him and got him a job at the Post Office. My dad thinks of him as his protégé and future son-in-law. It's the son-in-law part I can't stand."

"Becca's home!" Jeb leaned into the room, ducking his head as he walked through the door. Gretchen sucked in her breath involuntarily at the sight of this stick-thin, coal-black young man. His shape and color were Sunday's, exactly. She drank in the sight of him as he hugged his sister. "I missed you," they told each other. After what seemed like a long time, Latisha said she wanted him to meet her friend. He broke away from hugging his sister, but kept one arm over her shoulder. As he turned, Gretchen exhaled with relief; his face was nothing like Sunday's. Jeb had the same intense eyes as everyone else in his family; they protruded like marbles, which made him look as if he could see more than other people. He had funny, rangy hair that stuck out in random places, as if he had pulled on sections of it while thinking. "Nappy," Latisha described it. He smiled much more readily than his sister; Gretchen had the impression he smiled most of the time. Jeb welcomed her warmly, taking her hand in the same way his mother had.

Gretchen and Latisha offered to help her mother prepare dinner, but Mrs. Moseley said she had already cooked it and didn't need any help, so they just set the table. They would help tomorrow, she told them firmly. Zeke hovered around Latisha, who paid him no attention except to tell him to bring in enough Dr. Pepper's for everyone.

That first dinner, like all that followed, was delicious. Mrs. Moseley had roasted a pork loin, baked yams, and cooked mustard greens with a ham hock. They passed around the corn bread, with real pieces of corn inside.

Zeke asked Mr. Moseley if he intended to go fishing the next day and asked if he could go along. Gretchen asked where they fished around here and what they fished for. Mostly catfish, Mr. Moseley explained, and then asked if Gretchen had ever gone fishing. They all seemed interested to know that she had learned to fish as a girl and that she knew how to bait a line and catch bluegills and sunfish. Mr. Moseley seemed particularly pleased.

"Maybe we'll take you out to the Grover Grimes Catfish Pond Dam and see whether you can hook a catfish."

"Don't torture her," Latisha protested on Gretchen's behalf.

"I'd like to try it – really," Gretchen told them honestly.

Gretchen asked Jeb if he liked Howard University and what he was studying. It was as if she had pressed the "play" button on a tape recorder. He was studying engineering, and his real love was computers, enormous hulks of machinery that used a binary system to store large amounts of information and make complex calculations. Computers would replace many jobs people now did manually, and someday they might even be used to communicate with other computers, so information could be shared everywhere. It seemed preposterous, but his enthusiasm made it seem plausible.

Latisha bragged that Jeb was so smart he would be one of the people to invent such a system. Jeb ducked his head to acknowledge the compliment and then winked at Gretchen. Such an odd wink, like a frog, she thought, with the bottom eyelid coming up to meet the upper lid, as if his eyelid couldn't make it all around his big eyes. Odd or not, she liked him.

After dinner Mr. Moseley started a card game.

"Who's going to join me?" he looked around.

"I'm in," said Zeke and Jeb at the same time. Latisha and Gretchen joined them while Mrs. Moseley crocheted.

"What's your favorite game?" Mr. Moseley asked Gretchen. She blushed and told him the only card game she really knew was sheep's head, which everyone in Wisconsin knew but she supposed no one else did.

"Well, why don't you teach us, and then we'll know a new game," said Mr. Moseley without any hesitation. So she explained the game to them, that aces and all portrait cards were trump, with queens at the top and clubs the most powerful suit, followed in order by spades, hearts and diamonds.

"You take partners, but you don't know who they are at first." She recited her father's instruction on finding out who your partner was. Play your short suit to your partner, long suit through your partner. Zeke seemed perplexed not to know who his partner was at the outset, but Jeb seemed to welcome the new challenge. They told Gretchen to lead on the first game. She had mainly clubs and led the queen. Mr. Moseley played an eight of clubs, Latisha a seven of clubs, Zeke the queen of hearts and Jeb the ace of clubs. The ace threw eleven points onto her all-powerful queen.

"I guess I know who my partner is," said Gretchen and Jeb winked at her across the table. She asked politely if Zeke had any clubs, explaining that he was required to play them if he did and that, in any event, he was throwing away a powerful card by playing a red queen to her black. He had made a mistake and they allowed him in the first game to take back his queen and play a club. After a while, even Zeke caught on, and they all seemed to enjoy the game. Gretchen and Jeb became partners more than once and intuitively played well to each other. After a while, Jeb suggested they switch to a more familiar game, gin rummy.

"No way," Latisha declared, "that's no contest at all. Jeb counts the cards. You can't win against him."

Zeke went home without having any time alone with Latisha. But Gretchen stayed in the game, while Latisha joined her mother on the davenport, talking while her mother crocheted. Latisha had been right about Jeb, but Gretchen won one of the hands, and Jeb seemed to enjoy it.

Before going to bed, everyone had to take turns

in the single bathroom. The Moseleys insisted that Gretchen go first, as their guest, and showed her where to stow her towel. Mrs. Moseley came onto the sun porch with extra quilts for the girls after Gretchen was already in bed, sitting up with a book. Latisha's mother spread the quilt over her. Gretchen hadn't felt so cared for since her Grandma Etta had put her to bed as a child. She sat in the lamplight in this cozy house that reminded her of the cottage, imagining the lake beyond the trees in the back yard, and feeling like someone else's child at home.

The book she held was her Christmas gift from Sunday. It had arrived with his card just before she left for Mississippi, and she had just now opened it. It was an old, used, leather-bound edition of <u>Othello</u>, with text in German on one side of the page and in English on the other. The name Otto Karp had been written in German script on the cover page in the upper corner. Below it, Sunday had written, "In memory of our beginnings, love, Sunday." In the card, he wrote that he missed her and loved her. Gretchen caressed the leather as if it were the skin of his cheek.

Latisha broke her mood when she came in to bed. Gretchen had started to say something about how much she appreciated being with her family when Latisha interrupted her.

"Look, I saw what passed between you and Jeb, and I want you to stop it right now. You may think it's fine to have a black boyfriend where you come from, but you can't do that here. Jeb has a huge future in front of him, and I don't want to see him killed. Stay away from my brother!"

Gretchen looked up at her blankly. Latisha had no idea how far off the mark she was.

"Look, I wasn't trying to flirt with Jeb. I ... I promise I won't. I like him but not in that way." She could tell she was making no headway. "I can't tell you how grateful I am that you and your family took me in for this holiday. I promise I wouldn't do anything to hurt your family."

Latisha scowled without saying anything more that night.

For the rest of the holiday, Gretchen took care never to be alone with Jeb. She tried not to meet his eyes and drew no more winks. She didn't ask him if he knew Sunday. She spent as much time as she could with Latisha's mother, who impressed her as one of the most caring and discerning people she had ever met. As they cooked or washed dishes, Mrs. Moseley probed gently for what were Gretchen's study interests, where she thought she might be going in life. She encouraged Gretchen to follow her curiosity. Gretchen explained that the courses that were easy for her were not that interesting to her, but that she didn't know if she could meet the challenge of those that were difficult. "Go for what's hard, girl," Mrs. Moseley assured her; "it will reward you in the end." Her look was direct, stern and reassuring at the same time. They also talked books, and Mrs. Moseley was full of suggestions for Gretchen. "Read Helen Keller's autobiography. Read history; it will teach you all the mistakes people keep on making. Do you know Barbara Tuchman? She makes history sound like story telling." Latisha was mostly somewhere else when they had these talks, with Jeb, maybe, but not with them.

Gretchen did go fishing with Mr. Moseley and Zeke; no one else wanted to go. She managed to hook one catfish, and they patted her on the back as if it were an accomplishment. Together with the fish Zeke and Mr. Moseley caught, they had enough for dinner one night. On the night of the fish dinner Latisha tangled with her father. Zeke had gone home after dinner, and Latisha asked her dad to go out for a walk with her. Her tone of voice made it a summons. Mrs. Moseley looked up from her book but said nothing. It was chilly outside, and no one would think of going for a walk for the fun of it. Mr. Moseley zipped up his jacket as if he were buckling on a holster and followed Latisha outside. They were gone for about half an hour when Gretchen heard both of their voices close to the front door. They were shouting at each other. Gretchen thought she heard Latisha tell her dad to stop trying to control her life. She admired Latisha's courage. Mr. Moseley held the door for Latisha as they came in, and then they went into separate rooms.

Zeke didn't come for dinner after that night, nor for any of the remaining nights.

Gretchen tried to talk with Latisha that night as they undressed for bed, but Latisha was as distant as Chicago. She didn't want to talk about her father and she didn't want to talk about Zeke, so Gretchen let it drop. Latisha's distance lasted for much of the holiday, and she was edgy when they went to bed at night. Gretchen couldn't find a way to get through to her about anything, and she especially didn't know how to reassure her that she wasn't interested in Jeb. Latisha and Jeb spent hours by themselves, out walking or driving around, or just reading on the davenport, her arm draped around his. Gretchen wondered what it would have been like if she had had such a brother. Would he have been a buffer against her mother?

New Year's Eve was the girls' last night in Carthage. Classes started again on January 2, and they would spend most of the next day on the bus back to Chicago. Gretchen was surprised that the whole family was going to church on New Year's Eve, and Latisha was surprised that she was surprised.

"Don't you know about Watch Night?" Latisha asked. "Everybody goes to church on Watch Night."

"Why is it called Watch Night?" Gretchen tried to phrase her question carefully.

"In slave days, we were watching for Emancipation. Now we watch for the New Year, 'on our knees,' as my momma says. You'll see."

And so they went, in the middle of New Year's Eve, Latisha and her mother dressed in big, elaborate hats and fancy dresses, her father and brother in suits and ties, and Gretchen in her best skirt and sweater and a little woolen cap, her only hat. The faded little wooden church was even more crowded than it had been on Christmas Eve, and services had already begun. Some folks came as early as seven, Mrs. Moseley explained, and prayed until after midnight. Because they were 'late,' they were unable to find seats all together. Jeb, Latisha and Mr. Moseley sat at the end of one row near the back, and Mrs. Moseley and Gretchen sat directly behind them. The choir occupied most of the front of the church, and their voices made it seem as if the walls would pop out with the swelling sound. One song Gretchen recognized was simply a repeating chorus of "Amen," and people around her harmonized, each in their own voice. From Christmas Eve, she knew that Mrs. Moseley had a beautiful singing voice, a contralto, Gretchen thought, though she didn't know much about voices; and now Mrs. Moseley stood up and sang a solo of "Will the Circle Be Unbroken." Gretchen looked up at her with admiration; she had rarely seen or heard such genuine reverence. Throughout the evening, others spontaneously got up to sing. There was a sermon – and it was political – they were watching for deliverance from the violence of the past summers and for their rightful place as citizens in this 'great nation.' "Say it, brother," rang out a number of times during the sermon, once from Jeb. Mostly, though, the night consisted of singing, and by the end even Gretchen's tentative lungs felt full of new air. The family linked arms as they walked back home after midnight.

They slept late and had pancakes with syrup and bacon for breakfast. Mrs. Moseley rode with the girls and Latisha's father when they returned to the bus station in Jackson. Carrying five books under her arm, she told them she was going along to return books to the library in Jackson and pick up new ones. At the bus station, Mrs. Moseley hugged both girls. She thanked Gretchen for coming. When she held her own daughter, Gretchen could see that her cheeks were wet.

On the bus home, Gretchen tried to say something about Jeb.

"Forget it," was all Latisha said.

They each did a bit of their homework, talking a little but superficially. Latisha slept for a few hours, but Gretchen sat wide awake, hypnotized by the lights of oncoming traffic but unable to asleep. After trying to fall asleep, she felt cold and pulled on her heavy coat. She suddenly felt engulfed with the recognition that she was totally alone in this world and might always be. She wished for a mother like Mrs. Moseley or Sequoia, but that would never happen. She wished she could have her father back, but she couldn't get anywhere close to him without exposing herself to her own poisonous mother. Face facts, she told herself. You have no home to return to, anywhere. Sequoia may continue to be a source of support and caring, but she has made it clear that her home belongs to her and Sunday, not to you. And Sunday – despite what he said in his letters – appears to have left your life. You have lost the most important relationship you will ever have. Nothing you can do or say will bring him back. It's just how it is. You are on your own. Gretchen shuddered and pulled the hood from her coat up over her head. The bus driver had his radio on, and she could hear it faintly over the hum of the engine. Gretchen recognized Jerry Butler's "Only the Strong Survive."

She wasn't surprised to find that Latisha avoided her in the weeks that followed their return to school. When she caught sight of Latisha, she was either sitting by herself or with other black students.

Gretchen called Sequoia from time to time but no one answered. She decided she needed to make peace with Sequoia and wrote her a letter asking if she could take the bus up one weekend to visit her. In the letter, she apologized again for what she had said about Sequoia's mother. Sequoia called her a few days later.

"First of all," she said, "I understand your remark. At some point, we seem to have both decided that we're better off – or safer, anyway - without our mommas. I can't tell you whether it's the right decision for either one of us. I'll stop bugging you to make up with yours. You're a young woman now and need to make your own decisions.

"And yes, do come up one of these weekends. How about next weekend?"

So Gretchen took the Greyhound back up to Milwaukee, remembering as the bus pulled into the station the day that she and Sequoia had waited together for Sunday's bus from Mississippi. It was already a long time ago.

Just to see Sequoia towering over all the other people made Gretchen feel at home. When Sequoia hugged her, Gretchen caught a hint of the pine-scented soap Sequoia always used. She would have recognized her blindfolded. The apartment, too, smelled familiar and welcoming. Sequoia gave her Sunday's room to sleep in, and Gretchen walked back into it as if it were part of a museum, like one of those little houses refurnished to show visitors how people used to live in the old days. That disorientation might make it easier to sleep in Sunday's bed, but not much, she thought.

Sequoia spared Gretchen the effort of avoiding the subject of Sunday.

"Do you hear from him?" she asked Gretchen. Relieved, Gretchen said she used to get wonderful letters and that he had given her the book for Christmas, but that she hadn't heard from him since then.

"And his letters were always ambivalent, as if

he loved me but couldn't figure out how to make it work between us."

Sequoia sighed.

"I felt bad about turning you away at Thanksgiving and Christmas, but Sunday made it clear he wanted it to be just us. He didn't say what was going on between you, and I thought I shouldn't ask.

"I can't be the go-between for either one of you," she said, looking Gretchen straight in the eye.

"I know."

Sequoia's face took on a happier look. "But you've got a place here whenever you need refuge, or whatever, and Sunday isn't around. I love your company." Sequoia got up quickly, her face turned away. She walked over to the old upright piano and sat down.

"I've been playing a lot of music lately. Would you like to hear some?"

"Absolutely!" Gretchen wondered why she had never asked Sequoia to play for her before. Sequoia began to play Gershwin's "Rhapsody in Blue." The music was lively, jazzy, and a little wild as Sequoia played it. She played the whole piece. Gretchen could see from the angle of Sequoia's body that she felt happier and more relaxed as she played. Gretchen thought to herself that the next time she felt alone, she would conjure up this moment of Sequoia at the piano and the sound of her music.

By the time Gretchen returned to school from her weekend with Sequoia, she felt taller, stronger and better able to cope. She signed up for classes over the summer and found herself a tiny sublet to rent.

30
1967
Gretchen

Early in March, Gretchen took the train up to Milwaukee to visit Sequoia and to hear her jazz group play. She was excited to be invited, and Sequoia seemed keyed up in a way Gretchen had never noticed before. Sequoia excused herself to practice for a couple of hours Saturday afternoon, while Gretchen studied to the comforting backdrop of Sequoia's piano playing, interrupted occasionally by her starting over and repeating a sequence. Sequoia had grown an Afro, and her hair now created an airy circle around her head that glowed coppery in the afternoon light. She also wore some pale eye makeup that highlighted the whites of her eyes, and dark berry-colored lipstick that accentuated her smile. Gretchen had never seen Sequoia in makeup before, and she watched this new persona with great interest. When Sequoia dressed for the concert, Gretchen just said 'wow' softly when saw the dark green sheath that opened like a fan below her knees. Sequoia looked glamorous. Gretchen volunteered to drive, since it appeared to her it would be difficult for Sequoia to drive in that long dress. Sequoia gratefully accepted. She directed Gretchen to a big old church not far from Holy Ghost, which she had attended as a child. They drove less than two blocks from her grandparents' old home on Eighth Street, but Gretchen did not mention it or ask Sequoia for the short detour.

It was a Baptist Church. While Sequoia went backstage, Gretchen found a seat close to the front and looked around. The building had once had stained- glass windows, but most of them had apparently been broken over time, and now yellow glass replaced them. Bright cloth banners hung along both sides, some of them with Bible sayings sewn on them - one with the outline of a lamb, others with crosses in different colors and configurations. The pews were very old and cracked, though heavily varnished. They filled gradually, mostly with black people of all ages, but there were maybe twenty white people and even two mixed couples. A man who appeared to be the pastor of the church introduced the quintet. They had a silly name: Gimme Five. Sequoia swished in first, followed by an equally tall black man with a salt-and-pepper beard and Afro. Dark glasses hid his eyes. He carried his bass and blew a kiss first to Sequoia and then one to the audience. The drummer was a wiry, small, very young-looking white man who could have been Gretchen's age. The saxophone player also was white, a lanky middle-aged man with thinning, long hair tied behind his head with a leather thong. The last member was the flutist: a young black woman with a narrow Caucasian nose and small features whose marcelled hair was drawn back into an elaborate figure-eight-shaped bun.

It was the first time since high school that she had ever seen live jazz. Rapt with the interaction of the players, their expressions and cues to each other, she watched as each allowed the other solo time. Sequoia played with a fierce energy that Gretchen had never seen before, and her playing sounded professional to her inexperienced ears. She recognized a couple of Bill Evans pieces, but most of the music was new to her. When they finished, the group joined hands - the bassist actually broke in between Sequoia and the flutist to take Sequoia's hand – and together they bowed before a standing ovation from the audience. As the musicians filed out, Gretchen saw the bassist give Sequoia a big kiss as they passed beyond the line of sight of most of the audience.

As she drove Sequoia home, Gretchen couldn't say enough about how much she enjoyed the concert and how glad she was to have been included. Sequoia lay back on the seat with her eyes closed and a look of satisfaction on her smooth face.

By Sunday morning at breakfast, Sequoia's mood had changed dramatically. Distressed and agitated, she blurted, "You've heard about the draft lottery, I suppose."

Gretchen had in fact heard about it. It was a sore issue on campus.

"What is Sunday's number?"

"Low enough to make me worry."

Gretchen bit her tongue to avoid asking what Sunday's reaction was, and Sequoia did not volunteer. She changed the subject back to music. Gretchen also wanted to ask Sequoia about the bass player but didn't know whether she would cross a line with her about that too.

Before they said goodbye at the train station, Sequoia asked her if she would like to come to another concert. "*Absolutely,*" she told her without hesitation and Sequoia smiled broadly.

A month later Gretchen listened to a broadcast of Martin Luther King's "Beyond Vietnam" speech in New York. He complained of this country's taking young black men and sending them eight thousand miles away to guarantee liberties in Southeast Asia which they had not found at home. She sat in awe of his cadence, his dignity and his ability to draw the nation's attention back to civil rights.

In June Gretchen read in The New York Times that the U.S. Supreme Court had overturned a Virginia law against interracial marriage. The newspaper printed portions of the decision verbatim, and she found it so inspiring she cut it out and decided to send it to Sunday. Ironically, it was called "Loving v. Virginia." She wrote to Sunday that she hoped he felt as inspired by it as she was.

In July there were race riots in Newark, and later in Detroit.

Sunday never responded to her letter.

31
1968
Gretchen

The year was beginning well. Gretchen would graduate in June, and she had already been accepted into a graduate program in psychology at the University of California - Berkeley. She *loved* psychology; it completely absorbed her, challenging her powers of analysis and imagination at the same time. She'd developed her own theories about Norma's narcissism or borderline personality; it was easier to think of her as Norma now, not as her mother. But what drew her particularly was new research on attachment theory by John Bowlby and Mary Ainsworth. They theorized that the nature of attachments formed between infants and their mothers in the first weeks and months of existence shaped a child's personality for life. Gretchen held a vivid image of Norma's reaction to her birth: she would have turned away from her slippery red infant in disgust. Gretchen remembered Grandma Hilda's bragging that it was Bill who first fed her. Secure attachments, the theory went, allowed an infant the security to play, to leave the mother to explore and to return, secure in receiving a loving reception. Didn't fathers count?

In contrast to secure attachments, the theory held, some infants formed Avoidant Attachments. An infant with an avoidant attachment would avoid the mother during reunion, often preferring a stranger. Like every other psychology student, Gretchen was drawn to the theories that informed the mysteries of her own personality.

She wondered if it were possible for attachments made later – still early in life but well after infancy – such as hers with Sunday and Sequoia - to be just as powerful and life-lasting, especially for someone who had cause to avoid her own mother. She hoped the strength of such an attachment could augur as well for her future as that of an infant with a secure attachment. Part of her knew this was more her imagination than student analysis at work, but the thought gave her comfort and was consistent with the metaphor she had devised for herself - she was a tibia, a shinbone that had been broken and re-set and grew stronger and bigger through its healing.

Gretchen and Sequoia still visited each other. In fact, Sequoia had come to Chicago in mid-February and stayed at her apartment. She took real satisfaction in cooking a dinner for Sequoia, and Sequoia had clucked over the meal as if a master chef had cooked just for her. Gretchen smiled to think how she had obsessed over the prospect of this meal. Her first ideas had been grandiose. Inspired by the Indians in her neighborhood, she thought of cooking an Indian meal – and she had looked at an Indian cookbook at the library – but all the recipes called for about twenty spices each. She couldn't afford to go out and buy turmeric, cardamom, cumin, fenugreek, coriander, cinnamon and curry for just one meal. She had settled upon lasagna. It took her several hours to put it all together and figure out when those wide noodles were "al dente," but the dinner proved a success. She and Sequoia walked all over the campus, even though the weekend was bitter cold and the sidewalks were slippery with ice, and Sequoia promised to come to her graduation. That promise meant everything to her. Aside from her few friends at the university, she would have no one there for her. She had even thought of not attending her own graduation, but Sequoia ridiculed that idea.

They had worked out a comfort zone of avoided topics. Sequoia no longer prompted her to contact her parents. Certainly, her upcoming graduation ceremonies would have been a fertile occasion for such a remark, but Sequoia did not say it. Gretchen knew this omission was intentional and appreciated it as a sign of Sequoia's accepting her as a fellow adult and a friend. She had also learned not to ask Sequoia about Sunday, even though he too must be planning his graduation and future, and she knew Sequoia must be preoccupied with his plans. Gretchen herself wondered what he was doing; she imagined his becoming a professor someday. In what subject, she did not know – he would be adept in so many – but he was scholarly to the core, quiet and serious, someone who would write an important book in his field of study.

But Sequoia's and Gretchen's relationship was about just the two of them. Sequoia spent more of her time playing piano and her band, Gimme Five, performed often at local schools or churches. Gretchen imagined that Sequoia had built more of a life for herself in Sunday's absence. She wondered if Sequoia was as interested in the tall bass player as he had seemed to be in her. But she didn't ask, and Sequoia didn't volunteer.

She and Sequoia began to talk politics a little. Sequoia asked her who she would vote for in the first presidential election for which she was old enough to vote.

"Eugene McCarthy," she responded with conviction. "He'll steer this country out of Vietnam and support civil rights."

"Too stiff," Sequoia shook her head. "Not a chance. If you want someone who can be elected *and* promote civil rights, it's Bobby Kennedy. He's our man."

Even the usually relentless Midwestern winter gave every appearance of subsiding early in 1968. In all of March there was no snow, and forsythias and crocuses bloomed early outside her apartment building. She tried to imagine what it would be like living in a part of the world not weighted down by five months of winter. She gleefully imagined wearing sweaters instead of parkas in February. Some of her images of California originated in the Viewmaster she had received for Christmas as a child. Although she had not yet even seen California, she had heard that Berkeley was green in winter. Just that thought buoyed her. Life was looking good.

In early April everything changed.

She had bought herself a small television and formed a habit of watching the news in the morning while she ate breakfast, before going off to class or the library. On the first Friday morning in April, she automatically turned on the television.

She had not intended to – she was supposed to defend her senior thesis this afternoon and wanted uninterrupted hours of concentration before then. It was April 4, 1968: the news was that Martin Luther King had been assassinated the prior evening at a Memphis motel. The television flashed scenes of the anonymous balcony where he had been murdered, scenes from his marches in Selma, King at the pulpit, and King on the podium at the March on Washington. The station played all of his "I Have a Dream" speech. She sat down hard, as if a boulder had fallen on her and pinned her legs. For a long time, she just sat and stared, and the news alternated repetitively between the fact of the assassination and snippets from his years of spiritual activism. She was not able to cry. Nor was she able to do anything else. After a while, she turned off the television, but she sat down again and just stared into space. However much King's pacifism had been eclipsed by more current and radical heroes, this was a huge tragedy. Black America would feel wounded to the core. As for white America: what would it do? As she posed the question, she had no sense of how white America would react, but she realized she did not regard herself as of them. She had no sense of "her own people."

She knew she could not deliver her thesis today and would have to go to her professor's office sometime soon to beg for another time, if he would consider it. She wanted to take a walk, to go to the lake where she had heard King speak before a crowd two years earlier. She wanted to go to a Baptist church, where she felt her numbness could be converted to an emotional grieving. She wanted to offer her condolences to Latisha, even though she had not seen her for a couple of years. She wanted to be among black people and grieve with them. She wanted to hug Sequoia. She telephoned Sequoia, but of course there was no answer: it was Friday and she would be at school. She wanted to hear the deep, rich timbre of a black person's voice.

She turned on her radio, dialing to WVON, a local black station. Soulful hymns played on a station that usually delivered Motown sound. The announcer intoned, "In these troubled times, let all people of good will keep a cool head and not make Martin Luther King's dreams a nightmare. Let us remain nonviolent." It occurred to her for the first time that there might be angry demonstrations over this death.

So slow was she to muster herself that it was nearly one o'clock before she left her apartment. She had dressed in a dither; should she wear the clothes she would have worn to her thesis appointment? A glance at the clock told her she had better do so; there would be no time to change if her professor insisted on her delivering the thesis today. She almost left the apartment without her thesis, then grabbed it and all the related materials she had carefully assembled the night before.

The Quadrangle was strangely deserted. The few people she saw scurried as if to escape an impending thunderstorm. The door to the psychology department had a hastily penned sign on it - all classes and university events were cancelled due to the King assassination. Still dazed, she tried to open the door, but the building was locked. She could not even feel relief that her thesis appointment was cancelled. She turned around and decided she would walk to the lake as she had thought of doing earlier. To do so, she wound her way through the main part of the Quad, where she was relieved to see a group of maybe twenty black people standing in a circle, one of them in the center eulogizing King. She walked up to the group as if knowing this is what she had been searching for since hearing the news early this morning. As she stopped on the outer edge of the circle, her head bowed in reverence, a young man circling the perimeter of the group said to her quietly, "I'm sorry, but we'd like to be alone today. I don't mean anything by it." She mumbled "of course" or something just as polite and completely unlike what she ached to do, which was stay and grieve with this group. She walked away.

At that, her tears began and did not stop. She walked without intention, just letting her grief pour out. What had just happened in the Quad epitomized what had been happening over the last four years. This country had gone from the heady promise of real integration of black and white to a new segregation that blacks seemed to want as much as most whites.

She found herself on the Midway, one of the dividing lines of Hyde Park and the surrounding ghettos. On the South side, the Law School and the American Bar Center were draining people, all of them white, as if the buildings had become contaminated. All fled across the Midway to the North side, their steps worried and brisk. Gretchen walked east toward the lake. She began to notice some young black men – she thought they looked like part of the Blackstone Rangers gang – stopping some of the cars. Each time, the driver turned on his headlights and was allowed to continue. One such encounter happened as she walked by. She heard the young man say to an obviously nervous white driver, "Show some respect. Turn on your headlights and stay cool." As if grateful not to be assaulted, the driver turned on his headlights and drove away. All up and down the Midway, she saw this encounter repeated. Not one car failed to turn on its headlights.

When she got to the lake, the shore was deserted. Gretchen sat down on a bench and stared at the gray-green water. The sky was almost the same color, the horizon invisible. Her crying was finished, and she realized she was thirsty. She decided to go back home along 53rd Street and stop at a store for something to drink. A police officer patrolling a deserted 53rd Street on foot stopped her. He was the stereotype of "Chicago's finest" - white, beefy, small-eyed and blunt. He told her to go home; the streets were not safe for white people today. And when were they ever safe for blacks? she taunted silently to his back.

When she got back home, she drank two glasses of water without pausing and turned on WVON again. She heard Stokely Carmichael declare: "Go home and get your pieces; the white man today has declared war." More Negro spirituals. Then another announcement - a Baptist minister regretfully postponed the memorial service he had planned for that evening "due to the situation in the city." What situation? She turned on the television again and saw the beginnings of the riots that had begun to overtake many of the nation's cities.

Over the course of the weekend, while she hovered

around the television, much of Washington, D.C. burned, and soldiers were stationed on the White House grounds. In Chicago, the riots grew so severe as to be termed an "insurrection." Whole blocks of the West Side burned. Only the South Side stayed quiet, under the control of the Blackstone Rangers, the black gang so hated by the Chicago Police.

On Sunday morning, her telephone rang and she answered it eagerly. Like almost everyone else white, she had spent the weekend inside. The sound of another person's voice would be a welcome relief.

"Gretchen, I hope you're safe." It was her father. She had not heard his voice in over three years. How did you find me? she wondered. Why now? She could not stifle the love and the hurt his voice evoked.

"Yes, I'm safe. The whole South Side is quiet. It's a terrible quiet, though."

"I'm afraid I have some painful news for you." Idiotically, her heart leapt with hope. Had her mother died? She held her breath.

"Sequoia was in a bad car accident last night." She gasped and interrupted him.

"Where is she? I'll go visit her in the hospital."

"You can't. ..." The line went silent. "She died."

Gretchen gasped.

"She was hit head-on by a drunk driver and killed instantly."

"No," she wailed. No, no, no, no, no. "This is too much." She began to sob.

"I'm sorry." He paused while she continued to sob, as if to prolong even this remote connection.

"There's going to be a memorial service, I'm sure, and I'll let you know as soon as I find out.

"Gretchen, I love you. I've loved you from the moment you were born. I am very sorry about this ... separation between us. I would welcome seeing you any time."

She wept harder. For a long time, he kept the line open with no sound but her sobbing.

"It's your conditions I can't stand. I have to protect myself from my mother."

"You try to make me choose between my wife – your mother - and my daughter. I can't do that."

"I know. Call me about the memorial service." She hung up.

He did not telephone again until Monday evening. All day Sunday she had sat at home thinking about Sequoia, from the first time she had seen her lope into the record store like a giraffe, to every detail of the summer Sequoia had rescued her. All that day she did not eat. She had no appetite. But she woke in the middle of the night with a fierce hunger for Sequoia's baked chicken and mustard greens. All she had to eat in the house was orange juice and Swiss cheese, which she cut and devoured in hunks. On Monday the University re-opened, and she made a new appointment for her orals. She tried to study. To think about anything else was unendurable. When she heard her father's voice again, she did not even think to ask him how he knew about Sequoia. The memorial service would be held at the Mueller Funeral Home in Milwaukee on Saturday afternoon at four. She thanked him.

"How are you going to get here?"

"Probably the train. Things have quieted down in the city."

"Can I take you there?" His voice was quiet, tentative.

"Just you?"

"Yes."

"Oh, Daddy, yes."

So he picked her up at the train station. As the train pulled in, she could see him standing alongside the track, waiting like a lover in an old movie. He wore a suit and a tie and looked more somber than she had ever seen him. Welling up in gratitude at the sight of him, she tried to stash away her feelings by trying to recall if she had ever seen him in a suit before. She stumbled on the steps and ran to throw her arms around him. "Liebchen," he murmured, and held her close. She wished this moment would last forever.

In the car, he asked her many questions, as if to soak up all he could in this brief meeting. What attracted her to psychology? Was she looking forward to being in California?

Her hopes and ambitions tumbled out rapidly, so glad was she to speak with him. She wanted to invite him to her graduation, but did not for fear of arousing the familiar refrain that he would not come without her mother.

They pulled up to the funeral home, a modest red brick home with a brass plate on the front door. For a long moment, she just sat in the car, trying to collect herself.

"Do you mind if I come in with you? I'd like to pay my respects to her."

Stunned, she stopped herself from blurting out that he didn't know Sequoia. It gradually dawned on her that he must have been in contact with Sequoia for him to know so much about her own studies, even where she was. For a moment she just stared at him.

"You knew her too?"

"She used to phone me at work after each time she'd seen or talked with you, to bring me up to date."

Gretchen burst into tears.

Her father waited quietly until she finished. He smiled a little as she pulled down the mirror to wipe away the black circles under her eyes. She had worn makeup, knowing she would see Sunday on this terrible occasion. Now her eyes were red and barren of makeup. No matter.

"What do I say?" she asked plaintively. "I have no experience in funerals."

He gave her a gentle smile.

"I seem to remember you and your cousins playing tag at the last one. I had to tell you that was not how to behave at a funeral."

She managed to smile. "I promise I won't make *that* mistake again. Let's go in," she said with determination.

They paused at the doorway, with her taking in the room, which was small and windowless, with maroon drapes on the back wall. In front of the draped wall a closed casket lay surrounded by half a dozen wreaths, some of them in bright colors, even red. She remembered only white from her great aunt's funeral. A simple pulpit stood to the left of the casket and there were perhaps fifty chairs in the room. Of the thirty or so people there, not all of whom were black, she imagined many were other teachers at Sequoia's school, perhaps other musicians with whom she played, and a cluster of young black men of her own age, most likely

Sunday's friends. She recognized no one until she saw Sunday's head rise above the cluster of surrounding friends.

She followed her father, who walked straightaway to Sunday. He looked surprised and glanced uncertainly between her and her father. Her father took Sunday's hand.

"Please accept my sympathy. She was a very special and caring woman. She helped my daughter in many ways when I could not."

"Thank you, Mr. Reinhardt. I really appreciate your being here." That unforgettable deep voice. Sunday was all formality, which made it no easier for her to step forward.

She and Sunday locked eyes, and they both welled up. She could not muster words at all. She held out her hand to Sunday, and he took it with both of his, stroking hers. Neither of them said anything except with their sorrowful eyes. Then he turned to a mourner waiting behind her, and she walked away.

The service reminded her a little of the first Baptist services she attended with Latisha, replete with "Say it, brother" and "Amen" from the audience, except that the music was recorded rather than live. It was apparent the minister did not know Sequoia personally, though the details he provided were apt. Her generosity of spirit echoed with every speaker. One of them, she now recognized, was the bass player in Sequoia's jazz quintet; she had seen him before only behind dark glasses. His eyes were deep-set and underlined by wrinkles. He told them Sequoia taught them all to play with more intensity, for the love of the sound and the emotion of the music. He played a recorded excerpt from one of their concerts. She recalled the glamorous Sequoia she had seen in concert. Sunday did not speak, and she did not have another chance to say anything to him.

She and her father decided not to join the funeral procession to the cemetery.

"Do you have time for a quick supper before you catch your train?"

"Sure."

Over starchy pork chow mein and egg foo yung, they caught up with each other. She told him more about her studies and how she hoped to go into a clinical practice after getting a Ph.D. He shook his head in admiration at her ambition. He told her about Jim's new projects at the museum and about the room Jim himself had added to the cottage. Last summer had been the best fishing year they'd ever had, and no one knew why, but he was looking forward to the beginning of this season. He looked as if he were going to invite her to come to the cottage this summer. It was, after all, a place without Norma, but he did not say it. And she did not invite him to her graduation.

When he said goodbye to her at the train station, he hugged her again. "Know that I love you," he said, "wherever you are and whatever you are doing, just know that."

She climbed onto the Milwaukee Road train for the last time, waved to her father as the train pulled out of the station, and fell into a deep sleep all the way back to Chicago.

On June 5, Robert F. Kennedy was assassinated. On June 10, Gretchen attended her graduation ceremony alone. That summer, as she collated research for a psychology professor, riots broke out at the Democratic National Convention. The National Guard camped out in Washington Park in Chicago. The Chicago Eight - an unmatched group of activists ranging from a steadfast minister to an unruly anarchist to the Black Panther Bobby Seale - were arrested for disrupting the political convention. Normalcy was abandoned throughout the country. She spent as much of her time as possible in the library, thinking of anything else.

In August she packed up all of her belongings - four cardboard boxes of books, her typewriter and a single large suitcase of her clothing. She sold her television to a fellow student and arranged to mail the books to her student housing unit in Berkeley. She decided to go west by train, not only because was it cheaper - always the first consideration - but also because it would allow her a chance to see the spaces in between. On August 22, she boarded the California Zephyr and left the Midwest. Zephyr, she thought, a sweet wind to take me out of this miserable place into a new life. Whatever excitement Sequoia told Gretchen she should have felt as she left for college, she now felt as she boarded the train for California. As she felt the slow, powerful surge of the engine leaving Union Station, she smiled, relaxing into her seat and opening a book by Wallace Stegner that she had chosen because he was a Western author.

She read all the way across Illinois and the corn fields of Iowa, then slept. Dreaming, she was in a boat on a lake, on a sunny mild day, casting a line into the water. The boat drifted, and the slow rhythm of her casting and reeling relaxed her. Her father was in the boat with her, alternately fishing and rowing the boat toward another spot in the lake. She drifted awake, vaguely aware of moving through dark open spaces, then drifted back into the same dream, only now Sunday and Sequoia were in a second rowboat just next to them. Sequoia was explaining to Sunday how to cast for bass. Ever the earnest student, he cast intently but snagged his line and then patiently unraveled it, while Sequoia gave him tips in a soft, lulling voice. Gretchen felt such harmony with her companions that she wanted to stay in the dream forever. And indeed it continued for some time, now with her and Sunday in the same boat and her father in the boat with Sequoia. Birds sang from the shore of the lake; the heat made them all sleepy. She and Sunday anchored their boat and swam in the cool clear water, their bodies, now naked, floating beside each other, their hands linked.

Early in the morning, she woke and saw mountains for the first time. In the pale light of dawn, silhouetted against a violet sky, their snowy tips sparkled, vaguely pink. Riveted by this landscape, Gretchen moved to the observation car and did nothing but stare at this new world for the next two hours. They moved into the mountains, and the train audibly groaned with the climb. Fluttering aspens populated the lower forests. Firs formed a congregation of spires on the upper reaches. Like the train ride to the summer dacha in Dr. Zhivago, she thought, imaginary music swelling in her head. Now they paralleled a river, full of whitewater and huge boulders, surging westward with the same power as the engine that pulled her. Towering above them on either side were the steep walls of a granite canyon. She had no idea where they were, but it felt like heaven. Gradually the train, still paralleling the river, pulled out of the canyon into an open area with a town, where they stopped long enough for passengers to get out and buy refreshments. It was Glenwood Springs, Colorado. Gretchen got out and inhaled the clear thin air. Across the tracks was an imposing old hotel, the Hotel Colorado, its bricks the same color as the ferrous bare hills nearby. In front of it spanned a huge hot springs swimming pool, full of people. She bought herself some orange juice and a muffin, then returned to the observation car.

Crossing the parched desert of Nevada also fascinated her. For hours she saw no human sign. Sagebrush clung to the faces of distant mountains like the stubble on a black man's beard. The distant mountains lent color to the desert tableau – alternately pale green, rust and faint purple.

Gradually, she became aware that they were climbing again, and the low, once distant mountains grew into the majesty of the Sierra Nevada. They climbed again through aspen forests, then up to where occasional gnarled pines clung to rocky outcroppings. Tiny lakes appeared suddenly and then were gone. Lake Tahoe appeared on the left, a deep marine blue with sparkling white caps, a vast sapphire in the cleft of the mountain. Starting again to descend, the train passed towering Ponderosa pines, unerringly straight, striving for the sky. More tiny lakes, more surging rivers enlivened this landscape. Once again, the mountains gradually gave way onto flat land, this time some of it flooded for rice fields. On drier ground, they passed huge orchards of almond trees, fields of sunflowers and then something familiar – cornfields. Sacramento was the last stop before her destination, and she stepped out of the train in Berkeley as if transported to another planet.

Her first impression of the campus was that it was set in a park, the buildings on various hills, everything casual, almost haphazard, lacking the ponderous weight of the gothic University of Chicago. The town of Berkeley was scruffy, the main street lined with motley booths selling crystals, tie-dyed cloth, incense, sandals and other hippy paraphernalia. It was not long before she crossed the Bay into San Francisco, with its old-lady pastel Victorians and young women in granny gowns and lace-up boots. From the first look, she liked this city better. She dreamed that someday she would have her own practice in a Victorian building in San Francisco.

As she enrolled, she decided, almost on a whim, to give herself a new name, Greta. Gretchen was a name for a child. Greta was prepared to be a new person now, and the new name almost fooled her.

Part Three

32
1995
Greta

Greta looked down on tufted, white cumulus clouds from the window of the airplane as it neared Chicago. Up here, brilliant sunshine lit the clouds, which looked as inviting as deep white sofa cushions. But soon, she knew, they would buffet the plane on its descent into O'Hare. Below, the air would be gray, damp and chilled.

She had been making this annual journey from San Francisco to Chicago every November for – what was it? – nearly twenty years now for the annual meeting of the national psychological association to which she belonged. As in many recent years, she was to deliver a professional paper at this meeting. It lay on the tray table before her as she prepared for this national audience. "Racial Identification among Mixed-Race Children: Its Impact on Parental Attachment," by Greta Reinhardt, Ph.D. The meeting theme this year was cross-cultural issues, a focus within her own practice and research.

"You're too pre-occupied with race," her friend Marge had told her.

'That's because you're white,' she thought but did not say, would never say.

"How could I not be?" she'd answered. "It's a focus of my practice. It's a source of concern for my son." Not to mention her history with Sunday. She knew it was the history with Sunday that Marge thought she should have left behind by now. In some ways she thought she had left it behind. She told herself that Sunday as a person no longer felt so important to her. Sequoia still did, though. But the causes for her failure with Sunday, and with her sometime friend Latisha – weren't they racial? Why shouldn't she be pre-occupied with race? It remained a sharp scissors to cut some people out of others' lives.

She hoped her audience wouldn't share Marge's concern. She hoped for an audience who wanted to hear *more* rather than less about race. Everyone uses racial filters, she told herself, though usually not consciously.

She knew both aspects of her subject professionally and personally. She'd studied attachment theory with one of the original disciples of Bowlby and had become an expert in her own right in San Francisco, where she had lived for the past twenty-seven years. Her move to the West Coast cemented her distance from the mother she regarded as so damaging to her. She had had no contact with either parent, did not even know if they were alive, ailing or even still in Milwaukee themselves. They were more dead to her than Sequoia, whom she sometimes consulted in her head when she worried about some problem with her son Joshua.

She wondered whether she should have left him

with friends while she took this trip. She had been leaving him with the same family every November, but now he was fifteen, a recent transfer student as a sophomore in a small private school in San Francisco, and vulnerable to everything in life that was unfamiliar to him, including his new deep voice, which usually but not always sounded like a man's. Her eyes upon the clouds, she could see him vividly in her mind - tall, reed-thin, with caramel skin and unruly tufts of coppery hair. His green eyes were set exactly like hers beneath arching eyebrows that made him look perpetually quizzical. The bones of his face were hers too, as well as the shape of his head, but his full lips belonged to his other progenitor, whoever he was.

She had conceived him as deliberately and independently as she had made every other decision in her adult life. At the time, a physician had recommended she seek a donor with as many of her physical traits as possible, so that this child, conceived in so strange a manner, would at least resemble her physically. But she would have none of it, insisted on an African-American donor. The irony was that he did indeed resemble her closely in everything but his coloring. His sperm donor was reportedly an African-American physician, tall, dark and musical, an amateur tympanist.

Greta named him Joshua. That he would have the name of a strong tree was certain from the time of his conception. It was her way of honoring Sequoia, as she and Sunday had imagined so many years ago. She had been tempted, at his birth, to call him Tupelo, like "Tupelo Honey" because of his color; but she decided not to burden him with an odd name. His family origin would be unusual enough. Joshua trees are strong, long-lived, and distinctive, with spikes of honey-white blossoms. At birth, Joshua had given no hint of how he would later look. His eyes at birth were blue, his skin pale and his birth hair, which he lost within days, was black. She was determined he would be exposed to African-Americans. She lived in a mixed neighborhood, placed him in a public school with a significant African-American attendance, and cultivated friendships with parents of color. He looked neither white, nor Hispanic, nor Asian, certainly, nor truly African-American. She led him to believe that his being distinctive was an advantage, and it worked for a while. He certainly knew what it was to be chosen. He sailed through grammar school with his upbeat, outgoing personality and quirky sense of humor, which she imagined must have come from his donor.

But his first year of high school had been brutal, unexpectedly so. He had placed into the elite academic public high school in San Francisco, where well more than half of his fellow students were Asian-Americans. He could count on two hands the number of African-American students, and they hunkered protectively among themselves. At fourteen, he had felt marginalized by more than the usual adolescent demons.

She rallied by finding his present private school, whose eclectic population was more compatible. This school attracted many of the mixed-race families in the City, as well as children of same-sex couples. In this microcosmic rainbow, he seemed to thrive. But she had more than second thoughts about the artificiality of his school universe, a planned multicultural environment that sometimes resembled a contrived, multi-hued bouquet. As diversity was a goal of the school, a student's color or background became an attribute. Joshua qualified for a scholarship.

Whatever reservations she had, Joshua didn't share them. His upbeat persona returned in the new school. Girls of all colors admired his soft reddish halo. If you asked him (and of course she asked him) how he identified racially, he would quip "decidedly mixed" with a mock academic air or "I am the rainbow coalition, Man," with a black inflection.

This school was not as academic as his former public high school. And some of the students were from obviously wealthy families. While Joshua rode the bus to school, some of his classmates arrived in Land Rovers or Mercedes. She had not seen their homes, but wondered how he would react to the obvious economic diversity of this new school. He seemed more comfortable with it than she was, but that didn't surprise her; she'd worried throughout his childhood about how he would adapt to his differences. Such as not having a father.

As a young child, he'd tell his pals he had a mom but never knew his dad. As soon as he could comprehend the details, she explained how he had been chosen. She cultivated the notion that his family was all chosen, a coalition of long-held friends, most with children themselves, some gay, some married but mostly other single moms who had celebrated family holidays, Christmases, bar- and bat-mitzvahs and graduations together for years.

It pained her secretly that Joshua did not know his grandfather, but she knew the price of that connection would be a connection also with his troubled grandmother; and that was a chance she refused to take. In earlier years, she had tried to compensate by giving him painting lessons or taking him fishing, but his interests lay elsewhere. She learned to adapt to what interested Joshua. It amused her to no end when he took up taiko drumming, and he kept at it for several years with enthusiasm. Joshua was also mathematically and scientifically inclined. His current life goal was to become a geneticist. He was fascinated by the Human Genome Project, which would soon map the whole genetic structure of human beings.

Of course his drumming also reminded her of Sunday. Joshua had a bit of Sunday's reedy height and athleticism too; Joshua also ran track. She had always wondered what had become of Sunday, whom he had ultimately married, what life he was leading, what if any children he was rearing. She had never replicated that level of feeling for any other man. She'd told herself it was only five months, many years ago, when she was too young to know herself. But her professional training only reinforced the imprint he had left on her.

She fastened her seat belt and sighed as she stared at her notebook. She didn't really want to go to the conference this year. She would have preferred to stay home with Joshua rather than arrange for him to stay with friends again. After twenty years of this annual meeting, she could predict who would be at the opening cocktail party, who would cluster for dinner this evening, who would bore and who would brag in delivering their papers. She had decided to come again this year only because she had been invited to speak. But even that no longer gave her pleasure. She sighed again. This doubting herself on every subject was altogether too familiar.

Her dinner with Marge the night before had not improved her dark mood. A brilliant pediatric surgeon at the university hospital, Marge was perpetually in conflict with her male colleagues. A visiting surgeon from Holland had invited Marge to dinner. She'd been attracted to him and excited about a technique he was introducing at the hospital. At dinner, Marge and the Dutch surgeon had debated his theories in a way that only increased Marge's interest in the man. Afterward, she'd invited him to her home. Over brandy in front of her fireplace, her Dutch colleague confided in her. "It's too bad," he told Marge, "but what they say about you at the hospital is true. You're brilliant but argumentative. Behind those bright blue eyes is a penetrating mind, but not a woman's softness. You should ease up a bit, flatter your colleagues more. I feel like I'm on trial around you." Then he left.

Marge was turning fifty this year, a year older than Greta. She had lustrous pale skin and hair the color of dried wheat. "I no longer care about chairing this department someday; I'd just like to have one more good night of sex before I die. Is that too much to ask?"

Greta had not found any way to encourage her. In fact, she feared Marge might be speaking for both of them, and for most of their single, professional women friends. What men valued in each other, what Marge and she found exciting about the men who interested them, was that probing kind of intelligence that gave no quarter. But most men did not seem to value the same quality in them.

Looking out the window at the clouds, Greta reflected on Marge's comment. Was it really possible that neither of them would ever have sex again? It seemed too grim to imagine. She closed her eyes. Oh, to wake up in bed with a lover's hand draped over her ribs, a kiss at the back of her neck.... Were there people who actually lived with such luxury? She might settle for just a simple loving touch. Cynically, she thought: was there such a thing as a simple loving touch? Most touches were a way of saying: I want. The tap on the back: please make way. The child's insistent hand on the arm or thigh: look at me. The lover's tickle of the breast: get wet so I can enter you. The client's hopeful handshake: help me. Funny, how little she was touched as a child, except to be led forcibly across the street or to be spanked for some misdeed. She thought back, trying to conjure up her father's encouraging arm on her shoulder, or a kiss on the forehead, but no such memory came. Sequoia had hugged her several times, and each time she had been fortified with encouragement. Leave this, she thought: this leads nowhere good.

She scratched her shoulder unconsciously, at some miscellaneous itch. She remembered sitting on her Grandma Etta's lap, her Grandma leisurely scratching her back in unending, gentle arcs, and leaning back into her loving touch. She thought of Josh as a baby, of gently massaging his fat, soft feet as he nursed. Nursing had to be the best touch of all, the most reciprocal, harmonious and relaxing. She and he would both fall asleep as he satisfied himself. The amazing natural bounty of it - the more he drank, the more milk surged toward her nipples. She could squeeze her own nipple and arc the stream, like one of those rotund women in a Rubens painting. Too bad she had known Sunday when they were both too young to know what to do with nipples. She smiled.

When she said goodbye to Marge last evening, they hugged each other. The hug asked nothing from either one of them; it was part of the loving connection between friends. And Josh had hugged her goodbye, wishing her well with her speech. He would sometimes rub her neck after a hard day, or she would massage his shoulders or legs after a hard game. She was so lucky to have him. Even if there were never a husband or another lover, she was blessed to have this son.

Greta scrolled through her paper on her laptop, adding thoughts here and there, feeling considerably better about the days to come. By the time the plane landed, she felt satisfied with the work she had done and even a bit enthusiastic about the prospect of delivering her paper tomorrow.

As she stepped out of the terminal, a gust of cold wind nearly slammed her back into the door. She wrapped a scarf around her neck, turned up the collar of the winter coat she almost never needed at home and put on the red leather gloves she had bought for this occasion. She looked up. The sky was an undifferentiated sooty gray, threatening snow. The mid-afternoon light was faint; all the cars needed headlights. At least she no longer lived here. Leaving for California had been one of her best early decisions. Though she traveled here each year, she never visited the university or Hyde

Park. She was not interested in reunions of any kind.

One good thing about Chicago, and she noticed it every time she visited - she was back in a city where African-Americans were a large part of the population, and increasingly a part of every segment of that population. Fur-coated black men strode up Michigan Avenue. When she checked into her hotel, a young African-American woman staffed the desk. Her name tag read Latisha: Greta glanced up automatically. Not her sometime friend. This Latisha told her regretfully that they did not have her reservation, but Greta produced her confirmation slip and Latisha called out the manager, an elegant black woman with corn rows arced gracefully around her head. Her name tag read Doris Jackson. She scrolled through the computer, conferred with Latisha and then produced a room for her.

Greta's room overlooked the Chicago River, now draining backward from the lake inland, part of the City's effort to improve its appearance. Tour boats were moored at the docks below the street level. She suspected Doris Jackson had upgraded her room and smiled at her luck. She dressed for the evening cocktail reception, adding a red scarf around her neck and some eye liner to her pale eyes.

She heard a voice next to her ear as a man jostled her while they were leaving the introductory session. "Entschuldigung."

"No problem," she muttered automatically, and then looked up. She saw chestnut skin, a huge smile and cat-green eyes. "But why did you address me in German?" There was more curiosity than edge in her voice.

"Look at you," and he laughed, with a broad warm sound. "And look at your name tag, too."

"And I suppose I should address you in ...." She cast about a moment, recognizing a faint accent in his words, "German, also."

"Gut! Now we're cutting across stereotypes."

"Well, at least one of us is," she bantered. Tempted to ask him if he was really German, she decided to listen further instead.

They were walking side by side now, with the horde of registrants, toward the wine-and-cheese reception. She noticed how tall and gangly he was, reminiscent almost of Sunday so many years ago, but far lighter in skin. He pitched forward as he walked, as if eager to be in the next place. His hair was brown, not black, and he had a short mustache and beard that barely contrasted with his skin. His eyes were as intense, almost-yellow, as Joshua's cat Felix, and as unreadable, but that smile of his seemed to wrap around his face. He wore no name tag.

"A white wine lady, I presume?" He teased.

"Stop making assumptions about me - I want red," she tossed back jokingly. She always drank chardonnay.

They drank several glasses of wine together while standing in the crowd, making a game of describing other people in the crowd by their appearance. She knew most of these people, and this man's descriptions were hilariously apt.

"That man, the one with the vest and bowtie, talking to the thin man; he teaches at a Midwestern university. He's gay but married..." He paused, tilting his head slightly. "To another professor who writes voluminously and couldn't care less about his sexual orientation. He comes to these conferences to connect with the most accomplished gay psychologists he can find."

She laughed, putting her hand over her mouth. "He teaches at DePauw, and his wife is a professor of medicine who does write voluminously. I never thought about whether he's gay until now, and you could be right."

"Now you do it," he insisted.

"Not fair," she said, "I already know them."

"But do you?" he teased, and then fabricated clever personal stories about some of her colleagues that made her realize she knew only the slightest details about their personal lives. Too proud or stubborn to ask him where he was from - or knowing somehow she would get a misleading answer - she kept listening to his voice to get some hint from his accent. She found herself playing the game about him. She assumed from his brown hair that he had one white parent. Perhaps the son of an African-American soldier stationed in Europe. He seemed to know Chicago well, even some blues joints she remembered from college that would not be listed in conference guides to the city. Whoever this man was, it felt good to flirt with him.

As the crowd around them thinned, it became obvious that she - or they - should leave also.

"Have dinner with me, will you?" She didn't mind that the tone felt imperative; she liked it.

"Give me half an hour to freshen up and get my coat. I'll meet you in the lobby." She turned, then stopped. "What's your name?" She reddened.

"Howard. . . Howard Manheim." He thrust out his hand; she shook it and he put his other hand over hers. She reddened again. He walked away, turning back to smile at her.

Manheim, she thought, an odd name. One he made up? On the way to the elevators, she was waylaid by the moderator for her session tomorrow and spent some time with him reviewing the introduction for her presentation.

Entering her room, Greta rushed into the bathroom without even turning on the bedroom lights, realizing she had only ten minutes left before she was to meet Howard, if that was his name. She tore off her sweater, threw cold water on her overheated face and looked at herself in the mirror. She had not seen this woman in ... how long? A little perfume, a little make-up; she would not need much the way her eyes looked now after flirting with this man.

She flipped the lights on in the bedroom to find a softer sweater in her bag.

"Hey, baby." He lay, covered to his chin, in her bed.

"How did you get here?" Alarm crept into her voice. He could be a thief, a rapist, a serial killer. Anger climbed up her spine; this was *her* room.

"I told the desk clerk I had lost my key."

"And they gave you one?" Her voice rose into a false hysteria. "I'm tempted to call the desk right now - or the police."

"Why don't you just crawl into bed instead," he teased. "You look ready." Cocksure. She hesitated while anger, fear and – yes, attraction – jangled her. Also the old parental instinct that she should take no risks so long as Josh was dependent on her. How could she get into such a situation, at her age and stage in life? At the same time, an antic temptation to laugh bubbled up inside her. At twenty, she would have jumped into bed with this stranger. At forty-nine, a remonstrating voice took over.

"Look, let's just forget this happened. You climb out of this bed, get dressed and leave. I won't call the police, and we won't meet for dinner. Let's just say we both made a mistake."

"You just want to look at me," he grinned.

She fought a grin that played at the left corner of her mouth.

"I'm going to go back into that bathroom, which has a phone, incidentally. In five minutes, I'm going to come back out, and you're going to be out of here."

"Okay. I guess I did make a mistake. I'll leave."

The water dripped in the bathroom while she listened, trembling, for the sounds of his leaving. When she heard the door close, she sprang to latch it and fasten the chain. She spent the rest of the night alternately berating herself for getting into such an irresponsible and potentially dangerous situation, and for not giving in to her impulse just to climb into bed with him. She ate a room service dinner and disciplined herself to prepare some more for her presentation tomorrow afternoon.

Breakfast was served, as it was every year, just outside the plenary session ballroom. She served herself some fresh fruit and a tiny bagel before running into Herman Berkowitz, the pompous education chair of the association. He stopped her to remind her of how he had personally chosen her to participate in this important program; she nodded and bowed her gratitude sanctimoniously.

"Can I fill your cup?" A waiter asked. She held it out without looking.

"Decaf or regular, madam?" Howard stood next to her, smiling sardonically, coffee pot in his hand, towel over his arm, and a speaker's name tag on his lapel. His tawny eyes were expressionless.

She held out her cup without being able to say anything.

He poured slowly, obsequiously, while her face heated. Then he turned, clicked his heels ever so slightly, and walked away. A very superior little smile played on his face.

Howard Manheim was one of the featured speakers. According to the program, his specialty was forgiveness. He had worked in Ireland with Protestant and Catholic families who had lost sons or brothers or husbands in the troubles. He had spent the last year weaving in and out of Bosnia and Serbia, counseling refugees on both sides. Before that, he had done similar work with refugees from Uganda. His doctorate was in political science; he had taught at Georgetown and published on ethnic conflicts. His last teaching assignment had been in Berlin, his stopping off point for his refugee work in the former Yugoslavia. He was to speak on ethnic conflict and forgiveness.

He was introduced in reverential tones by the association president. Greta hung her head, not knowing whether he was a saint in his work with a James Bond-like proclivity about women, or whether she had just missed the evening of her lifetime, or both. Either way, she felt she had bungled the night before. At the same time, she argued: why should his credentials somehow legitimize his behavior?

He hunched over the lectern with the same

attitude of urgency she had noticed in the way he walked. His voice - and words - were warm and deeply caring. He gave examples of how people from various parts of the world who had been neighbors, with common problems and experiences and social events, later became entrenched enemies - and how forgiveness could be used as a technique to reverse the process. With the rest of the audience, she was moved by his fervor, the importance of his work, and his enormous compassion.

She lingered after the audience dispersed and the well-wishers had stopped shaking his hand. They were slow to leave. She didn't know what she would say.

"I was moved by ..." she began earnestly.

He interrupted her. "I overstepped my bounds. I owe you an apology. I'm always moving too fast," he said sheepishly, brushing back his hair with one hand.

"I guess hotel rooms are pretty easy after sneaking across international borders," she teased.

"Getting in isn't hard; it's what you find on the inside that can scare you." He laughed, reddening. "Would you consider dinner tonight? I'll meet you at the restaurant; I promise." He was still laughing. It was a round, warm laugh, the warmest sound she had heard in a long, long time.

"Yes."

They ate at an Indian restaurant he chose and both ordered curries so spicy that they went out into the cold November night with sweating faces. As he led her to a waiting taxi, he placed his hand gently on the center of her back, just below her waist. When they lay together in her room afterward, he stroked her back in tireless arcs, and his hand came to rest on her flank. She slept deeply.

When she awoke the next morning, he was gone. A bouquet of yellow roses was delivered to her room midday, along with a note: "Thank you for reconsidering. Howard." She did not see him afterward at the conference, or ever again.

But she brought one of the roses home and told Marge that she was convinced their sexual lives were not over.

33
1996
Greta

Greta raised the shades on the kitchen window facing the back yard. It was the first week in February, the beginning for her of spring in San Francisco, when the plum trees began to bloom and daylight hours lengthened just enough to stir memory of longer days. She smiled at the pink blossoms on her plum tree, barely discernable in the pale early light.

This was her favorite hour of the day, before Josh woke up, when she was alone in silence to contemplate her day. Today she would see Zoe, the young lesbian who had been debating with herself for almost a year now about whether to have a child on her own. Greta would have said, had she been her friend rather than her therapist, "Just do it! You'll be a fine mother and struggle at all the hard times, but you'll never regret becoming a parent." Of course, as a therapist, she would not say that to Zoe, and could not guarantee that anyone would not regret becoming a parent. Having a child was in fact the riskiest relationship decision anyone could ever make: you had no way of getting to know the child in advance, and your decision was irreversible. No wonder Zoe had hesitated for so long; she wanted to know what she could not know in advance, and she did not trust herself. Greta remembered well her own indecision, which had lasted far longer than Zoe's. For her, it hadn't been fear of who the child would be - rather, how could she know she would not behave like her own mother? She'd gone into therapy herself for two years over that question. Then, with sudden resolve, she had launched herself into motherhood like a hang glider catching the updraft off a cliff over the ocean, with all the wonder and excitement of first flight.

Last evening, Josh had given Greta new reasons to feel grateful for her having taken that risk. He'd confided that there was a girl in his class. So far, they had "hooked up" at parties (Greta would bite her tongue before asking what that meant) but he wanted to do something special for Valentine's Day. Should he send her flowers, take her out to dinner? Both? At sixteen, he was ready to tell someone he cared about her. Greta was touched that he trusted her and also amused at how he put it. "Don't ask me a lot of questions," he said, "just tell me what you think." So she did: flowers and dinner were over the top, but taking her to dinner would both show her he cared and allow him time to get to know her better, one on one. She helped him make a reservation at Destino, just in case the girl said yes.

Two new clients would come in today. Greta always looked forward to meeting new clients, to guessing the questions behind the questions that brought them to a therapist, the questions they dared not ask themselves outright. One was Roger Dawley, a twenty-year-old adoptee who wanted to meet his birth mother. He was coming to see her because the state recommended psychological consultation before granting information about birth parents. The other was Paula Hartwell, a fifty-year-old woman whose husband had been unfaithful for years.

Greta went upstairs to wake Josh. Although he could wake with an alarm clock, he still preferred her to wake him. She turned on a soft light in his room. He did not stir. She cupped her hand around his soft, coppery hair and wondered how much longer he would allow her to touch him this tenderly. She kissed him gently on his cheek, smelling that he needed to wash his hair. He opened his hazel eyes and smiled. "I'm up," he said, stretching. "Thanks, Mom." She looked at him once more, admiringly. He was one of those people whose skin and hair nearly matched, except in the summer when his skin got darker and his hair lighter, and they seemed nearly to glow with good health and spirits. Lucky girl, whoever she was.

Zoe arrived at Greta's office early, before Greta had even taken off her coat. She bounded in and sat down in a different chair from where she usually sat. Sitting on her hands and leaning forward, face flushed, she announced:

"I know what I want to do. I'm ready to become a mother!"

"How did you turn the corner?" asked Greta, keeping the wariness out of her voice.

"Summer has agreed to move in with me and

help me." Summer was the woman she had been seeing for about three months. Their relationship thus far had been stormy, full of dramatic pronouncements.

"How does that change the equation for you?"

"I realized I think it wouldn't be fair to a child to have only one parent. What if something happened to me?" She paused. "No offense." Zoe knew that Greta was a single parent.

"None taken."

"What if your relationship doesn't last? Would you be willing to share parenting with Summer even if she left you?"

Zoe looked as if Greta had socked her in the eye.

"You don't understand. It would be my child. We decided I would be the one to become pregnant."

"But I thought you said it wouldn't be fair for your child to have only one parent. If she has two parents and those parents split up, doesn't she then divide her time between both her parents?"

"But I don't think that'll happen."

"You can't know, can you?"

Their dialogue went on like this for the rest of the hour, and Zoe left sullen rather than elated. In the hour between clients, Greta took notes about Zoe's sudden readiness to decide. For months, Zoe had been on the fence, asking herself many relevant questions. What if the child were born with serious medical defects? What if the child had a personality Zoe would find difficult to live with? What if Zoe fell in love with someone who didn't want any children in her life? Greta was surprised that Zoe, an inveterate ditherer, would find this stormy relationship a quick fix to her dilemma.

Roger Dawley walked in and sat down uneasily on the straight-backed chair. A young man with pale skin and the coiled hair of an African-American, dressed in scrubs, he looked at her expectantly. Greta had arranged her office with three choices for her clients: a sofa for those who wanted to lie down during therapy, a comfy upholstered chair, and a straight-backed wooden chair. Greta's first impression was that Roger had never been in therapy before and was coming only because the state recommended it before releasing names and addresses of birth parents. Her initial questions of him confirmed that impression. She told him he was wise to follow the recommendation, that it implied nothing about a person's need for therapy. Such a consultation was intended only to aid a person in recognizing that he or she might be taking the lid off of Pandora's box. He started to relax and provided his history. He had been adopted at birth in 1970 through an agency adoption. His adoptive parents knew almost nothing about his birth mother, except that she was a white, unmarried college student. His adoptive parents, both of them white, were both mechanical engineers with AT & T.

"What sort of parents were they?" she asked.

"Dedicated, dutiful," he answered without hesitating. "They taught me the values of education and hard work. They were also honest with me. They told me I was adopted soon after I started school." He told her the information had come to him, even then, as a relief because he knew somehow he was not "of them."

"I can't describe it. It wasn't only that I looked different." He pointed to his coiled hair. "It was just this sense I had, that although they clearly cared about me, they just weren't my people."

A nursing student, he was drawn to nursing by a desire to help people, a trait that his parents comprehended in a very different way than he.

"I admire your insight. Who do you imagine your birth parents were?"

"Yeah," he smiled. "I knew you would ask me that.

"I've imagined my mother as a serious student who got involved with someone she knew she couldn't stay with. I see her as someone with compassion, who put me up for adoption because she thought I would be better cared for by a real family." He paused. "I'm clueless about my father. I see him as ...some outsider, someone she shouldn't have been involved with."

"Do you want information about her and not about him?"

"Well, I suppose if I open the box, I'm probably gonna learn something about him too. But I'm more interested in her." He shrugged slightly. I can't tell you why."

"What if you find her and she doesn't want anything to do with you?"

"Yeah, that's the tough question, and I've thought about it some. I suppose she could be so ashamed she wouldn't want anything to do with me."

"That, or she could have more selfish reasons. She might not want her current family to know that she had given up a child for adoption. Or, she might not care." Greta paused to see how he reacted to her bluntness. He nodded, without saying anything.

"That would be sad, but then you'd have to

realize that your compassion comes from you and not from her. You may be the origin of your own good traits."

He rewarded her with a smile.

"I've also thought about another scenario. She wants me into her life, and she's someone I don't like very much."

"Then what do you do? Are you stuck caring for her? Do you take on a responsibility for her even though she gave you up?"

"Now you got me. I didn't think of that."

She explored with him the possibility that he would have brothers or sisters. At each new turn in the conversation, she was impressed with his maturity and willingness to accept that important discoveries might not be welcome ones. When their hour had expired, Greta asked if he wanted to come back to talk about it more.

"Nah, I feel ready. Thanks." He shook her hand. "What do I owe you?" He wrote out a check and handed it to her.

After he left, Greta stretched. She was tired. It was one o'clock and she had another hour before her last client of the day. As she unwrapped her tuna sandwich and heated a cup of jasmine tea for lunch, she found herself speculating on Roger's birth parents: the father was a medical student who broke up with the mother, who never told him of her pregnancy. The mother was not a student at all, but a drug addict, and she had no idea who the father was. Greta had heard many stories in her nearly twenty years as a therapist, but one of the facts that kept her fresh was that every person had a new story. Some of her colleagues complained that there were only six or so stories and that, after hearing them repeatedly, counseling became stale. Greta disagreed. There were repetitive situations, but each person dealt with them in her own way. She saw human beings as endlessly nuanced, endlessly interesting in their decisions and inability to make choices. She counted herself lucky on days like this, to meet so many new people and to share the mysteries of their innermost lives.

She finished her sandwich and just sat with her eyes closed for a little while before her second new client arrived.

Paula Hartwell arrived on time and seated herself in the comfy chair. While she filled out the intake form, Greta watched her intently. Seldom had she seen such an arresting-looking person. Paula had tawny skin, eyes the color of topaz, and a mane of intensely curly hair burnished from yellow to deep brown. She held herself erect and threw the hair behind her with a toss of her head. Though slender, her arms were muscled. When Paula handed back the intake sheet, Greta did not even glance at it. She was transfixed by Paula herself, who sat in the chair with all the majesty of a stone lion in front of a building. Paula's arms lay parallel in repose on the arms of the chair, her long-nailed fingers curled around the ends.

Unaccountably, Greta found herself groping about where to begin. Seldom did she see someone so self-possessed. Relief lay in an open-ended question.

"What brings you here today?"

"It'll probably sound strange to you. I've been married – mostly happily – to a man for over twenty-five years. For nearly all of them, he's had occasional affairs, all short-lived." She tilted her head slightly, derisively, as if trying to shake off a fly.

"He goes off to a conference or professional meeting and beds some other professional woman, then he comes home and he apologizes. He confesses each time and sounds very sorry. In the early years, he used to tell me he wouldn't do it again, but he doesn't say that anymore. I'm just sick to death of it. I want it to stop. I don't want to hear any more apologies. I want to find out why, and I want to make it stop, if I can."

"Why are you seeking therapy, instead of him?"

"Why do *you* think? Because *he* won't." Paula's edgy voice revealed an impatience for too-obvious questions. She wanted to get right to the heart of it, without any time wasted.

"Why now? Is there something in particular going on now between you that makes this more pressing than it has been in the past?"

"No. I've just lost my patience." The edge was more pronounced, and Greta feared Paula would soon lose patience with her too. She took another tack.

"You know your husband and I don't. You've probably thought a lot about this over the years. What do you think might be the reasons?"

"I've wracked my brain over this. I can tell you all the things I've thought of and eliminated but I can't tell you what I think it is. Of course I wondered whether he was satisfied with me, but it's obvious to us both that we have a great sex life. It continues to be very satisfying, and it's even gotten better over the years. He clearly loves me. I've wondered whether he feels trapped in marriage, but it's clear he loves being married, and he loves being a father to our three children."

Greta wondered if Paula had waxed too thickly over the sex part but probed for other issues.

"Do you think he might feel inadequate to you?" Greta could see how anyone might be a bit intimidated by this fierce woman.

Paula laughed dismissively. She described his professional success - quickly tenured at UC-Berkeley, with years as a visiting professor at other prestigious universities, much published, honored for his teaching. Paula told Greta that although he was confident professionally, he was modest in speaking of himself.

"I'm an artist and a mother. No competition with him."

Greta wondered if Paula had the patience for a tangent.

"What sort of artist? Tell me about your own work."

Paula warmed to the question.

"I work in fabrics, make large tapestries, sometimes contemporary quilts. I also paint, mostly abstract oils. I show at crafts fairs, sell a bit but don't make a lot of money. I actually have one piece in the National Crafts Museum. I made this." She opened her arms to show the patchwork shawl draped over her shoulders. It had waves of variegated colors, red/orange/gold, and multiple weaves. The colors harmonized the different patterns and weaves. It was clearly a complicated piece made with great imagination.

"Can you imagine him feeling inadequate to your confidence, your creativity, or to some other aspects of you that he lacks?"

"He has no reason to be."

"Not my question. Might he be, even if he has no reason to be?"

"No." Paula shook her head, and her mane settled over her left shoulder. She was going to be a tough customer.

"How did you meet him?" Greta could see immediately that Paula liked this question.

"My father was – and is – a history professor. He used to invite his favorite graduate students over for dinner and ask them challenging questions about what was going on in the world. Of course, I was there too, a graduate student myself but not in history. He would never tell them I was his daughter. Sometimes we played a game called Diplomacy. It was a board game, with different players being different countries...."

"I remember it myself from college days." Paula smiled at her and continued.

"My dad always chose England; I would choose France. We would be secret allies and we thought we knew all the strategies. This one grad student – now my husband - chose Germany. No one wanted Germany in those days, but he chose it and caught onto our strategies right away. He was a gifted player; my dad and I were very impressed. He got invited back often, and he asked me out even though he knew I was the professor's daughter. I admired his nerve."

"You didn't think he was just kissing up to his professor?"

"No! It was obvious he wasn't doing that."

"What attracted you to him, besides his nerve in inviting you out?"

"He's probably the most intelligent man I have

ever met, very thoughtful and rational. I tend to leap into things, and he always thinks them through first. He was very tender toward me, and I loved that about him. I still do. And it turns out he's a wonderful father – very devoted to our children."

"What about his self-confidence with other women? Do you think he's trying to prove himself in some way?"

"That's the place where I don't know him, even after all these years. He's not the kind of man who obsessively flirts with other women when we're out socially. He's never, ever, given me any reason to be embarrassed or jealous socially." She paused, reflectively. "But obviously, something happens when he's out of town and I'm not around. So that's the person I don't know. It's always a woman I'm likely never to meet, as if he's careful not to embarrass me socially. But, still, it happens." More angrily, "And it's getting mighty old."

At least Paula had allowed an opening, some chink in the armor, some admission of what she had not been able to solve herself.

"Why do you suppose he always tells you afterward? It sounds as if it would be easy for him just to keep it quiet."

"Well, I would rather know than not."

"But is that why he tells you? What purpose does it serve for him to tell you?"

Paula admitted she did not know, had not thought about it from that angle. It was the end of the hour. Greta was both exhausted and relieved that she had found something to make Paula think about, something she had not focused on before. She hoped it would make her want to come back.

This woman fascinated Greta and she wanted to know her better.

"Do you want to set another appointment?"

"Of course. I'm here to work on this."

Greta drove home, listening to continuing professional education tapes on the way. She could muster only a simple dinner for herself and Josh. She broiled a couple of steaks, microwaved two potatoes and tossed a big green salad for them. He had had a good day: the girl – Cedar – had accepted his invitation to dinner on Valentine's Day. She toasted his good fortune. Cedar, she thought, what an imaginative name. She didn't think to ask him about it.

Since Josh was not old enough to drive without an adult at night and Cedar's parents had not wanted her to take the Muni at night, Greta drove them both to the restaurant on Valentine's Day. Josh held Cedar's hand as he walked her from the door of her home to the car. It was obvious from her body language that Cedar liked Josh. He introduced her to Cedar without mentioning her last name, and Greta asked a few questions to be polite, before trying to fade as much as possible into her role as driver so that Josh and Cedar could enjoy each other's company. Cedar had skin the color of her namesake and an erect, proud posture. Her hair was a neat bob of tight reddish-brown curls, just long enough to flop over her forehead as she moved her head. She had a radiant smile and a ready laugh. As the two got out of the car, Greta admired how good these two children of color looked together.

She reflected for a moment on how they

embodied the optimistic world she had imagined when she was their age. In a time when people had made caustic jokes to cover their fear of what would happen if Mai Britt and Sammy Davis, Jr. had children, she had imagined children of a lovely caramel color, like Josh and Cedar. More mixing, rather than less, had been her vision of a better world. Some of that had occurred, of course, but the world was immeasurably more complicated than her early imaginings, advancing and retreating simultaneously. Even in this city, at Josh's former school, he had had to choose whether to go with the black or white students, and he had found himself, by a variety of peculiar criteria (including how he dressed – he didn't want to wear loose pants hanging tentatively just above the crack of his butt), more comfortable among the white students. His current school, she knew, was a tiny enclave within the slightly larger tiny enclave of a liberal city.

She agreed to pick them up at nine and drove home to make dinner for herself. As she stopped at a cross light, Greta noticed several men carrying home bouquets of roses, and several couples – some of them pairs of men - walking arm-in-arm, themselves another part of the tiny enclave. Greta had no man in her life these days. There had been no man, to speak of, in her life for some years. It hadn't always been this way, this barren horizon. Twenty years ago her sex life was as wanton as a banana tree. Almost as soon as she moved to Berkeley in 1968, Greta began to shed her old life, just as she had shed her former name. As determined in sex as she was in school, Greta seized every opportunity that appealed to her. A drummer in Sproul Plaza who claimed to be from

Senegal – as black as Sunday but with a lighter, lilting voice – led her to a remote dell of trees on the campus where they crawled under the arms of a pine and ensnared their bodies for an hour or so, then sauntered off in different directions, like two leopards in a break from their habitual solitude. She met young men in all the usual places – coffee shops, cable car, Tower Records and Cody's Books. Always they were black – no one else held any appeal – and only once was there another student.

Darrell was, like Greta, a graduate student in psychology. Born of an NYU professor father and physician mother, he wanted to set up practice in some all-black community like West Oakland. He affected the speech of street blacks, though his real vernacular was more like her own and his street talk was never very convincing. They began by some debate in class, over an issue on which they took mainly the same side but with some nuanced differences, and they kept talking on their way out of class, to a coffee shop, and then to his apartment where they stopped talking altogether and just explored each other's body with their tongues. His body was salty, acrid and sweet in different places. She and Darrell carried on quite passionately, both in talk and in bed, for about six weeks, after which he decided he should be with a black woman. His only-too-familiar reason for leaving bothered her more than the fact of his leaving, but in those days there was such an abundance of men, that she didn't even bother to try to make anything last. If anyone had asked her at the time if she planned to marry some day, she would have shrugged, lifting her eyebrows at the futility of marriage. With men, it was like deciding whether there were any movies worth seeing on any given weekend. And then time passed, and such behavior became, well, inappropriate. Abundance had turned to drought.

As she looked back on it now, that period was so forgiving. AIDS had not yet struck. Antibiotics had conquered most STDs. The pill had eliminated fear of pregnancy. Sex without consequences. How unexpected it was to her that the sexual landscape for her son would be so much more dangerous than hers had been. He could not afford to be heedless.

Josh would be gone in only a few more years. She didn't know if she could adequately prepare him for the sexual landscape of his young adulthood. He'd got all the sex education in school, of course, and young people were trained to carry condoms. But how could a teenager know the consequences of not using them?

Too soon, Josh would have to rely on himself rather than on her. As Greta drained pasta for herself, she recognized she was sinking into one of her blue moods. Too soon, Josh would be gone, and she would be alone in this little apartment. At times like this, she thought: everyone wants to come to me for advice but no one wants to love me. Before she went out again to retrieve Josh and Cedar, she tried to lecture herself out of her mood. It did give her real pleasure to see that Josh and Cedar liked each other, and she predicted Josh would become a man capable of loving well.

It was with these thoughts that Greta went to work the next day.

Zoe was her first appointment this morning.

"May I sit here?" She said. "I never sit in this

chair." Greta watched as Zoe sat herself in the straight-backed chair.

"Wherever you like." It fascinated Greta to notice how much that choice said about her clients. When Zoe felt diffuse and rambling, she lay down on the sofa and free-associated. Usually she sat in the comfy chair. She had never sat in this one before.

"Well. It's hard."

Greta couldn't help laughing a little.

"The chair or what you're thinking about?"

"I think both." Zoe smiled, a little abashed. "You made me think last week. I realized this isn't about Summer; it's about what chances I'm willing to take. There's no way I can know what kind of child I might have, or whether the relationship with Summer will last. If I do this, I have to be ready to jump off the cliff." She paused, her eyes darting about the ceiling as if she might find a message there.

Greta said nothing.

"I can't promise this child two parents." She began to cry, then moved to the sofa. Greta remembered that Zoe's own parents had stayed together more out of determination than out of love for each other, then divorced after Zoe left home. Zoe had had a good attachment to her mother until she came out as a lesbian. Then her mother had rejected her. "All I can promise her is that I'll always be there for her, as long as I'm around. But I don't know if that's enough. Is it?"

"That's the most secure foundation you can give a child. What do you think?"

"I think I need to be able to promise I'll always love her. But how can I know that I will?"

"Not every mother does. But almost every

creature from geese to humans fiercely loves and protects its children. Why do you think you wouldn't?"

"I don't think I wouldn't. I just don't know if I would."

"In other words, you don't trust yourself that you would provide that love."

"That's true." Zoe stared off into space.

"Can you imagine your child doing anything that would cause you to reject her the way your mother did you?"

"No! I would never do that!" Her answer was instantaneous.

Greta shrugged her shoulders as if to say, 'well, then....' She said nothing. She continued to say nothing as the silence grew uncomfortably long for Zoe, who shifted back to upright on the sofa.

"You're making me answer my own question."

"That's the object, isn't it?"

They spent the remainder of the hour exploring Zoe's incipient shift from diffidence to confidence.

Paula arrived on time ten minutes after Zoe left. Today Paula herself seemed less confident. All her hair was pulled back into a rubber band, the ends ragged as a Rastafarian's, and her face was thin and jaundiced.

"What's wrong?" Greta began, since it was so obvious something was troubling her.

"My husband's just back from a conference in D.C., and this time he's concerned that his companion has some S.T.D. So he asked me to go see my doctor."

"Good grief!" Greta blurted. "So now it's your

medical burden too? What *is* he thinking? *He's* the one who should be in therapy!"

Paula smiled a thin smile. "That's why I'm here. I honestly don't know what to do any more."

Greta asked if Paula had ever given him an ultimatum. It seemed to her an ultimatum from Paula would be a powerful intervention.

"I've certainly thought of it." She paused. "But there's a part of him that is fragile. Remote and fragile. Most people wouldn't notice it. Our children sense it, but I'm not sure that even you would notice it. I don't know what it is or where it comes from, but if I actually left him, I'd worry about what he might do."

"Yes, but what about you? This seems to be taking a pretty big toll on you."

Paula sighed, without saying anything.

"Your husband's behavior is repetitive to the point of obsession. When did you last ask him to go into thcrapy?"

"I told him this week that I couldn't bear this by myself any longer, and that he needed to see someone also."

"What did he say?"

"He shrugged his shoulders, as if to say 'what good would it do?' But a day later, when he saw how miserable I was, he told me he'd think about it." Paula dipped her head, then folded her hands over her eyes and sat there like this for some minutes.

Greta let the silence draw out Paula's next thought.

"Would you see him, if I could persuade him to come in?"

They discussed whether Paula would like her to do couples counseling and what it would entail for Paula and her husband. They both agreed to consider it.

Greta's next client that day was Aaron, whom she had been seeing for nearly a year. Aaron had been married for over twenty years to a woman he had probably never loved, but they had two children together, one of them a brilliant student as he had been himself and the other born with Down's Syndrome. His wife Rebecca stayed home full-time to care for their disabled son. Aaron himself was a successful commercial trial lawyer who worked long hours. In recent years, Rebecca had developed fibromyalgia, that loose agglomeration of painful symptoms that could be eased with Vicodin but never cured. And, more recently, she had started to drink during the day, to a point that Aaron felt endangered their ten-year-old disabled son. When he came home at night, often Rebecca was sleeping. Their fifteen-year-old daughter had begun to care for her brother after school and to make them dinner, about which she had grown richly resentful. Aaron was wracked with guilt: he wanted to leave the marriage but feared what would happen to his wife and children. Greta tried to mobilize some action out of him.

"Could you cut your work load to come home earlier and help out with your son after school?"

"I'd lose my position in the firm; I'm expected to work this hard." She suspected he could not bring himself to tell his partners he had serious problems at home.

"Can you hire someone to help out in the afternoons?"

"Rebecca insists on taking care of the children herself."

"If you left and took the children with you, would you hire someone to help after school?"

"Yes, of course."

"Do you think that would be better for them?"

"I don't know," and he'd shake his head. For every solution there was an insurmountable obstacle. Listening to him for even an hour at a time was exhausting. Greta doubted he could bring himself to act.

When she came home that evening, Josh was studying at the kitchen table with Cedar, who blushed as Greta came in. She had a flash of memory of the first day she'd come home to study with Sunday and Sequoia came in with the groceries. Greta remembered vividly the fleeting mix of expressions on Sequoia's face. Dismay and welcome had both jousted there, throwing her off balance. Greta put a bowl of oranges on the table in front of Josh and Cedar, then made popcorn without asking them if they wanted any. At the first pop, she jumped. When she put the bowl in front of them, Josh looked at her quizzically. She gave him an opaque smile in response and left them.

Greta went to her own bedroom, opened the door to the tiny balcony and stepped outside, gulping in the soggy air. It had been raining for two days without respite, a patient, constant waterfall. "Dr. Reinhardt, why are you having an anxiety attack?" she asked herself aloud. They're having sex, that's why. Suddenly she was not Dr. Reinhardt. She was Gretchen, sitting at that table, feeling welcomed into an unfamiliar family who treated her warmly.

A random memory emerged - Sequoia used to make slices of bread with peanut butter and marshmallow crème and then left them to study. After eating the sandwiches, Sunday was still hungry for peanut butter. He brought the jar and a single spoon to the table, and they took turns spooning peanut butter out of the jar, grinning at each other with sticky smiles. That was well before they had sex. She remembered her first impressions of Sequoia, that strong, solitary, wise protector. Sequoia nurtured Gretchen's relationship with Sunday, her little brother and surrogate son. Greta wondered when Sequoia realized she and Sunday were having sex. Surely she must have known before Sequoia invited her to spend that summer with her.

Reflecting now as an adult, Greta assumed Sequoia knew from the beginning. It was brave of her, Greta reflected, to allow that in her home in those days. Sequoia could not have known how Gretchen's parents would react. And they were both under-age. But they were seventeen; Josh and Cedar are only sixteen. How could they be old enough for sex! How vastly different it felt as a parent, how much more frightening than it had been to be young and full of passionate certainty. Sequoia would have answered, 'you can't control them. They're old enough to have to learn for themselves.' Greta-as-parent rejected that notion. She would have to talk to Josh about all the unwelcome responsibilities of having sex. No sooner had she formed that thought, than she contradicted herself by thinking, he can't possibly be having sex, he just met her....

Greta-as-Gretchen thirty-two years younger recalled without effort her burning anticipation, the touch on her thigh that rippled up her leg and into her core, her fear of losing any sense of self, the hovering suspense, the merging, skin-to-skin, blood-to-blood, as if his flowed in her veins and hers in his afterward – all came back as if it were only yesterday, along with the sense, afterward, of connectedness to all that is whole and live and holy. Gretchen with Sunday had had the best of all possible births-into-adulthood, for which she would always be profoundly grateful and more than a bit nostalgic. What she wished for Josh was that he be able to make such a connection in his life, and then keep it throughout his life. But not now, not yet.

And what if he, like her, made that connection early and then lost it? Now, as Dr. Reinhardt, Greta recognized that having made such a connection with Sunday had made it ever so much more difficult – impossible, for her – to replicate it. But it might prove different for Josh. And, for her, having had that connection was unquestionably preferable to not having had it. Now, at nearly fifty years old, Greta wondered if her entire love and sex life lay in her past. It was an almost unbearable thought, and she pushed it away. She still occasionally woke in the middle of the night, burning with desire and wondering what dream might have brought it on. It had been a year since a man had touched her intimately, during that strange and magical encounter in Chicago.

Certainly this life she led was rich professionally and as rewarding as a parent as she could have hoped. *To love and to work – lieben und arbeiten* - that old prescription of Freud's for what an adult should be able to accomplish in life. The very fact that life's achievement could be framed in three small words – love and work – belied its difficulty. Most people could do one or the other well, but it was the conjunction *and* that made it so difficult. She had done the work part; that was clear. As a young adult, she would have substituted freedom for love in the equation; freedom was its own achievement, and probably a necessary antecedent to either love or work. Greta had achieved her freedom and in doing so had also recognized its essential loneliness. For her, love was the elusive component, unless of course her love for Josh counted. Through Josh, she came to realize that what she felt for him was a pure, deep form of love, a love that could survive even his rejection. Erikson had explained that Freud meant genital love, not, she thought, 'genitorial' love, the love of a parent for a child, or, for that matter, a child's toward a parent. She knew her life was preferable to those of her patients who had been in long, loveless and sexless marriages, like Aaron's and Rebecca's.

But what of someone like Paula, who clearly lived with love and also with intense pain? Greta would not trade with Paula; she would have left that husband long ago. She was still puzzling through the question of what kept Paula in that marriage. It might not be a good idea for her to see Paula's husband; she had formed a fairly negative impression of him as self-indulgent and weak – not someone she wanted to spend time with, even professional time.

By the time Greta came down to the kitchen again to make dinner, Cedar had gone home. Greta told Josh that Cedar would be welcome to have dinner with them the next time she came over. "Just let me know in advance, so I can plan for dinner," she told him. Their own dinner was unusually silent that evening, Greta unable to think of what she wanted to say to Josh and Josh not volunteering anything. She thought she should make a point to come home earlier in the afternoons.

It was another two weeks before Paula came in again. This time she looked better and stronger. Her hair curled in a vibrant mass about her narrow face; she wore makeup, an iridescent cinnamon-colored lipstick and nails polished to match. Greta could not remember seeing Paula with makeup before. Paula explained that she had an art show that was opening this afternoon. Would Greta come? Greta congratulated her. She explained that, although she wished she could see the show, she should not develop a relationship with Paula outside this room.

Greta asked if Paula had seen her physician and if she had been tested for any sexually transmitted disease. She also asked if Paula had regular tests for AIDS. Today, Paula was all efficiency and business. She had seen her doctor and had no infections. She had for some time been getting regular AIDS tests and had required her husband to do so also. Paula had spoken to her husband again about seeking therapy, but he'd said he was not ready. Greta was somewhat relieved that she would not have to answer whether she would see him.

"Don't you ever get furious with him for doing this to you?"

"I did, long ago. I even threw something at him, a plate, something stupid; I was drying dishes at the time. I told him to leave if he couldn't be faithful to me. Our oldest child was less than a year old then, and he started to cry. I tried to push my husband out the door, and when our son started to cry, he did too. He just crumbled. He went to our son's bedroom, lifted him out of the crib and cradled him until he stopped crying. I saw him holding our son, and I couldn't push him away. That little head lying so trustingly on his dad's shoulder. He's always been like that with each of our kids. Besides, my parents adore him. Sometimes I think they love him more than they do me. I ... just couldn't do it."

"Let's try a different tack. Do you mind if I ask you some questions about your husband's family?"

"Not at all; he doesn't have any family to speak of except for us."

"What was his relationship with his mother?"

"I knew you'd ask that. Like many black men, he had a mother who was done in, I think, by alcohol and maybe drugs too, and he came up with another relative as his mother figure. For Sunday, it was his sister."

Greta stopped dead. She stared at Paula with wide eyes.

"Did you say Sunday? Is that your husband's name?"

"Yes," Paula said offhandedly. "His mother named him for the day he was born. Why?"

"I knew someone named Sunday in high school. Where did he grow up?"

"Milwaukee."

Greta verified his age and the high school he had

attended. Now Paula stared at Greta, inquiringly. "What's wrong?"

"Your husband is Sunday Morgan," Greta murmured, her voice far away. "I'm sorry. I should have asked you his name at the very beginning." Greta shook her head regretfully. "I'm very sorry. I should not be doing therapy with you." Long pauses separated her sentences.

"Why not?" Paula looked mystified.

"Professional ethics compel me not to do therapy with anyone I know, or who has an intimate connection with someone I know." She spoke like an automaton. Greta had pulled so far into herself that only her professional persona could speak.

"I don't get it," Paula remonstrated. "That was thirty-some years ago. Have you even seen him since?"

"No. A couple of times in college. I went to Sequoia's funeral. That was the last time I ever saw him."

"You knew Sequoia too?" Paula sounded excited. "I think you may have a lot to add to this therapy. Did you know all our children are named after trees, in honor of her? Sequoia is a big hero in our family."

"For good reason. She is in mine too." Greta still sounded as if she was speaking through a fog. "My son is named Joshua for the same reason. Sequoia took me in for the summer before I went to college. I loved her." It was more than she should have said.

"Were you in love with Sunday?"

Another pause. "Yes."

"Well, you just might be the perfect person for me to be talking to," Paula said, strangely elated.

"Why are you so pleased about this?" Greta asked, from the same stupefied distance.

"Isn't it obvious? You could add a lot about his early years and how he looked on his childhood. You knew his mother figure. You're the perfect person to help solve this riddle."

"No, I'm not." Greta welled up, tried to hide her emotion. She glanced at her watch. Fortunately, it was the end of the therapy hour. "We need to stop now."

Paula took Greta gently by the shoulders. "Maybe I shouldn't be hugging you. But I hope you stay on. You could be a big help to us." She left, a detectible buoyancy in her step.

Greta sat down. For the better part of the next hour, she stared into space. Fortunately, she had an hour's gap before her next appointment. Her thoughts overlapped between the professional – lacerating herself for not getting the identity of Paula's husband from the beginning – and the personal. All the years she had wondered about this man, what he had done, how he had chosen to live, with what woman, with children or not.... All those answers lay available to her now from the person who could best supply them. And who wanted to, who thought it would be helpful to share this information. Why not proceed? Paula wanted to go forward, and her eyes were wide open. But no. Paula couldn't possibly appreciate the transference issues involved. Greta knew as a professional that she could not continue therapy with Paula.

Her thoughts returned to the personal. Sunday taught African-American history – what a good choice. And he had married such a strong, attractive, caring woman. He had made good choices, was a good father. Good for him, she thought. He had learned both to work and to love, that old prescription by which she measured her own failures. But wait: whatever made him obsessively unfaithful obviously interfered with his loving well.

These thoughts preoccupied Greta for all of the following week before she was to see Paula again. She was equally preoccupied with her own professional incompetence. Whatever else she had thought about herself, Greta tended to take for granted her professional competence. It was an arena of comfort, a place she could always go, even when she felt she had made a mess of her emotional life, had not formed a loving connection with a man, or had made errors of judgment as a parent. She usually trusted her professional instincts, felt she could intuit the right response to patients. She was good at patient relationships. Now competence was no refuge. She should have checked the names on the intake sheet when Paula first came in, instead of being so distracted by her appearance. At least she should have looked at it sometime. She should have stopped the minute she learned Sunday was Paula's husband. She should not have become enmeshed in this family that was not hers. She should have stayed away. Paula had become another loose rock underfoot as she tried to ford this stream.

One evening she sat herself down in her little study, an elbow of a room off the kitchen, and put Beethoven's Sixth on the CD player, using earphones to encapsulate herself in the music. Then she sat in front of her computer with the full intention of writing down her conflicted thoughts and making sense of them, as she sometimes did with patients who perplexed her. The music took her away, as it never failed to do, providing its own solace. She found herself remembering – it was the earphones that did it – her discovery as a child that the public library had listening chairs. On Saturdays when she was in junior high school she would sometimes take refuge at the library, check out a stack of books and a record – usually Tchaikovsky or Rachmaninoff – and sit in a comfortable chair listening to the record and reading her book for a whole afternoon. It was such a safe and enclosed environment, totally relaxed and peaceful. So too this little study, and the only sound was Beethoven. How could anyone combine order and passion and absolute confidence like Beethoven? Even after he lost his hearing, he continued to compose, with the surety of memory. She, by contrast, felt herself losing her way with Paula, too distracted, perhaps, by an appealing woman that she neglected to check for conflicts. And, even now, having discovered her mistake, she saw both that her history could in fact shed some light for Paula and the obvious fact that she couldn't trust herself to participate objectively in this enlightenment. As much as she might want for herself to know more, she could not aid Paula professionally because she could not act *for* Paula without injecting herself. And to whatever extent she might expose herself to learning more, she would be picking the scab off an old and deep wound. Greta did not trust herself not to find Sunday attractive even now. It would be only too easy to compound her mistakes and make more of a hash of this situation than she had already done. She must clearly withdraw from treatment with Paula.

Imbued with the confidence of this decision, she went to bed and fell asleep without difficulty.

Greta awoke the next morning from a deep, untroubled sleep. As she washed her face, she realized she had dreamt of Sunday. He had come to her as a client, under a different name, and then revealed himself after he arrived in her office. He was now handsome, lean but not scrawny as he had been at seventeen. His eyes reflected not only the quick intelligence he had always had, but warmth and openness and wisdom. He was graying, with a distinctive white spot on the left side of his head just over his ear. Yet he had no wrinkles, except the smile lines bracketing his mouth. In the dream, she felt grateful, brimmingly happy, that this man today was worth all the emotion she had spent on him over the years. This was a good man. She did not lust after him. She just felt happy to see him and know these things about him. They shook hands, then hugged, then just smiled at one another without saying anything for a long time.

Greta went to work that day with optimism and confidence, working with absolute concentration and clarity with her clients. She also forgot to call Paula to cancel their appointment for the following day.

Paula came in the next day with a determined air, taking over conversation from the instant she walked into Greta's office, overtaking Greta's resolve.

"I've thought about this all week, and I'm convinced you're the perfect person to help me.

I realize you might not be totally objective about those early years because of your own relationship with him, but I want your help. Besides, I've talked to Sunday about you. I didn't tell him you were my therapist, but I asked him if he remembered you from high school."

Paula gazed intently at Greta. "He doesn't remember you."

Greta dropped her pen. She bent over as if to pick it up. She felt as if her eyes had swum out of their sockets and flowed onto the floor. She could not look at the person who blew this poison dart. She could not even catch her breath. Greta needed to clear her head, stop the welling in her throat and eyes. Still bent over, she wondered if she could go on. She could have prevented this encounter with a telephone call, and now the wound was bleeding.

"Well, it was a very long time ago," Greta murmured. *How could he not remember?* Was that really possible? A hard irony to swallow, considering how much his memory had driven her all these years. It must be a lie. How far must he have traveled if he truly could not remember? He was lying. He wasn't. Greta desperately tried to recover her professional persona. Paula's answer had only revealed all the reasons she should not go down this path.

"Do you believe him?" Even as she asked, Greta realized the question triangulated them, drove a wedge between client and client's husband. It suggested her husband was lying. It was unfair. Or maybe not. Maybe it was just seeking an answer, a gauge of the communication between this woman and her husband. Greta felt her professional rudder slipping in this unfamiliar current. She should end this therapy, before she did any harm.

"Yes, I believe him. In all these years, I believe he has never lied to me."

Cheated, but not lied? The professional struggling to resurface, Greta told herself that even if Sunday Morgan did not remember her, she remembered him. And because of that, she could not ethically continue this therapy.

"I cannot help you, Paula. You need to find a new therapist."

Paula herself began to cry. Her eyes reddened, and a tear rolled down her cheek without her wiping it away. "I really think you can help. I'm *relieved* you remember him. I think you can help me understand."

Greta heard herself relenting, despite what she had just said. She told Paula she would think it over. She would call Paula with her decision. Even now, she could not fathom how she had moved away from her clear decision. It was unquestionably unethical for her to continue as Paula's therapist.

Driving home, Greta turned down the wrong street and forgot to stop for groceries. Only as she was opening the garage door did she remember she had not shopped. She closed the garage door again and drove to Safeway, where she wandered the aisles in such a state of distraction that she could not even think what to make for her and Joshua's dinner. She emerged from the store with a frozen pizza, orange juice, and a large box of laundry soap she did not need.

That Sunday Morgan lived in her own community, taught African-American history at Berkeley, was an astonishing – a monumental - coincidence.

That she should be doing therapy with his wife was beyond her imagination. Her powerful desire to know more about him overtook her. If she wished, she could drive past his house and catch a glimpse of him. But no, she would not do that. She would muster at least that much self-control.

This time, Greta did telephone Paula, half-terrified that Sunday himself would answer the telephone. Paula answered.

"Paula, it's Greta Reinhardt."

"Hi! Have you reconsidered? I so hope that's why you're calling me."

"No, Paula, I have to discontinue therapy with you. It wouldn't be appropriate to continue." She couldn't bring herself to say 'unethical.' "I'm sorry. I'll be happy to help you find another therapist who can work with you objectively."

"Another therapist wouldn't be you. It's you I want to help me. Won't you see me at least one more time, to help me through this issue?"

"All right." Greta felt obliged to see her once more, if for no other reason than to bring their therapy to a thoughtful conclusion. It was her own error that had created this problem. They agreed on a final appointment date.

34
Joshua

He stood next to Cedar as she opened her locker and pulled out her grey jacket and the books she would need for tomorrow. He stared at the even line of fine hair down the center of the back of her neck. He wanted to run his finger down that line. She turned around suddenly and asked if he would come to her house this afternoon to study. She offered no reason. He liked that about her; just when he thought he knew her habits, she would come up with something completely new.

"Sure."

"Follow me."

"Don't I always?"

She turned toward him, her eyes serious. "No, you don't. I wouldn't like it if you did."

Cedar lived within walking distance of school. As she opened the front door, Joshua thought he could smell turpentine.

"What's that smell?"

"I'll show you." She led him into a sunny room in the back. In it, an easel faced a back garden. A woman with huge, messy hair that glowed around the edges from the sun behind her, sat painting something unrecognizable on a canvas. She turned around, and he saw that she had yellow eyes, like his cat.

"You must be Joshua," she said. "I'm Paula, Cedar's mother. I'm glad to meet you."

"Hi. What are you painting?"

"I don't know yet." Seeing the quizzical look on his face, she added, "That must seem strange to you, but I often don't know what it will be until it's finished."

"I like the colors," he said, tilting his head.

Paula just laughed. "You're tactful," she said.

"C'mon." Cedar took his hand and led him into a different room. He looked around. It was full of books. On three sides, nothing but bookshelves. The fourth wall had more bookshelves, but there was a window and a desk in front of it. Another desk sat diagonally in the corner.

"This is a very serious room."

"It's my dad's study. I use it when he isn't here or if he's here and I'm able to read quietly, he lets me stay. You can use that desk." She gestured to the one in the corner and turned on the desk lamp for him. She sat down at her dad's own bigger desk and unceremoniously opened her geometry book.

"Is he away?"

"No, silly. He'll be home for dinner." She turned around to face him. "Will you stay for dinner?"

He nodded. "I'll call my mom."

He left a message on her office line that he would be eating dinner with Cedar and her family and home afterward.

Cedar looked intent on geometry. She drew shapes on a pad of lined paper. He couldn't stop watching her. She held her pencil weirdly, two fingers draped over it instead of one. He could no longer see the line of hair down the back of her neck, but watched the slight movement of her shoulder bone as she wrote. There was no chance he could concentrate on his own homework. He looked around at the books in the room, all neatly arranged by author and subject, like the books in his mother's office. These were mostly history, though. He wondered what her father did, but suspected she didn't want to be interrupted with the question, so he took out his own American History text and tried to read his assignment, about cotton, and the role it had played in causing the Civil War.

But it was impossible for him to study at her house. Pretty soon, her older brother Douglass came in, looked around the library and left without saying a word when he saw both desks occupied. And then her little sister Linden came in carrying a violin case. She curled her fingers around Cedar's head and kissed her on the cheek, then noticed him in the corner.

"You must be Josh," she said, without missing a beat. "Hi." Then she too left. He wondered what it must be like to live in a home with so many people in it. It must be distracting, he thought, though Cedar seemed not to mind.

Finally, when Josh was starting to wonder when dinner happened in this family, her dad came in.

"Hello, everybody," he called out noisily. Everybody came out of their various rooms to greet him, except for Cedar, who started to gather up her things from his desk. Her dad came into the room and touched the back of her neck gently. Just the spot Josh had been watching for the last two hours. "How's my girl," he said in a warm, deep voice.

"Hi, Daddy." She turned around and gave him a hug.

"Meet Josh," she said, and they both turned toward him in the corner.

Josh got up and shook her father's hand. How tall he was! And surprisingly dark, considering the color of the rest of his family.

"Welcome, Josh. I'm glad to get the chance to meet you." Everybody in the family seemed to know who he was.

At dinner, Cedar's dad asked him what he had been studying this afternoon. When he said the Civil War, Douglass and Linden smirked and rolled their eyes as if to say 'here we go again.' Cedar just looked down at her plate.

"I can't understand why cotton was a factor in starting the war." All three children turned toward their father, waiting for the lecture.

"Well, it wasn't a spark like the shooting of John Brown, but it was a key economic factor. Have you ever seen a cotton bush or tried to pick cotton?"

Josh shook his head.

"It tears up your fingers. It's work you couldn't pay anyone to do; only slaves would pick it."

"Sort of like the Mexican farmworkers here in the valley."

"Yes, that's a good analogy. It's backbreaking stoop labor that no one here wants to do. Cotton was big business, for this whole country, and for Europe too; everyone wore it. So the South needed their slaves, and it was easy for the North to be sanctimonious about it, because they didn't need slaves for their economy. The South continued to finance the war by selling its cotton to England and France."

"But why did England keep buying it? Didn't England abolish slavery earlier, in the 1830s?"

"Good point, they did. But England needed its cotton, and it was convenient to get it from this country. If they'd boycotted cotton from the South, we might not have had a war."

"Like our boycotting goods from South Africa during Apartheid?"

"Yeah. Too bad they didn't have a chance to learn from the future."

As he left their home after dinner, Josh told Cedar how helpful and interesting her dad had been in discussing the Civil War. "He should teach it." Cedar almost bent over laughing.

"He does," she said, "at Berkeley."

He turned red and reached for the door.

"I'm not laughing at you. He always finds a way to talk about history; it's a family joke. He must love you for bringing it up."

On the bus ride home, Josh read the rest of the chapter he couldn't focus on before dinner. He bounded up the stairs to his mother's flat, in love with all of Cedar's family. Although his mom called hello as he came in, he was suddenly conscious of how solitary a place this was. His mom sat reading in a corner of the living room, her feet curled under her. One lamp shone over her shoulder and the rest of the room was dark, still and lonely like a Hopper painting. She asked him how his day was, and about the evening, but all he said was 'fine.' He didn't want to dilute or expose or in any way alter by description the experience he had just had with Cedar's family.

35
Greta

Paula came in talking so rapidly that Greta could barely say hello.

"There's something I need to tell you," Paula announced.

Greta began to laugh idiotically. "You mean there's more?"

Paula smiled but did not join her laughter.

"I didn't tell you the truth last week when we met. I told you Sunday doesn't remember you because I so much wanted you to continue as my therapist. I thought somehow that might help persuade you to continue. I can see that you cared about him deeply - I knew that much from Sunday himself – and I can tell you still care about him. It may seem odd to you, but that's one of the reasons I want you to continue. I think you can help. And I trust you."

Greta looked at Paula guardedly.

"I'm sorry I lied to you," Paula said. "I must have hurt you. I thought if I told you he didn't remember, you would stay on with me. Of course Sunday remembers you. I don't know if you realize how powerful an influence you were on his life. He was more in love with you than he could admit at the time. I can tell you stories about the word games you played with your parents – remember Roots and Limbs, Branches and Vines?" Without pausing for Greta to answer, she continued, "I know what you wore to the prom, how you studied together and comforted each other when you didn't get into the college you each wanted. I know all these things. I've known them for years. Do you think for one second that this man does not remember you? I only said it to try to get you to continue. I clearly shouldn't have done it."

"How do I know you won't just tell me whatever you think I want to hear so that I will continue?"

Paula looked down at her lap. For a while, she said nothing.

"I'm not the solution to your riddle." Greta tried to keep up her professional front, but she could not leave it at that. "I don't appreciate your lying to me about Sunday, and I'm sitting here wondering if you knew who I was before you even called to see me."

"I can expl..."

"We need to stop now," Greta interrupted her. "I don't want you to explain."

Paula got up, slowly put on her coat, then hesitated, as if she were going to hug Greta and then thought better of it. She closed the door quietly behind herself.

Greta sat still for a long time, staring mindlessly into space. Her eyes went to the Sequoia tree that had been growing in the corner of her office for almost twenty years now. Soon after moving to San Francisco, she had bought it at Muir Woods as a little slab of bark with green twigs, intending to install it in her office as a sort of totem. It had grown strong and tall and straight, in front of the window behind her chair, as if Sequoia were looking over her shoulder. She felt anything but strong and tall now. The whole episode with Paula had been profoundly confusing. Had Paula just played her, trying to see who it was that Sunday had loved before her? Had Paula hid the truth for the reason she had given, hoping she could help Sunday professionally? Greta knew she'd made a professional mistake, but Paula was no victim. Just what bargain was it that she and Sunday had struck with each other over the years? At the moment, she did not want to know.

Greta got up to water the tree behind her, reflecting on how much like Sequoia she herself had become: contained, self-reliant, and solitary, pouring all her loving energy into her son. She had never taken Sequoia's advice to reconnect with her parents.

Odd that Paula mentioned "Roots and Limbs, Branches and Vines." It was a game Greta's parents made up in their early days in the little hut in Nevada, and then played with each other all during her childhood. It was a game of connectedness, of belonging or not. One person mentioned four things, and the other had to say which word did not belong, and why. There could be several right answers in any group, depending on whether one had a good enough reason to group or exclude. With roots, limbs, branches and vines, one could exclude vines because all the rest were parts of trees, or exclude roots because all the others were above ground. Her father tended to use biology as a criterion, her mother, linguistics. One of his games came to mind: titmouse, bush tit, bush mouse and wren. He and her mother had argued – or were they bantering? – over that for a long time. According to his logic, all were birds except the mouse. According to her mother, all had common word parts except wren. Her mother never allowed herself to be wrong. Her own puzzles were maddeningly tough: cattails, catnip, catkins, catalya. All plants. But the last had three syllables. Greta recalled her own first entry into the game: brown, black, grizzly, and red. Her mother excluded grizzly because it wasn't a color; her father excluded red because there were no red bears. Her mother insisted that there were red bears (weren't there cinnamon bears?) and that Gretchen simply didn't know how to play the game.

Norma (it was so much more comfortable to think of her as Norma, not her mother) seemed at this moment small and distant, not worth losing her father over. Greta could not summon up a sufficient memory of her childhood fear to justify the sense of betrayal she had felt as a child from her father. On the other hand, she could hear Sequoia's advice to reconnect with her father as if Sequoia were standing here today. Greta recalled her fury at Norma for cutting off her relationship with Sunday, but she had long ago recognized that he was on his way out the door regardless of Norma. Sunday had left for his own reasons, whatever they were.

Greta began to sob, big, hiccupping, wrenching gulps of breath and tears. All those losses, avoidable and unavoidable. And now here was Sunday, reappearing after more than thirty years, with a memory of her as detailed as hers of him. And children named after trees, like Joshua, because of Sequoia.

Paula did not easily let go. She telephoned Greta two days later.

"We didn't finish our session."

"I think we did."

"I don't know any more if this is personal or professional, but I still think you can help. There's something more I want to tell you, and see what you think."

"I don't think…"

"Please." This time Paula interrupted her, and she allowed herself to be talked into scheduling another final session.

Even before she sat down, Paula asserted, "I still think you can help."

Greta looked at Paula directly, for a long moment, with compassion. "If you think I am somehow the clue to solving this riddle, we may both be fooling ourselves. And I as a professional may not know to what extent I am participating in the fallacy."

"It doesn't matter. You have so much background knowledge; I know you can add something, whether it's professional or not."

"How?"

"I'm going to tell you something."

Greta waited, looking at Paula skeptically.

"He's always felt he lacked courage."

"How so?"

"For not coming back to you."

"That's nonsense; he went to Mississippi that dangerous summer." But she knew it was a lie, tactful perhaps, but a lie to cloak her own accusation that he had lacked courage to pursue their relationship back in those days when it would have taken courage to stay together. As if her mind had been etherized for the past few months, Greta began to wonder if this question of Sunday's courage was what had brought Paula here from the beginning. It certainly wasn't any preposterous generosity on Paula's part. Was Paula someone with risky curiosity? Was that why Sunday always told her about his affairs afterward? Did Paula get off on that? Or did Paula somehow actually think she could restore Sunday's fidelity by talking with her?

"Did you come here to seek help for him rather than for you? Is there something you wanted me to do?"

"I'm not sure. I wanted to see you. I wanted to see why he has been so preoccupied all these years, and to decide for myself whether he made the wrong choice."

"Have you decided?" Greta asked. How many wives would have faced such a question, she wondered. No one but Paula would have done it.

"What do you think?"

"I don't think he made the wrong choice at all. You describe a mostly happy marriage. Who's to say he and I would have been as successful?" Greta paused, pushing back unwonted memories (the ringlet of hair on Sunday's cheek came unbidden to mind, and she brushed her own cheek as if to remove it). What do I know about what makes a long marriage work, she thought. Recovering some professional thread to this conversation, she asked, "Isn't the question, really, whether you believe *you* made the right choice?"

"That's a circle: I did only if he did. But coming back to your other question, yes, there is something I want you to do." Paula stared at her with leonine huntress fixity. "I want you to see him."

Greta inhaled audibly, then held her breath, the withheld exhalation in yoga exercises. When she exhaled, she had recovered her stillness. Air filled her lungs again, this time without effort, and flowed back out again without conscious thought.

"None of us can know what will come of that. I'm more frightened of that than you apparently are." Greta realized she had said "will," not "would."

Paula looked at her with all the intensity of those fierce, tawny eyes. She shook her head, throwing her mane over her shoulder.

"I'm ready for it." Her mien left no doubt that was true.

"I'm not. I think Sunday must have found his courage in you. And I think we need to stop any pretense of my doing therapy with you. I think you've been leading these sessions from the beginning."

Paula smiled broadly. "My time has not been wasted."

At home that evening, Greta thought what courage it must have taken for Paula to seek her out like this. To want to know is one thing, but to take it to the step of forcing a new meeting.... Not many people would make that decision. She had no idea what she would do if she were Paula.

For herself, she thought that no good could come of her seeing Sunday again. She had already formed a negative opinion of him based on his philandering. If she disliked the man she now saw, she suspected he would make a mockery of too much of what she had held dear all her adult life.

Under the shelter of Sequoia, she and Sunday had shared no more and no less than all of their vulnerable, small lives up to that time. From the moment they had read together in Mr. Vitelli's class, it was as if they had recognized themselves in each other. Like reading the best of books and discovering with a silent and private joy that she was not alone on this earth; another being inhabited these pages who thought and felt as she did. It had been so easy for her and Sunday to spend time together; it was both as if they had always known each other and as if they were discovering another parallel world at the same time. His past had put hers into perspective. She had thought they were walking into their futures together, until she tried to embrace him as he got off that bus from Mississippi. His gaunt and hollow-eyed body was inaccessible. The book had shut, and she had never been able to reopen it.

It would be even worse if she now found him attractive, and instinctively she knew she would be attracted by him as a mature and accomplished adult. By whatever subtlety of Paula's that had drawn her into Sunday's family, she could not let herself be drawn in further. If she found him attractive, she did not trust herself to stay away. It was bad enough that she had continued her sessions with Paula after knowing of the connection; it would be that much worse for her to see him again. Greta knew it was best to stay as far away as she could from this proposition of Paula's.

36
Sunday

In high spirits, Sunday drove vaguely northward out of Boise. The conference had gone well and had ended. He had no more obligations before flying home tomorrow afternoon. It was a late Saturday afternoon in April. The winding, two-lane road paralleled a river bordered by aspens, just leafed-out, their new green back-lit by the slanting sun. With him was Marsha, a colleague he had known and liked for years, who for once had come to the conference without her husband. They had decided to drive out into the country a bit and then return for dinner. After dinner, who knew? The afternoon billowed with possibility like a spinnaker. Suffused with a sense of well being, he hung his arm out the driver's window, registering how good his eggplant-colored shirt looked against his dark, sun-burnished skin.

Marsha fed a Bruce Springsteen CD into the player. "Nostalgia," she smiled. She was just that much younger than he. Nostalgia for him roused Marvin Gaye and Tammi Tarrell, maybe The Four Tops. Marsha crossed her bare pale legs and leaned back, her fingers beating a small rhythm on the handrest between them. He glanced over at her breeze-blown sandy-colored hair, no gray yet. And few wrinkles, except at the outer corners of her eyes when she laughed, or furrowed her brow to think over a point in conversation.

"Do we know where we're going?" She asked.

"Yes. We're following this river to see where it leads."

"Perfect."

And so they wound their way into the dusk, watching the glinting aspens and river on their left and occasional farms on their right. There were almost no other cars on the road, which made the two city-dwellers feel privileged and quite apart from their normal lives.

After some distance on the curving road, Sunday spotted a vehicle in the distance behind him, a pickup truck. It gained on them steadily, apparently some local intent on getting home for dinner. And then it was on their rear bumper, aggressively close. Sunday searched for a wide shoulder on the right so that he could pull over and let the impatient truck driver pass. But for some distance the road snaked on narrow turns and afforded no place to pull over on the right. Finally, as the road straightened a bit, Sunday could see a small dirt road leading off to his right, ahead of them. He lit his turn signal and headed for it, to let the truck pass.

As the truck slid by them, Sunday glanced to his left. A pale, raw-boned man with eyes squinted in anger glared back at him. 'Dirty nigger.' Sunday could read this on the truck driver's lips without even trying.

Instead of speeding ahead, the truck pulled in

on the right shoulder ahead of Sunday and Marsha, and started to back up fast. Dust swirled around the rear of the pickup.

Instinctively, Sunday closed the windows and locked the car.

"I think our drive is over." As quickly as he could, he put the car into reverse to turn around and drive back. But the truck pulled in aslant in front of the car and stopped, blocking them. The driver got out. He loped toward them in a country walk. Scrawny was the word that came to Sunday as they watched him approach. He wore a faded red plaid shirt, unevenly buttoned and one side hanging out over his loose, hip-sliding jeans. On his left side was a leather sheath for a long knife, with a bone handle sticking out the top. The driver fingered it twitchily.

"Open the fuckin' window, nigger." He leaned over the driver's side of their car.

Reflexively, Sunday opened it, just as Marsha started to tell him not to. "Sunday, don't do it. Let me try to talk to him," she was saying. Sunday's mind was quickly receding into Mississippi, slowing him, mesmerizing him.

"Whatcha think you're doin' in my country with your white 'hore. It makes me sick."

"We are old colleagues and good friends. I'm here because I want to be, and I'm not anyone's whore," Marsha told him with quiet authority before Sunday could string any words together. "We didn't do anything to bother you and would appreciate you're leaving us alone."

"Bother me," he screwed up his face as if from a bad smell. "It bothers the shit out of me that you two come up here and think you can do your dirty business in my country."

Suddenly the driver had their door open and was pulling Sunday out, his right hand clutching Sunday's neck. The foot-long knife was in the driver's left hand. He gripped it as if it were part of his own body, pointing it first at Sunday's neck and next at his groin. The blade was filthy and crusted. Idiotically, its filth terrified Sunday, as if it mattered whether he would be dismembered by a clean or filthy knife.

All self-possession, Marsha was out of the car on the passenger side, holding her cell phone aloft.

"I just dialed 911. If you put that knife down, get back into your truck and drive away right now, we'll forget this incident happened and nothing bad will happen to you."

"Heh." The driver spat. "You think you're goin' to git any reception on that thing here? Just try." In an instant, he was in front of her. He seized the cell phone and threw it into the ditch behind her. He backslapped her face with his right hand.

"You stay outta this, whore."

Though taller than the driver, Sunday felt impaled in place, without strategy. He caught Marsha's eye and signaled her with a tilt of his head to run, just as the driver circled their car and pointed the knife again at Sunday's throat. All he could think of was his inevitable brutal death in the next few minutes or hours. He smelled sweat and stale alcohol on the driver's breath.

"Keep her out of this." Sunday recovered his voice.

The driver swiftly kneed him in the groin. As Sunday doubled over, he took a hard blow to his chin, knocking him to the ground. Another idiotic thought flitted through Sunday's brain: he had never been in a fight before in his whole life. So this is how it was. He crumpled into a lump on the ground, knees under him and arms around his head. He thought he could hear Marsha running away, back toward Boise.

With a flick of his knife, the driver split open Sunday's shirt, along his spine. He waited for the man to start carving up his back. What should I be doing, he kept asking himself and finding no answer.

"Heh. You're a fuckin' coward, too." With that, he kicked Sunday in his right ear. Sunday's legs reflexively stretched out, accidentally tripping the driver. He toppled like an old fence post. There was an elongated moment of stupid surprise on both of their faces. Then Sunday was on his feet. In falling, the driver had dropped his knife. Now Sunday grasped it in his right hand, testing his grip and the effect it had on the driver.

"I'm going to give you a second chance to stay out of trouble. Get back into your truck and drive away."

The driver sat with his legs bent in front of him, his arms on the ground beside him. Sunday did not know whether he was going to spring up and charge him, walk to his car, or just sit there and taunt him some more. The driver squinted, his lips curled down, hate emanating from him like a stink. Sunday realized slowly that he was shaking and that the man was not moving. He stood and the other man just stared at him for what seemed an eternity. Would he have to use this knife to save himself?

A sound intruded from outside the lock of their attention. An approaching car. The driver cocked his head, disbelieving. He got up slowly, wiping his hands on the dusty legs of his jeans.

A county sheriff's car loomed fast upon them, screaming to a stop between them and the road. The officer leapt out with gun drawn. For an instant, Sunday wondered if now he would be shot, since he was holding the knife. He lifted his arms slowly. Then he noticed Marsha in the car.

"Hold it right there." The officer was talking to the driver, not to Sunday.

The driver started to run for his truck.

"I said 'hold it right there!'" He raised his pistol. The driver did not stop.

The pistol cracked out two shots. The driver, one leg on the driver's seat, dropped the other, his left jeans leg darkening toward his ankle.

Marsha was out of the car, her arms around Sunday. "I felt so bad for running away; can you ever forgive me?" He looked at her in disbelief and started to heave. His shoulders shook uncontrollably. He wept. He wept until he had to seize breath and hiccups began.

"Forgive you? You have it all wrong. I was a coward. You were a lion compared to me."

Soon there was a siren, a second county sheriff's car, and the driver was taken away in handcuffs in it. Police tape was strung up, officers walked the area, searching the ditch. Sunday was helped into the sheriff's car while Marsha walked to their car. "This way, Sir," the officer had said to him. Sir: he was not expecting that. On the way to the Boise police station, he passed into a temporary but deep sleep. On waking, it was as if he had not slept. He read the words on a billboard they passed on the way into the city: "Find Your Best Life Here."

Sunday apologized again to Marsha at the police station. She was quiet but still apparently calm. He asked to call his wife. He was told they would need to give statements first. Randomly, he wondered if he could ever feel carefree again.

At the police station, he and Marsha were separated and each questioned in separate rooms. Sunday remembered the courtesy of the officers, the fact that they brought him coffee and a hamburger, but not much of the statement he gave. He and Marsha were released separately late that evening and driven separately back to their hotel.

He telephoned Paula from his hotel room. At the sound of her voice, his voice broke. He could barely tell her what had happened. "Come home," she told him, again and again, her strong voice a balm. Without seeing Marsha again, Sunday caught his scheduled plane home the next afternoon.

37
Greta

Greta's answering service phoned her early Sunday morning, as she and Joshua were having breakfast. Paula Hartwell had called at 6:48 this morning, said it was urgent. For some clients, every bump in the road was an emergency, and they could wait. But Paula Hartwell was different. She would not call early on a Sunday morning unless something were truly urgent. Greta excused herself to Joshua and phoned Paula from her study.

"Something terrible has happened to Sunday, and he needs to talk to you as soon as possible."

"Why?" For a split second Greta doubted her. Then she recovered. "Has he been hurt?"

"Not physically, but he's devastated. I've never heard him so despondent; he needs to speak to a professional immediately, and you would be the best person, for any number of reasons."

"What happened?"

Paula told her he had been at a conference in Boise, had taken a drive Saturday afternoon or evening with a white woman and some bigot had pulled them over, threatened them with a knife and roughed them up. Sunday was remorseful, frightened to the core. Greta gasped.

"Greta, I've never heard him this way. He sounds so ..." she paused. "Broken. He needs to speak to someone. You know his history; you would be the perfect person."

Greta's mind roiled with a memory of Sunday at the end of his Mississippi summer. With every bit of professional resolve she could muster, she resisted Paula's plea.

"It's just for that reason I would be exactly the wrong person. He needs to speak to a very talented professional, but it can't be me. I can refer you to an excellent colleague. I'll call him myself as soon as we get off the line." She could hear her voice as if another person were speaking, with chilly reserve.

" I really want Sunday to speak with you. He's in crisis. Why can't you talk to him?"

"Paula, I recognize he's in crisis, and he should see someone as soon as he can. But that person cannot be me." Silence on the other end of the line. "And it's not because I don't care. I'll do my level best to get him to a very talented colleague."

Paula consented to her making the call, but sounded disappointed and a bit distrustful.

38
Paula

Waiting for Sunday's plane to land, Paula wondered if he'd had sex with his colleague. She supposed so and that it was part of his remorse. From inside, one voice said 'good; maybe he'll be scared straight.' He had provided her few details on the telephone, but he had sounded far more frightened than guilty. She tried to imagine the encounter, but it had no more reality for her than if she had seen it in a film. She would have gasped at the tense parts and gripped Sunday's hand, been outraged at the injustice of it, and taken another bite of popcorn. What preoccupied her was how profoundly frightened he had sounded. The only other time she had experienced him as frightened was when their son Douglass had been hit in the head in a soccer game and lost consciousness. Sunday's hands had trembled in the ambulance. But that had been so different - it was fear for someone else; he himself had maintained his self-possession. He had known the right questions to ask, had comforted her. The Sunday to whom she had spoken in the middle of the night lacked all confidence. However weary she was of this latest infidelity – or attempt at infidelity - she was more worried about him.

The first thing she noticed as he walked tentatively down the airport corridor was his color - he looked like burnt-out charcoal. She did not notice that the right side of his face and his ear were badly swollen, until she tried to put her hands on either side of his face and kiss him. He pulled away, wincing, then put his arms around her as if needing her to hold him upright. Paula held him for a long time, tightly, trying to transfer from her body to his all the strength and resolve she could muster.

"I love you, I love you, I'm so glad you're home safely," she repeated, though she knew he was not home safely and would need a long time of convincing before he believed that. She nestled her face in his hair, inhaling the familiar, faintly soapy sweet smell of him and ran her fingers through the soft hair at the top of his neck. "You're home; it's going to be okay."

Paula spent the day doting on him, as did their children. Linden and Cedar made him dinner, a huge sloppy bowl of pasta with meat sauce they concocted themselves. Greta had left a message with the name and telephone number of someone she said was a gifted therapist; she had already spoken to him and he had agreed to see Sunday the next day. Paula called him and made an appointment for the next day. Then she called the university and left a message in the department office that Sunday had been injured in an accident and would not be in on Monday.

39
Sunday

Sunday felt at a vast remove from all that happened. He watched Paula and his children hover around him with a vague gratitude to be among them, but to say that he felt anything was a lie. He needed this remove; it kept the fear at bay. The dusk agitated him. He walked around the house and locked all the doors, then sat in a corner of the living room where he could see in every direction. He refused to budge from his corner to go to bed. That night he barely slept. Alert to every sound, he sat in vigil for hours.

He could not face driving the car, so Paula drove him to the psychiatrist's office. Sunday did not consider himself ready to talk to a professional, could not summon the wherewithal for so much speech. But the doctor – Sunday was amazed to see he was African-American – got him talking a little. He began to describe to the therapist what had happened.

"Was anyone with you?"

"Yes. A colleague."

"Man or woman?"

"A woman. She was white," Sunday added. The therapist raised one eyebrow, as if to say, 'so?'

"You'll see why it mattered," Sunday corrected him, and told the rest of the story.

Sunday met with the therapist daily for the first week. Within the first three sessions, Sunday began to talk about Mississippi. He remembered that he had accidentally seen the bodies of James Chaney and Michael Schwermer after they had been hauled out of the river. He had been at the courthouse that day to check on whether a family of voters had been registered, had gone to the colored bathroom down a back hall and then out the side entrance just as police were wheeling in the bloated corpses. That evening, he had told this news to the family with whom he had been staying. The eldest son, then in his twenties, had taken out his wallet and showed Sunday a yellowed newspaper photo of a young black man who had been hanged some years earlier just outside their town. "Why do you keep it?" Sunday had asked. The young man looked at him solemnly and said: "I don't ever want to get too comfortable and forget."

The therapist asked him about his wife. Sunday described Paula as someone who always knew who she was and what she wanted to do; she had a contained confidence. Thin, with beautiful tawny, tangled hair that she had never bothered to straighten, creative, an artist, a fantastic cook, an excellent mother.

"How did you meet her?"

The question made Sunday smile, for he always enjoyed remembering. "Her father was one of my history professors in graduate school. He often invited small groups of graduate students to dinner, for good food and invigorating conversation. We felt privileged to be invited, since he was one of the most brilliant professors. I thought she was one of us. She was seated across the table from me, and she kept challenging me with questions, throwing her long hair back over her shoulder when she had a new idea. I couldn't stop admiring her. As we all started to leave, she remained standing in the doorway, our professor's arm over her shoulder. At first I was shocked, but I was invited back."

"Did you feel he had chosen her for you?"

"I did." Sunday paused. "Yes, I did."

"Are her parents still alive?"

"Yes, and we're both close to them. They live in D.C., but we see them several times a year, and Paula talks to her mother nearly every day."

"Is Paula white?"

"No. Well, I mean, her father is black and her mother is white."

"Do you wish she were white?"

"*No,* and I don't know why you're asking," Sunday answered irritably. The therapist did not explain himself, but moved on to other topics.

Within a week, Sunday returned to his classes. The swelling had gone down and his skin was so dark that it was hard to see the bruises on his face. The normalcy of his routine, and the interest of his students provided some comfort to him. He was in a sufficiently early part of the curriculum – the move for liberation of the American slaves – that he could keep an academic remove from the subject matter.

With ineffable gratitude, he was able to resume his sex life with Paula. During the first few days back at home, he had watched her undress at night; and it had aroused in him only a vague fear for her safety. One night in bed, Paula spooned her body behind his, and began to caress him. It was so familiar, so predictably delicious, that his body responded as before. He traced the contours of her butt - the only place, he used to joke, where she had enough fat on her to caress. He turned over and sank his face into her hair, tasting her privately. Afterward, he sighed happily. "I've come back home," he said. When he was able to respond again the following night, he laughed aloud afterwards. "I really am back home," he said.

Sunday began to think and talk with the therapist about Sequoia. At first he was preoccupied with the contrast between her strength, her courage, her resolve . . . and his weaknesses. She had been such a good role model, had shown him such good character, but he had turned out to be a coward. It was just as well, he told the therapist, she could not see him now. For hours, they talked about Sequoia. He lingered over details, how confidently she loped into a room, too tall but strangely graceful. How she had visited him every week in the orphanage, taken him out for strawberry ice cream. How she had got him out of the orphanage and into a real school while he lived with her. Without her, he surely would not even have gone to college; he would have gone to Vietnam like most of his friends from his first high school, and maybe died, as nearly half of them had. None of them had had student deferments, and they were all drafted. Sunday had not spoken this much about Sequoia in years. Of course, he had told the children about her. She held a mythical place within the family and his children could recite Sequoia family stories. But this was more like singing a family history; he had become an African griot and Sequoia was his ballad.

The therapist asked him many questions about Paula.

"Is she your soulmate?"

"No,...but being a soulmate isn't ... essential, and she's such a good wife to me."

"What are your differences?"

"Well, she has courage and I obviously don't."

"No, that wasn't what I meant," the therapist said. "Where are the distances between you, the gaps in understanding?"

After a long pause, Sunday told him, "Paula never suffered any major losses in her life. She's had two good parents who loved each other, stayed together and are still alive. She doesn't comprehend not having a mother. Her parents to this day are a source of comfort and support for her. She's never lost a man she loved ... at least so far as I know. She always told me I was her first love."

"Was she yours?"

"No." He fell silent, and the therapist looked at him expectantly.

"There was Gretchen. Quiet, intelligent, preoccupied with her own troubled family, totally captivating to me in my last year of high school. We discovered ourselves in each other; we were so close we felt related. Sorta like siblings, but way too passionate for siblings." Sunday grinned ruefully. "She loved me with all the ... fervor ... of discovering someone who could be safely loved. And I left her in fear at the end of that summer in Mississippi." Sunday shook his head.

"Because she was white. Well, not exactly because she was white; that was too simple....

Because I could not for the life of me figure out how to make it work between us. We were going to college in different parts of the country. She was bound to meet someone else. And it wasn't safe for either one of us. Look what just happened – and this is 1996."

"Would you have married her if you hadn't gone to Mississippi?"

"Probably not."

"Why not?"

"Because I completely and utterly lacked the personal resources to try to make it work. I just couldn't do it."

"Were you afraid to lose her?"

"Totally."

"So you left her instead?"

Sunday pondered this on the way home, and at odd times while he was driving or walking from class. His answers made no sense. That time had been far more perplexing than he could put into words. He found a letter Gretchen had written him a few years before Sequoia died, while they were still writing to each other. Gretchen had urged him to have confidence, to live as if anything were possible. Anything else denied life. It was a letter he had never answered. It may have been her last letter to him.

"Back to Paula: are you able to talk with her about your losses?"

Sunday realized, of course, that he had kept his losses at bay. He had told her only the bare bones of his childhood, that he had revered Sequoia and her role in his life. He had even told Paula about Gretchen, years ago when they were first courting. The subject had come up because Paula was biracial, fair-skinned, and he was so dark. He had asked her whether she identified as white, would mind being confined to his black-skinned world. She had told him she trusted they would surround themselves with good, loving and interesting people and she didn't care whether most of them were black or white. He had thought her naïve, but he had believed her. He had married her and never been sorry about his good judgment in that.

"But do you feel she doesn't understand the depth of your losses?"

"Yeah. It's not that she doesn't care. I'm grateful for her caring. But there are places inside me she just can't know."

"Do you find it safer to be with Paula because she's labeled black than it would have been if you had stayed with Gretchen?"

"Well, it *is* safer."

The therapist, maddeningly, said nothing for a moment, and then he asked, "are you testing your own boundaries or courage or something when you repeatedly take up with these white women?"

Sunday and the therapist stared at each other. Sunday found himself grow hot; he would have been red if his skin were not so dark. He knew that no one could tell when his blood came up to his face. It was an old accusation, this crossing over to see white women (although one that Paula had not made, at least not explicitly – she didn't race-base anything), and no one could accuse him as effectively as another black person. In college, a few of his classmates had been dating white women, and they were put down for it - what were they doing at Howard if they were going to sell out in their own lives? Now the therapist had said it too, albeit more elegantly, and he felt insulted and diminished. He knew he would be lying if he said that race was not a criterion in this philandering. And each time he made such a connection, he felt such a release from himself, such a surge of freedom.... He knew it would not be easy to give up this habit. He was not so sure he wanted to. These were intelligent, open-minded women, and it was an incredible stimulation to spend an evening or a weekend with them.

The therapist was silent for the remainder of the session, a long time. And for all that time, Sunday did not answer. His embarrassment dissolved into nostalgia for the elusive pleasure of his time with these women.

40
Greta

A week after the Idaho incident, Greta telephoned Paula to find out how she and Sunday were doing. Paula seemed surprised and happy to hear from her. She told Greta that Sunday liked his psychiatrist and knew he needed to see him.

"Thank you," she told Greta. "Thank you for everything." To Greta, it sounded both heartfelt and dismissive. She felt Paula was telling her she had served her purpose and was no longer needed or wanted.

"I'm glad things are working better," she said, and they hung up.

A few days later, while she was mindlessly clearing the kitchen counter next to the telephone, she found Josh's school directory in her hands and paged through it idly. For no particular reason, she looked for Cedar's contact information. Next to her photograph, in which she stared intently and unsmilingly, was a familiar telephone number. Cedar Morgan was Paula and Sunday Morgan's daughter. Greta stared at it dumbly, wondering how she could possibly not have wondered why Josh's girlfriend had a name like Cedar, or why she had forgotten Cedar's last name. She stood there for some moments – had she lost all powers of attentiveness?

41
Paula

Paula's children asked her what she wanted to do for Mother's Day. Spontaneously, she said she wanted for all of them to take a hike together. The weather was predicted to be warm, and the idea of walking outside just appealed to her. To the rest of the family, hiking seemed an odd choice; it was not something they did together. But it was Mother's Day; they would indulge her. She wanted to hike on Mt. Tamalpais, only half an hour's drive, and to paint. Often she painted outdoors and then used the palette of her paintings for new weavings. The request made them realize she had not been painting for several months, which was unusual, but none of them had noticed until she said this.

"Can we still make you breakfast?" This from Linden, at eleven their youngest, but the caretaker among them.

"Of course, honey."

Linden cracked eggs and made omelets under Sunday's supervision, while Douglass cut green onions and grated cheese. Cedar was upstairs in her bedroom, where, Paula realized, she had been spending most of her time at home.

Cedar used to hover about Paula more. When she came home from school, Cedar was the child who wanted to see what her mother was painting or drawing that day. Often, she would sit with Paula and draw after school. She drew very well, especially portraits. Cedar had a knack for observing the attitude of a body, the tilt of an eyebrow or the particular wrinkle that identified the subject. But lately Cedar came home shortly before dinner, ate with the family and then retreated to her room. She did not seem unhappy, only distant. Paula made a mental note to try to draw her out more and find out what was on her mind.

Today Sunday had to call Cedar to breakfast. Paula watched her daughter come down the stairs, her hands behind her back. She had the self-possession of a young woman, Paula thought, not a girl; and she noticed with discomfiting recognition Cedar's erect nipples through her small tank top.

Cedar slipped a card in front of her mother's plate and sat down at the table. Paula could see that Cedar had made it herself. On the front was a drawing of perhaps a dozen African people sitting on the ground, the pink soles of their bare feet connected in a central circle, their toes as jaunty as embellishments atop a crown. This circle of feet was loving and playful at the same time. Paula recognized some of the faces. She was in the center of the picture, her hair a bit longer and more unruly than the rest, with her narrow face and wide smile. At her side was Sunday, darker than everyone else, also grinning broadly. Cedar, Linden and Douglass were also readily recognizable. A silver-haired woman with exceptionally long legs was also in the circle.

"Is that Sequoia?" Paula asked.

"Of course." Cedar grinned.

Paula found her own parents in the drawing, looking as they had in their fiftieth anniversary photo. And there were other young people, not all of whom she recognized.

"Who are the others?"

Cedar pointed out Linden's best friend Audrey, whose white skin and pale hair had been darkened for continuity, and Douglass' best friend Toby, similarly altered. "And that's Josh, with his back to us." He had somehow replaced Cedar's best friend Dusky. The whole circle had been beautifully and painstakingly done. Inside, Cedar had written, "We are a circle of love."

Paula was moved. Sunday looked over her shoulder, reading the card.

Cedar explained to them the people in the circle were playing an African game called "Osani." Each person in the circle must name something round, like the sun or moon or a bicycle wheel. In the next round, each person must name some 'round' association, like the family circle, a circle of friends, a sewing circle, a ring around the moon, the life cycle. As players fail to come up with a new 'circular' term, they drop out, and the one that remains is said to live a long and prosperous life.

"We are in fact a circle of love," Sunday said and he kissed Paula in front of their children. They giggled.

After breakfast, they piled into the car and drove across the bridge to Mt. Tamalpais. It was a day of dramatic, opaque clouds, threatening rain. Douglass didn't wanted to hike at all.

"We'll all gonna get just far enough from the car

before it starts to rain and we'll all get soaked and muddy running back."

"You won't melt if it rains," Sunday told him. "It's Mother's Day."

"It won't rain," Paula insisted.

"Look how gorgeous the sun is below those clouds!" She pointed. "I want to paint that." Cedar wanted to follow her mother and see how she translated those clouds and that light into a painting. Linden trailed behind, humming to herself.

For a while they hiked up and down crests that led to other crests, each lower and with a better view of the ocean below them. Douglass' opposition seemed to evaporate, and he and Cedar ran together along flat segments of the path. Paula found a path that she could see led down toward a rocky promontory and then further below. She wanted to go down and paint from the promontory. The path had a chain across it at the head and a 'No Trespassing' sign. Without missing a beat, Paula climbed over the chain and Cedar followed. Douglass took a running start as if to leap over it. Just then Sunday noticed the sign.

"Paula," he called down toward her. She was already on her way down. "You can't go down there. It might not be safe." She stopped and looked up at him disbelievingly.

"Obviously, I can. And I intend to."

"I'm not going down there," Sunday pronounced, as if it would stop them all. He took hold of Linden's hand just as she was about to walk around the pole holding the chain.

Douglass stopped short of the chain. "C'mon,

Dad. You can see the path. There's nothing dangerous down there."

"No." Sunday sounded huffy and prim.

"Sunday, don't be silly." Paula called up from where she had stopped.

"I want you all to come back here. You don't know who owns this land or what they'll do if they find us on it." He had adopted an imperious tone, as if telling a non-registered student he couldn't sit in on his class.

They all looked at him as if he had stepped out of another century.

"Yeah," Douglass said, in full sarcasm, "an army of warriors with bows and arrows will appear from just beyond that ridge and scalp us all." Still, he didn't move. Linden stood holding her dad's hand, waiting for the others to resolve this impasse. She had stopped humming and just looked around quizzically.

"I'm going down to paint on those rocks," Paula announced, pointing. "You can hike somewhere else that doesn't involve trespassing, and I'll meet you at the head of the path in an hour." She and Cedar continued on their way.

Douglass took a step, as if toward the chain.

"NO!" Sunday yelled. Douglass turned around and stopped.

"Why are you making such an issue of this? It's just a path." His face was losing its bravado. He wasn't used to his parents arguing, especially over something so arbitrary and simple.

"It's not safe." Sunday, still tugging Linden by her hand, laid his hand like an injunction upon Douglass' shoulder. So the two children followed him sullenly on a quite boring hike in a circle on the crest overlooking the rocks where Paula contentedly set up her easel and chatted happily with Cedar. Sunday looked down at them furtively at regular intervals.

After an hour – Sunday looked at his watch to make sure he did not return early – he and the two children returned to the head of the path and waited for Paula and Cedar to come up. Cedar turned her head and saw them; Sunday could see her turn back to her mother and say something but Paula did not turn around and she did not stop painting. The sun was starting to sink below the heavy cloud layer. A spectacular fan of golden rays leaked through a slit in the lowest cloud layer and lit the dark water.

"Paula," Sunday called, as if she had not noticed him. Cedar got up and started to pick up her jacket, but Paula kept painting as if nothing had interrupted her. Sunday could see Cedar say something to her mother and then start up the path herself, but Paula continued, undisturbed. When Cedar got to where her father was standing, he had his hands on his hips and an exasperated look in his slitted eyes.

"She said to tell you the light is really special and she wants to catch it," Cedar reported. "We should hike some more and come back in half an hour." Cedar tugged gently on her father's arm, but he jerked it away.

"It's time to go back."

"Dad, look at that light. Can't you see why she wants to paint it?" The four of them stood for a few moments, facing the ocean, Linden fidgeting with the tassel on her jacket, Douglass looking back and forth at his distanced parents, and Cedar admiring the glinting sun on the darkening water. None of them moved for several long minutes, and no words passed between them. Finally, Cedar challenged Douglass to a race to a boulder some hundred yards off. The two of them took off with whoops and dares, their knees rising high as they galloped along the hillside, a pair of chestnut colts.

Linden reached for her father's hand, but his hands were still lodged on his hips. Finally, he relented and took her hand. They watched together as Paula leisurely packed her canvas and paints and began to hike up toward them. She looked back for a moment at intervals, to catch another glimpse of the changes in the sun.

"It was glorious!" She said triumphantly, as she stepped back over the chain. Sunday said nothing. Douglass and Cedar returned, panting and grinning.

The children led the way back down the hill. Sunday and Paula fell behind, intentionally.

"Don't you think you're setting a bad example crossing over that 'No Trespassing' sign?" He waited a moment for her apology. "And what about not coming back when you said you would?"

"You think you get to call all the shots about trespassing?" She hissed. "Only break the rules you want to break? Who do you think you are, acting so sanctimonious in front of them? Don't you *ever* tell *me* not to set a bad example for the children!"

42
Sunday

Sunday was subpoenaed back to Idaho in late May for the preliminary hearing. The man who had attacked him and Marsha was charged with felony assault. Sunday assumed Marsha would be called to testify as well, although he had not contacted her, nor she him, since that day. Paula asked Sunday if he wanted her to come with him, but he could tell from the way she asked him – she was facing another direction and looking for some kitchen utensil in a drawer – that she had her own doubts about going. He told her no, she should stay with the children and he would manage it himself. He and Paula had not made amends for their argument ten days ago on Mother's Day. He thought she should have been more understanding of his fears – he was facing the subpoena even then and he got nervous anytime he was in a country setting, outside the city – and he thought she was, consciously or not, challenging him that day. Also, it was obvious to him that she still harbored resentment over his dalliances. How could she not?

He didn't trust himself about any aspect of this trip. Not only would he have to retell what had happened that day, he would also have to face his tormentor again. He harbored a deep sense of embarrassment, bordering on shame, on how feeble he had been in the face of a physical threat from a man much smaller than himself. He expected he would have to look at the man's face as he answered questions from both the prosecutor and defense counsel. He didn't trust his own ability to string words together into sentences in front of that man. And he would have to speak with Marsha again. He did not trust himself around her either. He feared his own capacity to walk to a witness stand, face both Marsha and that man, and answer questions about why he was on that road with her and what that man had done to him to punish him for it.

Of course he had spoken with his therapist about the upcoming hearing. But Sunday felt no support from him. The therapist had asked him to be aware of how he felt toward Marsha when he saw her again, and to come back and report to him on his own observations. *This wasn't a birdwatching hike*, he wanted to shout at the therapist, but he had said nothing.

His children, as it turned out, gave him the most support. They knew only that he would have to testify against the man who had attacked him and that the attacker would be there too. The night before he left, Douglass asked him if he was worried about what he would have to do. Douglass said he would be terrified if he had to do it, and Sunday acknowledged he was pretty scared himself. Cedar handed him a tiny package wrapped in white tissue paper and tied with a string. "Open it on the plane," she said, "and hold it in your hand in court." Linden just clung to him as he left the house.

Paula embraced him as he left, but there was no heart in it. "I hope this will make a difference," she whispered.

Cedar's gift was a small black beach stone, on which she had lettered in white pen, "COURAGE." He kept it in his pocket on the plane and in court, a tiny counterweight to his lofting fears.

He'd made arrangements to stay at a different hotel in Boise than he had stayed in before while at the conference. The district attorney met with him for several hours the day before he had to testify and rehearsed the questions he would ask him, along with the less friendly and more direct questions the defense attorney would likely put to him. He'd felt prepared.

The hearing itself took place in a nearly empty courtroom, before a judge with a disconcertingly childlike face, although the man must have been in his mid-forties. Witnesses were brought in separately. The only time he saw Marsha was in the moments before he was ushered in to testify, while she sat on a bench outside the courtroom, waiting for her turn. Her head down, she pretended to read a book on her lap, and they did not even look at each other.

Sunday was led so efficiently to the witness stand, where he swore on an old Bible held out before him to tell the truth, the whole truth and nothing but the truth, so help me God, that he did not even have a chance to look around the courtroom beforehand. He was on the witness stand, seated in an overlarge hardwood chair with just one armrest connecting to a flat surface, like a child's school desk. The judge sat about six feet to his right, at the same elevated level as he was, and the rest of the courtroom sat below them. At first he barely noticed the defendant; there were two tables with men in suits, and he recognized the district attorney at one of them. The judge – whose deep voice belied his childlike face – called the case, "The People vs. Fallows," and read the charges – aggravated assault and assault with a deadly weapon. Then the District Attorney stood up and walked toward him. Sunday felt a little better to see this slightly familiar figure approach him. The questions were simple, his answers rehearsed, and he began to feel relieved to be reciting rather than reliving what had happened that day. When the District Attorney finished, Sunday had begun to feel a little more comfortable at the tidiness of his presentation, and he surprised himself at how distanced he felt from the incident itself. Only once had he looked at the defendant, when asked to identify him, and the District Attorney had prepared him for this event as well, showing him in advance the mug shot of Daniel Fallows. Glancing at the defense table, only one of the three men in a suit looked as if he had never worn one before, and even the suit could not hide the ragged hair, narrow face and slit eyes of the man who had cut open his shirt with the large knife.

The District Attorney walked back to his table and sat down. Sunday felt his breath grow shallow and more rapid. The judge addressed one of the defense attorneys, and one of these men stood up and strode – menacingly, Sunday thought – toward him. When this man said 'Mr. Morgan,' Sunday heard the threat in his tone. *Now* Sunday was transported back to the day; this had become real and somehow frightening in an unfamiliar way.

He was, of course, asked insinuatingly just what he was doing there on that road with Marsha and where, exactly, they were headed; but the District Attorney had prepared him for these questions. He answered clearly and seemingly confidently in his professor's voice that they were co-participants in a conference of history professors and had taken a drive, intending to return a little later to their conference location (he was told to say 'conference location' rather than 'hotel').

When the defense attorney began to ask about the events themselves, he parsed them out with painstaking detail. Although Sunday had wanted to glide over them as quickly as he could, the District Attorney had warned him in advance that he would have to endure this kind of cross examination; and Sunday managed to give short, unelaborated answers. He wished, though, that he had more air in his lungs; his throat grew dry and he had to ask for a glass of water. He remembered one question in particular, although there were objections and the question became several separate questions but they all boiled down to the same question. In essence, if not in words, he was asked – no, accused – of having thrown down Mr. Fallows (a much smaller and frailer man than he, it was noted), seizing his knife and threatening Mr. Fallows with his own knife.

"It didn't happen that way. The Defendant tripped over my legs and dropped his knife when he fell. I got up and picked up his knife just about the time that the officer's car appeared. I never threatened him."

"So you would have this Court believe that Mr.

Fallows just accidentally tripped over your legs and that you did nothing to knock him down."

"Yes."

For an agonizingly long time, the defense attorney - a young man, burly but wily - asked the same question over and over in different words, trying to get Sunday to admit he had sprung up and turned on his attacker. Again and again, Sunday had to admit that he had been too frightened to do so. With repetition his answers made him feel as if anyone else would have jumped up and bashed the little bigot. At some point, Sunday remembered he was asked, sarcastically: "Were you really that frightened of this little man?"

"*This little man*, as you say, wielded a very large knife, and, yes, I was frightened. I thought he would kill me with it."

The District Attorney told him afterward that that answer had nailed it, and he seemed to gloat, hitting Sunday a little too hard on the back with his congratulations. Fallows was bound over for trial. All Sunday wanted to know was whether he would have to come back again to testify at trial. The District Attorney told him that they might be able to get Fallows to plead guilty, for less hard time; but the bottom line was that he would have to return if there were a trial and then his testimony would be before a jury.

From the courthouse, Sunday went directly to his hotel, asking the cab driver to wait while he picked up his already packed and checked bag. He flew home only a day after he had left. On the airplane Sunday asked himself, over and over again, in a variety of ways, why he hadn't just jumped up and disarmed Fallows. Any excuse, any justification, only shamed him. The plain fact of the matter was that he couldn't move: he was too frightened. Sunday wished the flight had a movie to distract him, but the flight was too short for inflight entertainment. It was, however, one of the longest flights he had ever taken.

His therapist was relentless, but Sunday kept coming back. Their dialogue continued for months. Sunday dreamt he was being herded, circled, like a steer by a cowboy, but he went willingly, wanting to know where he was being driven. The Man (he had started to refer to him in conversation with Paula as "The Man" and she knew exactly what he meant by it) hounded him about race-based issues. The strange thing was: he couldn't glean what The Man himself thought. Sunday thought about his famous colleague, whose core thesis was that America is becoming a post-ethnic society, apparently one so hybridized that there could be no tidy census categories like African-American (read Black, Negro, Colored in prior versions), Asian-American (by itself so broad that it engulfed Indians, Filipinos, Japanese, Chinese, Vietnamese, Pacific Islanders and Hmong) and Caucasian. In that America we would stop categorizing because we were all so mixed. Sunday had read his book and honestly praised the colleague's intentions and articulate effort, but he had also told him in no uncertain terms that he thought the United States was many generations away from such an idealized society. Other countries would get there first: Brazil, maybe, or South Africa. For whatever reasons, in its own tortured history, South Africa seemed quicker to forgive and embrace than the United States would ever be. We are in fact becoming hybridized, he knew. His own sister undoubtedly had Native American blood (he assumed Cherokee but would never know), and his wife was one-half Caucasian and had more white than black coloration. His caramel-colored children – especially pale Linden who in old parlance could "pass" – epitomized this hybridizing. But they were all identified as black, whether or not they wanted to be.

The real hybridizing was occurring, Sunday thought, among the vast and growing underclass. The last remaining melting pot of America lay in its underclass, the newest immigrants, the undocumented families from Mexico and Central America and China, and the generations of poor blacks. We are hatching a new generation of Vietnamese/black/Mexican-Americans, or Filipino/Guatemalan-Americans, with names like Precious and Destiny and LaRonde. How long would it be before his classes held students with such names? Not in his lifetime, he thought. They might graduate from high school, but very few of them were sufficiently educated to be accepted into the University of California. He taught at a state school, a public university, founded so that all who were qualified could obtain a college diploma and a white collar occupation. But it was now well beyond the reach of most public high school graduates. Public education through high school – which had rescued Sunday from the underclass – was now sentencing a whole new generation to stay there.

Although he didn't tell anyone else he did it, he looked each semester at his roster of students and guessed their ethnicity. Some were blatantly easy, like Tyrene Powell or Jesus Sanchez or Richard

Yu or Aaron Rubin, or even Ilyan Yarmulich. He would match the names with the bodies as they answered roll call on the first day. Tyrene would be the basketball star, and some time later in the semester the colleague who coordinated the teams would come calling to ask Sunday to raise his grade just a tad, so that he could remain qualified for the team. Jesus would have got there by sheer grit and determination and native intelligence. Aaron was most likely the product of a good private school in San Francisco. Sunday acknowledged to himself that he did his own racial profiling of his students, though he also made a point of grading exams solely by student number. He could tell, though; the voices came through.

Sunday did not share most of this internal dialogue with The Man. But when Sunday told him about the defense attorney's questions and his own shame at his answers, The Man understood instantly. No one, he told him, no one, could predict what he would do in such a situation.

"And if you had risen up in a heat of passion or courage or whatever you want to call it and had stuck that little man with his own knife, who do you think would be on trial? NO," the Man said, "you should not be ashamed. You did the right thing."

43
Joshua

Every day he spent at Cedar's house felt more amazing than the last. This afternoon, as he stood in the living room waiting for Cedar to get something from her bedroom upstairs, he stared idly at an old quilt hanging on the wall. It looked old and kind of ragged and he wondered why it hung there when everything else in this house looked spiffy. In the center of the quilt was a stitched portrait of an old black woman. A square of patches of different designs framed her. Knotted threads hung from the surface at different points.

"Hi Josh," greeted Paula as she came in from outside.

"I see you're admiring our prize quilt." She walked up to him. "Do you know anything about African-American quilts?"

"No."

"What about the Underground Railway?"

"Yeah, sure."

She began to tell him how quilts were used as signals for escaping slaves on their way north to Canada. Quilts contained secret designs, essentially a code for when to prepare to leave, when to leave, what route to take and how far to travel. "This is a wagon wheel," she pointed out, "this a log cabin, and these were tumbling blocks. When the tumbling blocks were displayed, it was time to leave, and the number and spacing of the rough threads told them how far to travel to the next safe house."

"How do you know that?"

"My mother collected these quilts and stories from old women who still remembered some of the codes, as told to them by their mothers and grandmothers. She's been threatening for some years to write a book about them, and my dad has been encouraging her; but she never seems to get around to it. So she passed the stories down to me, and I may have to do the same with Cedar." She laughed.

Josh thought he had never met such interesting parents. When he returned home and his mother asked him how his evening went, he just said 'fine' and disappeared into his room.

Greta

Just the way Josh had said 'fine' made her wonder if the evening had gone badly. There were infinite ways for an evening to go badly for a sixteen-year-old, but the one that preoccupied her was whether he had learned who Cedar's dad was. Not who he was, exactly; Josh would develop his own impression of that. It was strange enough that Josh and not she would get to know Sunday at this stage of his life. But the fact that she had known Cedar's dad in high school - Sunday could have told him that in just such a casual and innocuous fashion. Or Paula – it would have been Paula, not Sunday, since she seemed to have such a penchant for mixing things up – might have dropped the information that Sunday had dated his mom in high school. If anyone had mentioned Sequoia, it would have become obvious that the connection had been much more significant. All it would take would be Josh's asking Cedar how she got her name, and the answer would be the same as how he got his. Perhaps they should discover it for themselves.

She did not want to put an extra load on Josh's first high school romance by telling him she had loved Cedar's father in high school. But she also didn't want him to find out from Cedar's parents. That was selfish, she told herself silently. It might be better for her to take her cue from them and not tell too much. But it also wasn't fair to keep this from Josh. He would find out sooner or later, unless this relationship soon dissolved, in which case it wouldn't be a problem. "Magical thinking," she reminded herself: the problem with her profession was that it was impossible to make a simple parenting decision without overanalyzing it. But what was simple about this?

She did not believe in lying to her son, and holding back on this information felt like a form of lying. Of course, she had already perpetuated a much bigger lie than this. Years earlier, when Josh was in kindergarten, his school had a Grandparents Day. All grandparents were invited, and the children told stories about what their grandparents meant to them. The youngest children told the story to their teacher, and the teacher wrote it down for them on a card they could give to the grandparents. She had not even tried to contact her parents since

Sequoia's funeral. All these years later, she had no idea of how they lived, whether they were together, whether they were healthy, happy, sick or even alive. Despite all these years of going annually to Chicago, she had never once returned to visit Milwaukee. Never even looked them up in the phone book to see if they remained at the same address. A clean erasure of the past. What had been a healthy break for her in 1968 had become an impenetrable curtain. Mostly, it had been the least uncomfortable way for her to treat her family.

She had had some doubts when she was pregnant with Josh. Who would be his family? What if something happened to her? What to tell him? When he was old enough, she had told him the absolute truth about his own origins. Sometimes they joked about his anonymous "progenitor," though usually he was just the 'donor.' When Josh was still quite young, he asked his school friends one by one if any of them had a donor dad. He'd come home very excited to find that one of his friends also had one. And guess what, he'd announced: "she's got two moms!" Grandparents, oddly, were the more difficult absence to explain. She had dodged it until the day Josh had asked where his grandparents were, so he could invite them for Grandparents Day. Unprepared and almost panicked, she had blurted out that they died in a car crash many years before he was born. She apologized for his not having any grandparents of his own. The day had been saved by the parents of her long-time friend Debra, who lived close by. They were in fact fond of Josh and he of them. They stood in as his grandparents on that first and every other Grandparents Day until he went on to high school, where Grandparents

Day was not observed. They held an honored place at Josh's middle school graduation, and she had thanked them profusely for all they had done for Josh.

Whenever Greta had confessed guilt to Debra about the stand-in role for her parents, Debra told her it was a mitzvah: her grandparents got to have another 'grandchild' and they loved their adoptive role.

A lie with a good outcome, perhaps, but still a lie. A good outcome for Debra's parents, but a lingering problem for her and Josh.

She would tell Josh the truth about Sunday, but not now. She would decide later when was the right time – if he became serious about Cedar.

44
Sunday

On the Thursday before Labor Day weekend, Sunday drove to his faculty office. He wanted to spend a few hours on campus this week before classes began again, to put himself in place for the beginning of the year. His office was lined on three walls by bookshelves to the ceiling; on the fourth wall, where his old oak desk sat, a large North-facing window opened onto mature trees. He raised the shade to the top of the window and sat down in his chair.

Each year he began his undergraduate class on African-American History, an upper grade elective, in the same way. His first lecture would include three portraits of the same woman - a multi-faceted folk heroine of the Underground Railroad, a conspirator with John Brown at Harper's Ferry, and a wealthy woman of the Gold Rush days in San Francisco - Mary Ellen Pleasant. Students were easily captivated by her, and she embraced so many issues of the period. Start with a person and go to the issues, he believed.

He followed immediately by assigning something far more difficult and abstract: the *Dred Scott* decision

– not all 180 pages of it, but enough for students to absorb themselves with the tortured thinking of the U.S. Supreme Court justices who ruled that Dred Scott, his wife, and his two children were, at law, property, not citizens. He always included the section that distinguished between "negroes of the African race, and imported into this country, and sold and held as slaves" from "the Indian race" – "although they were uncivilized, they were yet a free and independent people, associated together in nations or tribes" who "have always been treated as foreigners living under our Government."

For Sunday, *Dred Scott* held great currency. It represented the body of legal thought that held the U.S. Constitution should be construed according to its original intent, which meant construing it in consideration of the conditions then existing. The Court expressed that it could not give more "liberal effect to the words of the Constitution than were intended at the time." *All men are born equal, with certain unalienable rights – except those born as property.* The flinty Massachusetts colonies had pass laws calling for arrest of persons of color who did not have passes allowing their movements. *In 1774 we were 'persons of color' – just as we are now. In the interim we have been negroes, colored people, blacks, and African-Americans, but isn't it interesting that we have come back to 'persons of color'?* Each of the colonies had its own miscegenation laws. Those learned justices – no one could doubt that – referenced the distinctions between citizens, freedmen and slaves in ancient Rome; the laws of France that automatically freed any slaves brought within its borders; and the details and ramifications of the Missouri Compromise.

Sunday reviewed his initial lecture.

Mary Ellen Pleasant was born a slave, with no last name, in Georgia in 1814. In her first memoir, she reported that she was the daughter of the youngest son of a Virginia governor, John Pleasants, and a Vodou priestess mother, making her mulatto. We are not told how her mother encountered this young gentleman. Like many other slaveholders of his time, he did his part to blend the races in this country. Mary Ellen's heritage from her vodouissant mother should not be overlooked. Apparently, as a child, Mary Ellen witnessed the killing of her mother by a plantation overseer who was disturbed by the influence of her Vodou practices on other slaves. Vodou, or voodoo as you probably know it, is not something to snicker over. This indigenous belief, principally among West African peoples, holds that divine spirit forces, when capably summoned, sometimes through real creatures such as snakes, help believers to live in harmony with the universe.

The child Mary Ellen was placed with an aging Quaker merchant known as Grandma Hussey in Nantucket, Massachusetts. The fair-skinned child was told not to reveal her race, and she passed for white. Here (he would show in power point) *is an extant photograph of her as an adult. If we trust the photograph, her skin looks too dark to pass for white, but you can see her Caucasian features particularly in her nose and lips.*

This placement with the Hussey family was a lucky break for the girl: they were abolitionists, but also, more importantly, they cared about her and educated her. She became a likeable clerk in the family's general store. After her term of service ended, the Hussey family helped her find a position as a tailor's assistant in Boston, where she met her first husband, James W. Smith, a wealthy flour contractor. The son of a Cuban-mulatto mother and white father, he passed for white. Smith owned a plantation near Harper's Ferry, which he inherited from his father. A participant in the Underground Railroad, Smith staffed his plantation with freedmen whose freedom he'd helped secure. Through him, Mary Ellen made contacts in the Railroad and abolitionist community, and she joined in these slave rescue efforts. James Smith died suddenly in the mid-1840s. Mary Ellen's memoirs reflect her ambivalence toward him. When they married, he had forbidden her from even notifying the Husseys of their wedding and otherwise prevailed upon her in ways that caused her to remark in those memoirs: "All I felt was that I had somehow lost my liberty all over again." Although Mary Ellen respected Smith and certainly enjoyed her station in life, she resented losing her own voice. When Smith died of unknown causes, she received a considerable inheritance from him. She continued her efforts with the Underground Railroad after his death.

Mary Ellen Pleasant contributed funds to John Brown, both for land and for arms. She purchased land in Canada to house the slaves that John Brown planned to set free near Harper's Ferry, Virginia. Although Brown's plan to capture the federal arsenal with only 21 men was something Mary Ellen considered reckless and hasty, she participated, both personally and financially. Disguising herself as a negro jockey (someone who was transported from plantation to plantation for horse racing), Mary Ellen Pleasant rode – with a white abolitionist pretending to be her owner - down the Roanoke River to alert the slave community of the impending insurrection and enlist their participation. Like John Brown, Mary Ellen Pleasant believed force was necessary to end slavery and she was willing to risk her life for the effort.

"I'd rather be a corpse than a coward," she reportedly said. When John Brown was captured and hanged for his part, a note from Mary Ellen promising more funds was found on his body. It bore the initials M.E.P., which the authorities misread as W.E.P. Mary Ellen fled, using the name Smith, and became a fugitive.

The P. stood for Pleasant, the name of the ship's cook, John James Pleasant, with whom Mary Ellen took up after Smith's death. Together, the Pleasants roamed between New Orleans and Nantucket by ship. This was a water route for some escaped slaves to Canada, but nothing is recorded as to whether this was part of Mary Ellen's work with fugitive slaves.

Sunday paused and rubbed his eyes, which, he noticed, were getting weaker. He might need new glasses.

Under the Fugitive Slave Act, escaped or former slaves captured – even in so-called free states - could be brought back and re-enslaved by their former owners. Persons who aided escaped slaves faced harsh penalties, and ad hoc courts ruled on these matters. Commissioners in these courts were paid double to return rather than to free captives. The Fugitive Slave Act of 1850 was part of a national compromise. As new states entered the Union, Southerners feared their entry would tilt the balance of slave and free states in the wrong direction. The so-called Compromise of 1850 allowed slavers to bring their slaves into free states without having to worry about losing their slaves in the process. This national Slave Act also ordered the return of escaped slaves. It might interest you to know that our own state, California, had a fugitive slave act of its own and actively participated during this period in repatriating persons of color to their former owners. Here are some newspaper ads from California newspapers of the period, offering rewards for the return of escaped or former slaves. He arranged transparencies of the ads to project on the screen in the lecture hall.

Mary Ellen Pleasant arrived in San Francisco on April 7, 1852, on a steamer from New Orleans. In 1852, San Francisco was a city of 40,000 people, only 464 of them African Americans, with men outnumbering women by a ratio of at least three to one. Many of these men were flush with money, and the rough town lacked many comforts. Services of someone who could cook or keep house were in high demand. Mary Ellen first offered herself as a cook, for good wages, while she invested her existing wealth in real estate. She opened a laundry on Jessie and Ecker Streets and soon set up several boarding houses where prominent men could live in sumptuous comfort and where she employed other persons of color. The employment market for African Americans in San Francisco at that time was phenomenal, particularly for sailors, cooks, porters and housemaids. The advantages to Mary Ellen's boarding house enterprise were several: she earned the trust and confidence of many of San Francisco's wealthy and influential men at the same time as she earned good money, found more people through whom she invested, and employed other African Americans.

She formed a close business partnership – and some say also a personal relationship - with banker Thomas Bell that lasted many years. She and he purchased a mansion and adjacent lot at 1661 Octavia Street in San Francisco, where she, he, his wife Theresa and the Bell children lived for more than two decades before Thomas' death in 1892. Here you see a photograph of the mansion. Incidentally, you can also find a plaque dedicated to her memory on the corner of Bush and Octavia Streets. *After his death, Theresa and Mary Ellen continued to live together in this mansion with Theresa's children and on a large ranch in Sonoma owned by Mary Ellen; but a series of lawsuits arising from his large estate, the ambiguities of ownership among Mary Ellen and Theresa and Thomas, and resentments from one of Bell's children, created a swarm of publicly-reported scandals in which Mary Ellen often figured negatively. Mary Ellen appeared as a witness in several of them, always portraying herself as a servant of the household. She dressed for court in those days with a bandana around her head and a shawl over her shoulders, to further her image as the servant rather than mistress of the household.*

In one of those lawsuits, brought by Pleasant as Theresa's representative, over the lot adjacent to their home, one of the appellate justices, reflecting the prejudices of the times, wrote:

"There is no apparent reason why this colored servant, without means, should seek to acquire the lot in question as her own property, and that either Bell in his lifetime or his widow, the Plaintiff, should have loaned her the money for such purpose....Hence

the unreasonableness – not to say absurdity – of the contention that the transaction was a bona fide purchase by Mary E. Pleasant – the colored servant of the Bell family – of the lot in question."

In the years after the Emancipation Proclamation issued in 1863, Mary Ellen began a series of lawsuits, several of them against the forerunner of the Muni Railway. A larger piece of her legacy is the law suit of Mary Ellen Pleasant v. the North Beach and Mission Railway, which went to the California Supreme Court in 1868. One day Pleasant stood at a cable car stop, her purchased ticket in hand, hailing the cable car as it approached; but the driver refused to stop for her, although there was room in the car. A passenger who asked the driver to stop testified that the driver had said: "We don't take colored people in the cars." Mary Ellen Pleasant sued the railway and recovered punitive damages of $500. In 1868, some ninety years before Rosa Parks refused to sit in the back of the bus, Mary Ellen Pleasant sued in her own name and recovered money from the cable car railway for failing to let her on the car. And Rosa Parks probably never even heard of her.

For so much of her life, Mary Ellen Pleasant had used her appearance for her advantage, by playing on people's assumptions of who she was. In the end, the court used those assumptions to rule against her. Why doesn't history remember her as a heroine akin to Rosa Parks? Was it because of her reputation as a madam? Or was it because her act was isolated, while Rosa Parks' refusal became a tipping point for the Civil Rights Movement in general? He always left enough time at the end of the lecture to engage the students in discussion.

Sunday's fascination for Mary Ellen Pleasant went well beyond her accomplishments. He was intrigued both by her resiliency and her chameleon-like resourcefulness: by her several names, and by posing alternatively as a male jockey or household servant, she eluded bounty hunters and law enforcement officials searching for her after the Harper's Ferry debacle. Once in San Francisco, passing as white, she charmed and entertained the wealthy and influential, lending them money and keeping their secrets; at the same time, she took an active role in the black community, giving them money, aiding others with their freedom. She taught Thomas Bell his financial skills and got him started. She may have been Thomas Bell's lover when she lived with him and his wife Theresa. Sunday admired even her deception, so necessary to her survival. He appreciated even her cantankerous side, her bringing several unsuccessful lawsuits to recover money and property that was only too easy for others to claim from her because she could not take lawful title to it. She had to gain others' trust to hold property for her and then suffer the consequences if others broke that trust. Sometimes he would temporize to himself: well, she could pass for white or black, while someone as black as I could never do the same. But he knew it went well beyond that. He could never say he would rather be a corpse than a coward. He would be the coward who survived every time.

Sunday closed his computer and locked up his office. He was ready to start the new semester, the first he would teach after the Idaho incident. He wondered if he would teach anything differently as a consequence. Sunday glanced at his watch, the new Movado Paula had given to him this summer for his fiftieth birthday. Even after the Idaho incident, she loved him, took care of his needs, and knew he would want something handsome and well-designed to wear on his hand. In the manner of well-matched, long-married people, he felt endlessly grateful to her. She was as reliable as an old habit. As reliable as Sequoia, actually, just as nurturing and just as strong. But as much as he admired them both, he envied them too, for their strength.

It was nearly noon. He had an appointment with The Man at two. He'd have enough time to walk about the campus for a bit with his thoughts, grab a sandwich from one of the vending carts, and drive back to the City in time for his appointment.

Sunday followed the path that meandered across the tiny stream and through the more wooded parts of the campus. He had taught at Howard, had guest-taught at Emory and several other colleges, but only on this campus had he found a haven. It was his seventeenth year here. The administration had no agenda for him other than academic excellence. He was not expected to be 'radical' or activist or innocuous. His students came from everywhere. He did not feel compelled to pander to any constituency. And his students continued to surprise him, defy stereotyping, and perform often beyond his expectations. His most promising graduate student was a forty-something white woman from Louisiana whose research and thesis in progress were on the relationship between antebellum plantation wives and household slaves and how those relationships changed or were maintained after emancipation. Like his other students, she seemed to appreciate him. He'd been granted a faculty teaching award several times. He had a good life here.

Winding his way back toward Sather Gate for lunch, Sunday stopped for a falafel sandwich from Ali's Alimentaries. Who would think of such a name? He conjured up someone in Ali's family, perhaps with little grasp of the English language, poring over a dictionary to find some clever name. And who was this middle-aged, middle-eastern man whose teen-aged son now put just a little bit of hot red sauce on his falafel? By what tortuous route had he, or his parents, come to this place? Sunday was so black that sometimes people asked what part of Africa he came from. While he didn't mind such questions, he knew enough not to ask them of others, including Ali. Sunday took his sandwich to a bench on the grass. He could not help noticing that posters and tables were back on Sproul Plaza. Classes had not yet started but freshmen had arrived for orientation. "Stop the Palestinian Massacres," read one banner hanging from a table piled with pamphlets. At another table, draped in a rainbow flag, someone who could be either a man or woman handed out small rainbow buttons promoting equal rights for gays and lesbians. Sunday wore no buttons. He never had.

Perhaps he would tell The Man today about Mary Ellen Pleasant. His therapist knew that Sunday referred to him as The Man. In fact, when he first heard it from Sunday, the therapist put his hand up to his mouth to hide his grin and started to shake with laughter. He had a face as round as a chocolate truffle, the color of milk chocolate actually, Sunday thought (although he usually hated skin color being described like food or coffee) and all the subparts of his face were round too. Big round protruding eyes that saw everything. Cheeks like tiny round balloons tethered by the laugh lines around his mouth. A genial face, unlike Sunday's own lean and solemn one. But the geniality masked the incisive mind behind it; and Sunday still, now four months into this process, both feared and felt challenged by The Man's questions. Yes, he would find out if his therapist knew of Mary Ellen Pleasant.

As it turned out, Sunday's therapist did know something about her. After a pause, his eyeballs lofted, The Man recalled "a folk hero from the Gold Rush days in San Francisco, part of the Underground Railway, a notorious madam. She parlayed her sexual favors into creating wealth," he said, relishing the last detail.

Sunday grimaced.

"You got her all wrong, man. She..."

"Are you trying to ape her, sleeping around to gain some favor for yourself?"

Sunday recoiled, scraping his chair on the floor as he moved it away from The Man. He looked away for a moment, then lashed out.

"Who the hell do you think you are? You're supposed to be here to help me, not hurl insults at me. What is this, anyway?"

The Man looked at him hard, his eyes bulging.

"What do you do when you get really angry, Sunday? I was just trying to bait you now. Where does your anger go?"

"Do you really think I have sex with women to gain influence?"

"No, I don't. And I don't think you do it for all

the usual compensatory reasons that black men play around. But you sure *act* the stereotype. It looks ugly; it hurts your wife; it may someday hurt your career, even though you think you're careful. And it almost cost you your life this spring, out in Idaho. So why do you do it?"

"Why do you think I come back here, week after week?" Sunday's voice rose. "It doesn't exactly give me confidence that you don't know either."

They were both silent for several long moments, only the sound of Sunday's agitated breathing in the room.

"What do you do with your anger, Sunday?"

"I don't get angry that often. I try to stay calm. I'm still angry at you, though."

"Yeah, I see. But what are you going to do about it? I'm not here to solve this issue for you. You got mightily scared in Idaho - as anyone would - and you may think you're cured of this nasty little habit of yours; but I don't think so. That fear will fade and the tempting adventure of this will call to you again, unless you get a grip on whatever it is you're trying to make up for."

Sunday took a deep breath.

"Actually," he began, acidly, "I was going to tell you something about Mary Ellen Pleasant that resonated with me."

The Man sat back in his chair, and waited. Sunday said nothing.

"I know I'm being hard on you. I care about what you do. And I'd really be happy if you told me what you came in here to say."

Sunday was quiet for a while longer, and The Man waited patiently in his chair, rocking back very slowly.

"She managed – from a childhood harder than anything you or I ever saw – to gain the courage to ride around in disguise, risking her life to save slaves, to work with John Brown on his reckless, doomed scheme, escape and keep doing the same kind of work. I call that courage. I could never say 'I'd rather be a corpse than a coward.' I could never do what she did. I admire her, man. I'd overlook a whole lot of other things she might have done and keep admiring her for what she did do."

"You don't think it took courage for you to go to Mississippi in 1964?"

"I think that's part of the problem. Mississippi scared the shit out of me. I don't remember any of the details. I've tried to think of whether there was some particular incident, but that whole summer just ruined me. I was less of a person after that."

"What would you have done if you had been 'more of a person'?"

"For starters, I wouldn't have abandoned Gretchen. There were so many more things I could have done during that time. I did no civil rights work whatsoever. I dodged the draft by going to college and graduate school. I kept my head down, man, every day of my life. I wish I had more of whatever made Mary Ellen Pleasant tick."

"Sunday, when you went to Mississippi, did you help register any voters?"

"Sure. That's what we were there to do."

"And were those people glad you helped them to register?"

Sunday nodded slightly, remembering how fearful some of those people had been.

"Do you think it's nothing that you teach a whole new generation about our history? That you've published and been honored as a professor? That you have stayed married and in love with a really special woman for over twenty years and are rearing three good children? Whoever Gretchen was, don't you think you have a wife you really love?"

Sunday looked down, said nothing.

"What did Mary Ellen Pleasant do when John Brown got caught? Did she stick around to read the note the authorities found on him? Did you think she was a coward for running away from *that* scene?"

Sunday looked toward the window.

His therapist let the silence run for the remaining twelve minutes of their session. When he called the session over, he acknowledged that Sunday had a few things to think over.

As he drove home, Sunday still felt galled. His head ached. He didn't like the way his therapist had spoken to him, as if he had not been speaking the truth.

Sunday slammed the front door, without intending to. As he tossed his keys onto the end table, they slid off, clattering to the floor. He cursed.

Paula came out of the kitchen, her eyes like traffic warning lights.

"What is it?"

She pulled him by the arm into the kitchen and swung the door shut behind them. "It's Douglass."

Sunday's stomach clenched. He began to ask whether their son was okay, but Paula put a finger on his lip. "Just listen," she said in a low voice. Douglass and his friend Toby had gone to Walgreen's after basketball practice to get a coke. Toby had supposedly lifted some batteries and put them into his jacket. A store employee had seen this and come after them. Toby ran out of the store, and the store manager yanked Douglass into a back office until the police arrived. They had found nothing on Douglass – it wasn't clear whether Douglass even knew whether Toby had stolen anything – but they gave Douglass a rough time. One of the officers hit Douglass across the face when he'd refused to give the name of his friend. He had the beginnings of a black eye. After being hit, Douglass revealed the name and address of his friend. They took both boys into the station and then released them to their respective parents. Both boys were charged with petty theft and had dates to appear at Juvenile Hall.

"How's he taking it?"

"You know Douglass; he's internalizing most of it. He wouldn't tell me much, but he was able to cry it out with me. I just sat and held him for a long time. He needs to talk to you."

Of their three children, Douglass was the most like Sunday. He looked like a paler version of his father, a honey-colored scarecrow. Quiet and observant as an owl, a serious but shy student. He had only a few friends but was tight with them, and Toby had been a friend for years. When Sunday entered his room, Douglass was hunched over his desk with a calculus book open. He didn't turn around, though he had said "come in" forlornly when Sunday knocked.

Sunday put his arms around Douglass' shoulders and brought his face next to his. Douglass' hair smelled as sweet as a baby's, but his body threw off the acrid smell of sweat.

"Your mother told me what happened," he said gently. "What do you make of all of this?"

Douglass turned around. "Toby was my best friend. How could he do this to me? He decides to lift some dumb batteries from Walgreen's and then runs off and leaves me to take the hit for him."

"It took some courage and considerable loyalty for you to stand up to the police for him." Sunday gently touched the corner of Douglass' left eye. Douglass winced.

"But then I ratted on him when that cop slammed me."

"You had to tell them. By the way, it was the right thing to do."

"I didn't know whether Toby had taken anything. I figured they stopped me just because I'm black and Toby was hanging with me."

Sunday left that alone.

"Did you ever see Toby lift anything before?"

"Yeah. He does it a lot. He thinks it's cool. He likes to try to put something by the people in the stores, thinks they're stupid and he's smart."

"Did he ever ask you to try it also?"

Douglass stiffened a bit and allowed that Toby had tried more than once to get him to take something.

"You call that a good friend?" Sunday prodded. "Did you ever take anything yourself? I want you to look at me and tell me the absolute truth."

"No, Dad. Honest. I thought it was kind of stupid."

"I believe you, and I'll go to bat for you. You shouldn't get into trouble for this. But you also won't be spending any time with Toby after school for a while."

Sunday took his son's shoulders to reassure him. Then he turned and started to walk out of the room.

"Dad...." Sunday turned around again. "Why do I feel like such a coward?" Sunday stood still and took an audible deep breath before he turned around to face his son.

"Son, believe me, you were anything but a coward. You stood up to the police. You were loyal to your friend even when he didn't deserve it. That's not being a coward - no way - ever. You hear?" Sunday grabbed Douglass by the shoulders, harder than he had intended, and Douglass flinched reflexively. Sunday stared hard into his son's pale eyes and repeated, "You are *not* a coward."

Douglass smiled at him weakly.

After dinner, Sunday took the dog out for a long walk. He wanted no company. He took off in a direction that would be all uphill for as far as he wanted to walk. The dog pranced ahead, jogging left and right at the temptations to her nose. He felt oddly proud of his son in this episode, for daring not to tell the police Toby's name. Sunday wasn't particularly worried that the Juvenile Hall matter would be resolved unfavorably. Paula would explain it all to the Judge or whoever was in charge, and he felt confident the charges would be dismissed. Douglass had good values and he'd had the courage to stand up to the police. Sunday would get the badge number of the officer who had hit his son and have Paula file a complaint against him. That burned him. But what troubled him more was that Douglass was echoing his own sense of cowardice. Sunday wondered what he might have done to signal this to his children.

He turned this around in his head for a block or more, his mind going nowhere enlightening. And then the pleasure of just walking took over. He grew warm from climbing the hill, loosened his jacket, and turned around to look back from a hilly vantage. What he saw was the water of the Bay, graying from pale blue in the dying light. A solitary light on Alcatraz, and the flow of headlight beams on the road in front of Crissy Field. The night was mild and windless. It reminded him again how benign the climate was here in San Francisco compared to Milwaukee, or even D.C. There were no thunderstorms, no crackling lightning, no blizzards, no tornadoes, nothing in the natural environment to waken him in fright. Well, except earthquakes, but he had found them oddly exhilarating.

He found himself thinking of a moment in one of his last classes the prior spring, in a discussion of Martin Luther King's assassination. He'd described the riots that followed immediately after King's shooting, and then the way the country had turned to focus on Vietnam rather than on civil rights. A flaxen-haired girl from Iowa raised her pale right arm and asked why some acts of terror seemed to move everyone to stand up for their rights and others seemed to frighten everyone into silence. Her question sparked a discussion of what moved people to march when they knew they would get beaten or hosed, to register to vote when that might lead to the KKK burning their house at night, or to integrate a school when they knew they would be ostracized or beaten. As if catching her suggestion, a young blood from Oakland had said that black people were braver than white people because they had to be to live in this country. "What about Michael Schwermer?" He had lobbed back at the young man. "Hadn't he been killed in the summer of 1964? What about the white man who'd volunteered to be first off the bus on the Freedom Ride from Montgomery to Jackson?" What was it he had said at the end of class? *Sometimes we don't know from what source we draw our courage; it rises when we most need it.*

Or not. Had he really said that to his class? It must have been a student who had said that. For himself, it would have been a lie. Or was he quoting someone else? The statement came back to him at various times after that class, which took place only a month or two after the Idaho incident. Whose statement was it? His own son Douglass had drawn on some spontaneous source of courage this afternoon while the police were questioning him. But, instead of recognizing his own bravado, he accused himself of cowardice. Sunday forced himself to revisit the incident in Idaho. Had he not grabbed the knife as soon as he had the opportunity? Don't let yourself go too far down that road, he told himself; you got that knife by accident and you don't have a clue what you would have done if the highway patrol had not appeared in the next moment.

It was fully dark by now, and Sunday had reached the top of the hill. The Bay was now inky, a band of pale ripples reflected from the light on Alcatraz. The dog panted expectantly, eager for more. He paused for a moment, on the corner of a park, trying to decide whether to go back down the hill or into the park. On the corner ahead of him, at the far end of the block, he could make out two figures, young men slouching on the park steps. A third approached them from across the street, and the two jumped up. They huddled for just a moment. Then the third figure loped across the street again, disappearing into a car. Sunday decided to turn around and go back down the hill, not wanting to become a witness to a drug deal. At that moment, a patrol car appeared on the far corner, and one officer leapt out. Quickly he collared one of the two young men. The other took off with the speed of a track runner. He could hear but not see what the officer was doing to the young man who had not run.

Sunday turned around, yanking the dog in close to him. He began to walk faster down the hill, back toward his home. *The speed of a track runner.* At once he remembered what he had done in Mississippi. In the same synapse he knew why he had forgotten all these years. It was still a long walk back down the hill. But all the way home, all he could hear were the cries of the young man being beaten - and the terrified, panting breath of the young man who had run away thirty-two years ago. They had been walking home from an evening meeting, sharing some innocuous story, when the four white men jumped out of the car.

Paula greeted him at the door, trying to read his mood.

"We have a solid young man," he told her. "We need to deal with the cop who hit him and with Juvenile Hall, but it's going to be all right."

"We need to reassure Douglass," she said, and he agreed.

They spoke easily, as they always did, about

how to take care of their children. Then he went upstairs to undress for bed. He was not inclined to tell Paula what he had remembered. There was something else he needed to tell her. Sunday decided he would tell his therapist, since he had earned the right to know. But, he also thought, the person he really wanted to tell was Gretchen.

When Paula came up to bed, Sunday was sitting up, book in hand as usual. His reading light was on, but he was not reading. He watched her undress, admired her straight back and the proud toss of her unruly hair. He felt an immense gratitude.

She came to bed naked, as usual. He folded himself around her, his left hand holding hers between her breasts. They often fell asleep in this position.

"It won't happen again," he told her.

"You've never said that before." Her voice was measured, cautious.

"I wasn't able to."

They lay there silently for some moments, listening to one another's breath. His was too rapid for him to fall asleep. He continued.

"You could have punished me. You could have left me long ago. I was begging for punishment and dreading it at the same time."

"It would only have done more harm to leave you. That much I knew."

He held her tightly and kissed her shoulder.

"You've always known more than I did. I owe you all my happiness in life."

She turned to face him, separating their bodies.

"You've given me happiness – and pain - in equal measure. You better mean what you say."

She turned over and moved so that their bodies no longer touched. He lay awake long after her breath had fallen into the slow rhythm of sleep.

45
Joshua

Cedar. Aromatic cedar. Like the chest in which his mother kept extra blankets for cold nights. When he used one of those blankets, he fell asleep with its scent. For Cedar's birthday in May, he'd bought her a small cedar-lined box. The sales lady had called it aromatic cedar and told him it would keep its scent forever and ward off harm. Most of their friends who had a special guy or girl had their own special song, but Josh and Cedar were led by their sense of smell.

Aromatic Cedar. Her own aroma was more like spiced oranges, but salty when he tasted her skin. Hungry Cedar. They devoured salted mixed nuts when they studied, asked their parents to cook more spicy dishes for dinner. One Saturday they walked down Valencia Street in the Mission, looking for a cheap ethnic restaurant to try for lunch. Wandering into an Indian market, they found a wall of spices, all in bins with ladles to scoop into little bags, not like the bottled spices in Safeway. Following their noses – and sometimes the attraction of color, which led them to the golden bin of turmeric – they lifted lids and leaned in close to sniff. It was not long before the saleswoman, a rippled, substantial woman in a pumpkin-colored sari, asked them what they were looking for. Inspired, Josh asked her what was the best-smelling spice they sold.

The woman paused for a moment, as if deciding whether they were worth taking seriously. Her brow furrowed as she looked skeptically at these young colored people. As if on impulse, she suddenly gave them a broad smile and told them they needed to mix spices to find what smelled best. “Chat masala,” she told them, “that’s what you’re looking for.”

“Do you have any?” They asked, in unison.

“I’ll mix it for you,” she told them, and then set to the task as if she knew she was making them a love potion. She leaned over this bin and that, the skin above the waist of her sari rolling from side to side as she pinched a little here, a larger scoop from there, stopping at more bins than they could count. In a few minutes, she shook the small plastic bag in which she had collected her mixture of spices.

“What do you think?” She held out the plastic baggie as if it were a masterpiece.

Cedar sniffed it first and inhaled too deeply. She sneezed, and they all laughed. Josh smelled it next and thought he had found nirvana. “What do you mix it in?” he asked her.

“Fruit, any kind of fruit - mango, melon, banana, even berries, though we don’t have berries in India.” She smiled conspiratorially, as if knowing what they would do with it.

“How much do we owe you?” asked Josh, the practical one.

The woman angled to the counter, the folds

around her waist making small waves with each step.

"$1.76."

They thanked her, paid the small sum, and skipped out of the store and up the street a bit before letting themselves inhale it some more.

"I won't sneeze this time," Cedar promised.

"Cinnamon, definitely cinnamon," she pronounced. "But what else?"

Impulsively, Cedar licked one of her fingers, dipped it into the bag, pulled out her stained finger and began to rub it on one breast, then the other, just below the scoop neckline of her shirt.

Josh licked one of his fingers, dipped it and put it into his mouth.

"Melons," he pronounced. "We definitely have to try it on melons." And they laughed and laughed, skipping down the street.

Of course he had asked her how she got her name. Months ago. "Because I smelled good, and my skin was red," she'd told him. "My mother knew I would be red cedar right from the start." She didn't get to the tree part at all.

At her house, they divided the packet into two separate baggies, one for him and one for her. Her home was full of siblings, so they could not try to taste anything on each other. Josh was so frustrated that he left; the temptation was too much to contain.

Cedar kept her packet in her room, spreading a bit on her breasts and behind her ears when she knew she would be with Josh, as if it were exotic perfume.

Josh took his home and actually asked his mother how to use it. She looked at him quizzically and asked him how he had got it. He told her he and Cedar had wandered into an Indian market and asked for the best-smelling spice. "Did the woman tell you how to use it?"

"On fruit," he said. "She mentioned mangoes or melons." His mother smiled mysteriously, bought a cantaloupe the next day and sprinkled the spice on it for dessert.

"What do you think?" she asked him.

"Yes!" they both pronounced when they ate the melon.

"It has a lot of cinnamon in it, but it's not just cinnamon," his mother said in her most studious manner. Then she looked at him curiously.

"I don't know if I should do this," she said, and disappeared into her library, returning with a book marked with a post-it.

"You may like this poem," she said. "You don't have to read it now."

Josh took it to his room later and read it the same night. It was titled "The Cinnamon Peeler" by someone named Michael Ondaatje, from Sri Lanka. The man in the poem worked as a cinnamon peeler. At the end of the day, he reeked of cinnamon, and, when he made love to his woman, she smelled of it too. The poem was erotic. The cinnamon peeler had to wash the smell from himself so as not to arouse the suspicion of her "keen nosed mother." After he married his lover, when she walked around her village, her scent advertised that she was the cinnamon peeler's wife. Josh wondered how his mother could know what he was thinking.

He wrote out the poem for Cedar but he didn't tell her how he had got it.

She read it right away, then looked up at him

and said, "I don't care if the whole world smells you on me." She let him kiss her spiced breasts for the first time and then laughed at his stained lips. But she wouldn't let him go further. "I'm just not ready," she told him.

46
Greta

Paula telephoned Greta one day at her office after they had not spoken for several months.

"My daughter Cedar is dating your son."

"I know." Greta paused for a long moment while neither of them spoke. "I guess I can't escape your family no matter what I do."

They both laughed. It was friendly, welcome, ice-breaking laughter. Greta read relief in Paula's laughter and realized that she welcomed the sound of her voice again.

"You know this is inevitable, don't you," Paula said teasingly.

"What?"

"You're connected to this family no matter how hard you try not to be." Greta could hear the smile behind Paula's pronouncement.

"I guess I can't control this part of it, even if I wanted to," Greta acknowledged. "Not that I do. Cedar is a lovely young woman, and Josh seems to be in love with her."

"Undeniable." They both sighed.

"And you didn't start this one, did you?" Greta accused, jokingly.

"Nope, it's all them. They met at school. They did this themselves."

"You realize this is coincidence upon coincidence. We couldn't have dreamed this up if we had tried."

"Right. We get to watch it play itself out."

"What's your prediction?" Greta asked.

"I don't do predictions," Paula answered. "But, just as a heads-up, I think you are soon going to get an invitation to dinner at our home."

"You sure know how to torture me."

"I do," Paula answered. Greta heard the friendliness in her voice.

"I just want to know one thing," Greta said. "How do I know *you*?"

"There's that," Paula acknowledged. She paused. "Can't we just know one another from school?"

"Except that we don't. I'm never there, even if you are," Greta pointed out. "I met you at one of your art fairs, and we became friends after that," she suggested.

"That works for me. By the way, there's a women's art fair coming up at Fort Mason, and I'd love for you to come and see what I have made."

"I'd like that too, and now there's no reason not to."

Only two days later Josh came home and asked her if she would come to dinner at Cedar's parents' home.

"Her parents want to meet you," he told her. She just looked at him, but he gave no hint of irony.

"Of course," she said. "I'd love to meet Cedar's parents." This came out in a level, almost professional voice. He could hear its falsity.

"What's wrong? Don't you like Cedar? Don't you want to meet her family?"

"Sit down, Josh. I need to tell you something."

His face registered worry. He sat down quickly, sinking into the kitchen chair.

She sat down too, across the table from him, her body slumping into the stiff chair. She looked into the warm brown eyes of her son. She willed herself not to look away.

"This is not your fault, and I wish I didn't have to tell you this, but you should know it."

His face registered trouble.

"Many years ago, when I was in high school, Cedar's dad and I fell in love. You've heard me speak of Sequoia. She was his mother-figure, his older sister actually. She was a role model for us both. Cedar's dad went off to work in the voter registration project in Mississippi the summer after we both graduated from high school, and we broke up after he came back. I haven't seen him in all these years."

"No shit." He looked at her as if she had grown to double her size.

She was amazed to see him smiling. Grinning, actually.

"Why are you smiling?"

"I can see why you'd like him. He's cool."

She laughed, relief loosening all her muscles, and relaxed into the chair.

"How is he cool? I wouldn't know. I haven't seen him in almost thirty years."

It was Josh's turn to laugh now; he knew something she didn't.

"He talks the same way you do. He's a little nerdy, but he's really cool. I can't explain it." And

Josh started to laugh, first a little and then she started too, and soon they both were laughing so hard they were crying.

"I guess you don't mind," she said. "I was worried that this would burden you and Cedar."

"So tell me," Josh said, suddenly serious, "does Cedar remind you of him?"

"Not at all. I wouldn't have guessed." She answered without hesitating. But then she paused, relief still flooding her. "But I can't believe you were both named in honor of the same person. It makes me feel as if you were related."

"She's my non-sister."

"Right; she's your non-sister. She may be your soul mate, but she is definitely not your sister."

"Mom," Josh looked at her with a seal's eyes, "do you like Cedar?"

"I do. And it's obvious she really cares about you." She paused. "Just give it time to breathe."

He got up out of his chair and went to hers, hugged her awkwardly.

"Go to bed," she told him, wiping the wetness from the corners of her graying eyes.

47
Sunday

A week after the session in which his therapist had provoked him about Mary Ellen Pleasant, Sunday sat down again in the leather chair that faced The Man. They both began to talk at the same time. Sunday wanted to tell him what he had remembered from the summer in Mississippi, but his therapist started first to say something about Pleasant. They both paused, and then his therapist extended his hand to indicate Sunday should begin.

"I know what happened in Mississippi."

His therapist nodded, his eyebrows raised in two identical arcs.

Sunday described how he had come home from the last session and learned what his son had done, and how Douglass too had seen the world in terms of his own cowardice. He described his walk afterward, the street arrest of the supposed drug dealer, the arrested dealer's cries, and the echoing footfalls of the one who had run away, as well as his own mirroring recollection.

"I was coming out of an evening meeting with another team member, a white guy. We were walking home, laughing and talking. About what,

I can't remember. I know we were relaxed and it felt so good to laugh. Took away so much of the tension of what we were doing. We'd talk for a while and then one of us would say something that would bring back whatever we were laughing about. I'd heard a couple of car doors close, but I assumed they were our own team members who had a car, getting in to drive home. I remember we were told to drive or walk straight home and not mess around." Sunday glanced down and his brow wrinkled as if he'd smelled something bad. He hunched over in his chair.

"Nathan – that was my teammate – started laughing again, and he couldn't stop. He bent over holding his gut; he was laughing so hard it hurt. I turned around to look at him. I saw four old white guys not twenty paces behind us, two fat guys in overalls and two skinny ones. All of them with kerchiefs masking the bottom halves of their faces, like farmers working in the dust. Or bandits in an old Western. Red kerchiefs, like farmers wear around their neck to catch their sweat. Two of them carried baseball bats. One of the fat ones was rubbing one of his hands up and down the bat, like he was warming it up. I slapped Nathan hard on the shoulder. 'Run!' I told him. But I don't know if he even heard me. I turned around and ran away as fast as I could. I didn't even look back 'til I knew they weren't close behind me. I was about a block away when I looked back. I could see that Nathan was down, kinda curled up. I could see them hitting him with the bats and kicking him. I turned around and ran all the way home."

When he finished, Sunday looked back at his

therapist like an eager student who'd found an answer to a difficult question.

His therapist leaned back in his chair and ran his hands up and down his legs and knees. "Amazing," he said softly.

"Did you find out what happened to your friend that night?"

"Yeah. He was beaten badly. His jaw and several ribs were broken. He woke up in a local hospital and in a few days his parents had him flown home. I never saw him again."

"What do you think he would have said about your running away from those four men?"

"I don't know, but I reported it to our team supervisors, who told me I had done the right thing. I didn't believe them, but I guess my story helped prevent my friend from being arrested for attacking four white guys. At first I planned to write or call my friend, but I never did. After a while, I couldn't because I felt I had just made matters worse by not checking in on him afterward."

"Do you remember his full name?"

Sunday looked out the window again, his eyebrows knit. "He was a Jewish student from Topeka...Spiegelman. Nathan Spiegelman." Sunday shook his head. "I haven't thought about him in all these years." He paused. He wanted to become a lawyer. I wonder if he did."

"Why don't you try to find him?"

"Oh yeah. That would be good. I'm the guy who left you to be beaten some thirty years ago. Remember me? By the way, did your jaw ever heal? Sure; I could do that."

"Try thinking about how you would react if you were he and you received a letter telling you how he had felt bothered all these years about running away. You might be surprised."

Sunday shook his head disparagingly.

"Okay. Don't. Just a suggestion." His therapist cocked his head sideways and looked at Sunday a moment. "I'll change the subject – sort of. Do you think Mary Ellen Pleasant should have stuck around when John Brown got caught and had herself hanged with him? Didn't you tell me you admired how she used her wits and ability to disguise herself to resurface in the West, no longer a fugitive?"

Sunday opened his mouth, then closed it and looked out the window again.

"Okay, try this. Do you think your son Douglass should have withheld Toby's name and got a worse beating? I don't think so."

Sunday winced but kept his eyes on whatever lay outside the window.

"Sunday, have you ever heard of a false paradigm? All these years, you seem to have seen your life through the sole filter of whether you're a coward or a hero, and you've condemned yourself almost from the beginning. Life is more than a quest for a badge of courage, don't you think? You've succeeded admirably at most of life's other challenges; why don't you try forgiving yourself for running away from a beating in 1964?"

Sunday dragged his eyes away from the window and turned them on his therapist. "I also left Gretchen."

"Maybe you should have. Sounds like she had a troubled background and had issues of her own. You two went to school a thousand miles away from each other. Most relationships wouldn't have survived that."

"Are you going to suggest that I try to contact her too?" Sunday asked sarcastically, a hint of a smile on his face.

His therapist tilted his head and stared at Sunday, waiting.

"She referred me to you." Sunday smiled triumphantly.

"You mean Greta Reinhardt is Gretchen?" He just shook his head. "This world is way too small."

"I always wondered whether she'd told you that when she made the referral."

"Now you know." His therapist kept smiling and shaking his head. Then he stopped. "But let's talk about you and Gretchen and don't distract me with my colleague Greta. I guess I don't have to suggest that you look her up. How did you find out about this connection?"

Sunday explained that Paula had been seeing Greta professionally and that Greta had stopped the therapy when she learned that he was Paula's husband. And, to add to the bizarre coincidences, his daughter was dating Greta's son.

"You're testing me now, Sunday."

"Truth is always stranger than fiction, isn't it?"

"So have you seen her?"

"Not yet."

"And I bet you're wondering what to say to her when you do." The therapist paused for a moment. "Let's come back to Gretchen and why or how she haunts you."

"I don't know. I didn't think about her that much before Paula discovered her, except to feel I hadn't ended it well. Every once in a while I'd think about her and wonder what she'd made of her life and what our life would have been had we tried to make it together."

"What did that look like?"

"I imagined a lot of harassment as part of our daily lives, and I thought I probably couldn't have withstood that, even if she could or would have. It was hard for me to imagine anything further."

"So you thought maybe you'd test that by taking other white women out for an evening or weekend or whatever?"

"Is *that* what you think?" Sunday leaned back in his chair, straightening his arms and gripping the armrests.

"I don't know, Sunday. What does it look like to you?"

48
Greta

Paula invited Josh and Greta to dinner on a Sunday evening in mid-November. That would keep it from going late, since Monday was a school day. Paula gave her directions to their home on Pine Street, only a short distance from her office, as it turned out.

She stood in front of her closet, dithering about what to wear. Ordinarily, she gave it little thought. She had a closet full of mostly brown and black loose pants, loose sweater tops and shapeless jackets. She wanted Sunday to see that she was still thin. But that was obvious, no matter how shapeless her clothing. And she didn't want to be drab. She thought of all the colors Paula wore; she was a blazing streak wherever she went. There was nothing in this closet even close. She remained in this silent stupor for some minutes, before she heard Josh's footsteps outside her bedroom door. She grabbed a sweater-jacket that had some color in it, tweedy hints of red and orange and brown, that she seldom wore because it was so very thick and warm.

"Are you almost ready?" Josh leaned his head into her bedroom, around the door.

"Almost." She gave him a flustered look, and he returned a slow smile of recognition.

"Mom, you look fine. Remember all those times you told me it doesn't matter what you wear, so long as it's clean?"

"Yeah. That was then and this is now."

"Can I drive? I know the way." He had just got his license.

"Okay. Just give me a few minutes." He left.

She looked at her face, wondered about make-up and dismissed the thought. It had been too long. She stared at this unsmiling face in the mirror, trying to find Gretchen in it. Her face was still narrow; bones don't change, and her hair, still flaxen, was paler but not gray. She pulled it up and back with combs, plumping it around the sides a bit instead of just pulling it back over her ears as she had done as a girl. Her eyes were still the blue of late evening, her best and only notable feature. Lines bordered her thin lips, giving her a more solemn expression than she had had as a young woman. She sighed. She was who she was. This evening was not going to be about how she looked.

In the car, she asked Josh to describe Cedar's brother and sister.

"They're both really smart, but they're quieter than Cedar. Linden is kind of shy. She plays the violin. Douglass looks stringy but he's actually an athlete; he's a miler."

Greta looked at him quizzically.

"He's a track runner, runs the mile. And he's really into math. He wants to go to MIT."

"His dad was a runner too, in high school." She glanced off into the dark space in front of them. "Only he ran the 100 yards."

The Morgan home was a Victorian on Pine Street, painted pearl gray with white trim, near Fillmore Street, in a neighborhood that had been all black in the seventies but was now chic and mostly white. Rectangular bay windows bowed outward from both the first and second floors. The house was meticulously maintained, with flowering plants on the tiny front porch and Victorian numerals for the address on the door, which had a knocker.

Paula opened the door and welcomed them. A thick black lab lumbered to the door and licked Josh's hand in recognition, its tail wagging. She had to work her way around the dog to enter.

"Cedar's in the kitchen," Paula said to Josh, and he disappeared in that direction with the big dog following, leaving Paula alone with her for the moment.

"I'm so glad you're here, Greta." Paula stepped back and took her coat. She looked about her. The entry was all dark wood, probably the original for the house, and a brightly colored North African rug lay on the floor. She could see the doorway and garden-facing window of Paula's studio and asked if she could see it. Paula gladly led her into the studio, and she admired the abstract painting on the easel. It was full of dashing lines, very much in motion, more energy in the lines themselves than in the color, which was muted brown and black. She looked around the room itself and liked everything about it. The back wall faced a garden. At some point the windows must have been enlarged to expand the view. She imagined lots of light would grace this room during the day. Various postcards of paintings and sculptures and painted sketches were tacked up on a wall adjacent to the easel.

"My father would have loved to paint in this room," she said without thinking. "He had just a tilted table in the attic in our house."

Paula looked at her thoughtfully, her head tilted inquisitively. "Was your father an artist?"

"Yes." She absorbed Paula's why-didn't-you-tell-me-before look. "We therapists aren't supposed to talk about ourselves."

"But now you can." Paula smiled with particular satisfaction.

"He was a wildlife artist for the natural history museum in Milwaukee."

"How lucky you must be; you can go see his work any time you like."

Just then a small, caramel-colored girl poked her head into the room. Her face resembled Cedar's, but her look was more contained, and she wore her hair tied tightly back.

"Mama, the sauce is boiling. Should I turn it down?"

"Greta, this is my youngest child, Linden." Linden came forward and said "hi" as she tentatively shook her hand. The three of them went into the kitchen, which also must have been remodeled because it was light and open and, like the studio, had a wall of windows facing the garden. It looked like a professional kitchen, with gleaming pots hanging from hooks over a chopping block island.

Paula briskly took the sauce off the heat and thanked Linden for letting her know.

"This is a room for serious cooks," she said admiringly.

Paula told her everyone in the family except Douglass enjoyed cooking.

"Not everyone likes to do everything, but among us, we can put a good meal on the table."

Linden looked behind her and brightened. "Dad, will you help me with the yams?"

As if in slow motion, she turned and faced Sunday for the first time. She noticed at once the spot of white hair on the left side of his head; the rest of his hair was salt-and-pepper. He was still lean, though slightly thicker around the waist. He grinned at her. The lines on his face gave him more expression than he had had at seventeen.

"Hello, Gretchen." That voice. *Say it again,* she pleaded silently. *That James Earl Jones deep voice.* "Or - I should say – hello, Greta."

She laughed, and he did too. "It's my grown-up name."

"It's good to see you," they said in unison. Paula looked at them both with a mysterious satisfaction.

He looked at her with a slightly helpless, where-to-begin expression and excused himself to help Linden with the yams. Greta watched Sunday's hands as he began to peel the cooked yams and help Linden do the same. His thin long fingers were those of an older man, lined and bulged at the joints. She asked if she could do anything to help, but Paula told her that dinner was in capable hands and led her into their living room.

She smiled as she looked around. Like hers, the room was lined with books, some on shelves and others piled unevenly beside chairs. Paula went into the other room to get her a glass of wine. She settled into a large plush chair. Soft piano jazz music played from somewhere. Paula returned with a glass of pinot noir for each of them. She took one sip and tasted cherries. From the kitchen came an aroma of cooking meat.

Paula asked her about her artist father, and she found herself talking about the birds and landscapes he used to paint, as if she had seen his work only last weekend. He loved nature, she started to explain. "He painted every detail realistically because he said he couldn't improve on nature's design."

Sunday walked in, his own glass in hand, and sat down on the sofa next to Paula, his knee touching hers. "I've left the kids in charge," he said. She noted his loose, easy posture, utterly comfortable in his beautiful home. He wore gray pants and a v-necked plum-colored sweater with a muted plaid shirt collar underneath. She looked at the couple before her and imagined them posed on that sofa, in the soft light, for a photograph of a successful couple in some feature magazine article. Only they did not seem to be posed - just totally comfortable and glad to have her with them. She felt bathed in an unfamiliar ether, nostalgic and new at the same time. She would have been happy to continue to sit there, invisibly, as in a movie theater, and watch this family entertain. Yet she was compelled to be present and participate.

Sunday asked her about her work as a therapist, and she began to describe her practice. "How did you choose this field?" he asked, and she told him how she had become interested in psychology in college and attachment theory in graduate school.

"It's not what I would have imagined you'd do," he said.

"What did you imagine?"

He cocked his head to one side, highlighting that odd white spot that she had seen in her recent dream, and paused.

"Art history, perhaps, or literature, teaching something at a college or graduate school level," he said, and then leveled his head. "But I'm glad you went into therapy," he added. "You not only helped Paula and me but also referred me to my own therapist."

Greta demurred. "I think very highly of him."

Cedar rescued them by swinging open the kitchen door and announcing that dinner was ready. She watched in near amazement as each of the children, including her Josh, brought serving dishes to the table. Josh carried the main dish, a lamb stew with lemon slices garnishing the platter. Linden carried the bowl of yams, and Cedar carried a huge salad. Douglass set a bowl of rice on the table and Paula told everyone where to sit. She put Greta at one end of the table, Josh next to her and Sunday across from her. Cedar sat at the head of the other end of the table, with Paula on her right and Douglass on her left. Greta admired the whole feast while Sunday served her from the platter.

For a while the children dominated the conversation, with Douglass' science fair project and a funny story about how he had nearly evacuated the school one day with a sulphurous concoction he had made. She participated sufficiently to draw out the children, Cedar in particular, but somewhat automatically. She still felt powerfully as if she were watching a film - preferably one on a video that she could rewind and replay again and again after this night - and she wanted more than anything else simply to be able to watch it play itself out. She became aware again of the background music, still the same gentle jazz piano. She had heard it before.

She looked up and caught Sunday gazing at her.

"Bill Evans?"

"Yes." Sunday smiled.

"Do you know this particular piece? I've heard it before but can't quite remember."

"Some Other Time," he said without hesitating.

"I do remember. Sequoia played this for me once when I visited her. She was rehearsing it for a concert with the group she'd put together. I heard them once in concert when I was in college."

Sunday looked at her with naked longing. "I never got to hear her group."

"I'm sorry you missed them." She grinned. "I think Sequoia might have had a thing going with the bassist. In any event, they sounded good, and anyone could tell she loved to play music with them."

She began to tell Sunday how Sequoia had taken care of her that summer after high school, even about fishing at the hidden lake on her birthday.

"I know that lake," he said, "she used to take me there too, when I was little. But I hated fishing, so she stopped trying to teach me."

They laughed together, remembering the woman who had mothered them both. She found herself wondering whether Sunday could find that lake again.

Linden looked back and forth at them quizzically, following this conversation. "Are you related?" she asked.

She and Sunday each gave the same smile of recognition, looking at each other for a long time without saying anything.

"Practically." It was Paula who answered, from down the table.

But no one explained further, and Sunday led the conversation elsewhere, telling Linden she may have got some of her musical talent and interest from Sequoia. He avoided saying 'my mother' or 'my sister.' Greta asked Linden how she chose the violin, and Linden explained that her teacher had suggested it, since she had long fingers. She told them she might want to move on to some other instrument, like the bass. "See, it is Sequoia," Greta told her.

When they had finished eating, all the children – again as if on cue – stood up and cleared the dishes. Paula went into the kitchen with them to prepare the dessert. Sunday and she were left alone at the table, facing each other, their wine glasses emptied, their eyes soft. For some moments, they said nothing, just smiling and smiling at each other, as if this were enough to satisfy all that had not happened between them for so many years.

Paula came in with a persimmon cake that she and Linden had baked. Josh carried a pot of coffee and put it on a trivet on the table. Linden passed around a sauce to pour on top of it. The cake was delicious, and conversation lagged momentarily while everyone savored the tart/sweet dessert. Greta had the sense that while she was not looking, Josh had joined another family.

Douglass, Cedar and Josh began a discussion about rap music, their voices growing loud as they argued with each other. Douglass thought all rap was just thugs being crude. Cedar and Josh jumped all over him in defense of rap, and soon all of them were throwing around names like Black-Eyed Peaz and Eminem and Notorious B.I.G. that she would not have recognized but for living with Josh.

She glanced at Sunday as if to say, 'aren't you glad we're of another generation?'

Sunday asked, "How's your dad?"

She suddenly looked stricken.

"I don't know," she answered quietly. "I haven't seen him since Sequoia's funeral." Without turning her head, she glanced to her right at Josh, still loudly engrossed in conversation with Douglass and Cedar, defending the imaginative rhyme of rap.

Sunday gave her a look that was pure Sequoia but said nothing.

"You're right. I never took Sequoia's advice." She looked down. "I try not to think about him – or about Norma either. I had to get away from her, and in the process I lost him." She paused, and her voice dropped further. "It's not a very good report, especially from a psychologist." She was still looking down at her plate.

"I suspect you're stronger than Norma now," he said. "Why not try to contact him? I remember how much he cared about you."

She looked up and gave Sunday a plaintive look. She could not find any words.

"It's always easier to give someone else advice." He shrugged slightly.

Paula got up from the table again to clear the dessert and again all of the children helped.

"Did you ever marry?" Sunday asked her. She looked down at his fingers, casually twirling a coffee spoon.

The question burned her. *And were you ever faithful?* She wanted to ask, furiously. She took a moment. "No."

"Josh?" He asked.

"Anonymous donor," she replied. "No love lost there," she added quietly.

How had he cut so quickly to her bones? *Let me just watch the movie and not have to be in it.* "What is that music?" she asked. "It's unusual to hear jazz flute, and it's not Lateef."

"That's Buddy Colette, 'A Man of Many Parts.' " Sunday got up and handed her the CD sleeve. "Do you still listen to jazz?"

"No, not much," she lied.

When the others came back from the kitchen, Cedar said, "Let's play osani."

"What's that?" She looked puzzled. Everyone else around the table, including Josh, knew what it was.

Cedar explained it to her, and she found herself charmed by both the concept of the game and by Cedar herself. Each person was to name something circular and continue doing so for several rounds; in the next stage they were to name concepts associated with something round or circular, like a family.

"Okay, but someone else start, and I'll try to catch on," she said.

They agreed to start with Josh, on her right, and go around to her at the end.

"A sleeping cat," he said, grinning.

"Venn diagram," came from Douglass.

"The planet Venus" was Cedar's contribution.

"A ball of clay," added Paula.

"Oranges," said Linden.

"A doorknob." This from Sunday.

"I can tell you've all been playing this a long time," she said, struggling to be clever enough. "A bird's nest."

"Should we keep going with round things or go on to the second round?" Josh asked. "Bad pun," Cedar joked, but everyone wanted to go right to the second round.

Josh opened, "Family circle."

"Planetary orbit," said Douglass instantly.

"The circle of life, from the Lion King," said Cedar.

"The sky in Van Gogh's 'Starry Night'" injected Paula.

"An orchestra," added Linden.

"The shadow under a tree, at high noon," added Sunday.

Fueled by Paula's art reference, she added, "The halo over Jesus in Renaissance paintings."

"A team," from Josh.

"A perfect conjunction of Venn diagrams."

"An igloo," from Cedar.

"A ripple in a pond," added Paula.

"A song sung in round, like 'Row, row, row your boat.'"

"Good one, Linden," said Sunday, and then paused a long time, as if he were struggling to find an answer. Finally, he said "Othello," looking intently across the table at her.

She glanced quickly at Paula and found herself inordinately pleased to see a puzzled look on her face. Greta felt suddenly very warm, as if she were having a hot flash. She gave Sunday a quick look of pure gratitude. The rest of the family moaned.

"No credit," Douglass proclaimed, "nothing round there."

"Wait," Linden injected, "I get it. It starts and ends in 'o.' Pretty clever, Dad."

Paula declared that she could not follow this and indicated it was time for the children to start getting ready for bed and school the next day. Taking her cue, she thanked Paula for the evening with her family. She stood up from the table, draped a hand over Josh's shoulder and moved toward the front hallway.

Paula gave her and Josh quick hugs at the door. She paused in front of Sunday, then held out her hand to shake his and thank him. He took her hand in both of his, and again she felt a wave of heat radiate from her chest down the rest of her body. Sunday told her he hoped that Josh and she would come back soon. His eyes retained the intensely personal expression of the moment he had mentioned Othello.

She felt euphoric as she left the Morgan home. She found herself humming, almost inaudibly, "Will the Circle Be Unbroken." As she and Josh left the penumbra of light from the house, she could see little clouds of her warm breath in the cold, dark air. With one word, Sunday had managed to convey to her alone – with their families watching – the whole length and depth of their relationship, from its origin thirty-two years ago, as if nothing had interrupted it. She felt whole.

She cheerfully tried to link arms with Josh as they walked to her car, but he pulled away and she agreeably let him walk by himself. Neither of them spoke. She was sweating by the time they reached their car, only a short walk up the street. She took off her jacket and laid it on the back seat.

"What's wrong with you, Mom? It's cold out."

"Hot flashes." It wasn't the first time she had had them, so Josh knew what she meant and just shook his head.

"Can I drive?"

"Not tonight." She slid into the driver's seat.

Even before she started the car, Josh began.

"So why did you tell me your parents died in a car crash?" His voice vibrated with anger and betrayal. He had obviously heard Sunday's question and her answer.

He could not have found a more vulnerable moment.

"I'm sorry." Long pause. "I lied to you then, and I've worried about it ever since." She avoided looking at him, staring ahead into the dark.

"Apparently not enough to tell me the truth. So what's the story?" He was almost yelling. "And at least you can turn on the heater. You may be hot, but I'm freezing in here." She still had not started the car. She turned the key and put the heat on, but made no move to start driving. For a long time, she remained silent and still.

"There is no way to apologize to you enough," she began. "Let me drive us home and I'll start to tell you the story when we get there."

"Don't make up a new one on the way," he said acidly.

They were silent for the remainder of the drive home. She felt so flooded with all of the evening's emotions that her feet felt heavy, and she drove slowly. Josh groaned with impatience as she let another driver cross in front of her instead of taking the right of way at an intersection. She could not say anything, could not think of how to begin to explain, could not form the words, could not move her tongue. She longed to be back in the single-minded joy of a few moments earlier.

When they got home, she fumbled her keys in the door. Josh half pushed her out of the way and used his own keys. She turned on the light over her usual chair in the living room and slumped into it. She noticed how drab her apartment looked after where they had just been. Josh paced back and forth, accusing.

"All my life, I thought I had this tiny little family, just you and me and a group of friends you called family. I didn't question it because you told me always to tell the truth and I assumed you were telling me the truth." He paused, gaining strength and volume. "What was the story you told me? They died in a car crash? How convenient!" He pounded his fist on the wall, putting a photograph on tilt.

"Do I have brothers and sisters too? Any other relatives conveniently dropped out of existence?" His voice was breaking now. He sat down, and thrust his head into his hands.

"So who's my real family?"

She had no idea what thoughts would come out. She opened her mouth as if knowing any explanation would be futile, inadequate, self-pitying, inexcusable. She closed her mouth, swallowed, and leaned forward in her chair.

"I never got along with my mother," she began. "I adored my dad, but he would not protect..." she halted and started over. "I got so angry with my mother in my senior year of high school that I left home right after graduation. I stayed with Sequoia and refused to see my mother. My dad would not see me without my mother being there also; he was that loyal to her. I was too angry – and maybe afraid also - to see her, so I cut off contact with both of them. It turned out that my dad and Sequoia talked from time to time, and he kept up with what I was doing through her; but when she died," she looked up at him as if to see if he would question her death too, "my dad and I lost track of each other. I don't know if he's still alive or if they're together or what."

Now Josh looked exhausted. He hesitated over what question to ask first. Minutes passed while they both sat in miserable suspense.

"So what happened between you and your mom?"

"She wouldn't let me see the young man I loved." As she said it out loud, it sounded flat, boring, banal and trivial. "There were other things, earlier. Once she nearly killed me when she drove off the road, and who will ever know if that was on purpose or just a freakish accident. But the last straw was that she wouldn't let me see Sunday when we were in high school."

"Oh, shit!" Josh got up and stormed up to his room, slamming the door.

She sat in her chair for a long time before she too got up to go to bed. Her body rescued her: she fell into a deep, long sleep. The next morning she got up late. She dressed in a rush, and when she went into Josh's room to wake him, he was already gone. When she went to the kitchen to pour herself a quick bowl of bran flakes, she discovered Josh had already left the apartment. She telephoned his school, suddenly worried that he might have done something rash, but was reassured that he had arrived on time and was in class.

Since her first patient would arrive at ten and it was now only 8:20, she decided she had just enough time to take a swim. By working her body, she might rest her roiling mind. She grabbed her tank suit and goggles and drove to the pool just a few blocks from her office. As she stood at the edge of the water, she took as a sign of luck that there was one free lane; she would not have to swim up to or around someone else. As always, the first ten laps were laborious, a reminder that her limbs were getting older; and then she lapsed into a more relaxed rhythm. Odd, she reflected, that she was the only one in her family who swam. She had tried to introduce Josh early, with vacations in warm places on the water, but he had taken to running instead. Her dad had loved the water, but only went in to cool himself off. He mainly spent his time in a boat, fishing. And her mother never liked getting her hair wet. Only Sequoia loved to swim. That summer they lived together, they went to the beach, even though it meant getting taunted. And they'd had that unspoiled birthday surprise at the little hidden lake. She wondered if she could find it again. Sunday knew it too; maybe he knew how to find it. Now, there was someone else she could ask, someone else who inhabited part of her history.

As she pushed off from the rim, she realized she had lost count of the laps. When this happened, she 'fined herself' by starting again to count at the last lap she could remember. Now, the lapse set off the larger recrimination. She had lied to her son about something fundamental. He might never trust her again. He was going to be confused about his origins for some time to come, maybe years. And she had embroiled his girlfriend's father in the whole story. She was the only one to blame for this fiasco. She began to swim faster, as if that could take time off her sentence. Josh might never forgive her. She could sympathize with him if he made that decision, but she didn't know if she could live with herself if that's what he decided. She didn't know how to live without him.

She inhaled water and choked. Refusing to stop, she coughed at each exhaling stroke until her breathing rhythm returned. For all of her doubts in advance about having a child, Josh was now an indispensable part of her. Before this debacle, she was beginning to realize how hugely her life would change once he went off to college, how dependent she was on his company and on her ability to cook for him, talk to him, even just to wake him up in the morning. He gave shape to her life in a way she was convinced had more depth than a husband would have, although she had no basis for that comparison. She could not have imagined as a young person just how profound it was to be needed in this way. Her clients needed her too, but her sense of utility to them was so far removed from this very immediate, invisible bond, this lifeline with unlimited tensile strength. Her dad must have felt this bond; everything intuitive in her being knew it. Yet she had broken off all contact with him because of Norma.

She looked up at the big clock and recognized that she had just enough time to get out of the pool, dress and get to her office in time for her first client. She had completely lost track of the number of laps. As one who never swam without counting, she just shook her head now at how stupid it seemed. For the first time in her life, she began to look at how her father must have felt at her leaving – her abandonment of her own parent. She shook the water out of her ears and dried hastily. For years, she had treated clients who felt beleaguered by their sense of abandonment by their parents. How could she not have looked at it before from the other end? How did the parents feel whose children had abandoned them? Here she was, fifty years old, well more than halfway through her sorry life, professionally employed for her empathy and insight, and she had never even visited this emotional space. It was suddenly, blindingly, obvious to her that she needed to make amends to her father, if he was still alive. Her mother – she would think about that later – was a mere obstacle, a rock to be rolled out of the driveway. She could do that.

She strode purposefully into her office, arriving just moments before her first client. Jacob was a fifty-two-year-old man who had been seeing her for the past two years. His marriage was in deep trouble. Three years earlier, he and his wife Sarah had lost their only child Claudia, a nineteen-year-old who had been raped and murdered in the woods outside her college campus. Claudia had been the fulcrum of their marriage; their whole lives had turned around her. Indeed, it had been their desire to have a child (Sarah then being thirty-eight and fearful of going through life without a child) more than their attraction to each other that had led them to marry. Now Sarah was sixty and unshakably convinced that her life was over. Sarah herself had been in therapy with one of Greta's colleagues for the same two-year period, and the two of them consulted from time to time with the consent of their clients. Throughout this two-year period, Jacob had wanted to keep the marriage together, while Sarah had, on and off, wanted to divorce.

"Good morning, Greta," Jacob's deeply lined eyes looked genuinely cheerful.

"How are you this morning?" she asked. "You look cheerful."

"I think I am. I think... something is changing with me. This morning when I got up, it was dark and cold, as always. But when I looked outside, there was the most beautiful orange sunrise. Just as the sun came over the dark horizon - you could actually look at it without hurting your eyes, it was this giant orange orb – I thought it was so beautiful I wanted to take a photo. I decided to go outside, watch it come up and walk here.

"On the way, I walked past a school. Small children were being dropped off by their parents and going inside. Ordinarily, I would have walked a block to avoid even being reminded of such a scene. But I kept walking through this pack of mostly eager, animated young faces, and it made me feel good instead of bad. I suddenly saw these children as a source of ...renewal... and hope, not as a reminder of Claudia. Actually, for a few weeks I've been feeling ready to feel good, if you know what I mean. At home, I'd have to hide it, of course, but I think I'm ready to live again and be happy again."

She paused a moment, appreciating his resilience.

"And you are hiding this from Sarah because you feel she isn't ready for it?"

"That would have been my first answer. But I think I'm hiding it because I don't want her to shoot me down. I don't want to lose this feeling."

"So if you gave her the chance to share it – to take joy in this beautiful sunrise, for example – it might deprive you of the capacity to enjoy it tomorrow?"

"Yes, exactly." He looked at her with recognition of what he 'should' be doing, "It's so new; I feel I might lose the capacity to feel this way again. For three years, all we have shared is misery. I'm beginning to want to get away from that."

"And so you're thinking of leaving her to get away from all that misery?"

"Yes."

This was the first time she had heard him speak of wanting to divorce.

"Well, that is certainly one of the things you could do, and, goodness knows, Sarah herself has given you this opportunity many times. But it also seems to me that part of the 'glue' for you, in this marriage, has been that you two are the only ones who share the full history of this wonderful young woman. You two have borne witness to all the joys and miseries of that experience."

"Well, if it's only misery that Sarah can remember, I'm beginning to think that I should move on, so I can remember the joyful times and try to recreate some joy in my own life."

"Understandable," she paused. "But you spoke a moment ago about how vulnerable these new feelings were. You seemed to distrust whether Sarah could appreciate them, without being willing to test them. Let's just look at what it would be like if you called out to Sarah to look at that orange sunrise with you and see if she might appreciate it."

"She was already off to work. She leaves earlier every morning, it seems."

"Let's try a weekend, when she's not working. What if you suggested to her, for a change of pace, that you two get up on a Saturday or Sunday morning and watch the sun rise, then go to breakfast or take a walk together in some place you think is beautiful."

"I did something like that in Claudia's first semester at school, when we were still both down about her being away, and it was a real failure. Sarah just told me she'd rather be at work than out wandering the streets." He gave a disgusted look. "Or something like that."

"And then everything changed, when the worst imaginable happened." She noticed his head sink. She continued so as not to leave him there. "When parents have been wounded that deeply – and only you two can know how deeply that is – there's a natural tendency to wall yourselves off emotionally from any further harm. And we've discussed many times how well defended Sarah is. What you are talking about now is quite big: the rebirth of a capacity for joy. It's vulnerable for you now because it's so new. But I suspect you have found something that you're not going to lose by exposing it to Sarah. True, you are going to feel misery again in your life, and she may 'shoot you down,' as you say. But are you sure you don't want to give her the chance to share it?"

"I honestly don't know. Part of me is willing to try, though I know what she'll do. Another part of me just wants to grab this new chance and run with it."

"'If you 'know what she'll do,' you'll try to make whatever that is happen. But you were surprised yourself by this new feeling. Why not leave room for being surprised by how she might react? It takes a strong person to show his vulnerability, and it looks to me as if you are regaining your strength."

"I never thought about it that way."

When she stepped into her apartment after work, she could feel that it was empty. Josh's cat came out of his room, mewling for food; Josh usually fed him when he came home from school. Also, Josh normally phoned to tell her when he would be there, and she knew his athletic schedule. He was not scheduled to be home late this evening. She picked up the telephone to listen for messages, but there were none. Her mind leapt to the possibility that he would not come home. Her terror of his running away warred with her rational mind telling her he was too sensible to do that.

But there was nothing rational about the situation she had created. She hung up her coat and swim suit and towel. Ordinarily she would begin to cook dinner for herself and Josh, but she had a strong feeling he was not going to come home for dinner. She found herself walking from room to room, not knowing what to do and not being able to sit down, like an anxious dog. She stood in Josh's room as if looking for clues, then as if he were never to return; but this made her frantic, so she walked out into the hall and then into her own room. She opened the door to the little balcony that overlooked the garden; the cold air rallied her.

It was dark, but she could make out the naked frame of the plum tree, where a lone bird perched in stillness. The telephone rang, and the startled bird flew away.

It was not Josh's voice on the line, but Paula's.

"I just wanted you to know Josh is here, so that you don't worry about him."

"Thank you." Her own voice had no gratitude in it.

There was a pause. She could visualize Paula thinking about what next to say.

"Um, Josh is refusing to go home. He seems to be angry about a conversation you and he had last night. We've been talking to him about how he needs to go home to talk to you, but we haven't been able to persuade him just yet."

"Will he talk to me?"

"I'll try again, but I asked him to call you and he wouldn't."

"Is he there with you now?"

"He's in the other room; Sunday is talking to him."

She found herself profoundly embarrassed that Paula and Sunday had to bear the brunt of her stupidity. It made her so ashamed she could hardly be even civil with Paula.

Paula took a chance. "Greta, let him stay here with us just this one night. We won't let him stay any longer. It's a safe place for him to cool off, and – believe me – Sunday will be good at talking sense into him. We had a situation recently with Douglass that I didn't tell you about, and Sunday helped him immensely."

There was no immediate response. She gritted her teeth, knowing this plan made sense and hating it at the same time. She wanted to demand that they send Josh home. At the same time, she knew such a demand would heap more shame on her because he would not go. Most of all, she didn't want Sunday and Paula to see this vulnerable flank of herself.

"Paula, I wish I could relieve you of this burden, but it sounds like I can't. Thank you for taking him in." She hung up quickly, before Paula could say anything else.

She stood staring at the telephone for a long time. *She* should be the one dealing with Josh, not Paula and Sunday. *She* was the professional, not the one leaning on others with her problems. That a former client would be the repository of her own most vulnerable mistake grated on her. Although she could see through her anger enough to recognize that Sunday might be just the very best person to put her lie into a sympathetic historical context, she could not get past her sense of deep embarrassment.

She opened a can of chili and ate a peanut butter sandwich with it. Not a dinner she would ever have with Josh. Maybe this is what she would be doing a lot more often when he was gone.

She took a long bath, thinking of the statement in Sylvia Plath's autobiography that there were few problems a hot bath could not cure. Afterward, she went straight to bed and attempted to read a novel. Of course it was impossible to concentrate. But she looked up from her book and recognized that this night was about Joshua, not her. He was the one having to absorb a huge altered reality about his family. And he had wisely chosen to take refuge with a family who cared about him and who could even tell him a bit more about his missing grandparents with an objectivity she herself lacked. Joshua was in the best place he could possibly be tonight. With that, she fell asleep.

She awoke again at four, and could not return to sleep. She felt alarmed and vigilant, imbued with the memory of an old dream she had had when she was three months pregnant with Josh. Today she knew it was a dream, but on the morning it had first happened – coincidentally or not, on her mother's birthday – she didn't recognize it as a dream upon waking. She had spent an entire morning in hiding, imbued with a paranoic fear that her mother was stalking her in San Francisco. In the dream her friend Mauna, whom she had known since their first weeks in graduate school, had telephoned her to warn her that Norma was in town and looking for her. In the dream, Mauna had recognized Norma straight off. On a seedy block of Market Street, Norma had approached Mauna and grasped her arm. Her fingers were talons and she had the penetrating eyes of a hawk, Mauna reported. *I need to find Gretchen*, Norma had told Mauna.

At seven she telephoned Josh, offering to bring him fresh clothes for school. She apologized again. He told her to bring the clothes but not to come in. "I'll be home tonight," he told her in a flat voice.

Gratefully, she went to his room and picked out what she thought was his favorite shirt, clean jeans, underwear and socks.

When she got to the door of the Morgan home, she had a fleeting temptation just to leave the bag of clothes on the doorstep. But she rang the bell. Paula answered, reached out to give her a hug. She stiffly accepted it and thanked Paula for her help.

"You and Sunday did my family a real service last night."

"Don't forget how much you helped my family. It's the least we could do."

She gave Paula a quizzical look.

49
Joshua

Since the dinner with Cedar's family, Josh had been reflecting on what a pathetic life his mother led. Fifty years old and never married, she lived this tiny life with him in this faded apartment in Noe Valley. Tiny kitchen with cracked dishes and unmatched pots hanging from the ceiling because they didn't all fit into the cupboards, tiny bathroom he had to share with his mom (he didn't even have a whole shelf for his shaving kit and deodorant), tiny bedroom with its long dark wall and little window glancing out onto the back yard, and living room lined with bookshelves, CDs, a worn sofa and his mom's reading chair in the corner. He had grown up with her cobbled-together family of friends, all single women, some of them mothers she had met when he was in preschool. Until now, he had not minded that he didn't have a regular family.

There was Marge, the surgeon, who couldn't mention any man without sarcasm. "Sorry, Josh, no offense," she'd say, automatically, and then continue. He liked Anita better; she had a daughter his age who was pretty cool, but probably smarter than he was (she went to University High and looked at him in a way he felt was condescending), and Anita spoke well of her former husband. Mauna, too, was all right; she seemed to care about Josh as a real person. She always remembered his birthday with small presents that told him she knew who he was. And her two sons, Jamal and Kinte, were friends, though they went to a public high school and he didn't see them that often. He had to admit these women were not bad for friends, but now he could see from being with Cedar what a real family was like. These women were nothing like a real family. Now, it turned out, his mother had actual relatives, a mother and father whom she had completely cut out of their life and hidden from him. He dreaded Thanksgiving, only a week away, when this whole motley group would gather around yet again, as they had every year of his life, each bringing their own favorite dish. They'd move the kitchen table to the living room, link it with a card table, and cover them with Indian bedspreads as tablecloths. Sometimes other friends would come – a mother whose children were with their father that day, a colleague visiting from another country, or some other orphan one of the others knew from work. They rotated who would cook the turkey, and this year it was his mom's turn.

At Cedar's home, there would be just their own family, with Cedar's grandparents coming from D.C. to stay with them for a week. Cedar's mom would cook the whole meal with help from everyone in the family, and they would all be together. He wished he had such a family. When he grew up, he would marry, have at least three children and create such a life. He would have Thanksgiving at his own home, and invite his mom to see what it should be like. He wished he could spend this Thanksgiving with the Morgans.

What kind of mother wouldn't even invite her parents to Thanksgiving? What was wrong with her? Here she was a psychologist, his icon until now of the wise parent who understood people. He had relied on her for advice, with his friends, even with Cedar. She seemed to know – most times – how not to intrude on him when he needed privacy, and to offer suggestions that were mostly on target. But now? How could she give her clients advice about their parents when she didn't even know how to treat her own?

He came home after school on Tuesday because Mr. Morgan had told him he should, and he was going to talk with his mom for the same reason. But she had a lot of explaining to do. He put his jacket on his bed and just sat for a while, staring at the walls of his room. It needed new paint; the color was faded and it was full of scuff marks. He and his mom had painted it together when he was eight. He had chosen a particular tone of blue – almost turquoise. She had warned him that it might look too intense on the big walls and talked him into a slightly lighter shade of the same blue. Rolling the color on the walls, they had both gotten themselves full of paint spots. And they had made plenty of mistakes; the sides of the doors had irregular blue marks on them from where they had affixed masking tape crookedly. But at the end of that day, they had felt mighty proud of themselves. They'd ordered in pizza and ate it sitting on the living room floor, and he had slept in her room until the new paint smell went away.

On the wall over his desk and computer was a

bulletin board, with a small pencil drawing Cedar had done of him when they were still just friends and photos of him and Cedar with their friends at a party. Also there was a small photo of him and his mom leaning against the rail of a ferry in the New York harbor on the way to the Statue of Liberty four years ago when he was in seventh grade. To the left of the desk, just next to the door, were faint pencil marks up the wall, measuring his height at various ages; they did it every year on his birthday, without fail. Two years ago, he had grown two inches, and there was the largest gap from the line below. He needed a new set of drawers, too, he decided; these had been here since he was four years old. This place needed new life.

Josh poured himself a glass of apple juice from the refrigerator and sat down in his mom's wing chair in the corner of the living room. It was starting to get dark in the room, the light graying through the old drapes, but he decided not to turn on the lamp. He hardly ever sat here; it was his mother's chair, and he had only sat on her lap here when he was much younger and she was reading to him. It was pretty comfortable, though the left arm had frayed and a bit of the white stuffing showed through the old brown upholstery. The brightest things in the whole room – and the only new things – were the newer books. She bought books all the time, stacking them on the floor until she read them. Some of the bookshelves had two rows of books in them, one in front of the other, all organized by subject matter and alphabetically, as if this were some old library. On the one wall not covered with bookshelves there were four photographs – not of their family or anyone they knew – these were by real photographers. One depicted a ragged, poor black family on a wooden porch, all barefoot; another, a group of diamond miners in South Africa, handing heavy loads up a hill from one man to the next, their skin shiny with wet mudstains. There was one taken in a black church, half the congregation standing, their arms up and mouths open, joyful and half-crazed, clad in big hats and fancy dresses. The last was one of Martin Luther King, taken from the back, looking out on the hordes of people congregated on Capitol Mall in 1963. Her precious relics.

His mother was starting to get old. Her face had lines, not just at the corners of her eyes and around her mouth, which made her look sour when she was not smiling and unconscious of anyone looking at her, but also in her forehead, not counting the curved scar over her eyebrow, which made her look worried even when he thought she wasn't. He had a hard time imagining her at his age, and the thought of her being in love with Sunday then was too weird. She looked plain next to him. She didn't care how she dressed. Sunday was the opposite; he had clothes that made him look elegant. Josh himself didn't focus on clothes enough to say what it was, but Cedar's dad looked *put together* all the time. It was true that his mom and Mr. Morgan had talked at dinner like people who knew each other well, but more like old friends or relatives who hadn't seen each other in many years. As he thought about it, it was hard to imagine her with any man, because he couldn't remember her in a relationship. She was just his mom, and, in truth, he had sometimes appreciated having her all to himself.

She had told him the other night that her own mother had broken up her relationship with Cedar's dad. He tried to think how he would feel if she did that to him, but it lay outside the realm of his imagination. If someone else – he couldn't imagine who it could be – would try to end his relationship with Cedar, he would be furious. He would run away, maybe, but the idea was so far-fetched that it had no reality. His mom would never do that. If she didn't like Cedar or what he was doing with Cedar, she would tell him what she didn't like. On the other hand, he couldn't imagine her lying to him; and now he knew she had done so, and about something that really mattered. So he felt on guard against this new person inside his mother.

50
Greta

When she opened the door, she sensed that Josh was home. No lights were on in the house and no voice greeted her ("Hey Mom" usually hailed from his room), but she felt his presence. It wasn't just that Paula had promised he would be home; she actually felt him in the house. Relief flooded her veins, along with a hot flash. They were coming predictably at the end of each day now, but never mind. Even if Josh was very angry, he was where she could speak with him. She hung up her gray coat, slowly, taking stock of where Josh might be and trying to imagine his state of mind.

He sat stiffly erect in her chair in the corner of the living room, his arms atop the arms of the chair. He was only slightly more than a shadow in the corner of the darkening room, and she could not see his face clearly.

"I want to talk to you," he said imperiously, as if he were the parent.

"I'm glad. Tell me what you've been thinking." She sat down on the sofa, where he would have to turn his head to look at her.

"Why did you hide my grandparents from me?"

"I wasn't trying to hide them..." she began, and then shifted off her defensive tone. "Let me start over. When you were little, you caught me completely off guard when you asked if you could invite my parents to Grandparents Day. I couldn't explain my ...rather tortured history... I didn't know how to tell my very young son that I had hated my mother and felt I needed to escape her, so I lied. It was a shortcut, a dead end as it turned out. Once I had told you that, I couldn't tell you that they were alive and living in Milwaukee – if, in fact, that's still true. I didn't want to dredge up my past, and I didn't want you stained with any part of it. I wanted to create a different kind of life for you."

Josh sat silently in the chair, like a too-young prince on a throne. She could discern the features of his face now, and see that his eyes were stern and confused at the same time. Not a muscle moved in his body. He did not even blink. He was trying hard to maintain a prosecutor's demeanor, but she sensed his doubt that he could carry it off.

"Josh, I know this was wrong. I hope you'll learn to forgive me. Over the years, it seemed to me less harmful just to let it rest. I've been asking myself the last two days how I could or should have corrected this before now, but I haven't come up with any answers. No parent is perfect," she finished lamely.

He hmmphed in disgust. "That's just what Mr. Morgan said."

What else had Sunday told him? Of all the people on this planet who knew what secrets parents shielded from their children, Sunday might top the list. He was likely, then, to be forgiving.

"What else did Sunday tell you?"

"He told me to ask you about your mother." Josh shifted in the chair to face her, crossing his arms across his chest and burying his hands in his armpits. "He told me you didn't have the same mother I have." His face had softened, his eyes grown inquiring.

"That was a generous thing for him to say." She looked down and picked the pills off the elbow of her sweater. Josh remained silent. She had to look up at him. He was obviously waiting for her explanation.

"I was seventeen when I left home. I went to live with Sequoia, as you might remember. When I left, I hated my mother with a passion. I resented her in a way I can't dredge up now. I was afraid of her all my childhood, and I felt I began to live only after I left."

Josh remained silent, waiting for more.

"Josh, I don't like telling grievance stories. I had a bad relationship with my mother and I couldn't wait to escape her."

"Well, you must have carried a pretty big grudge to stay away all these years."

"I must have – because I adored my dad. But I held a grudge against him too, for not protecting me from her, and for not being willing to see me without her."

"Protecting you from what? Did she abuse you?"

Strange, how fluent today's children are with the language of abuse, though Josh used the word incredulously. She was far more uncomfortable than he with the word.

"When I was seven years old, she took me on a drive in our family's new car and drove us both off the road, into a steep ravine. I was terrified. My father promised me he'd protect me from her, but he didn't." She heard her own voice as Gretchen's, the child.

"I thought she didn't want me. She always treated me like I was in her way, preventing her from living the life she wanted...."

"Were you hurt?"

Greta looked at him, as if to say: *wasn't it obvious*?

"I meant in the car accident; sorry."

"I had what must have been a mild head injury. I was in the hospital for several days. But I had no 'long term injuries.' I was just terrified of her."

"Did she ever hit you?"

"On my thirteenth birthday, she broke my arm." She shook her head. It was more than she wanted to tell him. "Josh, are you hungry? I'm starved."

"Sure, but I don't want to stop. I'll order a pizza; don't move." He bolted out of the chair and ordered a pizza, rattling off the toppings (mushrooms, green pepper and olives) that she liked rather than the sausage he preferred. When he came back, he sat down on the floor, facing her on the sofa. He asked again about her mother hurting her.

"Yes, she lost her temper a lot and hit me unexpectedly. I learned how not to say or do anything to provoke her, but sometimes it came out of the blue." Greta looked out the window, as if some rescue were to be found there. "Josh, I don't like talking about this."

Josh looked pained himself. "What about your dad? What did he do when that happened?"

"It didn't usually happen in front of him, but on my thirteenth birthday he and my grandparents were there too. He just sat there and my grandma had to pull her off me. He was afraid of her too. When they argued about something, he always gave in to her. After the car incident, he promised me she wouldn't drive again, but after a year or so, she was driving again and would sometimes take me along. So he was no help. My Grandma Etta – her mother - used to distract her, which was helpful, but she wasn't around enough after my parents got their own apartment. And then she died while I was in high school." She looked at Josh, staring at her intently. "Yes, she actually died."

"I believe you," he said. He got up and sat on the sofa next to her, put his arms awkwardly around her shoulders. She began to cry, at first trying not to let him know, a silent tear dropping on his arm, but then, with his arms around her, she let go and began to cry, harder and harder, until her shoulders shook and she gasped for air. He did not let go, just held her, his head resting lightly over her left shoulder, his hair soft as a towel.

When the doorbell rang, she jumped up, grabbed a twenty from her purse and gave it to Josh. She fled to the bathroom to dry her eyes, while he paid for the pizza. Josh put the pizza on the old Indian table from Cost Plus that passed for a coffee table, and they ate it in the living room, he cross-legged on the floor, she on the sofa, both of them talking about anything else.

The next morning Josh told her calmly at breakfast that they were going to look up her parents and visit them in Wisconsin if they were still alive. He thought Christmas vacation would be a good time to go.

"It would be cold, much colder there than

anywhere you've ever been. It would be better to go in summer."

He looked at her as if she just didn't get it. Then he hugged her and told her they would look up the phone numbers after school that evening and make their plans to visit his grandparents over the holidays.

* * *

The phone rang during the last ten minutes of an hour. Assuming it was Josh, who knew to call between clients, she answered eagerly, stopping just short of saying 'hi, Josh.'"

"Hello, Greta." It was Sunday's voice.

She caught her breath. "It's you."

"Yes, it's me. After all these years."

She paused, and he continued. "I was wondering if I could take you to lunch someday soon."

She was silent for several breaths.

She could almost hear him sigh. "I promise I won't make a pass at you," he joked, almost drawing a laugh from her.

"Well, in that case, how can I say no?" Her voice sounded almost relaxed.

They arranged to have lunch at a small café not far from her office on the Wednesday after Thanksgiving.

That day dawned cold and clear; one could see for miles from a hilltop on such a day. But there were no hilltops between her office and the café. She wrapped her neck in a gray velvet scarf and put up the hood on her coat. She could see only the ground in front of her.

At the café, she peeled off the heavy gray coat

she had bought for Chicago winters, loosened the scarf, and lay them next to her in the booth. She had arrived first. The café was already decorated for Christmas, and arcs of tiny white lights were tacked along the tops of the windows, which themselves were painted to look like frost. People walking past outside were shadows in motion, not recognizable.

Sunday found the booth before she saw him. He gave her a wide smile and slid into the seat across from her, deftly removing a red wool scarf from his neck at the same time.

"It's a day for hot soup," he proclaimed, rubbing his hands together, as casually as if they had lunch together all the time.

She answered in the same casual vein. "I go to the gym to swim most mornings, but it was too cold to even think of it today."

They chatted for a few moments about her swimming and his running and told each other how good they looked after all these years. They ordered their food. Sunday paused.

"There's something I want to say to you, and I know it's many years too late." He looked at her searchingly, but she wouldn't meet his eyes. She gave no sign of even having heard him. She looked down at a small vase of holly and evergreens on the table and fingered the outlines of the holly leaves, one by one, giving only a slight start when one pricked her finger.

"I was a coward for leaving you. I must have hurt you, and I let you down at a very bad time."

She still didn't look up. He'd spoken softly, but not *that* softly. She sensed him waiting. She could feel him wondering what her reaction would be, whether she would forgive him, reveal her anger, or tell him how much he had hurt her. Just as he was about to ask if she'd heard him – she felt this coming – she gave a small gesture. A shrug. She had not dismissed his apology at all, but there was nothing to be done about it now. Or, rather, there was. She could say something to absolve him, perhaps lighten his load.

She looked up and met his eyes.

"It's not about us anymore." Her look was steady and calm and open. "We can help Josh and Cedar have a different time of it than we had."

Sunday's shoulders relaxed. She had given him enough, without having to absolve him.

"We can," he said, and his whole face smoothed, as if he'd been driving on unfamiliar streets for a while and just recognized where he was.

The waitress delivered their bowls of chili and cornbread. She wrapped her fingers around the bowl, and Sunday put his over his bowl, to catch the warmth.

She spoke. "There's something I've always wondered about. What happened to you in Mississippi? Can you tell me now?"

"I want to. You know, I was only recently able to remember it – with the help, by the way, of your therapist friend. The memory came back to me suddenly, and as soon as it came to me I wanted in the worst way to tell Sequoia – and you too." He shook his head slightly. "And now you ask.

"One night, I had just left a meeting with another worker, a white guy named Nathan. We were kinda pumped up and happy from the meeting, laughing and not paying attention to what was going on around us. At some point I realized there were four white men behind us – older guys, with baseball bats. I tried to warn Nathan, but he was bent over laughing so hard that he must not have heard me. I began to run. I don't know if I assumed Nathan was also running ... or if I just ignored him and ran to save myself. They beat up Nathan. I could hear them behind me, but I didn't stop ... I just kept running. I didn't stop to help him. I found out afterward they'd broken Nathan's jaw and a couple of his ribs. He was in the hospital for about a week and then went back home. I never even went to see him in the hospital."

"That must have been devastating." She put one of her hands across her mouth, as if to stifle some larger reaction.

"It made me feel small. I couldn't talk to anyone about it, not even you or Sequoia. I knew I wasn't a man who could brave whatever it would take for us to be together in those times."

When he finished, she used the back of her hand to wipe something off her cheek but said nothing for a long time. She remembered his talking about his friend Nathan at the beginning of that summer, but also that he stopped talking about anything in Mississippi at the end of that summer.

"No wonder you broke it off with me." She looked away, trying to imagine carrying his fear. "Why didn't you tell me at the time? I want to think I would have understood."

"I couldn't talk about it to anyone." He repeated, then paused, as if thinking back. "Yeah, on one level you would have understood. But you would have tried to persuade me to keep going anyway, and I would have had to tell you outright what a coward I was."

"Anyone in his right mind would have done what you did. There was no way you could have saved Nathan that night." She kept her comments to that night. There were many things he could have done afterward that he didn't do. Like tell her outright. She'd trusted that the two of them were close enough that he could at least have told her.

"Eat your chili," she said finally. "It's going to take me a while." She began to eat her own, and its spiciness warmed her.

"I think Sequoia must have guessed something like that." she said finally.

"I still miss her." She paused, remembering. "She seemed to be training me to live without you, not trying to put us back together again."

Sunday laughed, shaking his head. "I can tell you this: she had a different sermon with me."

"For real?" She looked up with genuine surprise.

"Oh yeah." Sunday was still shaking his head, smiling. Gradually, his smile wilted and his voice caught. "You're the only other living person I know who remembers her." She put her hand over his, and he laid his other hand on hers and looked down.

"She's sometimes still here for me," she began. "When I'm trying to figure out how to be a good parent to Josh, I sort of consult her in my mind.

"It was so strange when you and Paula came to my rescue a few weeks ago. I resented it at the time, and I was embarrassed, but you helped him to understand, in a way that I couldn't, what I had told him about my parents. It was almost as if Sequoia were around to give him advice. That you knew me then and knew who my parents were ... and could talk to him ... was a huge gift."

They ate the rest of their chili. As he was about to pick up the check, she blurted, "I'm going to say something really selfish."

"You're entitled."

"In some very foolish way, the reason you broke it off makes me feel better, like it wasn't because of me personally ... only that I ... was the wrong color."

"*You* were the wrong color?"

"Well, I guess it doesn't matter much which of us was the wrong color, only that we didn't match at the time." She cocked her head. "Do you think it would be different today?"

"Between us?" She felt him backtracking fast.

His discomfort spurred her. "Yeah, if you were single, would you still think we were the wrong color for each other?"

He leaned back. "It's just hard for me to imagine being single; that's all."

She had her answer and she changed the subject, telling him about her upcoming trip to Milwaukee with Josh. He told her he thought he could find the lake where she and Sequoia had fished; he'd look at a map and give her a call.

Outside the café, he gave her a hug. From him it was more than a hug, more like an attempt to revive a frostbitten soul. He held onto her tightly for some time before they parted.

As she walked back to her office, she found herself irritated. As comforting as it was to reconnect with him and reflect back on Sequoia, the conversation left her feeling raw. She rewound it in her mind several times, trying to pinpoint where it had gone off track. What had happened to him was truly devastating, and many people would never have gotten over it. That was undeniable and deserving of her empathy. That he couldn't tell her or Sequoia at the time was understandable. But that he just allowed their love to drift away, over all those months, and never say anything, and that now, decades later, he still couldn't imagine crossing the color line – except in his repetitive escapades – was unfathomable. Now more sad than irritated, she wanted to guard against thinking he epitomized more than his own limitations. He needed Paula's strength, she thought. He was incredibly lucky to have her. Together they were outstanding parents.

What would she have done if he *had* stayed with her? Did she have any better answer for that than he? How would she have dealt with his weakness?

And yet, they knew each other's vulnerabilities at the time and were able to give each other comfort. He knew her early history better than anyone else she knew, and even now he used it to help her with Josh, to help Josh judge her less harshly. If they had stayed together, he would have helped her be less resigned. She would definitely be a better parent, and she would have had the courage to become a parent earlier. They would have had more than one child. If she had stayed with him.

She looked around her. She had walked past her office, by more than a block. She'd never done that before. Glancing at her watch, she recognized she still had half an hour before her next appointment. She pushed her wool scarf up around her ears and kept walking.

If she had stayed with him. Knowing herself, it was entirely possible she would have left him. It was what she had done with her parents. There were so many thousands of ways to imagine how she and Sunday would have lived their lives had they stayed together through the Sixties. All of them labyrinths, with multiple paths to choose. Imagining an alternate past was like flying over one of those cornstalk labyrinths farmers constructed these days, after the harvest and the stalks had dried, recognizing from the air that there was a pattern, glimpsing the map in a moment of overflight and trying to remember it, so as to walk it on the ground afterward. Impossible to reconstruct, except in the imagination. One could learn it only by walking it.

What would she say as she walked back into her father's life now? Bringing Joshua would be a form of offering, of her own humbling recognition of the mistakes one makes as a parent. She prayed her father would still be alive to receive them. She thought now for the first time of what would have happened if her father had left her mother. It would have meant his leaving her too; fathers didn't get custody of their children in those days. She would have been left alone with her mother, with no cushion. He must have known that then. He did what he could to follow her after she left, until Sequoia died. He did what he could to protect her and yet stay loyal to his wife. He did what he could.

Sunday too had done what he could at the time. Neither of them had done enough to satisfy her, and others might well have been stronger or wiser in their place, but she was standing here now, whole enough, in the middle of her life, with a healthy optimistic son, useful work, and the strength to keep on walking into the future.

51
Sunday

Sunday got up early the next morning, as always, to run with the dog. He dressed silently and ran down to the dog run along the water at Crissy Field. When he returned, it was still too early for anyone else in the family to be up. He drank orange juice and ate some toast with peanut butter. Today was Friday, his day without classes. Usually, he would write or prepare lectures. Today he decided to take a long walk along Ocean Beach. He left a note for Paula telling her where he had gone.

The sun was just rising as he parked the car along the beach. The ocean was calm, small ridges of white foam sparkling at the edges of the dark water. He decided to leave his shoes and socks in the car. He walked barefoot in the soft dry sand, heading southward because he could go farther in that direction. For a time, he just concentrated on how the cool sand worked the muscles in his feet, his mind otherwise unoccupied. The color of the water lightened gradually as he went on, though there was no sun. A gray sky hung over the gray-green water, and the sand too was gray and cold underneath his feet. It had taken him over thirty years to look into himself, until he too was graying. He had spent more than half his life – all his adult life – running away from issues he should have faced at the time. Only now, with The Man's help, could he even look head-on at running away from Nathan in Mississippi and Gretchen in Milwaukee. He thought about writing to Nathan, who might, for all he knew, be an established lawyer in Topeka – or anywhere – now. Composing the letter would be more difficult, he suspected, than finding Nathan. But speaking with Gretchen – Greta - yesterday gave him heart. Even if he couldn't find Nathan, it might be worth trying to write the letter. He might learn more by trying to put words around what he had buried all this time. As for Greta, she seemed so spare, so thin and serious – especially when he saw her in the same room with Paula. But Gretchen had always looked thin and serious; they had both been like that at seventeen. He had fashioned for himself a far more comfortable life than she had, and he could tell that his was far richer in love. He sensed that she had poured all her love into her son Josh and that Josh would grow up to create more love around him than she had in her lifetime.

He liked Josh, almost like another son, and found himself trusting Josh with Cedar. Sunday remembered how easy it had been to talk to Gretchen, even about the most painful elements in his life, and he imagined it must be that way for her clients too. At their lunch, they had found that same place of comfortable connection, not only with each other but also with Sequoia. This thought alone gave him peace. He trusted that Greta would understand a great many more things he might try to tell her, without trying to make his explanation into something else, some other kind of relationship between them that he did not intend or even desire. He believed she would continue to understand him and not even need to forgive him because she had already skipped that step long ago: she simply *knew* him.

His calves began to ache, so he moved closer to the water, onto the hard wet sand. It was colder but easier to walk on.

What had happened in Mississippi was stark and frightening – as was the episode in Idaho, but they both seemed primitively simple compared to larger issues in the world today. Race in this country had become a far more diffuse issue. As a professional in San Francisco, he lived in an island of relative safety. He had plenty of company among black professionals. He had learned the comforts of privilege. The poor struggled as they always had, but with less attention paid to the black poor. Who was to say the immigrant poor, the Hispanic poor, the suddenly poor suffered any less? Sunday had come to believe it was more important to focus on the poor as poor rather than on the poor as black - not that he had done anything about that other than make the point in his classes.

The world was both better and worse on the subject of race relations. Mandela had helped move South Africa out of apartheid and into a country with forgiveness as a model for addressing the crimes of the past. But the Hutus had slaughtered the Tutsis in Rwanda just a few years ago without any intervention from the rest of the world.

The world of his teen-aged years presented the overriding danger of nuclear elimination, as the Soviet Union and United States muscled over who would dominate the arms race. In 1963 everyone had clung to the radio, wondering whether Kennedy would start an inevitably fatal nuclear war if the Soviets broke through the Cuba blockade. Today the planet seemed less threatened by nuclear explosion than by the likelihood of polluting itself to death. A slower death by cancer than by war. There was plenty to fear: terrorism in the Middle East, an overpowering earthquake and tsunami, random street violence, an auto accident on the highway. You could walk in that fear every hour of every day if you chose to and not exhaust the possibilities.

Maybe he would write a book about Mary Ellen Pleasant. She must have known fear in her life, yet she continued to sally forth on some new daring effort at each turn. He might learn from her by reading more about her. He might visit the university that owned her papers and read her own record of what she wanted the world to know of her. There was more to her than his prepared lecture, which was now so familiar to him that it had grown stale.

Sunday moved closer to the water, let it wash over his bare feet. It was bracingly cold, but the small waves coming in tempted him. He waded in up to his ankles without bothering to roll up the bottoms of his jeans. For some time he walked on like that, until the water no longer felt cold. And then he ran, water splashing his legs and fresh air filling his lungs.

* * *

Acknowledgments

I am enduringly grateful to many people who inspired me and assisted in improving this book. To Gladys Veidemanis, my original spur. To my husband Al for his discerning ear and unfailingly good judgment. To my daughter Kavana for her enthusiastic encouragement. To my mother for sharing old stories and her love of literature. To my friends who read prior drafts of this novel and gave me honest criticism: Peggy Bennington, Mauna Berkov, Sherry Cassedy, Jane Ginsburg, Lee Jordan, Neil Mayer, Laura Otis, Pamela Pierson, Susan Rutberg, Dee Samuels, Madeleine Simborg, and Michelle Washington. To Jeanne McMann, for her leadership at the Thursday Morning writers' group and her encouragement and fine editing. To Grace Eslava for patient technical assistance. Finally, to all those who critiqued my work at the 2008 Squaw Valley Community of Writers; each of you enhanced this novel.